Acclaim for Jim Lewis's

THE KING IS DEAD

"*The King Is Dead* takes the father-son conflict and deftly weaves it into a 20th-century American fable. . . . Lewis proves he can evoke intimate sadness within big stories. That's the mark of real tragedy—and real art." —*The San Diego Union-Tribune*

"Jim Lewis's sterling novel of politics, race, fidelity, and regret is a model of literary economy . . . an epic worthy tale packed into a brisk 260 pages. . . . This is grand fiction." —*Texas Monthly*

"Genealogy counts for everything in Jim Lewis's absorbing diptych of self-discovery. . . . An effective examination of the search for truth in a divided family." —*The Seattle Times*

"*The King Is Dead* is little less than a landmark, a moving-on outwards and upwards from midlife inertia, with all the attendant cries of release, towards something sad, illuminating, songful and shivering with life." —*Time Out* (London)

"[*The King Is Dead*] does what novels should and so rarely do: encompass a great deal in a limited space, pass the inessential, and enlarge life." —*The New York Sun*

"A beautifully sculpted narrative [of] political chicanery, domestic infidelity and murder. Magnificent!" —*Independent on Sunday*

"Like the classic Southern novelists (Faulkner, Warren, Percy) Lewis writes as though he means for you to enjoy it. . . . *The King Is Dead* shows that Lewis has become a novelist to reckon with." —*San Antonio Express-News*

"A gripping novel that flashes over 50 years, exposing the way in which an instant can shatter a life."   —*The Times* (London)

"A Faulknerian tale of crossed destinies . . . masterfully told. . . . Compellingly readable and brilliant in design and style. . . . Startling and memorable. . . . Jim Lewis is a writer to relish."
—*The Commercial Appeal* (Memphis)

"Jim Lewis is a writer of the same heavyweight stature as Franzen and David Foster Wallace. There is much to admire in how Lewis narrates his melancholy saga of love, betrayal, shame, loss, regret and disappointment across the generations. . . . A short review can barely do justice to the artfulness and deep intelligence of this novel. Above all, Jim Lewis persuades you that a single reading of his work is not enough."
—*Scotland on Sunday*

"*The King Is Dead* is a marvelous book, and with it, Jim Lewis has come into full possession of a powerful literary voice whose main qualities are the hardest to come by: integrity, empathy, narrative allure, and wisdom. Lewis's moral intelligence purges his prose of every false move and cheap convention, burrowing ever closer to the truths about the pull and stain of heritage. This is a book of impeccable artistry."
—Jeffrey Eugenides, author of *Middlesex*

"A refreshing throwback to the old baroque school of Southern writing, but with the difference that the fatalism, to which novelists like Faulkner and even Cormac McCarthy were as addicted as they were to whiskey, is absent."
—*The Austin Chronicle*

"Lewis writes near faultless, witty, warm prose and his diverse characters spring to life. *The King Is Dead* is a novel with both ideas and heart. Long live the king."   —*Irish Independent*

JIM LEWIS
THE KING IS DEAD

Jim Lewis was raised in New York and London. He has taught philosophy and literature at Columbia University, and has written about both politics and the arts for many magazines, journals, and museum catalogs. He has published two previous novels, *Sister* and *Why the Tree Loves the Ax*; and written a screenplay, based on a short story of his own, for Francis Ford Coppola's Zoetrope Studios. He lives in Austin, Texas.

ALSO BY JIM LEWIS

Sister

Why the Tree Loves the Ax

THE KING IS DEAD

JIM LEWIS

———

THE KING IS DEAD

VINTAGE CONTEMPORARIES
Vintage Books
A Division of Random House, Inc.
New York

FIRST VINTAGE CONTEMPORARIES EDITION, OCTOBER 2004

The Library of Congress has cataloged the Knopf edition as follows:
Lewis, Jim.
The king is dead / Jim Lewis.—1st ed.
p. cm.
1. Motion picture actors and actresses—Fiction. 2. Racially mixed people—Fiction.
3. Crimes of passion—Fiction. 4. Fathers and sons—Fiction. 5. Politicians—Fiction.
6. Uxoricide—Fiction. 7. Tennessee—Fiction. 8. Adoptees—Fiction. I. Title.
PS3562.E9475K56 2003
813'.54—dc21   2002043288

Vintage ISBN: 0-375-71400-6

Book design by Dorothy Schmiderer Baker

www.vintagebooks.com

Printed in the United States of America
10 9 8 7 6 5 4 3 2 1

For Wool

THE KING IS DEAD

PRELUDE

There was a woman named Kelly Flynn. She was born in 1720 to a Dublin banker, and raised in London, where her father had been sent to service a loan from the King. At court she met and married a Belgian furrier named DeLours; together they had nine children, and six of them died, four from disease and two through misadventure. One who survived, an intrepid boy named Henry (b. 1745), cut short his schooling to join the Army and was commissioned as an officer.

The Empire was widening into the subcontinent and there was a great need for resourceful men. Henry DeLours was clever and brave, and he was sent to Calcutta; while there, he met an Englishwoman named Elizabeth, the daughter of a fellow officer. He married her, and they produced five children. One of them, a daughter named Mary (b. 1770), returned to England to attend boarding school.

During a tour of Cornwall, Mary met an older man, a printer named Samuel Crown, who admired her, courted her, and soon won her hand. They returned to London, and their children were William, Theodore, Olivia, and Georgia, each following on the last by a little over a year. It was expected that the male children would join in their father's business, but Theodore (b. 1790) was willful and wandersome, and as soon as he came of age he sailed for America, looking to make a fortune of his own.

For a time he clerked in a law office in New York. Each evening he went home to his small, dark room and wrote to his mother, describing both the faith he held in his future and the hardships that were testing it: debt, the dismissiveness of the men for whom he worked, the desolation he felt in this new, strange city. But he was frugal by way of defense, and he soon managed to amass a small amount of cash, which he used to purchase a few acres of land in Kentucky. He planted tobacco, labored, prospered, and within a few years he'd expanded his estate to some three hundred acres and two dozen slaves; by the age of thirty he had come to sufficient prominence to run for a local judge-ship, and, with the help of some casks of whiskey that he had delivered to the taverns on the eve of election day, he won.

It was 1820, and Judge Crown was unmarried. Instead, he took a Negro woman, a slave named Betsey, who served in his house. He brought her into his bed almost every night—Apollo may not forgive me but Pan assuredly will, he wrote in his journal—and soon she gave birth to a son, a light-skinned boy named Marcus (b. 1821).

When he was a child, Marcus's mother told him that his father was a house slave from up the road, but by then he'd already heard rumors that he was sired by the man who owned him. The cook would cluck about it and shake her head; the footman would tease him in their quarters at night; but he never sought to confirm or disprove the story of his origin. He didn't dare, still less when Theodore at last found a wife, with whom he could have children who were legal and sanctified.

One midnight Marcus ran away from Crown's farm, toward a leg-endary North. In his pocket he carried eighteen dollars, a sum that his mother had pilfered, penny by penny, from the household accounts, and which she'd given to him along with instructions to find his way to Ripley, Ohio. Under darkness, Marcus ran through fragrant fields; in morning towns, on broad bright days, he purchased food by pretend-ing to be on an errand from some nearby estate, where the Master had a sudden need for a particular cut of meat, or oranges to make a punch, or bread to serve to an unexpected guest. By afternoon he would be sleeping in the cover of a thick forest or down at the bottom of a ravine.

In a week he came to the south bank of the Ohio River, which he followed east as far as Ripley. He could see the town on the other side of the water, but he was afraid to cross to it, and he waited at the river-side four days and nights, for what he didn't know. In order to stave off hunger pains he slept as much as he could; in his dreams he heard women's laughter. At last he was discovered by the freeman John Par-ker, who ferried him across the water and sent him along the Under-ground Railroad, northwest to Chicago. Fifteen days after leaving his home and his family, Marcus landed in the living room of a boarding-house on the south side. Not knowing what his own surname might be, he called himself Marcus Cash, and soon he was working as a laborer on the docks of Calumet.

Judge Crown's farm began to falter, he owed money to every merchant within fifty miles, and bill collectors came by regularly to dun him. In the summer of 1840, Crown got into an argument with a barmaid over a glass of beer; he became belligerent, he became violent, and she struck him in the temple with an ax handle. He lingered on for a delirious few days, and then he died. To help pay off the debts he'd accumulated, his wife sold the slave Betsey, Marcus Cash's mother, to a plantation in northern Mississippi.

By and by, Marcus Cash met and married a mulatto woman named Annabelle, eleven years his senior, a widow with three boys of her own. She had long soft braided hair, she could sing as sweetly as a flute, she cocked her hip and swept back her skirts. Within a year she was pregnant with a daughter they named Lucy (b. 1843).

Lucy was fair-skinned and full of feeling, and she needed more attention than her parents had to spare. What's more, she was so much younger than Annabelle's three boys that they scarcely thought of her as a sister at all, and as soon as she reached adolescence each in turn made advances on her. Marcus Cash walked in on the third and administered a whipping to him; but the incident suggested a danger that might recur on any wicked day, and soon Lucy was on her way to school in Philadelphia with instructions to study charm, to keep her legs pressed together, and to pass for white as well as she could, whenever it was possible.

When the War Between the States began, the Cash men watched and waited, and as soon as colored troops were allowed to enlist they joined up. Marcus died at Milliken's Bend, when the tip of a bayonet tore his heart in half; one of his stepsons died of gut wounds received by gunshot at Fort Pillow, another of pneumonia contracted in the mountains of West Virginia, and the third of inanition while marching through Arkansas.

By then Lucy Cash had returned to Chicago, and after Appomattox she and her mother moved south to Memphis, Tennessee. At Annabelle's insistence they pretended to be a young white woman with her aged and loyal servant—but in truth the older woman was nearly insane. Memphis had been in Union hands since the middle of the War, but she wanted to be within defaming distance of the former

Confederacy: The two of them moved into a rooming house and the girl took a job sewing for a local tailor; and every evening Annabelle Cash would venture out onto a bridge over the Mississippi, where she would spit down into the water, and let the river carry her insult down.

Years passed—ten years, fifteen years. Lucy Cash had become a spinster, while her mother died a long, slow, puzzled death. The daughter was thirty-two; it was unlikely that she would find a husband, and a child was almost impossible to conceive. The daughter was thirty-three, thirty-four. And then one summer morning Annabelle awoke with a chill, complained briefly, and died, leaving Lucy Cash alone with her inheritance.

What happened then became a legend in Memphis: Lucy Cash moved out of the rooming house and into a small but elegant place on the north side of town. She hired a cook and a handmaid, bought chandeliers for the house and dresses for herself, and began to throw parties for young women and men. Within a year she was among the city's most prominent belles, fifteen years too old but no one seemed to care; the yellow-fever epidemics of the 70's had killed many of the younger women who might have been her rivals, and besides, the gatherings at her home were so elegant, so lively, the hostess was so charming and so duskily pretty. And in time she had her suitors: a pale and wealthy middle-aged man with a horse farm, a young rich gadabout, the blond boy born to a prosperous merchant, and the son of a minister, named Benjamin Harkness.

Having a keen sense of the mystery of salvation, Lucy Cash married the minister's son. Her wedding took place just a few days before her thirty-seventh birthday, and exactly 280 days later the first of her four children were born; they would be Sally Harkness (b. 1879), and then Benjamin Jr. (b. 1880), and Charles (b. 1881), and finally Katherine Anne (b. 1883). The two daughters were prolific from a young age, producing a total of eleven grandchildren for Lucy Cash, none of whom she'd see or hold; she died of tuberculosis in 1892, revealing only on her deathbed, and only to her two boys, that she was one-half Negro.

In 1899, at the age of nineteen, Benjamin Harkness, Jr., went north to work for big steel, staying briefly in Philadelphia before being sent out to San Francisco to oversee the development of supply lines from the port. It was an unruly town, and being the grandson of a minister born to the privilege of wealth, he took full advantage of the sins of the Barbary Coast. By day he shuffled papers in his Russian Hill office; at night he gave syphilis and cirrhosis a run to see which could kill him first. In the end, the waves preempted both; stumbling home from a wharfside saloon late one night, he fell into the Bay and was drowned.

Charles Harkness was a dull and dutiful man, less ambitious and less lively than his brother, but his blood survived. He finished college, married a woman named Alice, and became a wholesaler of dry goods. Around Louisville, Kentucky, where he lived, they called him Gain for the number of his offspring: Charles Jr. (b. 1904), George (b. 1905), Diana (b. 1905), John (b. 1906), Robert (b. 1906), the twins Mary and Elizabeth (b. 1908), Patrick (b. 1910), David (b. 1911), and the second twins, Emily and Irene (b. 1913).

As soon as she was old enough to leave the house, Diana went north to New York—to study art at the city's great museums, she told her father, but in reality to play amid its prosperity. Many nights she came home to her Riverside Drive apartment giggling and trailing black feathers from her boa across the lobby; many mornings she sat on the edge of her bed and wept—in despair at her loneliness, in pity because she was lost. Later, she would marry a bad man named Selby in a lavish church wedding; six months passed and she had her first son, Donald; a year and a half afterward she divorced her husband, not telling him that she was going to have another child. It was a second boy, Walter, born in 1925 in his grandfather's house in Louisville, but cared for by Diana, until one day in 1937 when she stepped in front of a car on West Oak Street, was struck and thrown, lived on for three more days, and then passed away.

When Walter Selby was eighteen he enlisted in the Marines and was sent to fight in the Pacific War. In 1945 he came home a hero, finished college in two years on the GI bill, and then went to law school at Vanderbilt. Afterward, he settled in Memphis, the home of his great-grandmother, where he went to work for the governor of Tennessee. He met a woman named Nicole, he loved her more than love knew how; he married her and they had two children, a boy named Frank, and a girl, four years younger, named Gail. This book is their annals, twice-told and twofold.

PART ONE | SHOT

Dearest Father:

You asked me recently why I maintain that I am afraid of you. . . .

—Franz Kafka, "Letter to His Father"

1

Nicole's hand was warm and damp. Three-thirty had come, the Governor hadn't called—nor had anyone else—and Walter Selby had gone home lively to his wife, happy to have some time to spare before dinner. He was still thinking about work, running phrases for a speech through his head, but he wasn't thinking hard. It was an afternoon toward the end of May, and he was enjoying the last hours of sunlight, along the street, under the shade of the pin oaks. To see his own house in the late sunlight of a spring weekday was a rare pleasure, and not one he wanted to squander.

To see his own wife. He parked in the driveway and emerged into a noiseless world; some money had bought that quiet, that still and green street. He could hear his steps on the walk, the hiss of the spring on the hinge of the outer door. He had his key in the lock and he paused to prolong the homecoming moment. These were instants he liked to savor: the border, and just across the border, where he would call Nicole's name and then wait for her to answer, wait and wonder where her voice would come from, where she would appear. In the years since they'd married the process had taken on a formal quality, and the closer it came to ritual the more it delighted him; the smell of his own house delighted him, the weather dampening, the day-late hour, the light lengthening across the lawn, his anticipation lengthening along the front hall.

It was a Wednesday, and the Governor was back in Nashville, appearing at a hearing in the State Senate about advisory appointments; he would be strolling amiably down the aisle right about now, dressed in his thin grey penitent suit, a half smile on his face while he shook alike the hands of men he enjoyed and men he despised. Then he would take to his table, sit down slowly, and drop a tablet of bicarb into his water glass to distract his interlocutors while he composed himself. The water would remain fizzing at his elbow until his remarks were done, at which point he would stand up, take the glass and down its contents quickly, and then stroll out of the room again, smiling again, shaking hands, whispering.

The Selby house was quiet. Frank and the baby would be in the park with Josephine, the nanny they'd hired soon after Gail was born. This was Nicole's own time, the part of the day when she could do what she liked, and Walter seldom interrupted her with so much as a phone call. There was some mystery in every marriage, or else there was no material left for later intimacies—for the hours after the children had been put to bed, to save and to spend, repairing the ragged forward edge of their affairs. Away from others, away from work, toward the night.

He stepped inside and called her name. There was a long silence, and he began to wonder if she was in the backyard, so he headed through the house. Along the way the light stepped down into the darkness of the living room where the blinds were drawn, up a notch in the rear hallway, and then up again into the illumination of the kitchen, which, with its south-facing windows, its formica and its reflecting metal, was as bright as a room could be. He stood there, blinking, then he turned and started back into the living room and saw her standing in the doorway, with a look on her face that he couldn't quite describe: surprise, the satisfactions of a day, and worry or a question. She smiled a little. You're home early, she said.

Short day, he said. She was wearing black slacks and a simple blue sweater; her hair was down, and once again he was struck. The man who first burned clay to make china: Wasn't this what he was after? This face, in age? He put his briefcase down on the kitchen table and crossed the room to her, taking her shoulders in his hands. How beautiful, even on a bright, unglamorous afternoon; her cheeks were slightly flushed, her pupils were dilated, her lower lip hung slightly on the flesh. He hugged her; her nipples, half hard, pressed against the upper edge of his abdomen. He stepped back and looked at her from arm's distance.

What is it? she asked.

I was just about to ask you the same thing, he said. What is it?

Nothing. What do you mean?

He shrugged. Nothing, he said. He drew her toward him again, leaned down and kissed her cheek. Neither of them smiled. He reached for her hand, a gesture he had made a thousand times before: he loved the feel of her palm against his—soft, cool, and dry—how her fingers would begin to tremble when the contact, plain at first, quickly grew awkward and unnatural, and then settled again into something comfortable, as each of them abandoned the tiny flickers of will that made their fingers clench, and peace was achieved for two. It was very much like marriage itself, he thought, where some small part of one's self was deliberately, happily, allowed to die. But that afternoon her palm was damp—slightly hot, and slightly damp—and small and subtle though the difference was, it bothered him. He felt a clinging sensation, moist and cloying; it was like putting on a still-wet bathing suit, and he disengaged his hand from hers and rubbed his palm, slowly and almost unconsciously, against the hip of his trousers, and then bade her good-bye for a time so he could shake off the office day.

He was upstairs changing into home clothes when the children came back from the park; he could hear them burst through the door, hear Frank boasting loudly about a game. I hid in the sandbox! he said. All the way down and in, and they couldn't find me, no matter how hard they tried. Not even Josephine could find me, could you?

No, I couldn't, said Josephine. And I looked and I looked.

And then finally I had to come out and show them where I was, or they never would have found me, ever. —Daddy!

Walter was coming down the stairs, watching the tableau below him: Nicole had taken the baby from Josephine; Frank was struggling to get out of his muddy clothes. In the hallway? said his father. We don't get undressed in the hallway. Frank. Come on, now. Son. Frank.

The boy said, No one could find me!

I heard, said Walter. Now go around back to the porch and take your clothes off there. And then you can tell me all about it.

Later, Walter drove Josephine home to South Memphis, his big brand-new blue Impala gliding down the streets, passing into the colored part of town, with its neat little houses set a short way back from broken sidewalks. Thursday, Friday, Saturday, Someday, he thought. And when Someday comes, what happens? He knew very little about the woman on the seat beside him, now holding her glossy black purse tight against her middle. She was good to his children; she had several of her own, all of them now grown. She had a husband at home who worked hard for a paycheck that always seemed to fall a little bit short of the week's expenses. How big was their bed? And how well did they sleep? No better, no worse, this year or a hundred years ago; because bed was where the world reached its level, the one place where all the efforts of the State—his efforts, his State—came to nothing. This Negro woman beside him, the room she was traveling toward, the man she would meet there: When the blinds were drawn and the lights turned off, and she lay down beside her husband, the lying-down would exist in its long kindness, no matter what was done to help them or to cause them to die. Then was all work futile? He pulled up to the curb before her house and turned in his seat to face her. How are you doing? he asked.

Well, Frankie's reading better . . .

No, I mean you. How are you and your husband doing? He couldn't remember the man's name.

Josephine shrugged. We're getting by, she said . . . And she hesitated, waiting for him to say something else, then looked over and found him gazing at her, his expression split between the half smile on his lips and the darkness in his eyes. She didn't want to know what he was thinking, so she made her good-bye and stepped out of the car, leaving Walter to nod and say, See you tomorrow, and pull away from the curb.

Promptly at seven, the family Selby sat down to dinner, but Walter was distracted, hardly listening to Frank as he recounted his boy's day. Throughout the hour he could feel the sensation of Nicole's nipples against his chest. Well, she wasn't feeding Gail anymore, was she? Was it a thought, then, that had gotten into her and then started out again? He could feel her hand on his; the sensation had somehow stuck to his palm and wouldn't dissipate. He felt it, beneath the skin and below the veins, behind the bones, between the nerves.

Little Frank didn't want his food, he said something about the food, he complained about the food. I don't like this. Mommy? he said, his gaze wandering off to one side. He really needed to learn to look people in the eye, thought Walter, if he was ever going to get the things he wanted. —Can I have something else? said Frank. Please? Can I? Please, please, please? He pushed his rice around his plate a little bit with his fork and then slumped down in his chair, his mouth set against any obstacle to his appetite.

Nicole was talking to the boy, but Walter wasn't listening; he was trying to follow a rustling in the rearmost hollow of his mind. She looked at him with wide eyes. Could you help me? she said. Could you help me with this?

Frank, do what your mother says, said Walter gently, looking at her rather than the boy. She returned his gaze with a questioning and concerned expression, and the boy was looking at both of them. Gail began to cry and Nicole reached for her, so suddenly and swiftly that the baby screamed. Oh, now . . . I'm sorry, she said softly, almost singing. I'm sorry, don't cry. —And just like that the baby stopped. Outside, it had begun to rain, the drops picking up where the baby's tears had left off. Everybody could hear it, each of them in the room, everyone in the city. There was no thunder, no sound of wind, only the piano splash of the rain and the smell of wet leaves. Can I have a hot dog? said Frank.

Shhh, said Walter. And then pointlessly: It's raining.

Nicole was still for a moment, and then she spoke to the boy in a whisper. Only if you promise to eat it all. All of it, she said. Frank promised, so she rose from the table and went to the kitchen. Walter watched her go.

After the meal he helped her with the washing up while the boy sat with his little sister; they stood side by side before the sink, but aside from an occasional accidental brush against her hip, or a mutual grazing of fingertips as he handed her a plate, he didn't touch her. He didn't watch her undress that night before bed, or cup her shoulder and smell her neck as she fell asleep beside him, slowly passing him into dreams. He lay awake for a long time, his arms stretched behind his head, while he pondered the prodigal inching of her blood, and the damp heat of her hand.

2

One hot night nine years previously, Walter Selby had found himself alone in the parking lot outside of a baseball stadium, a vast concrete pool set in acres of asphalt down by the river. The game was done and the crowds were leaving but he'd become separated from his companion, a pyknic reporter from the *Press-Scimitar*, in a ruckus that had begun when an elderly woman suddenly struck her cane down on the head of a passing teenager. Now he was wandering between and among the parked cars, trying to find his man. Thirty minutes had passed since the last out had been made, and still the crowds were milling. Every so often the headlights on an exiting car would swing by, causing shadows to wheel across the way; he wasn't sure which gate he and the reporter had used to enter the stadium, earlier in the evening, still less where they'd parked the reporter's car. And the lights, and the groups of ghosts, marked only by their voices, which passed him in the summer darkness.

There, about thirty yards away, stood a rounded figure, much like the rounded figure he had lost. The man was standing in silhouette against the downward raking light of a stanchion; Walter started that way, but as he approached the figure turned, smiling at a passing woman with a mouth full of gold, and it was another man, no one he knew. He stopped again and sighed. A car went by, boys and girls hanging out the open windows and cheering loudly.

The woman, a woman-shadow, was coming his way. She came closer and closer, until she was within touching distance; then she stopped and looked up at him, though her face was still hidden in the shadows. Well, said the woman, shaking her head. I can't find mine. You can't find yours, either, can you?

He said nothing, because he could think of nothing to say. An old sedan approached them, its lights illuminating her for just a moment; she had dark hair and pale skin, and fine, taut features, and she was about to smile, but the car passed and her amusement was given into the darkness again, leaving him with the impression that he'd barely missed seeing something uncommon, a notion nudged a little further on by a trace of her perfume, loosened by the passing car from the kingdom beneath her clothes. He hesitated; she was still smiling in the night. At length he said, No. I was right behind him, but we got separated coming out.

The moon was half round; occasionally its shine would be slowly occluded and then revealed by a night cloud, and the slow shuttering of the moonlight added to the woman's superlunar appeal. I had some friends here, she said solemnly. They could be anywhere. I don't even know how I lost them. She spoke quickly and cleanly, with a kind of confidence that she might have learned from the movies. For that matter, she continued, I don't really know where I am. I came along because I didn't want to sit home. She made a wry face with such force that he could feel it in the darkness.

You're in Memphis, Tennessee, said Walter. Where the lost can hardly be distinguished from the found.

She started at the sharpness of the sentiment and then settled. I think you're right, she said. I think you're right. I'll tell you what, then: You look for my friends, and I'll look for yours. With that she took him by the arm and began to walk him in the same direction from which she'd come. Now, don't tell me your name, she said. But tell me what your friends look like.

My friend . . . He had almost forgotten his friend altogether, and now he could hardly picture the man. There's just one, a little round fellow. I don't know. He looks like everybody else, only a bit more so. And yours? If I'm going to look for yours, I'm going to have to know.

Oh, she said. I lied about that. I don't really have any friends here.

Came all by yourself, did you? Halfway through the sentence it occurred to him that she might be telling the truth, however improbable it may have been, and he pitched the tone of the last words down, so she could take them for sympathy or take them for mockery, either way if she wanted.

Yes, she said sadly, protruding her lower lip in a facetious sulk. No friends. Oh, well. Who needs friends? All of these people. —She stopped in her tracks and gestured around the parking lot and then widened her eyes at him. And only you are gallant enough to help me. No, she said again. Which, after all, means you're going to have to take me home.

I have no way to get home myself, he reminded her.

Well then, we'd better find who we're looking for or we'll have to walk, she said.

They began to wander this way and that, they stopped to let a honking car pass, and he stole another look at her in the ruby glow of its taillights. Then they were walking again. There was something quick and supple about her stride, as she effortlessly adjusted her pace to match his. In time they came to the edge of the lot; there was a field of tall grass, and in the distance they could see the lights of cars gliding slowly along the access road. Hm, she said. This may take all night.

—All right, she said, grabbing his arm a little tighter, turning him back toward the stadium. New rules: My name is Nicole Lattimore.

I'm Walter Selby, said Walter Selby. She smiled again, just as they emerged from the shadows, and this time he could see her face whole and happy, her pale blue skin and perfect countenance, and the grin set within it, so broad that her lower teeth showed like an animal's—a figure of joy and absolute appetite, world-conquering, generous and overflowing, and so powerful upon her face that she squinted as if she too was blinded by it. Overhead there was an airplane climbing the sky, moving upward, outward from the surface of their beautiful blue-black globe. By his side there was this flawless creature, smiling and announcing her name, and he knew what he wanted.

—Stoney, she said loudly. Stoney! In the near distance a tall dark figure was loading something into the back of a sedan; the man turned at the sound of her voice, ducking his head as if it would help him see farther across the night. Nicole? Then they were at the car and all the doors were opening at once, and they were surrounded by five men, the youthful products of reason, peace, and prosperity. Oh my, said Nicole. I don't know how I got lost, but I've been looking for you for almost half an hour now. This is Walter: he's been helping me find you.

Hello Walter, said one of the men, speaking for all of them.

He's lost also. Maybe we should give him a ride. She turned to him. Where are you going? He gave one last glance around the parking lot, now mostly empty. I suppose I should probably wait here a little while longer, he said.

No, no, she said. We can give you a ride, we can take you home. It's the easiest thing in the world. Walter, this is George. He's driving, and you have nothing to worry about.

They piled into the car, a big black Ford: Walter, Nicole, and two other men in the backseat, three more up front. Well, Nicole said to no one in particular, I was really worried. I was really worried, even with Walter here, and even though he was so nice. I thought I was never going to see you again, ever. With that she fell silent, but Walter listened very hard for her thoughts. He was thirty-three then, and she was only twenty-one.

To his other side there was a slight pale boy named Peter, who began to speak. You know, George, he said to the man at the wheel. You are the only man in Memphis who knows exactly where he's going. —The car bounced over a rut in the road, and Nicole fell against

Walter, her slight weight briefly lingering at his shoulder before she righted herself again. Peter continued. Your name's Walter, is it?

Walter nodded.

Tell us about yourself, Walter.

Peter . . . said Nicole.

No, no, Peter went on. I'm curious. I mean, what do you do? Aside from rescuing lost women in parking lots.

That's not enough? said Walter. My God, man. The training alone: months in the wastelands of the Arctic, years studying female physiognomy, perfecting the Reassuring Smile, the Unflappable Calm. This suit, for example: Do you think I simply fell into it this morning? Oh, no, my friend. It's the result of decades—decades, I say—of research into color science . . . the psychology of texture . . . the evolution of animal skins. Ah, you know, John Thomas Scopes was one of ours.

The car was quiet, Peter's wit had been broken by the time Walter had finished his second sentence, and only Nicole was smiling. Hers was the discovery: let the boys be less smug for it.

I work for the Governor, said Walter. I'm a speechwriter, an aide.

Again there was silence, and then Peter spoke again. The Governor, is that right? Tell me this, because I've been wondering. Has he met the newly crowned Queen yet?

The Queen? said Walter.

Elizabeth the Second. I wonder if she'll ever come to visit us, said Peter wistfully. Well, never mind, we have our own Queen. We have our Queen right here. He reached across Walter's legs and touched Nicole's knee, a gesture, it seemed, as much to her silence as to the girl herself. Then he went back to staring out the window and making fun of George's driving. The others began to go over the baseball game, making jokes, telling tales. When they got onto plays they had seen, fantastic and legendary moments, Walter spoke up. —I saw a triple play once, he said. This was in the minor leagues, though. In San Diego, while I was stationed there.

Stationed? The other man in the backseat lifted his head and leaned forward so he could crane around and look at Walter. Stationed, as in the Army? They were too young to have fought in the War, or even to remember it very well.

Marines, he said. He could feel a change of consciousness in the girl beside him, a soft click as she came a little bit more alive.

A thin-faced, red-lipped boy in the front seat turned. There were tears of excitement in his eyes. Selby, he said. Isn't that right? Corporal Walter Selby. I knew I recognized you.

What's that? said George, peering up at Walter through the rearview mirror.

Isn't that right? said the thin boy again.

Yes, said Walter.

You came to my school to give a talk, about five, six years ago. —Walter frowned, not from forgetfulness but merely to disavow any vanity, but the thin boy misunderstood. Oh, you probably don't remember, he said, as if remembering were a weakness.

Eddy remembers everything, said a weary man sitting beside Walter, who until then had said nothing at all.

You were awarded the Navy Cross, said Eddy. Yeah. For distinguished something, valor and bravery or something. Boy, you stood up there . . .

What's the Navy Cross? said George.

A bit of ribbon, said Walter, and a bit of bronze.

Did you fight Germans?

You don't use a navy to fight Europeans, said Peter.

Of course you do, said George. There's a whole ocean between us. They had U-boats. They had a navy.

I fought Japanese, said Walter softly.

The car was quiet. They were passing over a bridge, the water below was pitch black and as smooth as glass, and Nicole reached over and briefly touched Walter's arm.

Then they were at his door, and she was stepping out of the car, leaving him room to exit. Good night, you all, he said.

Five good-nights came back. He stood on the sidewalk, slightly turned away from Nicole, as if he couldn't quite bear her brightness full on.

Thank you for taking care of me, she said.

You're welcome, he said. It was a pleasure. Good night. He nodded gently and started up his walk, looking back at the girl when he was halfway to his door. She was standing beside the car, she smiled at him again with her effortless jubilation; then she waved good-bye. And she climbed back in, and the car drove off, leaving him there in the quiet of his neighborhood, in the center of his tiny little lawn, which stretched for miles and miles to his lighted front door.

3

Back in the days when days were new, Nicole had met a man named John Brice. That was in Charleston, it was early in the fall, and all of her friends had thought he was strange. Yes, they said, he was handsome, lean and graceful, but he was strange. To begin with, he'd just appeared on the street one April day—Nicole had seen him standing outside the Loews in the middle of the afternoon, waiting all by himself for a matinee to begin—and then again, there he was on Broad Street a few days later. After that it was time to time; he was always alone, often with his hands thrust into his pockets. Sometimes it seemed as if he was dancing a little bit, dancing to himself as he went on his way. She'd seen him, a tall slim fellow with refined, almost feminine features and his hair combed back.

At the time she was just out of her parents' house; an only child, imaginative and open. She'd spent two years in junior college, and then she came home again, took an apartment with a girlfriend named Emily, and started working in a women's clothing store called Clarkson's: some dresses, some underthings. Just a job, although she took pleasure in the details of the place, the feel of her fingers stretching over satin or the resistance of a band of elastic. Mr. Clarkson was usually at home, tending to his sick wife, so most of the time the store was hers; she even had keys to open it in the morning and close it at night, with only an hour or two toward the end of the day when he would stop by to empty the till and deposit it into the bank across the street. Otherwise, there she was, alone amid the cloth, the silks and nylons, and the ladies who came in.

This man, he must have been new in Charleston but he strode down the sidewalk as if he'd put a down payment on the whole town. That was something you noticed right away. Still, she didn't think much of him; he was not-quite-regular and all alone, and it didn't take much to make a young man wrong for a girl, in that city, in those days. At first she couldn't quite tell what it was, exactly, and then it came to her: there was a slight eccentricity in the way he dressed, nothing that most people would have heeded, but she had an eye for the way a man put himself together. He would pass her on the street, wearing a pair of black dress shoes, perfectly acceptable, except that the laces were mouse-grey, and he had doubled them through the eyelets before he tied them. Was that on purpose, or couldn't he shop for something as simple as shoelaces? One evening when she was walking home from work she saw him standing outside a florist's in a seersucker suit, quite a nice one, actually, with narrow stripes of a deep rich blue; but it was a little bit late in the year to be wearing summer clothes, late enough that you would've thought he would be cold; and his belt was a few inches too long, so that the extending tongue turned and fell a few inches down over his hip. It was just the kind of thing she would notice, and she crossed the street instead of passing by him; but he turned and watched her all the way down to the end of the block, and she could feel his attention dragging on her at every step.

Then he came into Clarkson's. It was a Tuesday, late in the morning, and he opened the door, peered in for a second, and then slipped across the threshold. He didn't say a word, he just moved among the dresses and the blouses, along a line of girdles, back and around and back again, while she followed him from behind the counter and thought, What is this man doing? He took a little half step sideways— very gracefully—and she stood perfectly still. Then he did a little dance, maybe, a few subtle steps almost too soft to be seen at all, a slight gesture with his hip, his head cocked. He glanced up at her, studying her face, and she would have reddened before his eyes—but just then the telephone rang, she looked down at it, and he suddenly turned and left the store before she'd even had time to pick it up.

Then there was her father's fiftieth birthday party, marked by a family gathering in their house outside of town—she remembered the weekend well and long afterward. So goes the tone of a time: not just forward over everything to come, but seeping outward too, in every direction, like wine on the figures of a carpet. She helped her mother in the kitchen, there was an aunt who got drunk at the party that evening, and wept noisily all night at something no one else had noticed and the woman herself couldn't explain. That night Nicole slept in her old bedroom and listened to her parents in the room next door, arguing in soft voices and then, worse, giving in to that silence which had frightened her so when she was a child, and still made her uneasy. Poor father: a few years after she was born he'd contracted a fever, which was polio and paralyzed his left leg from the hip down. Poor mother: a local beauty alone with an infant, her husband quarantined and per-haps never to come home. By the time he recovered they were strangers again, the large family they'd dreamed of was not to be, he retreated into hobbled quiet, and she wore a seaside cheerfulness everywhere but on her mouth's expression. Now Nicole listened as her mother sat heavily on the edge of the bed, and her father cracked his knuckles as if he would break his fingers right off.

The next day she was back at work, and that very afternoon John Brice appeared again. The same man, he walked around the store a lit-tle bit and then left. But she knew he was going to come back again, she knew she was going to know him, and she waited for him; a few days went by, and then right when she'd decided to stop thinking about it, he opened the door and came in. He had a look, didn't he? Not just his expression, which was ready, but his clothes. This time he was wearing a grey double-breasted suit and a wide blue-and-grey tie, a foppish outfit, kind of high-toned, she thought, although he wore it very casu-ally. He ambled up to the counter where she stood. Hello, was what he said.

She should have just said hello in return. Instead she fell back on her shopgirl manners. How may I help you? she asked.

He paused. I was just looking, he said, and motioned to the inven-tory with one long pale hand.

Anything in particular? she said

No. . . . He shook his head a little.

Maybe if you tell me who you're shopping for, I can recommend something. The sun outside the windows shone down on an empty street, and she looked up and read the name of the store imprinted backward on the inside of the day-dark yellow glass.

What's your name? he asked. She didn't expect that, and she hesi-tated. It was something she didn't want to give away, because she knew she'd never be able to get it back. Come on, now, he said, and made her feel foolish.

Nicole, she said at last. Lattimore. It was as if all the dresses and underthings were filled with silent women, watching women: were they smiling or shaking their heads? It didn't matter anymore. It was done, really, with that. She gave him her name, and that was all he needed.

4

On the third weekend after they'd met he invited her for a drive down to Sea Island and she accepted. He had a huge blue car, a Packard Coupe that he'd bought almost new a few weeks after he'd arrived in town; he came to get her at the hour they'd set, just past dawn, and parked outside her apartment building, but he didn't ring her buzzer. She only realized he was there when she grew impatient waiting and put her head out the window to see if he was coming; then she went hurrying down to him, though she didn't chastise him for not coming to her door. It seemed like one of his things, she could let him keep it if he wanted.

It was a long way, and chilly, and he drove fast, flying along the edge of the ocean, beside inlet and alongside islet, blue outside his window and green outside hers. On Sea Island they bought a basket lunch from a general store, then parked by the ocean and scared the seagulls off the sand with the car horn. Later, they kissed until her lips were sore and her tongue tasted just like his. They arrived back in Charleston that evening; it was too late for dinner, really, but he was hungry, so they stopped for a hamburger. She asked him what he intended to do with his life. She thought it would be a good way to begin to get to know him.

He didn't hesitate and he didn't look away. I'm going to be a band-leader, he said, and for a moment she couldn't imagine what in the world he was talking about. Play the saxophone, jazz, he went on, and he held his hands up, one above the other, gripping an imaginary instrument and wiggling his fingers. Jazz, jazz, jazz. New York, Chicago, maybe Los Angeles. I'm going to be famous.

At first she thought he was joking; it had never occurred to her that a man could have such an ambition, that wealth and fame could be studied, rather than simply stumbled upon by those with improbable access to the unreal. Oh, you are? she said teasingly, and she saw him wince. I'm sure you have the talent, she added hastily, and you certainly look the part. But isn't it difficult to break in?

Sure it is, he said. He paused. I've got a little luck, he admitted. My father, over in Atlanta—he has some money. He stopped again, as if he was suddenly embarrassed by the rarity of his fortune. My father is what you might call . . . a wealthy man. He doesn't much approve of what I'm trying to do, but he's willing to support me for a little while.

Then why did you come to Charleston?

My grandfather had a house here, he said. When he died, he left it to my parents, but they never use it. So I came up here to get away, to practice—you know. To get myself ready.

Ready, she thought. Odd syllables. Was she ready, herself? The more she thought about the word, the stranger it became. —And here was the waitress with the check, it was time for him to take her home.

5

Things about him that she loved: He was tender and devoted. He was funny, and though she'd never actually seen him on stage she was sure he was very good, and so dedicated that he was bound to be successful. He needed her in order to be happy, and he never hid the fact. He never hid anything: he wore all his emotions on his face—ambition, amusement, amorousness. He had that odd, faintly extravagant style, not just in his clothes but in almost everything he did, from the drink he ordered—a martini, bone dry, three green olives, on the rocks—to the language he used when he was excited. He was optimistic all the time, and negotiated the world with an ease that couldn't be gainsaid.

Things about him that she never could be comfortable with: He spoke to her as if he were trying to coax her over a cliff. He judged the world immediately around him severely and without sympathy. He was moody. He had no other friends but her. Many things had come easily for him—money, for example, and self-confidence, and a sense of purpose—and he didn't understand that those things didn't come for her at all. He could be stubborn and impatient. He was more sure of his feelings for her than he should have been, and there was no reason why he might not change his mind. He was a field in which disappointment grew.

In later days they would go to the movies, and afterward he would do imitations of all the parts, the leads, the character actors, bit players, the women too, his voice cracking comically as he reached for the higher notes. Some of his impressions were startlingly accurate, and some of them were just terrible, and the worse they were the more she adored them. Then he would drive her back to her apartment, and, because she had no radio, they would sit outside her building, listening to swing while they kissed under the shadows of a tree—once for such a long time that the battery ran down, and when it was time for him to go home he couldn't get the engine started, and he had to call out a truck to come help. After that he made sure to start the car every half hour or so, letting it idle for a few minutes while they went on with their talking, necking, talking, their raw rubbing at each other.

Oh, how much she loved that car, the shallow, intoxicating smell of its upholstery, the chrome strips—like piping on a dress—that bordered the slot where the window sat, the white cursive lettering on the dashboard and the fat round button that freed the door of the glove compartment. These were elements with which she shared her sentiment. Did he ever know? His keys hung from the ignition on a chain that passed through the center of a silver dollar, the thick disk spinning when the car shook; it was emergency money that his daddy had given him back when he first learned to drive, though when she pointed out that it might not be spendable with that hole in the middle, he just smiled as if she'd deliberately said something amusing.

He might have had some money but he had no telephone, so he would call her from a public booth in town, not always the same one; he would be standing by the railroad terminal, in the library, on a street corner. She couldn't call him at all—she never quite knew where he was—and she grew more and more frustrated with waiting. She tried to show him but he didn't seem to notice. He called her at home on a Thursday night at nine. I can't talk right now, she said. Let me . . . she sighed. Well, I can't call you back, can I? she said pointedly. Call me tomorrow. —And with that she hung up on him and went back to her reading, though the page in whatever it was trembled, and the letters shook themselves out of order. When he called her at work the next day, from a phone booth in a filling station, he never asked her what had kept her from him the night before. Wasn't he curious? Didn't he care? All that evening she was in a sullen mood: All right, she said shortly, when he suggested another movie; she sat upright in her seat in the theater, and neither stopped him nor responded when he put his hand on her arm and then slid his fingers down to her wrist, from her wrist to her knee, her knee to her thigh. He started up between her legs and still she didn't move at all, so he withdrew.

He took her to a cocktail bar afterward; she hardly said a word the whole way there and sat across from him, rather than beside him, in the darkened booth. Are you all right? he said. He was wearing a beautiful grey shirt.

I'm fine, she said, her fingertip playing distractedly across the lip of her martini glass. She waited a moment, and then she said, I don't think we should date anymore.

He widened his eyes and slumped back in his seat. No? he said.

I'm sorry, said Nicole. I just don't think we should.

No? he said again, as if he was hoping that No said twice might mean Yes. Will you tell me why?

He was hurt, and whatever gratitude she might have felt for his exhibition of caring quickly gave way to guilt, so she drew back from her anger and offered him a deal. She couldn't bear to wait by the phone, but they would be fine if he would call her regularly, at work just before noon to make plans for the evening, if plans were to be made; at home before nine if there was nothing to say but hello.

It was their first bargain, and he kept his end carefully, mornings and evenings. There was nothing romantic about the routine, not at first; it was just John calling the way he had promised he would. And then it was romantic, after all, and October turned into November.

6

Now tell me, because I don't know, she said one afternoon. Where do you live? He had arrived at her door in his car again, and it had occurred to her, not for the first time, that she didn't know where he was coming from. He seemed to prefer it that way; anyway, he never volunteered to tell her. If she had to ask, she would ask: Where do you live?

He shrugged. Up in the woods, a few miles out of town, west. She waited. It's just a little house. He traced an invisible house in the air with his fluid hands. Up in the pines, about ten miles from anywhere.

At night it's so quiet, all you can hear is the wind and the wolves carry-ing on.

Is that right? she said with a smile. She wasn't sure what to believe, but that was how she thought of him from then on: John-of-the-Pines when he was being quiet and sweet, John-of-the-Wolves when he had his long tongue in her mouth and his hands all over her. That was a world, and a town, and a tenure.

She told her parents she was dating a man, mentioning it to her mother in their garden one Saturday afternoon and counting on her to convey the news to her father. And what does he do? her mother had asked. She was wearing a sun hat that hid her eyes, but her tone of voice suggested that she was asking for an appraisal rather than an inti-macy, as if being a lady was a business, too.

He's with his father's firm, said Nicole, quite startling herself with the ease with which she lied. Something to do with wood: forestry, lumber, paper, something like that.

He sounds very promising, said her mother, as she primped a gar-denia. Your father will be pleased. When will we meet him?

Soon, said Nicole. We'll make a date and I'll bring him by, she promised, but somehow she never did.

One morning John Brice made his morning call from a booth out-side the supermarket; he was in there, just wandering around the aisles, looking at all that food, and he decided on the spot to make her a dinner.

When?

I was thinking tonight, he said, and she sighed to herself, disap-pointed that he was treating an occasion she found momentous with such lightness of intent.

All right, she said. Tonight, then. Let me go home and get myself fixed up, and you can come by for me at seven.

Hot damn! he said suddenly. Dinner tonight! I'll be by at seven. —And he hung up the phone before she could ask what she could bring.

At seven he was at her door, and as he walked her to the car he ges-tured at the paper bag she was carrying. What have you got?

A pie, she said. Store-bought, I'm sorry. And a bottle of wine.

He kissed her. Wine, oh, wine, he said, and kissed her again. Spo-dee-o-dee!

He took a county road back up behind the town, beating softly on the steering wheel to the rhythm of the song on the radio. In time he turned down a bowered lane, and she asked herself if it was so wise of her to have come along, after all. I don't really know that much about him, she thought. Do I? He was leaning far back in the front seat with his knees almost resting on the dashboard, and he didn't appear to be looking at the road at all; it was as if he were navigating by the treetops. Then he slowed and turned down a driveway, up under the trees they went, and he watched with her as his headlights swung across the front of a little gingerbread house standing in a clearing.

You don't get to see too many houses like this anymore, he said. Not really. This was a bootlegger's house, going back to the last century. This was where they stored the whiskey, up here in the woods. Casks of it. That's how my granddaddy got rich. He exited his side of the car, and she stayed in her seat until he came around and opened her door, not a courtesy she would ordinarily have waited on, but it seemed appropriate to the occasion. There was a wide wind coming across the hills; it was chilly, and she shivered. He put his arm around her and began to walk her to the door. He left the place to my folks, he continued, but they don't want to be reminded that there's some dirty money mixed in with their nice clean cash, so they stay in Atlanta. I always knew it was here, though, and when I had to leave Georgia, I knew I was going to spend some time here.

Why did you have to leave? she said, and she stopped, as if she was going to refuse to walk any farther if there was something wrong with his answer.

He turned, serious as a funeral: They were looking for me. Because . . . —she stared—I shot a man in Reno.

You did what?

Now he was singing, in a hillbilly voice: Just to watch him die. . . .

She started to back toward the car. John.

I'm joking. I'm just joking. Nicole. It's a song, one of those new songs, he said. I didn't have to leave. Not like that, like you're thinking. I wasn't in trouble. I just had to leave because I didn't want to be there anymore.

John Brice's house smelled of the walnut boards they'd used to build it; she noticed that as soon as they walked inside. There were four rooms: kitchen, dining room, sitting room, study. This is my place, he said. The light from the lamps was as dim as an old man's eyesight, and the pictures on the wall were dark and dignified. It wasn't the sort of house she expected, and then she remembered that he wasn't the one who had decorated it; the only sign that it was his at all was a saxophone balanced against a music stand in one corner. The rest was rather gloomy. It needed a lighter touch, something a woman would do, and she allowed herself to imagine for a moment. . . . There's a big old cellar that's empty, he said, and a bedroom tucked up under the eaves, upstairs. You can't tell it's there from the outside, in front, but there's a window in back. She nodded; what was this talk of bedrooms, anyway? He took her jacket and hung it on a peg on the wall.

She looked at the saxophone again. Will you play me something? she said.

Maybe later, he said, taking her by the hand and leading her into the kitchen, where he hugged her so hard she cried out and then laughed. I'll play you something I wrote for you.

Dinner was good, she didn't know any boys who could cook, but John Brice got together a meal, broiled some steaks with a dry rub made from his grandfather's recipe, and made mashed potatoes. Now the wine was done. Standing in the quiet kitchen, the dishes piled in the sink, the only light coming from a fixture over the stove, and she wanted to say something to him about how lovely the evening had been, he was before her, beside her, and—how did it happen?—he was behind her, and there was a hole in the back of her that she couldn't see and couldn't close. It ran all the way up to her heart, which was pounding and pounding, in anticipation of being crushed. Shhh, she said, and there was quiet. She didn't want to miss anything; she wanted to feel every fluttering of experience. Don't worry, he said, but she wasn't worrying.

There he was, groom and spouse. Come here, he said, although she was already in his arms. He put his hands under her blouse, resting them gently on the warm flesh of her hip. How close did he mean to come? He kissed her, more than once but less than many times; then he led her by the hand into the living room and laid her on the couch. His hand was on her breast and she tipped her head back a little bit, a reflex; she didn't know what she wanted. He murmured something, she couldn't make out what, and she couldn't tell whether he wasn't talking or she couldn't hear. She looked all the way across the room to a window. The moon had risen away, climbing up so far that it had disappeared, there was nothing but blackness where the sky would be, and all she could sense was the smell of John's arms, the wetness of his tongue, his murmuring beneath the noise she made when the boundary broke, the tears and gore leaking out of her, making a mess, and the wind in the trees outside.

She had helped him rend her from the word *Miss*. What a good sport: so lovely: what a lustful thing. She wasn't sorry to see it happen, but she lay awake for some hours afterward, gazing on her rags and tatters, until she roused him from his sleep and insisted he take her home before morning. By the time they got back to her house the sun was nearly up and she was exhausted, really so tired she could barely make it the last few steps to the door.

The next day she found that there was little she remembered about those final aspects of the night before: the smell of walnuts, looking at herself in the bathroom mirror, and then taking a cool wet washcloth to her bloody thighs and carefully rinsing it clean in the sink when she was done. He said he had a song for her, but he hadn't had a chance to play it, had he? She remembered his last kiss of the night, which penetrated past her mouth all the way into her skull.

7

Emily in the living room of their small apartment on Chapel Street, sipping at a gin and tonic in the dust-amber heat of a Saturday evening. Emily, who worked as an assistant at a furniture importing firm and had lunchtime trysts with the married man who managed the place. She was wearing one of his dress shirts, open to her navel, and she was giggling as Nicole described the night before. Then she resumed her usual air of lassitude. How bad was it?

It wasn't bad at all, said Nicole. Which is not to say that I actually enjoyed it.

Did *he* enjoy it? —She took another sip of her drink. As long as *he* enjoyed it, darling. We do what we can.

Nicole frowned. I don't know. I didn't ask.

Oh, I'm sure he enjoyed it, said Emily. They usually do.

Speaking of which, how did you get that shirt? said Nicole. Did you send him back to the office bare-chested?

That's one of those secret tricks we kept women have. How to build up your wardrobe, without his wife being any the wiser. I wonder if I could write that up for one of the magazines. Tips for a Fallen Angel, by Anonymous. She sipped at her drink again. So. My little Nicole has a lover.

I suppose I do, said Nicole.

Hurrah, said Emily. Another wicked girl.

I suppose I am.

Then we'll have each other to talk to in hell. Bring along a parasol: I hear it's hot down there.

Well, I may pay for it on Judgment Day, but I'm going to get as much from him as I can in the meantime.

Nicole! Emily laughed.

Jezebel, if you please. Jezebel, harlot, hussy, trollop, any of those will do.

Slut, said Emily, and was immediately sorry she'd said it.

But no, —Slut, said Nicole emphatically, even as she reddened at the word, and wondered if it was right.

8

On the way home one night, John Brice confessed to a future he'd obviously worked out in detail, so much so that it was more real to him than the car he was driving and the road it was on. We're going to go out west, we two, he said. We can go to Los Angeles, get out of here. I'm going to put together a band, get a house gig at a big fancy night-club. Get rich, live in a house up in the hills, with a hundred rooms and picture windows that look out on the lights. We'll go to parties every night, drive down Sunset Boulevard in a big silver convertible, we'll know the names of all the important people, and they'll know ours.

But the whole of his speech was an opposite to her. Everything he said, when he was in that kind of mood, told her in forfeiting terms that he wasn't the man she had been waiting for. Because she didn't want any of that: really, not at all. He frowned a little when she failed to answer, but he didn't say anything more. What did he care if she was silent? His will was all he needed. How did he do that? she wondered. She sometimes thought that he wanted to kill her, or at the very least, that he didn't care whether he killed her or not.

Over the course of the following few weeks she spent almost half her nights at his house, conscious each time that she shouldn't be there, she was opening up for something to go wrong. At first she kept forgetting to plan ahead, and she had to wear the same clothes to Clarkson's the next day and worry that some busybody matron would notice, and know at once what she'd been doing. Then she wised up and left a dress or two at his house; her wanton clothes, they called them. Gin bottles in the liquor cabinet, red moon in the sky, songs on the radio. She had just started to get used to it, sex and all the setup it required, she had just started to enjoy it, when he tested her reach again.

He made another dinner one night in early November, a big ham, greens, cornbread, and she had only been able to eat a little of the mountain he piled on her plate. Afterward, he stood from the table, fixed her a drink, and then began to pace. Here's what I'm thinking, he said. I have to, if I want to do. . . . She didn't give him any look that helped him. It's time, he said. It's past time. I've been here, I stayed here longer, because I wanted to be with you. And I still want to be with you, but I have to go. So I'm going to go, up to New York. And I think you should come with me.

She frowned, she didn't think he was all that serious. New York? The words meant nothing to her. I'm not going to New York, she said. I've never been and I'm not ready to go now. Why do you want to do that? I don't. What do you want to go up there for?

He said, Everything I need is up there, all the people I want to meet.

People? Meet?

Other musicians, songwriters, arrangers. I can't stay around here forever, I've been here too long already, I can't stand it. It's time for me to go.

She thought she was everyone he'd ever want to know, and she went cold, inside and out. Well, you go to New York if you want, she said. I'm not going. You go make yourself into a big man. —She made a mockery of the last two words. If he noticed he ignored it.

I want you to come with me, he said. I'm asking you to come. Nicole. Nicole. I have enough money to keep us for a while.

She shook her head. You're crazy. Go if you want, but I'm staying here.

She thought that was the end of it; either he would go immediately and leave her to childlike Charleston, or he would stay for a while and change his mind. But she was wrong: they talked about it all through the following days; always he said he had to go, always she said she wouldn't, and always there was the next day, the next discussion, dissection, dissension, another day of putting off disaster.

It'll be so easy, he said, on the drive back to his house one night.

It's not easy at all, said Nicole. My family, my friends are here. You and I are here. She waited a moment, gazing at a cream-colored quarter moon out the window on her side of the car, but he said nothing in response, and when she looked over at him his stony face was illuminated in the glare of an oncoming car.

That was December 1st, and she felt the ends of things overhanging. Three days later he disappeared, just like that. He didn't warn her, he didn't explain. His calls stopped coming, and she waited, she thought it was because they'd fought. But a week went by and still no word, so she borrowed a friend's car and drove out to his house, only to find it empty and dark. Then she realized he'd left for good and without a good-bye. He'd gone to New York.

She imagined that the city had swallowed him as soon as he set his first foot down on the sidewalk. In her head New York was hell, and he was innocent but there he was. Hell, because there were so many, many people, none of them had faces, and there was no escape, and no way for them to love each other. She couldn't imagine what kind of experiences he might be having. She tried to picture it, but all she could see was his back as he walked down the street, because he, too, had lost his features. She worried and wept; she'd never realized she was capable of such misery.

She would be tempted to ask the women who shopped in Clarkson's: Should a woman travel to hell in order to be with a man she loves? Seven dollars and fifty cents for a girdle. Three dollars for nylon hose, beige, package of three.

9

One sunny Friday morning just after New Year's a woman came into Clarkson's, someone Nicole had never seen before: bleached blonde, her makeup hastily applied and unflattering, no smile and no gaze. Maybe the woman was thirty, maybe thirty-five; she shopped a little bit, she looked around at this and that. She took a dress down from its stand and turned it forward and backward to get a better look. There's a fitting room in back, if you'd like to try that on, said Nicole. The woman merely nodded, replaced the dress, and turned away to another part of the store, where there were lacy underthings. Just about then Nicole realized they were running out of the tissue paper that they kept below the counter, so she went into the back room to get some more. When she returned the woman was gone, and it was only an hour later, when she was going through the store, primping the stacks, that she discovered an entire shelf full of hosiery missing, and she was halfway to the stockroom for replacements before she realized that the woman must have stolen them. How very strange, the more so since they were different sizes, and so she couldn't possibly have had any use for them all herself. Well, thought Nicole, I'll have to tell Mr. Clarkson, and he won't be happy about it. He can't really blame me, though. Who would have thought a woman was a thief? It made her sad to think about it, and sadder still to think she had no one to share the story with.

10

Nicole put a sign on the door of Clarkson's that said:

CLOSED FOR LUNCH OPEN AGAIN AT 2:00

She locked the front door and stepped out on the sidewalk. It was chilly, and the sky was shallow and grey as ashes. She hurried the few blocks home. In her mailbox there was a small lilac envelope with the address of a high school friend's parents engraved on the back flap. —And a letter from New York City. She opened the lilac envelope immediately; it was an invitation to the girl's wedding, and she put it down on her kitchen table and sat suddenly. Well, weren't they all grown up? She had no way of explaining how such a thing could be happening.

She went to a tea shop for lunch; she ordered, she ate, she wondered where the new year was taking her. Back at the store, an empty afternoon, she opened John's letter, accidentally tearing right through the return address, which was just as well: she didn't want to know exactly where he was.

Dear Nicole:

Please forgive me because I don't write very well. I'm sorry I left without saying good-bye. I didn't know what to say. I love you very much but I had to leave Charleston. I wanted you to come with me, but I did not want to fight about it anymore.

New York is even bigger than I thought it would be. Yesterday I saw Robert Mitchum right on the street. I am playing with some fellows, and they are very good. I hope that someday I will see you again. Please do not be angry with me. Write to me at the address on the envelope if you want to.

Love,

John

She'd never seen his handwriting before; it was crude, unschooled, a cursive script with wide, fat loops, as if he were roping down each word. She could imagine him buying the paper at some corner store, reaching into the pocket of one of his suits for his billfold, with that funny expression he got on his face whenever he spent some money, his eyebrows raised as if the transaction was a surprise to him and he was a little bit worried that he'd get it all wrong, somehow; she could picture him sitting at his desk in some cheap hotel, brown eyes swimming; she could see him putting the letter in a mailbox and then disappearing into the crowds on Broadway; and then she couldn't see him anymore. She folded the letter slowly, put it back in its envelope and put the envelope back in her purse. Through the plate glass in the front of the store she could see an old man in shirtsleeves and a white panama hat, shuffling off to the left.

John Brice had ventured to Babylon with his faithful genius about him; and if that was where he wanted to be, what was hers to add? He didn't love her, she thought. He didn't mean it; either he was living in a dream or he was lying. So sooner or later he would have grown tired of her and he would have started to hate her, and she'd be alone and not so young anymore, and stranded in New York City.

The door opened and a woman came in, and without breaking her gaze through the window, Nicole said, May I help you?

Darling, it looks like you could use a little help yourself, said Emily. I was going to invite you to lunch, on me.

Nicole blinked in surprise. I just ate, she said.

You look like something just ate you.

I got a letter, you know—she gestured—from John in New York.

He still trying to get you to come up there with him?

Nicole shook her head. No, she said. He's gone.

Then forget about him, said Emily. You're twenty years old. There'll be another, believe me. There'll be another.

But Nicole wasn't sure there'd be another at all. What if he was the only one, ever? For a few days she thought about writing him back, but she couldn't have told him anything; it was a madness that started anew each evening, a paralysis in her blood that prevented her from sending so much as a note to him. It was too much for her: the weeks of wandering around with a blank look on her face, an entire symposium she conducted all by herself. Answers, another idea, another question. She never did decide what to say to him, where to start, what good any of it would do, so she never wrote back to him at all.

11

One morning in early March, Mrs. Murphy with the red hair and white gloves came gliding into Clarkson's, accompanying her fourteen-year-old daughter for her first brassiere, in preparation for her journey to the city's most exclusive finishing school. She got to chatting with Nicole while the girl was in the dressing room. Now, love, a woman like you can't spend the rest of her life working in a place like this, said Mrs. Murphy. Mr. Murphy's cousin works for a radio station in Memphis, and he was just telling us how they were looking for a girl to work there, someone to help around the office. Maybe you should call him, Howard Murphy. He's in the directory. —Oh, look, and here's my baby all dressed up like a woman. Lift it up a little, honey. In front. In front, just a little. The girl watched as her mother slipped her thumbs under the top edge of her own cups and tugged them gently upward. The girl did the same. —There you go. Mrs. Murphy turned back to Nicole and unsnapped her little black clutch. We'll take three, she said with a small smile, and drew out a carefully folded bill with her fingertips.

Thus Nicole took herself to Memphis. She called Howard Murphy: The radio station was looking for a Gal Friday, they were hiring— yes, right away, if she was qualified; she mailed a letter detailing her skills and received a phone call two days later; she took a train out for an interview and returned to Charleston to find the job offer waiting for her; she made up her mind, she accepted, and she made plans; she packed a trunk with dresses and effects, and she moved, walking through the door of her new house—a tiny little furnished place a woman at the station had found for her—only six days after Mrs. Murphy had stopped into the store.

There was so much to do, and so much that was different: the wider accent and stronger sibilants, the lights on Beale Street, the new fortune of a new city. Now she and John were two giant steps apart and facing farther away. Maybe a seam in her mind had come undone, all of her love had spilled out into Memphis, and Memphis didn't care at all, and swept it away. But there was this: the strangest thing. She began to miss John's car terribly, it was a helpless assignment of her affections, and she wrote in her diary that if she were to sit in it again she would fill it with tears. Then she tried to put it out of her mind; but every so often, and for a few years afterward, she would turn her head whenever a car of a similar blue went by on the street, knowing it wouldn't be John, knowing it wouldn't be a happy day even if it was. Still she turned her head, because she was looking for herself at twenty.

12

Walter Selby's throat was stopped with visions; sex trickled down it like whiskey, the blood behind his eyes was doped a desperate shade of blue, and nonsense verse rang in his ears, a singsong of refraction and perfection. When the car pulled away that night, with Nicole in it, the neighborhood was quiet and he was dazed; already she was not just gone but missing. He went into his house, took his jacket off, and walked to the bathroom to wash his face, pausing before his reflection and rubbing his cheeks with his hand so that his features distorted. Then he shook his head, took one last look at himself, and walked into the living room, where he lowered himself slowly onto his couch. Over and over he went up to touch the night's events; again and again he retreated, as if he were unsure that they were real. He opened the telephone directory and looked her up: and there she was, a plain entry in the order of names—and there was her address, a road he recognized. He gazed at it briefly and then closed the book and carefully put it back beneath the base of the phone, as if this small gesture of control would be sufficient to prove that he wasn't such a fool after all, he hadn't lost his dignity and he wasn't a boy.

He didn't sleep well that night; he didn't work well the next day. He arrived at his office dead tired and distracted and paused in the dark cool hallway before the door pane of frosted glass. Behind that door, and every door on the floor, and every floor in every building, there were men and women conducting the business of the day.

Q: What were they making?
A: Everything but love.

He entered and his secretary looked up with a slight grimace. The Governor's called three times already, she said.

He's still in Nashville, isn't he? said Walter, worrying for a moment that the man might be holed up in his suite downtown, on some surprise visit to his western constituents.

He's in Nashville, all right, the secretary said. He's upset about something. —The phone rang, she answered, Yes sir, she said. He just walked in.

Walter Selby nodded, went into his office, and picked up the receiver. Selby, the Governor said. He made no introduction, he needed none: his voice—soft, insistent, and musical—could not be mistaken. Where were you last night, my friend? I tried to call you about a half dozen times. There's a senator from Knoxville who wants forty thousand dollars attached to the Parks bill for some war memorial, and we don't have it. He's threatening to make a big deal about it, and it's going to make us look like we don't care about the war dead. Forty thousand dollars. Of course, it's his brother-in-law who's going to build it, but who's going to listen to me on that? War dead . . . War dead. . . . Forty thousand isn't a lot, but we don't have it. We don't have the money: we just don't have it. And you're off at a ball game. . . .

The Governor knew everything, that was given; the Governor was a magic priest of populism, a genius at the whip, and Walter hardly noticed the trespass. Instead, he found himself trying to remember what he had just heard, the words and the Governor's exact intonation, so he could relate it to Nicole when he saw her again. The Governor had become a portrait of the Governor, and all its colors were richer than real. Are you listening to me? said the portrait, its voice heavy with political emotion.

Of course, said Walter. This is Anderson we're talking about.

This is Anderson, said the Governor. I need you to get him to back down. I need your voice: you talk to him. Appeal to him. If that doesn't work, think about what we've got that he wants more than he wants a war memorial, and then tell him you're going to take it away from him. —And without so much as a good-bye, the Governor hung up the phone.

13

Now, Senator Anderson, the Governor has asked me to call you and talk to you about this war memorial. The budget's tight as can be . . .

I know it is, said Anderson. But, goddamn, I've got over two score dead boys from this district, three or four of them from the most prominent families in the state and all of them good supportive people. —Supportive of the Governor, too. They've given up their sons, and they've been waiting almost a decade for some sort of official recognition. You, of all people, should understand.

Yes, said Walter. I understand. I honestly do. And you can have the money. You can have it.

This gave the Senator pause. I can have it? he said, a little more quietly.

Sure you can, said Walter. All we have to do is find something else in the budget to take out.

Something else? said the Senator.

Yes. So I've been going through it again.

I'll bet you have, said the Senator. What are you trying to tell me?

Well, here it is. It's not your district, but Strachey right next door's got about fifty thousand tied up in this little tree-planting business. He wants to prettify the highway from Crossville to Cookeville. Walter slipped his hand under the waistband of his underwear and gently, thoughtlessly, cupped his scrotum.

. . . That's his wife's project, said Anderson softly. There was an old silence on the line. The Senator had held his office since the days when his district was lit with kerosene, and was reelected at the end of every term on a platform of sentimentality. He had never been much of a statesman, and he was growing tired.

In time Walter spoke. Is that right? he said.

You know damn well it is. You know if you try to kill his wife's beautification program, he's going to come after you.

That's all I could find. We can handle him.

God Almighty, said Anderson. He's going to come after *me*, if you tell him why. I need him for the new maternity wing on the hospital. The man thinks, because he was born in his mother's bed, that's good enough for everyone.

Anderson was starting to drift. Walter Selby was nodding silently and absently drawing a poplar tree on a sheet of official stationery. That's all we've got, he said. What do you want me to do?

You tell the Governor . . . Ah. —Anderson sounded close to tears. You tell the Governor I handed him this county on a silver platter.

He knows, said Walter Selby, but I'll tell him again. The budget was safe now, and he could afford to humor the man. How's your own wife doing? Still got a thousand recipes for rhubarb?

Yes, said Anderson, but all the life was out of him now. She's published them in a book.

That's fine, that's great. I'll have to go find a copy, and you give her my best.

I will. . . . Well, I guess I better go now, said Anderson. He was sixty-eight years old, and his only son had passed the last thirty years drooling his supper down his chin in the Nashville Home for the Mentally Impaired.

Go on. I'll talk to you tomorrow, said Walter Selby.

There were some reports in a stack on the corner of his desk; he glanced at them and then turned his chair around so he could look out the window. The morning sun was crooking through the branches of the tree outside; overhead, a pair of perfectly formed cloud puffs were gliding across the dark-blue sky. Life was short and singular and the State was on his desk, the day was bright and angled toward the evening, and Nicole was the name of happiness. He nodded softly to himself and then turned back to the day's work.

14

He waited that night until nine, and then he found her name in the phone book again, took the telephone receiver from its base and quickly dialed the number, already beginning to pace the floor before the rotary had returned to its resting place from the last digit. There was a pause, within which he could have planted an oak tree. Then the line began to ring, —rang again, —and rang seven times before he reluctantly hung up. Having made the effort, he found it almost unacceptable that it should have no effect, and for several minutes afterward he was unable to sit down; instead, he walked the length of his living room and then returned to the telephone and dialed her number again, with the same result. He was needled and stung, now. A police car passed outside his window, siren whooping into the darkness—not a common occurrence in that neighborhood—but by the time he got to his front porch it was gone. There in the driveway sat his car, big-shouldered and black. He considered driving over to her house. And what would he do there? Wait outside. In anticipation of what? He couldn't say, he wouldn't have been brazen enough to try to approach her whenever she finally came home. Where was she? There was nothing for a man to be, but lonely.

At last he went to bed, if only to close his eyes. Through the sleepless hours he saw her telephone number, he saw her friends, he saw the car they had ridden in. He saw everything but her face; she was so beautiful that her features had disappeared, as if in a blindness begotten by the brightness of her smile. He spoke out loud. You are a fool, he said. Go to sleep. And he went to sleep.

15

Late the following afternoon the Governor called. I'm coming in on Thursday, he said. We've got a brand-new firehouse opening up down in Smollet, and they asked me to come cut the ribbon. —There was great enthusiasm in his voice: the Governor liked openings of every sort, schools, hospitals, TVA projects, all things municipal and structural. He would drive two hundred miles through rain and fog to sit for an hour on a podium in some county seat and speak for five minutes on the occasion of the opening of a new Hall of Records, be it little more than a spare room in a courthouse. Write me something, will you? the Governor commanded. Get in a few lines about the utilities program we've been pushing here, but don't make it look like Nashville's trying to cram anything down their gullets. Just remind them, somehow, that we're well aware that it's our state, our resources. You know how sensitive those people can be.

How long do you want to go? said Walter.

Not very, said the Governor. We can save the big show for some other time.

Walter made an assenting sound, and there was a silence; then the Governor took an audible breath: exhaustion, concentration, or just air.

. . . What else? said the Governor.

What else?

What else do you have for me? Anything?

Nothing big, said Walter.

Well, tell me something small then.

For a second Walter considered mentioning Nicole. If the Governor didn't already know, he'd want to be told, and he'd like the story; he'd have a little file on her in a day. No. He spoke up. There was an accident out in Farragut, a school bus went off the road and down into a gully.

Ah, that's terrible, said the Governor sorrowfully. How bad is it?

So far, not too bad, said Walter. A couple of high school kids with broken bones.

That's bad enough. We've got roads in this state that haven't been repaired since Davy Crockett was in the legislature. Have the papers gotten hold of it yet?

Some local editions, round about where it happened.

Ah, shit. Get me the name of an editor out there. I'm not going to say anything, but I want to know who I'm not saying it to.

The editor's name was McAllen, then Walter sat down to write a few remarks for the Governor to speak in Smollet. History, promise, revenue. He considered calling Nicole when he was done, but anybody could have interrupted him—his secretary with some papers, the Governor on the line, officials and lobbyists, and others and others.

16

It was four days further before he reached her; at last one evening she answered, and when she did he was so surprised that he didn't know what to say. There was a bar of silence. May I speak to Nicole Lattimore, please? he asked. This is she, said Nicole, her voice giving nothing away, not surprise, delight, or suspicion. It was a certain reserve that she'd learned since she came to Memphis, no more than a polite and professional way to answer the telephone.

He reached up and touched the knot of his tie with his fingertips, to make sure it was straight. This is Walter Selby, he said softly. We met the other night, I guess it was about a week ago, at the ball game, in the parking lot afterward. I hope you don't mind my calling.

Not at all, said Nicole, who just moments earlier had been measuring the century for solitude. She put her fingertips down on the edge of the table before her and listened while he made his way through an invitation, a date, dinner. The simple fact of his attention was gratifying to her, and so was his obvious nervousness. She hadn't had much in the way of romance since she came to town; the boys in the car had been friends, that's all; one of them worked in the advertising department at the station, the rest were his pals, and after a bit of jockeying they had settled for adopting her as a sort of mascot. It was just as well: she'd needed a few weeks to set up her little house, a few more to acclimate herself to her new job. The radio station was big and busy, and they needed her everywhere, all the time, answering phones, fending off salesmen, fetching reels of tape, cataloging 45s.

But Walter Selby was an important man, wasn't he, and he was asking to take her out to dinner. She felt, for the first time in a very long time, an advantage on the world. She wasn't frightened of him. She agreed to dinner; she saw just how it would go, on that night and the nights to come. They would talk, maybe they would laugh; they would date a little bit, now and again; perhaps she would touch his bare chest with her hand and burn away a little misery; and then one way or another it would end, and she would be six months older.

Later that week he came to her door in his Custom, carrying flowers and wearing a dry smile. He'd spent fifteen minutes at the florist's, but now, as he rang the bell and waited, the flowers looked strange to him, like glass, and he could hardly remember what they were called or see their colors. Blue, light blue, red, bled. Nicole came to the door and he bore down for an instant, taking in her smile and scent and skin. She greeted him warmly and invited him in while she found a vase, but he came no more than a few feet over the threshold; the house was so small, he barely fit into it. She kept talking to him as she walked back to the kitchen: This is terribly sweet of you. I haven't had flowers in here since I moved in. I know I have a vase, somewhere, I'll have to rinse it out. You don't mind waiting, I hope. —She trimmed an errant leaf off one of the stems. There, she said, and turned around to find him nowhere. She laughed and called, Walter?

I'm here, he said from the other room.

All right, make yourself comfortable, said Nicole. I'll be with you in a moment. And thank you for these, they're beautiful. —She could hear nothing from the next room, and she imagined him standing politely, just inside the door, patient, still, and willing to wait.

He took her out and took care of her. She didn't have to think about anything except how to be winning and pretty, and that she could do. At the table he spoke some, playing with the cuff of his white shirt. He gave up a little bit of family history, a word or two about his time in the service, and how he'd come to Memphis afterward.

She was judging him gently as he spoke. He knew things and had a thousand secrets to tell or not to tell. His hands were clean and strong: they had been purified by war, whatever war had been. He was older, and he was lovely, in his way. Do you like him, your Governor? she asked.

She'd expected a simple affirmative, but Walter Selby paused a little, as if the question was entirely new to him; and he smiled to himself, thinking about words of praise and what they were worth. *Like* would be misleading, he said at last. No one likes anyone when anyone is governing. But he's a brilliant man. His job is to make the state prosper, and he does well on that account. —Walter looked around the dining room and then leaned in, and Nicole leaned in to listen. But I'll tell you how he does it, he said softly. Not too many people know this. Every night our Governor goes down into a dark room in his basement, lights a black candle, swishes some whiskey around in an ivory bowl, and waits for the Devil to come whisper in his ear. And the Devil tells him everything he needs to know for the next day. —He wagged his finger. Now, that's a secret. That's how it's done.

He sat back and smiled, and Nicole smiled too, but more thinly. You're joking, she said.

He's a complicated man, said Walter.

She lowered her eyes and let her mouth go soft from relief. I suppose he would have to be, she said. The question is, what does the Devil want in return?

Oh, said Walter, Old Scratch won't ever go wanting for a pleasure ground, as long as he's got the State of Tennessee.

You're a cynic, said Nicole.

I'm hopelessly in love with a slovenly queen, but she scorns my affections; when I try to dress her in suitable robes or better set her table she turns her haughty back. Sometimes I sulk to cover my shame. Then morning comes and I try her again.

That's sweet, said Nicole, and she smiled as if she'd swallowed the sun.

The conversation wandered from there: back to his time on the campaign, forward to Memphis, back to Charleston and her schoolgirl days, her parents, Emily left behind. In the minutes the table vanished, the restaurant dissolved, the city pitched away all its pettiness. He asked her about the radio station; he'd met the owner once during the Governor's campaign. Oh, it's very interesting, really, she said. I don't quite understand it all yet. I don't know much about music, except for the Hit Parade; but something's going on that's got all the fellows at the station excited, and you wouldn't believe the sorts of people who come through.

What are they like?

Wild men, she said, laughing. Just wild men. They come up out of the swamps, they come down from the trees, and they never say anything but they yell it at the top of their lungs. She leaned back in her chair and crossed her legs. My job is to be very nice and friendly and try to make sure they don't burn the place down. She reached for her wineglass, and a small silver bracelet slipped out from under the cuff of her sweater and glittered in the candlelight as it dangled from her white wrist. It's like they're fighting a war. —She grimaced. —I'm sorry. That must sound to you like a very silly thing to say.

No, said Walter.

You being a hero and all that, she said, and thought of the word's possible meanings for the first time when she said it.

He frowned, on familiar ground. They gave me a medal. They could have given it to anyone.

That's not true, I'm sure, said Nicole, though she wasn't. You were in the Pacific?

He didn't want to talk; he wanted to watch her, but she had turned the table back to him, and he felt obliged to take it. The Philippines, he said. Some of the South Sea Islands.

What was it like?

He lowered his eyes. What to tell? The islands were beautiful, he said. Everything was huge and green. I was very young.

Nicole nodded solemnly, because the hour had suddenly become solemn. She had intended no such seriousness, and neither had he; but there it was. Eddy was very impressed with you.

I hardly remember what I did, he said. It was a good long time spent bored and waiting, and a few short moments of absolute terror. When it was over, I didn't know where I'd been or who I'd hurt. She nodded again and swallowed a question, one she often wanted to ask afterward, always with the same terrible curiosity, a sickening lurch made more shameful for the fact that she felt like she was seeking it. Who did you kill, Walter?

17

He had been eighteen when he joined the Marines, a year behind his brother Donald's enlistment in the infantry. He had shipped out from San Diego to Honolulu, and he'd gone, as much as anything, because he wanted to get out of the South. There was no reason why he chose the Corps, except that the story of the sea was so distant from the story of his family, and he had an eighteen-year-old's desire to exploit the distance and impress his dead forebears. A few weeks in training and there he was, waiting in Hawaii to be cast into battle.

There were ten thousand troops on base, all sorts of men, with all sorts of reasons, and many with no reason at all. Walter had never seen such an array, such opposition and jumble: from fair to tan, from soft to savage, from swift to slow. They came and went through the barracks and depots; they rambled along the dry roads, falling in and out of patterns like glass chips in a kaleidoscope, according to ties of time and origin, inclination and impulse. They spent days maintaining their gear, cleaning this and oiling that, and nights lying on immaculate, evenly spaced bunks in their barracks, waiting and boasting, with the smell of the sea all around them, and the long rhythm of the surf as it repeatedly gathered itself and broke against the shore.

Within a few days a set of alliances had formed, gangs among them: Irish from Chicago, the Northwest Loggers, college boys, they found one another and fell in as easily as if they were following orders. Walter was a member of the Austral Gentry, heirs to the manners and the land from the Carolinas to the Mississippi, from the Mason-Dixon Line to the Gulf Coast. There was MacIntire, Hamilton III, Lukas from the hills of Georgia—good boys all.

There was one more fellow, a small, wiry man from the outskirts of New Orleans named Chenier. He was a little bit older than the other men, and he looked older than that, because his skin was rough and dark from standing in the sun, and his nose had been flattened in an adolescent fistfight. He was a Cajun; most of the men on board could hardly understand him through the meal of his accent, and this, too, separated him a little bit from the others. He smiled crookedly, smiled slightly madly, and spoke in a crazy dirty French mumble. During his days in stateside camp a sergeant from Louisiana had dubbed him Coonass, and he carried the name with him, all through his deployments.

Some of the men took in his dark skin, his mumble, and his nickname, and decided he was a Negro, if not in whole then in substantial enough part. Warren from New Hampshire may have been the first to suggest it, one evening while he stood at the base of his bed, peeling wide papery flakes of sunburnt skin from his shoulder. I don't know about all this work outside, he said. A civilized man doesn't stand in the sun. The invention of culture was simultaneous with the invention of indoors: palaces, cathedrals, libraries, legislatures. —He made a gesture like a man sprinkling a pinch of salt, and the skin fell from his fingers to the floor. —Where does an evolved man eat? In a dining hall. Where does a wise man lay his lovely wife? In the darkened privacy of his chambers. Oh, the sun is a fearsome thing: the Greeks called him Apollo, the son of Zeus himself. The Egyptians called him . . . What did the Egyptians call the sun god, Brammer?

Fuck if I know, said Brammer.

Warren peeled at his skin some more. Everything the sun sees, it destroys, starting with a man's own flesh. Myself, my father, his father, and his father before him, all treated the sun with a healthy respect, and the Warrens have always been the paler for it. Now the Corps asks me to stand in the sun all day, just so my rifle won't get lonely. Hence, I burn. It is the mark, I say, of a civilized man. —He gazed imperiously around the room. Now, Chenier, for example, doesn't burn. In fact, Chenier is getting mighty dark. Where you been, Chenier? On your own little Africa campaign? —Laughter all around, and the conversation turned.

Then a unit had been finishing maintenance on a cannon when one of the men spotted a slick of oil beneath it. It was evening; the sun was red on the horizon. Sergeant isn't going to like that, said a Voice of Fearful Mourning. Somebody's going to have to stay behind and get it cleaned up.

Let the nigger do it, said a Voice of Young-Old Dudgeon.

He meant Chenier, and Chenier, who was on the other side of a crate of shells and didn't hear him, accepted the assignment without knowing why it had been left to him, spent an hour on the job, and then ran to the mess, where he sat at a table with two of his battalion mates, who rose pointedly from his presence and took themselves across the room.

Well, an argument went, over boilermakers and under a bitter yellow moon. Coonass was a black man, snuck in by the Department of the Navy under the guise of being white, because Roosevelt wanted to prove his principles. No time better than a war, when great masses of men shifted around the world, and all societies were transformed. Somebody had to be planning it: somebody had to be keeping track, from start to finish. One Negro man in the Marine Corps.

Chenier paid no mind. He'd heard worse, he'd done worse. He was thirty years old, his teeth were still strong enough to bite the head off a penny-a-pound nail, and his hair was still thick; he didn't care what young men thought. It was just as well they left him more and more alone, to fall back on his tangled inner tongue. He wrote to his wife in Slidell, telling her it wouldn't be long until the day he climbed back into bed with her, and banged her until the walls shook.

Then there came a Wednesday night when leave appeared, like an alignment of the planets, for Lukas, Hamilton III, and Walter Selby. It was a fine night, a fine fortune, the palms were rustling, the wind was up, and the three men strolled the walks with careless ease. At the motor pool stood Chenier alone, dressed in his immaculate uniform and a sour-smelling aftershave. He nodded hello to the boys and turned back to his obscure thoughts. Hamilton III took the others aside in a spirit of gallantry born out of the tedium of waiting, as surely as his ancestors' had been born out of the tedium of the fields. Listen here, he said. I don't care what those boys say. Coonass is a man of honor. Coonass is an upstanding representative of the values and tradition of the United States Marine Corps. And Coonass is going to accompany us on a goddamn drunk.

Walter Selby went to Chenier and made the invitation, and Chenier accepted with a shrug, neither ungrateful nor quite glad.

Where were you going, anyway? Lukas asked him as they started into town.

Don't know, said Chenier. Just going into town to get a drink, maybe look at the femmes go by.

The femmes, said Hamilton III. That's good. What kind of femmes do you like?

Chenier said nothing, but he smiled broadly in response, his wide lips curling back immodestly.

We'll see what we can do, said Hamilton III.

They began at sundown in a bar on a hillside and progressed down toward the water, as if in a dream of drowning. In one dark beery place they became bogged down—Lukas wanted one of the waitresses and insisted on staying until he could proposition her—but in time they moved on. Their faces grew red and their eyes grew wet, ten o'clock came at Lonesome Bob's, the Best of Honolulu, where they ordered rum and coconut milk and stared at the center of the scarred round wooden table.

> *I left a girl in Abilene*
> *I left a girl in Abilene*
> *Prettiest girl I've ever seen*
> *Waits for me in Abilene.*

I want to go dancing, said Lukas. Let's go find us a dance somewhere. You a dancer, Coonass?

Chenier nodded, his face serious and proud. King of St. Tammany Parish, he said. Ain't nobody better.

There's a big band down at the Regis Hotel, said Walter. Let's go, then. Let them swing.

Let them swing, said Lukas, and they rose a little unsteadily and started back into the night.

The hotel ballroom was dark but the bandstand was bright, the music was hot and loud, and Chenier could dance just as he said, jitter-bugging furiously, with his hat clenched in one hand and a local girl grasped by the other, his lined face shining and a smile fixed upon his features. Walter watched him with a combination of curiosity and admiration, as if the other man were an exhibit of some sort, a demonstration of human physical skill taken beyond the practical and into festive excess; and he danced one song himself, with a tall, heavily made-up woman with straight black hair and ocher skin, and then retired to the bar, where Lukas and Hamilton III were waiting.

Look at that man go, said Lukas. Chenier had loosened a button on his dress shirt and his legs and arms were flying this way and that. —He looks like a goddamned rooster trying to fly. Can't compete with that: let's get drunk. Bartender! You got any bourbon in behind that fancy bar of yours?

Then it was midnight and the band members were taking their bows, there was applause all around, and the three of them were as blind as worms, as bent as worms and with as little left to lose. Last hours on earth. Outside, the palm trees were being whipped around by a dark Pacific wind; inside, Hamilton III was lecturing to no one. My mother . . . he started, and then he stopped again, as if mentioning her was all he had intended. Coonass had come off the dance floor soaked in sweat, his hair as wet as if he'd just stepped out of the ocean. A big round-faced sandy-haired boy was waiting for him at the bar, watching him as he came across the polished floor, finally laying hands on the bar top and huffing for air as he gazed down to the far end, where the bartender was wiping up a spill.

Tell me something, nigger, said the sandy-haired boy. He wiped his small bent nose with the back of his hand and sucked back the water from his lips.

Chenier shook his head. Not so, he said, though he was so breathless it came out in a single slurry syllable. It made no difference at all. The sandy-haired boy put his hand on Chenier's shoulder and squeezed a little.

Tell me, how did you get in here? You're a sneaky little son of a bitch, aren't you? Sneak your way into a white man's Marines, where you don't belong. Sneak into this hotel.

Down the bar Walter noted a certain dissonance in one corner of his consciousness, but it was late and he didn't want to look, so he turned slightly, facing himself a little farther toward the dance floor, where a pair of Red Cross girls in chiffon dresses were holding hands and giggling about something.

You're crazy, Chenier said to the sandy-haired boy. I don't need no trouble.

Yes, said the boy. Yes, yes, yes. Yes, you do need trouble. Why don't you come outside, and I'll show you what you need? Come outside, and I'll shove your black head up your black ass.

Chenier said nothing and didn't move. The sandy-haired boy smiled and nodded to a pair of friends who were standing in the corner; the two friends smiled back, and then turned and left the bar. Idly, Walter watched them go. He studied his hands; he gently rocked his glass. Chenier caught the bartender's attention. Shot and a beer, he said, and he cocked his head up to look at the chandeliers in the mirror behind the bar.

You can't serve him, said the sandy-haired boy. The bartender made a puzzled face. Don't you know who this man is? the boy continued. The bartender shrugged. This man, said the boy, is of the African race. Now . . . now . . . now, I don't know how he got here, I don't know who he lied to, or what. I don't even know why he's trying to pass. They've got plenty of places of their own. But I'll tell you this, he insisted, leaning over the bar top. You keep serving him, and no white man is ever going to want to come in here again.

That's enough, said Chenier. In the dim light he suddenly looked very much older, more formidable as a man, but also more frail.

It's not even close to enough, said the sandy-haired boy, leaning in, and Chenier sighed. Come on outside, and we can settle this real quick.

Can I get a drink, my friend? said Chenier to the bartender.

Why don't you boys take care of whatever you've got between you, said the bartender. Go take care of it, and then you can come back in and have a drink, O.K.?

The sandy-haired boy waited while Chenier stopped by Walter's end of the bar to pick up his hat. By then Harrison III had begun the saga of his mother, her many marriages, her money, her mansion. The Cajun paused and leaned in to listen.

What's going on? said Walter.

I don't know. . . . said Chenier, slowly. This boy here seems to have a problem with me.

The sandy-haired boy smiled and spoke loudly from down the bar. I'm going to teach your nigger friend a lesson, he said, but Walter made no effort to argue with him; he was too drunk to quite register the insult, there in such crimson luxury with women and music; it caused him little more than a thought to the wind outside and his home back home. There was a bit of banal silence, and then the other two were gone.

The Cajun died that night, beaten to death in five minutes in the night behind the hotel's service entrance, by three men who were never found. At the end there was steam coming off of him, but he was shivering, and the last thing he saw was a big dirty grey cat licking at his ankle. Skk, said Chenier. Skk.

It was only when the M.P.s entered the ballroom that Walter, Hamilton III, and Lukas realized that anything was wrong at all. They'd noticed that the Cajun was missing, and they knew he was in some kind of trouble, but they'd figured it was just going to be a little bit of pushing, something in the dark that any one of them might have confronted. Maybe he'd made friends with the sandy-haired boy and gone off to other pleasures. No.

The policemen separated them and brought them back to the station; there they were questioned, one by one: What are your names, and what unit are you from? Where have you been tonight? What have you been doing? Who was your friend? Who was he talking to at the bar? The three of them, Hamilton III, Lukas, and Walter himself, had hardly looked at the boy long enough to see him; they had heard the word *nigger*, and that had told them everything they needed to know. You didn't see him? said the investigating officer to Walter. Your buddy goes out to fight three other men, and you don't even see who it is? Why didn't you go with him? Why didn't you help him?

Walter was eighteen years old and had nothing to say, though a mad tear of dishonor slipped down the side of his nose. The drinking had long since left him, and their loss was strange; no one was supposed to get hurt until combat, and then only gloriously. No one was supposed to die upon dancing. Back at the base the three who were still alive had their last conversation. God damn it, said Lukas. Why'd the son of a bitch leave us? Why didn't he ask for help? But all of them knew that they had done something too indecent to be washed away by sunlight or sobriety, or even the war to come. They had been careless and star-cursed, and Chenier had died.

18

The following week Walter Selby boarded a transport ship bound south for the Gilbert Islands. Riding on the back of the giant grey-green ocean he waited patiently to die, to be cut in half by a shard of metal come whistling down from the empty sky, to be thrust upward on a column of fire, to tumble overboard and drown in the deep—not so much because he deserved it as because he was out of moral luck. Instead, the seas turned gradually blue, the islands appeared, the gorgeous jungles, coral reefs, a lagoon, a beach; forward and forward, under the palms and pandanus and in the event, he discovered how clever he was at killing men, and he killed every man he could.

19

He came home half skinned, with a nice medal to cover his rawness. His brother Donald was waiting for him in Louisville with a handshake and a proud smile, belied only by a little tightness around his eyes, where the war would not be forgotten. Everyone Walter met wanted to congratulate him, to call him, hire him; there were car horns blowing all over Louisville, and the lights burned in the house through the night. College went by quickly; he had a history professor who insisted he was made for public service and coaxed him into attending law school at Vanderbilt. Six years after peace had resumed, there were still people who remembered how well he'd done when war was at hand, and when he graduated he was asked to help out with a local campaign, a congressman whom no one believed stood a chance of reelection. And then, to everyone's surprise, his candidate had won, and Walter felt a deeper and deepening satisfaction. After the War there would be no wars but that for the security and justness of Tennessee. He'd been offered a job in the Congressman's office, but he declined: the Congressman himself was not inspiring, and his seat, in the lonely east, had no power to lend. What's more, Walter liked the campaigning, the knowing, moving, and fixing. He was a young man with an authority that seemed inborn, thoughtful and stern, an educated man who nonetheless liked to get down on all fours and fight, a formidable man getting more formidable, a force to be feared or a comfort to those he cared for.

One winter afternoon, Walter received a call from a state senator in Nashville. He had heard a bit about the man: soft-spoken, frank, well trusted by his wan constituents, who had voted him into his father's office a few years after his father had died, and kept him there for more than a decade. He was known to be thoughtful and thought to be fair; all his legislation had been sheer windmilling to the State's higher machinery, but the people in the small towns, the failing farm communities and the middle poor, loved him for his promises and his undisguised contempt for the old men in the capital and Boss Crump's machine in Memphis. He was more interesting than most, and Walter went to meet with him.

The senator had an elderly, tremulous factotum waiting in his anteroom who guided Walter into the office, disappeared, and returned a minute later with a tumbler full of Tennessee whiskey, a seltzer bottle, and a porcelain bowl filled with ice, which he set down on the table by Walter's elbow. The Senator will be with you shortly, the factotum said, and took his leave again.

After a few minutes, the door opened and in came a small slight man with a great big round head, and hair and eyebrows so white he might have been an albino; but he was merely old, and stripped clean of color by the speed with which it happened. Walter stood; the senator shook his hand softly and motioned him to sit again, taking a wine-colored leather chair himself and drawing in a long breath.

Walter Selby . . . said the senator, gazing at him frankly. You're a big fellow, aren't you? That's good. I like that. He took a moment to look at the papers on his desk. Walter Selby: I've been hearing about you. Walter nodded, and then there was silence, but for the airs of the house around them. At length the senator spoke again. Do you know how far it is from Memphis to Sugar Creek? he said.

About five hundred miles.

Four hundred and seventy-five, said the senator. That's a long way. A lot of highway. Our truckers are getting shaken down all along it. We have to do something about that. We've got to help the farms a little, as much as we can. We've got some classrooms with forty-five children in them, and others with just two or three. It doesn't make any kind of sense. We've got utilities up in arms about the TVA, and people still don't have power in some parts of the state. No power. No lights, no refrigeration, no radio to listen to after dinner. There are people who believe that the only solution to our problems is World Government. —The senator paused to taste the words. —World Government. Over there in Memphis there's a group of businessmen, meet in secret every

Thursday night at the Badger Room to discuss the establishment of a . . . World Government. There's another group, meets in secret every Monday at noon in the back room of a luncheonette on Union Avenue, to discuss how to thwart the first. —The senator held his hands up in an attitude of prayer and pushed them against each other. You see? he said. Two opposite and equal forces. I've taken them both aside and told them how much I appreciate what they're doing. Told them, I can't come right out and endorse you, of course, but you have my tacit support and my gratitude. And they do. As long as they keep pushing against each other, they can't push against anyone else. —Here the senator shook his head sadly. Sweet Jesus, the state's crawling with lunatics. Half my job is keeping them howling at the moon, so they don't start howling at me. I was talking to a doctor down at Vanderbilt the other day, man working on an immunization program. A good program, too, and I'm going to get behind him. Then I asked him: When are you boys going to come up with a vaccine for foolhardiness? That would solve about half our troubles right there.

Walter smiled slightly.

All right, said the senator. Let's talk. —He leaned back in his chair, paused, and then leaned forward, until Walter could smell his clean breath and barbershop aftershave. I saw what you did in that campaign. I watched you pretty closely. You've got your war record but you're not riding it all over the state. You've got family ties here from a long ways back. I know all about it, don't you worry. Nothing to be ashamed of. There's probably a little colored blood in all of us.

What? said Walter.

Old Lucy Cash, she did what any woman in her position would have done.

The name had come from so far back that Walter had to pause and think.

You didn't know, did you? the senator said softly.

That's my great-grandmother.

She was a colored woman from Chicago, said the senator. High yellow, a lovely girl. She wanted to pass, so she came down here.

Walter shook his head, looked down, and studied his blood—the same blood now, but it felt burnt. Where did you get this from? he said.

Well, you know, I looked into things, said the senator. I wanted to know who I was talking to. The important point is that it's not important. Do you see?

Walter nodded and said, No. A pause. No, of course it's not important. I bet half the people in Tennessee have some Negro blood in them somewhere.

That's right, said the senator. That's what I'm saying. But I don't think people are quite ready to hear that yet. Not today, anyway. Maybe tomorrow.

Maybe, said Walter. Tomorrow. Is that why you and I are meeting?

Oh, that's just a little part of it, said the other man. We have so much work to do, you and I.

I suppose maybe we do, said Walter.

I can tell you're a virtuous man, and a practical man, and an eloquent man. You represent the future of Tennessee, and you carry it well. One of these days you're going to be an important figure in this state, perhaps even the country as a whole. —The senator paused and gestured needlessly to the papers on his desk. I've been talking to the state party chair, going to dinners all through the wards. I have solid support. I'm going to run for governor, and I think I'm going to win. But I need you, Selby. I need you to go down to Memphis for me and watch what goes on. Keep an eye out, keep Crump's men at bay. I need you to write some speeches for me, to get these people out to vote. So, said the senator, and he lifted his head and smiled. What can I give you to make you sign on?

Later, Walter would wonder what Nicole was doing at just that instant, what beauty of girl-in-body she was performing on the stage of her hometown. But he wasn't thinking of her when the senator first charmed his loyalty from him, even as an ideal to come. He wasn't thinking of the people, he wasn't thinking of history: there would always be room for the state and time for the century. He was thinking of the senator, and the magic he'd wrought from the past, making Walter a different man, though in no way he could tell. The news of the color in his blood was meaningless; but the way it had been delivered was a little miracle, a perfect manifestation of knowledge in the service of authority, and authority as guarantor of knowledge: a system sufficient unto itself, which the senator had put on display just to show that he could. He was an inevitable man, and his campaign would be steered by the stars. Walter shook the senator's hand that evening and began his phone calls and visits the following afternoon.

In November the senator became the governor, and Walter became his aide—his speechwriter, his adviser and confidant, his bully when a bully was needed, and his eyes in the west. There was an office in Nashville and another in Memphis, with a room or two in Knoxville and Chattanooga. You can have Memphis, my perfect man, the Governor had said to him, as he stared and smiled up at Walter from his seat behind his desk. But I want you to beware, for me and for yourself. —He spread his hands, as he did whenever he was about to take a rhetorical liberty. These are parlous days, he murmured. Women and children cower in doorways whilst crime runs free in the streets; there are Communists all the world over, and our enemies come to us disguised as brothers; the South is bearing a New World, and the midwives in Washington have filth upon their hands. And the poor can't bear their burdens any more. Et cetera, he said. Et cetera. —The Governor smiled again, now more broadly, with the delight of a small man who's just been challenged by a big man he knows he can beat. Just help me keep these sons of bitches off my back, he whispered, so I can get some work done around here.

Didn't Walter walk in Tennessee? And didn't he take every stride with confidence and pleasure? You can rely on me, he said.

20

He had stories to tell Nicole, and he told them well. Men and women he had met along the way, histories veiled and exposed. The Governor had served his first term without reducing the state to ruins as his opponents had predicted, and for that he was elected again. Then the bosses had started coming around: local power brokers, ward captains, industrialists, preachers of distinction. Each time he finished one anecdote she asked for another, and each time he complied. What had been said in the room, that made the electric utility keep prices down until spring. Who was sent to the Baptist ministers, to convince them to allow trucks to carry cases of liquor on the Sabbath. Who got the contract to build the airport runways, in exchange for what contribution to which of the Governor's causes.

Tell me another, and I'll give you another kiss. It was a warm October night, and they were sitting on his porch swing. Stories for kisses;

her hair smelled sweet but her breath was slightly sour; every time it shocked him, made her kisses more real, which in turn made them more fantastic. He would have told the entire history of Tennessee for her kisses.

Well, he said. There was a fellow I met in Chattanooga, ordinary man, ordinary size, little pink bald head, he must have been about fifty, maybe fifty-five years old. I met him at an American Legion Hall, but I still don't know what he was doing there. The Governor was giving a speech, I was waiting outside, and there was this man. I don't even know how I got to listening to him, and at first I didn't know what he was going on about, something about a man named James Ewell. Every time he spoke of this man he used the full name: James Ewell. That's what I noticed first, as I tried to keep up with him.

Well, it turned out James Ewell was a neighbor down the road, and James Ewell had a daughter named Evelyn, about seventeen years old. —No wife, his wife had died when the girl was a baby. This too went on for a while—James Ewell, Evelyn Ewell, the farm they lived on—until it last came out that the daughter was a crack shot with a rifle, best all-around shooter in the county, and James Ewell was as proud of the girl as could be, and he was very close to her. Very, very close. You know? Closer than anything. People used to wonder about that.

All right. James Ewell and his daughter used to go hunting together in the woods, the man said. James Ewell and his daughter, they would disappear for a day or two and come back with their truck loaded up with deer. Until one day when the daughter come into town alone, walked calmly into the police station, and said she had shot her Daddy, out there in the woods. It was an accident, she said: she'd been following a buck through the trees, and the next she knew the old man was lying on the ground with a bullet through his neck. And now no one knew what to do; the girl never missed, that was the legend. But what proof did anyone have? And so they let it go with her tale to cover it.

An interesting story, Walter had said to the man. What can I help you with?

Well, I'll tell you, said the man. Now this selfsame daughter was going around with his own son. I don't want the boy to end up dead, and I don't want to tell the girl *no*, and the goddamn chickenshit police won't do a thing about it, said it wasn't anything they could do. (And here Walter apologized for his language, but that was what the man had said; and Nicole just smiled and nodded.) But I saw your Governor was coming in to talk, and I wanted to ask him for his help.

I'll tell him, said Walter. You leave me your name and how to get hold of you, and I'll let the Governor know all about your problem.

The man had been disappointed by that. He wanted to put his case to the Governor himself, but Walter had said that wouldn't be possible; he was very sorry. Still, he promised he would do his best. He handed the man his notebook and a pen. —Well, all right, said the man, and he scribbled down his name and an address on a rural route.

Of course, the Governor had wanted nothing to do with the man, his son, or Evelyn Ewell, but Walter himself had been curious, and he'd checked up on them with the local law, a few months later.

And? said Nicole.

Son and girl were happily married, had a baby on the way; and the old man wouldn't talk to either of them, so sure was he that doom was still making its grim course toward them, delayed only for a few years, which, as far as doom was concerned, was no time at all. —And for all I know, said Walter to Nicole, they're still living just like that. He paused and looked at her thoughtful face. What do you think? he said. Was the man making it up? Am I?

Nicole blinked. Oh, no, she said quickly. Neither of you, no. I believe you. I believe him. You can tell by the story that it has to be true. Even if it isn't true. Don't you think?

I do believe you're right, said Walter, pushing the swing back with his legs and letting it glide gently forward again.

21

Walks in the evening, beneath a dark, humid sky that reflected backward on the day. They would stroll along the riverfront, stopping here and there to peer into the water; or park at the edge of the wealthy streets east, and wander up the roads, looking through fences at gardens. One evening they had dinner and then dropped by the zoo an hour before closing time to watch the elephants get ready for bed. He kissed her, and all his ideas went dead by the contact, like lights burned out by a short circuit, leaving only one thought dangling down in the darkness: *Farther.*

He reached for her, but she stood back with a slight smile on her lips. I think I should go home now, she said.

He nodded, straightened up, and smoothed down his jacket. Yes. All right.

He took her home, kissed her once more at the door, and let her go. She stood inside the threshold and licked her lips. Walter was gentle, polite, considerate. He was stable, he was staying. He was a man, then, worldly and resourceful. So he was staying. So good, she was glad. The next time they went out, he kissed her again at the hard dark end of the night, and she pressed forward into him, where it was closer still to midnight, venturing in, with her kiss returned, toward everything he knew. That night she took him home; and the nights afterward she did or didn't, depending on how she felt: whether it would be too much to be with him, or too much to be alone.

22

The Governor called Walter. Now, what's going on with that accident out east? The one with the schoolchildren.

Nothing much, said Walter. Some of the parents are looking to throw a man in jail.

Who?

Anyone they can think of. The bus driver, the school board, the farmer whose property the road passes through. Other than that, nothing's going on. Nothing at all.

Good, said the Governor.

No, I don't think so, said Walter. I think we have to do something. Do what?

Lean on the legislature little bit, maybe put a phone call in to a contractor, let him suggest how dangerous the roads are, and how easy they'd be to repair. —He could sense the Governor taking off his glasses and polishing them with his handkerchief, as he had done a thousand times before. —I can do it myself, said Walter.

No, said the Governor. I think we need to lie low on this one, now. We're weak down there, and they don't love us. They're suspicious of us, whatever we do. Let them run around awhile, like hens in the yard when the rooster's been gone too long. When they're done, we'll come in with a little humility and a little common sense. A word like *taxes* will die on our tongues. We'll get what we want, and we'll give them what they need.

Yes, said Walter, and he thought: Remember this, too, so you can tell it when the time comes.

23

COUNTRY

The singer had been drunk—well, he was drunk damn near every night. And since night was the larger part of what he knew, he was drunk pretty much all the time. Before dawn, he'd pissed himself again, and the woman beside him—what was her name?—had woken him up by yelling at him. Get up! she said. Wake up, get up. She shook him for a good five minutes before he raised his head.

Now, come on, honey, he said. Don't be a bitch, all right? I've got enough of that at home.

The pants to his suit were on the floor at the foot of the bed; one boot was on a chair, the other shoved halfway under the couch; he couldn't find the jacket, and he guessed he'd lost it somewhere the night before. That was a four-hundred-dollar suit. He got that suit from old Nudie out in L.A., and he'd paid cold cash for it. And now where was it? All gone, for this chippy.

There was someplace he was supposed to be, but he couldn't remember where. He'd have to call someone who could tell him. In the meantime, he could use some coffee. He could use another drink, but coffee would do, coffee and maybe a few pills. They were in his jacket. But where was his jacket? You don't know where it is . . . said the singer, out loud but to himself.

There it was, crumpled up in a corner of the room, and he slipped it on. All right, then. . . . He reached into the inside pocket, searching for his billfold. Now, I had a lot of money in here, and now it's gone. His voice had taken on a slightly harder tone. You wouldn't know anything about that, would you? he said to the woman, who was sitting up in the bed. She looked nervous, she wasn't sure how mean a man he really was. Shit, don't you worry about it, he said. I was going to give it to you anyway.

Well I'm not a whore, she said. You don't have to talk to me like that.

Now the singer had that taste of metal in his mouth, a taste he hated, and a whinge in his head. It came from the chloral hydrate pills, he knew, or it came from them being all gone, but there was nothing he could do about it except twist his tongue in his mouth and suffer. He said to the woman, Lend me ten bucks, will you, darling? I've got to get somewhere.

Where you going? she said. You going to leave me to clean all this up? She gestured to the piss-damp sheets.

Got to, he said. And I've got to use your phone. Where is it? She said nothing, just stood and went to the window. He looked around the room, while she watched him warily. God, what a skinny man, she thought. A wrong move, a misstep, and he might break himself right in two. How did a man so skinny end up hung like that? He would have hurt her the night before, but he was only about half hard. She watched him with a puzzled expression while he found the phone and dialed his wife. The woman could hear him: Billie Jean, honey, he said. I'm supposed to be somewhere, and I don't know where it is. You've got a schedule there somewhere, don't you? Go find it, will you? He paused, and a voice came twittering on the line. . . . I'm with my buddy Skeeter, he said. More noise from the phone. No, I'm not, he said. I'm with my buddy Skeeter. You want to talk to him? He took the phone down from his ear, and, with his back to the woman in the room, he raised his face to the ceiling and called, Hey, Skeeter. Come talk to Billie Jean. He waited a few moments and then spoke into the receiver again. Well, he's on the crapper, but he says to say hello. Now, honey, go get that schedule for me, will you?

While he waited for his wife to return to the phone, the other woman stripped the bed, peeling back the sheets with her thumb and index finger and muttering to herself: It's not so easy to get stains like this out of good cotton sheets. And still he ignored her. At length she heard him speak again. That's right, that's it, he said. Now go on down to—what is this, December whatever. There you go, he said. Now, where am I supposed to be? Where? All right then, he said. Thank you, honey, you saved my ass again. What would I do without you? I'd be as helpless as a one-legged man in a room full of cockroaches. I do love you. I do. —And with that he replaced the receiver.

Damn, he said to the woman in the room with him. It's almost New Year's.

The taxi came about twenty minutes later. Hey, I know who you are, said the driver, as the singer was folding himself painfully into the backseat.

No you don't, said the singer. I know what you're going to say, but I'm not him. I just look like that poor son of a bitch.

No, you are, said the driver.

Take me downtown, said the singer.

Yes, sir, the driver said, and he pulled out onto the road.

The singer hunched down in the back of the car and pulled his hat down over his eyes, while outside winter Memphis turned in the chill. He bent over a little bit farther, until his face was right above the floorboards, staring down; and he vomited long and hard.

Shit God, said the driver. What the hell are you doing back there? No answer came. I can't have you doing that, said the driver. I don't care who you are. He pulled over to the side of the road. Open the door at least, and take your head out, try and make it over to the bushes over there. But the singer just sat on the running board with his head down between his bent knees, driveling rheum onto the cold pavement. When he was done, he took a handkerchief from his pocket, wiped his face, and climbed back into the car.

O.K., let's go, he said.

The driver pulled away, shaking his head but saying nothing. He could clean out the back of the car, but the story would be good for years. Where we going? he asked after a little while.

Down to the Peabody, said the singer. I think I have a room there, I'm supposed to meet with some man later on, some politician fellow from Nashville. Wants to meet me. I don't know why. Then I got to play downtown somewhere, and then we're going to Shreveport. —Not you and me. Me and the band.

The car dropped the singer off at the hotel and he stumbled through the lobby, everybody staring at him. What they were staring at, he didn't know; so he looked a mess. Shit, but they would have looked a mess too, if they'd been through what he'd been through. Did they expect him to keep his pecker dry every night? Well, it wasn't going to happen. Maybe one of them knew Billie Jean and was going to call her and tell her. Then he was going to have to go home to her screaming and crying and packing her bags, and that would be hell. He ducked and hid his head a little, but he had to show his face at the desk. Hello there, said the little man with a smirk. How can I help you?

You can start by telling me what room I'm in, said the singer. Then you can give me the key.

Of course, said the desk clerk. —They always said, Of course, no matter what you asked them to do. You could say, And now you can kiss my ass, you dumb son of a bitch; and they'd say, Well, of course, sir, if you'll just give me a second to step out from behind this desk. You don't mind bending over, sir? —You'll be in Room 702. And I have a message here for you, from . . . The clerk looked down at a piece of paper. I guess it's from . . .

That's all right, said the singer. I got you. He reached over and took the paper and his key from the clerk's hands, and then turned and ambled over to the elevator, just a little hitch in his step to testify to the night before. He stopped on the other side of the lobby. The note read: *Meeting with the Governor at 5. Dinner after. Check in the auditorium at 7:30. Showtime is at 8. Sold out. Someone will come get you at 4:30. This is an important man, and we don't want to keep him waiting.* There were four dashes underneath the lines, and beneath that there was his manager's signature. When he reached the room the singer looked for a clock and found it on the night table. 11:30.

He called the record company, he knew the number by heart, but he dialed it wrong, and some woman picked up. Who's this? Where's Lester? he said.

No Lester here, the woman said, and she hung up the phone so quickly that he had to stop and rescue a little minute for himself. Then he dialed again and got through.

What is he, some politician or something, right? said the singer. The governor, or something. Of Tennessee. . . . He was tired, and sat on his freshly made bed, his suit jacket and shirt open, exposing his pale and fragile chest. What's his name? —What's that? —All right, all right. My back is killing me, you know, and the pills don't do much good anymore. I've got to lie down for a little while, I'm just going to lie here and get some sleep. You have the hotel ring me at four and I'll come down. I'll get dressed and I'll come down, and you can pick me up. —Shit, I wouldn't do this, you know, except I owe you so much money. So I got a big white house and all the furniture Billie Jean can buy, and I'll come down and say howdy to the Governor, if that's what you want. I'll do whatever you say. I will. But now you listen to me. When this is all over and you've got all your money, you can kiss my ass good-bye. Do you hear me? You and those Jews you have down there. You all can say good-bye. Shit, yeah. I'm going to take my business somewhere else. Because, listen. I didn't have you when I was just a little kid singing songs on the street, and I was doing O.K., then. Hell, I was doing better than I am now. —And you can take my ex-wife with you. She'll fuck you right in half. It'll be good for you. Teach you something. Politician. . . . I was singing on the streets of Louisiana, of some little nowhere town, Louisiana. Where were you? That's what the Lord said to Job, you know. Where were you when I made the world? That's what I'm saying. That's what I'm saying to you. You want me dressed up, cleaned up, go meet the goddamned Governor. Why? I'll sing him a song, and he can hump it all the way back to Nashville. It's wintertime and I'm twenty-nine years old, and I'm . . . I've got to get all through the mountains tonight, to get to Shreveport. What's this Governor going to do for me? What's he going to do for you? Keep you out of jail, where you belong. Don't matter to me. I'll be gone. Dead. —He's gone, they'll say. I wonder what I can get. The songs. That big white house. Maybe that ex-wife of his, or his pretty little widow. Well, you're not getting one fucking penny. You want me to dance like some wind-up doll for your Governor? Has he got some law on you? I'll bet. I know you've got all money and all down at the Statehouse. Well, I don't care. I'm O.K. and fuck you. What do you think of that? These folks . . . these folks. . . . They're coming into town for a show, and I'm going to give them a show. I'm going to give them everything I've got. Everything I've got. How much do I owe you? Thousand. Six or seven or eight thousand. I'm going to pay you, as soon as I can. I've got the money coming to me. It's coming to me, and then I'll pay you, just like I said I would. I'll pay you and then you can get off my back. . . . Ah . . . my suit is all . . . I . . . the jacket's wrinkled, and . . . I need a cleaner or something. Can you send somebody up here? I was going to go to sleep, take a nap, but I don't think so anymore. I'm not tired. I want to get my suit cleaned. I got nothing else to wear. Hang on. *Hang on.* Let me bring the phone over to the window. I want to look out. . . . Look at that. The sky. It's going to snow. It's going to snow. I think it's going to snow. Where do you suppose the ducks go when it snows? —You know, I've got this new song. It's going to be a big hit, I'm telling you. It's going to be a whole another thing. It's got a jazz part to it, kind of. It's a whole new thing. Want me to sing some of it for you? You're going to own it anyway. You might as well hear some of it, right? Where's my guitar? Where's a guitar? Where's my goddamned guitar. Jesus Christ, help me. Never mind. You'll hear it tonight, if you come. You know, you know. . . . You know, I never see my boy anymore, his mama won't let him come with me. As if there was something wrong with what I'm doing. She doesn't think there's anything wrong with the money, though. When I get off the phone with you, I'm going to call him. I haven't talked to him since Christmas Day. I got him a dog; did I tell you that? Just a little puppy. A boy and his dog. You know what it is about a dog? They bark, and then they bite. No two ways about it. Nothing deceitful in that. . . . Ah . . . God, I'm tired. Going to sleep now. Listen to the radio, maybe. Then I'm going to sleep. You can wake me up when your Governor's ready, and I'll come down. I'll come down. I'll be down. All right. I'll come down. . . .

Hours later, the telephone began to ring, and it kept to its ringing, over and over again; just ringing in the room, sound over the sleeping man. Out the window the sun was setting early over Memphis and a wind was up, causing the clouds to move rapidly across the dark sky. The singer wasn't dreaming. The room was undisturbed, not a chair pulled away from its original position, not a drawer opened; nor had he pulled the sheets back. He slept naked from the waist up, his flesh pressing against the bedclothes, but he wore his pants and his boots. The phone rang, the phone rang. At last he stirred, turning a quarter of the way over and mumbling something to no one. The phone rang. He was awake, then, but he'd slept on his right arm and it was numb, and when he reached for the receiver it wouldn't go. And still the phone rang, until at last he managed to knock it off the hook with his hand. Immediately there was a tiny little sound from the earpiece. He began calling back to it: Just hold on a minute, O.K.? Just hold on. I'm coming, he said, as he sat and looked blankly around the room. Finally he reached with his left arm and took up the receiver. Yeah, who's this? Outside the Mississippi swam and swallowed whatever light was left.

A man from the record company was waiting downstairs. He went into the bathroom and splashed cold water on his face, turning his head one way and then the other and watching himself: he wasn't a movie star, but he could write a song. Then he put on his shirt, and put on his jacket, slipped the string tie into a pocket, and strolled from the room.

The elevator was empty, and the golden light reflected off the brass, making the little room feel rare and wealthy. Now he started humming, some tune, he didn't stop to think what it was. He tapped his foot slowly and hummed a bit louder, while the elevator slipped down through the hotel, and by the time he reached the bottom he was in a pretty good mood.

There in the lobby was a man from MCA, a little round fellow with thin, slicked-back hair. He was sitting low in one of the easy chairs, and it took him a little while to get to his feet. Well, hello, he said, smiling broadly. There you are. We were beginning to wonder. . . . We were going to send somebody up and make sure you were O.K. The singer said nothing; he just stood and smiled a little bit. Well, said the man from MCA, here you are, anyway. So that's good. He reached out and patted the singer on the shoulder, and spent a little whiskey breath on the afternoon.

Car outside? asked the singer.

No car, said the man from MCA. Same hotel. The Governor is staying in this same hotel. All we have to do is turn around, get back on the elevator, and go right up to see him. He smiled again. Easy as can be. Are you ready?

The singer nodded. I'm ready, he said. Ready. Let's do it.

Well, all right, said the man from MCA.

The singer began humming again as he crossed the lobby, and he sang a little bit under his breath:

> *T for Thelma,*
> *That gal's made a wreck out of me.*

What's that? said the man from MCA. New song? Is that a new song you got there?

The singer shook his head. That's Jimmie Rodgers, he said. You ought to know that. What do you do up there, anyway, at the record company?

Oh, you know, said the other man. A little bit of this, a little bit of that. A little bit of everything, I guess. Some publicity, some bean counting. Counting beans. I'm a vice president, myself. I guess I do whatever I can.

Well, that's Jimmie Rodgers, anyway, said the singer. That's a song. . . . Now they were at the elevator.

That a number you sing? said the little round man.

I might, said the singer. I might sing it tonight.

Well, all right, said the other man. Jimmie Rodgers, you say? I'll have to go find that. What's it called?

I can't remember, said the singer. I'll let you know when I do.

Up in Room 845 of the Peabody there were two men in suits, nice-looking fellows, well-dressed and clean-shaven. One of them was old and small, bespectacled and canny-looking. The other was younger, a big fellow with an earnest face. The singer stared at him for a while. Then the man from MCA said to the singer, Now, I want you to meet the Governor. The singer stepped forward a few paces and put out his hand, and the old man extended his. How are you, Governor? said the singer. The handshake was limp, and each man silently blamed the other for not putting his powers into the greeting.

I'm well, thank you, said the Governor.

And this is . . .

Walter Selby, said Walter Selby. The flesh hung from the singer's bones and his body seemed consumed by a waste, as if there were a mine fire burning in him, and a crushing without, so that his chest had collapsed.

Selby? said the singer. Is that your name? Walter nodded. All right, then. Selby. —Now, Governor, what brings you down to Memphis?

Well, said the Governor, I figured I ought to visit the people who elected me. So I'm trying to get around a little bit, before I have to go back on up to Nashville.

Nashville, yeah, said the singer. How's it going there? Are you taking care of us?

I'm doing my best, said the Governor, making straight talk among men. And I think we're doing all right. We're working on some bills, some law enforcement. . . . There are men trying to take food out of the mouths of honest working people. Fortunes being made by criminals. You can bet we're doing our best to take care of that.

Well, that sounds mighty good, said the singer. Mighty good. There was a lot of the hills in his voice, and Walter wondered if the Governor was being had a little.

If the Governor noticed, he wasn't letting it show. We hope so, he said simply. We're doing what we can. And how about yourself? I hear your name everywhere I go; I hear about you everywhere: this, that. How many songs do you have on the Hit Parade right now?

Oh, I don't know, said the singer. He really didn't know, and he turned to the man from MCA to ask, but the man from MCA was picking at a plate of food that had been left on a dresser by the window, and he hadn't heard the question. The singer shrugged. There's usually a few, he said. Right now I got. . . . He paused, looked up into the corner where the wall met the ceiling, and started to count. Some time went by and he seemed to forget what he was doing. The Governor and Walter Selby began to shift, and the singer returned to the conversation. Three, I guess, he said.

Anybody else got more than one? asked the Governor.

No, said the singer, I don't think they do.

I'll be damned, said the Governor. Now tell me. How do the record companies make some songs hits, and other songs, they just kind of disappear? How does that happen? He said all this as if he was simply very curious to know and thought that the singer might be able to explain it to him.

But the singer just shook his head. I don't know anything about that, he said. I'll tell you what, though. You come out to the show tonight and you can see what I got.

The Governor raised his eyebrows, smiled, and turned to Walter. Can we do that? he asked. Have we got time?

Walter shrugged. When do you start?

Eight o'clock, said the singer. Grove Street Auditorium.

I think we can make that, said Walter. I should double-check, but I'm pretty sure we can catch at least part of it.

Well, all right, said the man from MCA, who had returned from the window with a chicken wing in each hand. You just come on down, come to the back door and ask for me. My name is Ruskin, and I'll bring you right in.

24

From the wings of the stage the singer looked much bigger than he had in the hotel room: there was something original and mean about the man, a whole new way he came to town, towing his temper behind him. Out in the audience the people sat politely, clapped loudly after each song, and some of them cheered and a few of them hooted. They'd come out of the alleys and in from the farms for the night: a dollar-fifty to get in, clean clothes, a shave, hair slicked down, and not one of them was smiling. They knew all the songs, and they watched the singer perform as if they were worshiping bad luck.

He went through ten or twelve numbers in a little under an hour. Then he took his leave and came offstage, shining with sweat and trembling. He stared right through Walter Selby and only just recognized the Governor. The boys in his band were directly behind him, and while they waited for their encore they shifted and remarked to one another how the show had gone. The singer stood in the wings, just a foot or so out of sight of the audience, and listened to the clapping with his head cocked a little bit. There was no way to tell what he was waiting for, but when the moment arrived he simply stepped back out onto the stage. The band started to follow, but the singer motioned for them to remain in the wings, and they stood there, watching like the rest, with slightly puzzled expressions. There was a pause, a hush after the welcoming ovation had ceased but before he began his final song. A little rustling in the back rows, like rain in another county. The singer spoke: I want to leave you all tonight with a song by a man, I'm sure you all know who he is, we owe him a lot, music owes him a lot. A great American singer. His name was Jimmie Rodgers. —There was a brief round of applause.

We should get going, said Walter to the Governor.

I want to send this song out to a fellow I know, said the singer. An old friend of mine. He's having some trouble, like we all sometimes do. —The Governor put his hand up, to stay and watch. —I just want to tell this fellow . . . I know just how he feels.

The singer strummed a slow chord on his guitar and began.

T for Texas, T for Tennessee
T for Texas, T for Tennessee
T for Thelma
That gal's made a wreck out of me

If you don't want me mama
You sure don't have to stall
If you don't want me mama
You sure don't have to stall
'Cause I can get more women
Than a passenger train can haul

There were scattered laughs through the auditorium, and a cheer here and there. The Governor smiled, and Walter took a step closer to the stage.

I'm gonna buy me a shotgun
Just as long as I'm tall
Gonna buy me a shotgun
Just as long as I'm tall
I'm gonna shoot poor Thelma
Just to see her jump and fall

From there it was excruciating, endless, verse by crawling verse, without sound or movement from the audience, without mercy from the singer. Not a second passed, but the song went on; not a look was lost, and Walter began to feel his nerves stripping in the back of his neck. Now there was no story left, nor song, but the last long note in the singer's throat, which filled the room like a bitter scent, and he was done.

The singer came off the stage and the Governor stepped in front of him, undeterred by the sweat dripping off the other man's suit or the slight grimace on his mouth. That was a fine show, the Governor said quietly. Really a fine, fine show. . . . The singer made no reply; he was thinking about something else, or perhaps about nothing at all, and he sauntered away.

On the way back from the auditorium the Governor said, Well now, you see, that's the best we have to give. And it's no less than anybody else's, and maybe it's more. Walter was looking out his window at the city and said nothing, but he wondered to himself if the man had seen the same music he'd seen, because there was no less or more about it at all. The songs were carefully done and they captured their audience, but they were neither art nor amusement, nor solace, nor democratic odes: they were facts, and they would be known. Later that week, he stopped by a store and bought a few of the singer's records, carrying them carefully home, where he played them all one night, sitting on his couch while Nicole lay stretched out along the cushions, her head in his lap. Are you going hillbilly on me? she teased, and soon afterward she was asleep, her face smooth and untroubled in dreams, while he listened to song after song and wondered what he was hearing. Was this the real sound? Was this the world they were all negotiating? He didn't like the music, but he couldn't get it out of his head, neither its trouble nor its thrill, and he heard the singer's voice for days afterward, following him as he walked briskly down the polished halls of the Governor's office building.

25

Now, now, while the sun is still high; the nation is coming into town, everyone will be there for the Great Rebuilding. A man needs to gather together the few things he loves. Already entire lives have been done and undone, fortunes transfigured, futures made for good or ill. Marry me. Marry me in Tennessee.

One midmorning, Walter's secretary knocked twice on his door and, as was her habit, entered without waiting for an answer. She found him sitting in his chair, which was pushed back from his desk; he was staring at a small black box that lay in the center of his blotter. Mr. Selby, she said. John Jones just called from Nashville? He says the Governor needs to know how many members the Teamsters have, county by county. He says he thought you might have the numbers down here, and can you put together a memo. —Selby had turned his eyes up to her, but his head was still angled toward the desk, and the mute little reliquary before him. He neither nodded nor frowned. Mr. Selby? she said again. I'm sorry. Did you hear me?

Yes . . . he said.

There was a silence in time. Then you have the file, the information? asked Selby's secretary.

Mm, he said, in a manner which might have meant either yes or no. Mr. Selby?

He rolled forward in his chair, leaned over, and placed his hands on either corner of his desk, resting his weight on his outstretched arms. In this box is a ring, he said. It was my mother's, her engagement ring. —He paused, his secretary stood unmoving, though she was still thinking about the Teamsters. Walter spoke to some grey place behind his eyes. My father gave it to her, in New York, in 1922. . . . I never met my father. When she died she left it to me, and I'm about to give it to a young woman—to try . . . to give it to a young woman. He met his secretary's eyes. I'm going to propose to her this evening, he said.

Oh, said the secretary, and smiled, wondering why he wasn't smiling himself. How lovely, she said.

Wish me luck, and tell Mr. Jones he'll have his information by the end of the day.

Good luck, said his secretary, but by then his gaze was gone again, and she smiled once more, this time just to herself, and noiselessly left the room.

That night Walter took Nicole to a fine French restaurant downtown, the tablecloths white as bedsheets, the little lamp on the table glowing dimly, a featureless waiter nodding at their order and disappearing. He had the ring in the pocket of his jacket, and from time to time he would reach in and touch the box with his fingers. She'd noticed the gesture, but she didn't ask him about it. It only took a part of her thoughts to contemplate it, and she never did guess just what he had in there and why he couldn't keep his hand off it; wasn't it something, how quickly she'd come to love him, how little she understood him?

Afterward, he drove her down to the river's edge and parked by the side of the road at the end of a bridge. For a time he sat behind the wheel of the dead car, watching the water beyond the windshield. Is something wrong? she asked, and he slowly shook his head. —Not at all. Come for a walk, come walk on the bridge with me.

They were in the middle of the span, and the pavement below their feet seemed to be rising and falling very slightly, as if it were the water underneath that was still and smooth, and the world above, and all its hard and tangible debris, that had tides and was tested by the moon.

He took her arm, his hand almost encircling it. Nicole, he said. I have something I want to say.

It was a speech he had written over the course of the preceding days; the occasion was meant to be spontaneous, but he wanted it to be perfect, so he kept returning to his words, simplifying, making sure he was saying everything he wanted to, simplifying again. He took notes and arranged them this way and that, and soon enough he had something settled, and he couldn't help but know it by heart, though doing so made him more nervous rather than less so, since it meant he had nothing to think about while he spoke. Nicole, he said again. She waited. He was careful to keep his eyes on hers as he delivered his delicate oration. It's been nine months now since we met, he said. Not a long time, but long enough for me to know that I love you. —Either the tears in her eyes were making her smile, or her smile had brought tears to her eyes. She wanted to say something like Thank you, but kept silent. So I understand, he said, what lies in the heart of every man who is truly happy, and not chasing his own sad vanity into a dark corner. And I'm asking you to be my wife, and I want to be your husband. He paused and studied her face for some kind of response, but she was thinking so many things—so soon but she wasn't surprised, she knew, so sweet, his safe hands, this clean turn—that she couldn't show them all and ended up showing almost nothing.

He drew the jewelry box out of his pocket and held it at his side, looking down at his hand as if he was a little bit puzzled at its purpose. I've had this for a while, he said, and then in one swift motion he brought the box up and held it out to her. She reached for it almost without thinking, and opened it. It was my mother's, he said. The provenance was a surprise and Nicole's thoughts flew, and then settled again, even deeper than they were before. It's so beautiful, she said, because it was.

He hesitated. He had planned to say more, but now her radiance was a shame to shadow; still, she should know. Nicole, he said, before you decide whether you'll take it there's something I want to tell you. I don't know if it will make any difference to you at all, but you should hear it.

Still she held the ring, now slightly confused. Was it hers? Was he? He sensed her discomfort. I just want to tell you, he said.

She nodded.

If you're going to marry me, if we're going to have children. . . . He paused. There was a barge moving beneath the bridge, and she felt herself grow slightly unsteady as she tried not to watch it. How bad could this be? He was watching the barge himself, as if he were thinking of leaping. She waited and waited. This is about my family, he said. That we're not . . . all of us . . . going back . . . white. Do you see?

She didn't have the faintest idea what he was talking about, and she waited for him to say something more. He turned back to her and held her gaze. Here it is: My great-great-grandfather was half Negro, he said; and so was my great-great-grandmother. I thought you should know that, that I've got some colored blood in me, one-sixteenth. I thought you should know.

She said nothing, because the moment, which had been perfectly beautiful, now had become quite peculiar. The uncanny image of a pitch-black baby with her features danced into her head and then out again. Perhaps she heard Walter's heartbeat; certainly he heard it himself. Ah. . . . He paused for a very long time. Some people care about these matters, he said. It's all right.

Oh, she said. And then, Oh, again. I don't. Care. I don't care, at all. She stopped again, and mused over the possibility that she should feel offended. But when she looked at him he was so obviously, utterly relieved and helplessly grateful that she decided immediately to let the matter drop. I don't care, she said again, and she went to him and kissed him.

He couldn't smile. He wanted her to say Yes. Are you saying yes? he asked. Does that mean yes, you'll marry me?

She laughed and said nothing; she wanted to play the occasion, let it stretch and turn. How long could she make it last before the iridescence died? Three, four, five. . . .

For Walter there was a hole where his happiness should have been, and he almost reached out to grab her, to shake some answer out of her. Instead he planted his hands forcefully in his pockets. Nicole, he said. —She didn't say a word, stared at him as if she couldn't see him. —Nicole, will you marry me?

. . . Yes, she said at last, and she wished the word was an hour long. I'm saying yes. —And he took hold of her arms and pulled her to his chest, startling her with the violence of his embrace so that she laughed again.

Good, said Walter Selby. Good, that's great.

The bed: It was king-sized, white and warm, and hadn't they had fun picking it out, in the department store downtown? They'd walked hand in hand among the displays while the sales help watched; but as soon as she sat down on one, a wide white mattress on a box spring with a curved wooden headboard looming over it, a man came over and said, Can I help you?

She laughed, and the salesman blinked for a second at the force of her delight. We're just looking . . . for a bed. She laughed again at the very idea.

This is one of our finest, said the salesman. He was wearing a tight-fitting blue suit, and he had a thin mustache. She wondered what his own bed was like, and who, if anyone, he shared it with. Well, everyone has a bed, she thought, but none of them are as fine and comfortable as ours will be. We're getting married, she said to the salesman, and this is going to be our very first bed, so it has to be just right.

Well, there's plenty to choose from, said the salesman. Right here we have every new advancement in mattress design. Now you take this . . . and he turned them toward another set. Go on and sit down on that, if you like. —She sat. —There are three hundred coils in that mattress, said the salesman. Three hundred coils to keep you well supported. Guaranteed, no restlessness at night, no backaches in the morning.

Hmmm, she said. Is this the best?

This is the best, the salesman replied.

Then we'll take it.

That bed would be worn to a hollow, later by years. That was where he would discover how to make her gasp, how shameless she was with her mouth, swallowing him and asking for more; that was where he would smell the changes her body went through in a month. In that bed she would abrade her face on his rough evening stubble until her features were burned; they would invent words for rank things and jubilant things; they would sweat and shout. Bed of congress and stubborn slumber, where she would train herself to sleep on her side, with his hand cast over her bottom breast and his hot mouth at her neck; she would learn to abide his occasional thrashing through his dreams—but he was lovely when he slept, mannish and still soft. Bed on sugared, sour mornings, where they would turn to each other, turn again, and turn themselves all inside out.

27

Charleston that June was hot and damp. It had rained throughout April, and rained some more in May, until the ground just couldn't hold any more. Up by Jacksonboro the Edisto had overrun its banks, and even the ocean seemed to be as full as it could be; it gathered and groaned. June was the date of Walter and Nicole's wedding, and Charleston was the place, but the reception had taken at least three months to plan. Her father, it transpired, had long harbored big plans for his only child's wedding, an expression of pride and sentiment that surprised both Nicole and her mother. He had begun a special savings account some years past to pay for it, he had every intention of mounting as lavish and impressive an event as he could; and while he had little interest in the details he encouraged her to be ambitious and spend freely. It was to be the greatest demonstration of his fondness for his daughter, and his ability to send her into the world in grand style.

There were invitations to be designed, the wording to be chosen, the envelopes to be sent and returns to be tallied; a caterer and a menu to be chosen; music; a hall; and above all a dress to be found, bought, fitted and altered. Event had come to event, the lists had lengthened, there was more food, more cloth, more glass and more light. They chose place settings and made seating arrangements, and Walter, struck, moony, the world's most fortunate man, withdrew into his good fortune and agreed with whatever Nicole suggested.

But the more compliant he became, the more she resented him, and as the date approached her anger grew, until she wondered who it was that she was marrying, this man with no opinions. Then came one weekday when she wanted to call the wedding off. Well, if you don't care, then I don't care, she said to him. Maybe we should just forget the whole thing. And with that she stormed out of the restaurant where she had met him, fabric samples for the tablecloths in her bag, and went straight home to call her father and tell him that she couldn't go through with it.

But her father would have none of it; he had become so intent on the occasion that he simply dismissed her panic, as if it were little more than an annoyance. You're worse than your mother, he said. *She* tried to have me arrested for abandonment, just because I went into town to have a whiskey while she was testing recipes for beef stew. Walter Selby is a fine, fine man. You go get him and make up with him, and stop this nonsense right now.

So she did: she found him in his bedroom, sitting perfectly still and fully clothed on the edge of his bed, with an odd sort of expression on his face, part bereavement and part puzzlement, like a man whose happiness has been snatched from under him so quickly that he's still searching for the moment of disaster, though it's already come and gone. She kissed him and he hardly changed expression, but his hand went to her cheek and rested there.

Then the day was upon them. A parade, a processional. Everything was ordered, the line of aunts and uncles, there; the ribboning flow of children bearing props—rings and hats, books, flowers, —there. She'd seen such luxury before but never been the cause. Suddenly she wondered if she was worth such an occasion, with everyone watching. How bright was the jewel? How fine was its reflection?

Emily was her bridesmaid, she had slept over in an extra room the night before, and it was Emily who came in to wake her in the morning. Out her window the sky was grey from horizon to horizon, threatening a downpour that never did come. Wake up, beautiful, said Emily, and when she turned her back, Nicole went to the mirror to see herself. Well, they all say this is supposed to be the happiest day of your life, said Emily. Is it the happiest day of your life? And Nicole said that it was, though she hoped for even happier days to come.

The morning was orderly, the movement, from station to station—breakfast with her parents, dressing, waiting for relatives and friends to come by—went off without the slightest faltering. There was only a minute or two when she was alone in her room, while Emily was off finding someone who could fix the tiny silver buckle that held the strap on her shoe; she filled the quiet by thinking of who she had left behind to get to that day. There were boys she had imagined as her husband, always a boy, for as long as she could remember. There was Billy, for example, a crush from the second grade: where was he? Already married, and she remembered hearing that his wife was on her third baby. That was one she was happy to have missed. There was Roger, who taught her how to tell fibs to her parents; there was Thomas, who took her to his high school prom. And then, of course, there was John Brice; she flinched at the thought of his name, and something inside her abdomen flipped over. Well, everyone loses the first. Still, she could hardly keep from thinking how it might have been had she followed him. A terrible mistake, she was sure. Yes, it would have been a disaster, and how wise she was to have forsaken it. She wondered where he was now, and what he would think when he found out that she'd taken someone else's name and affixed it to her own, never to be removed. Nicole Selby: say it again, and she turned John Brice out of her mind.

It was hot, even in the morning, and she worried that her perspiration would stain the wedding dress. Emily came back with the shoe and then left again, and then her mother came in, to touch her hair. Only her father was entirely calm. There he was, quietly hobbling over to the bar to make sure that there was enough liquor, chatting easily with a few male friends, telling a joke or two.

The time ticked away, one more minute, one more, an hour. She was in her room, and Emily was helping her with the very last of the adjustments to her dress. Somewhere across town, her husband-to-be was waiting for her, and she wanted very badly to go to him. Are we ready? she asked Emily. The other girl was fussing with her stockings, and really she couldn't stand it, she couldn't take it anymore. Almost, said Emily, and then she made one last adjustment and reluctantly rose to her feet. Now, she said, staring at the bride with a ravenous look. Now you look perfect.

The Governor was flying in from Nashville; there would be a car bringing him along any time now, and everything was going to change when he arrived. Already there was a stirring throughout the wedding party, a slight anticipatory pomp among the men. In the hallway outside her door she could hear her father calling to Walter's brother, Donald, who had come in from the Midwest earlier in the week, another side of Walter, a little older, a little less brilliant. But somehow, in the time since he'd arrived, he and her father had become very close, laughing together at jokes that no one else had a chance to hear. It was too bad Walter's mother couldn't be there; she would have liked to meet the woman, let her know that her son was going to be well cared for. Strange, how the flavor of family seems like such a fixed thing when you're young, and then, after all, it proves to be as mutable as flour, which takes on the taste of whatever it gets mixed with.

She knew this would be her last period alone, if not ever then as a girl. What did those old paintings show? Those perfect paintings, fashioned by wise old men: the maiden gazing upon the fluttering, departing bird. But Emily was right. She felt perfect—she felt like she looked perfect—she felt like she looked like she was perfect. The hunt was over and the prey had won. Her mother was waiting for her downstairs, wearing a look of bittersweet loss, as if the time of her own life had come crumbling in on her, all at once, all this morning. Oh, honey, the older woman said, and that was all she said. Her father was waiting on the front lawn, dressed in a black tuxedo, a white shirt with a batwing collar, and a tie composed of alternating diagonal stripes of black and silver. He was beaming, jingling the car keys in his right hand, his left hand thrust into the pocket of his pants. He delivered her an ostentatious bow and gestured grandly to the car waiting at the curb, a Cadillac Brougham he'd rented, to take his only child away. Nicole stepped lightly down the walk and slid gently into the backseat; the car was new, and smelled of leather and glass.

There was a room on the right side of the Presbyterian Church, and she waited there, while her parents went outside and greeted the arriving guests; Emily was with her, gossiping about this and that, but Nicole wasn't really listening; she was barely breathing.

Walter was waiting in the back of the chapel, Donald beside him, holding a pair of rings in his pocket, bands and bonds. The season they circumscribed was meant to last as long as time itself, an unbreakable term with no beginning and no end. The organ began, there was the smell of flowers, the groom took a breath, stood up tall, walked down the aisle, and waited for his bride. Everything thereafter was simple; it was the conclusion of an effort that had dilated, expanded, become enormously ambitious, and then had all its ambitions fulfilled. He loved her, he said he did, she said she loved him too, and they were married.

28

Walter stood at the reception, the very last to speak. I don't know how the world works, he said, his own words moving him to shortness of breath. I don't know how history works. I only know this: that every event in my life, whatever meaning it may have seemed to have had at the time, must have been leading to this moment and this union, which justifies and sanctifies every hour that I've lived, blesses everyone that I meet, makes beautiful every place I visit. I know I've done nothing to deserve this day, and these friends, still less this perfect partner; but I will do everything in my power to preserve her faith in me, and to ensure that she's as happy, now and forever, as she's made me.

You see that? whispered the Governor, to whoever happened to be standing next to him. That's my man.

29

A Knoxville judge named Finder was implicated by the *Tennessean* in a baby-bartering scheme. Young mothers, poor and never married, were brought before him on charges of neglect, and the judge would find them guilty. He would order the infant taken away, sent to a wealthy, childless couple in New York or Hollywood, who would, through a complex string of intermediaries, send money to His Honor in the form of legal fees. He, in turn, would pass envelopes of cash to a police sergeant, his brother-in-law, who would take to the streets to find another unfortunate woman.

Finder had been nominated by the Governor himself, and Walter, newly wed and ten feet tall, left the next day for Nashville, where he stayed all week, moving from office to committee, talking, repairing and rebuilding the estate and affairs of his fellow citizens. Nicole had been unable to hide her disappointment when she learned that her new husband was going to be gone for so long; Walter would miss his wife as much and more, but the Governor had a notoriously poor record of judicial appointments, and the Finder story was beginning to inspire broader condemnations from pulpits and editorial offices around the state.

On his way one afternoon to meet with the reporter who had first found the story, Walter's brow was as dark as a big black bear's, and his stride through the Statehouse was huge: his head scraped the ceiling and his shoulders brushed the walls; his footsteps rang on the floor like a sledgehammer striking stone, and his testicles made a loud clacking noise as they struck each other, like billiard balls at the break. His breath was a hurricane; ahead a clerk turned a corner, found himself faced by this storm, dropped a file folder and ran back the way he'd come, leaving scattered reams of documents to churn in Walter's wake, and the foundation trembled and grown men stood aside, while secretaries peeked from the safety of their offices to see Leviathan pass. Turning a corner he came face-to-face with Finder himself, pacing outside a review-board hearing. The judge was in his late forties, thin and balding, and he started when he saw mighty Walter Selby. Good Christ, I'm glad you're here, said the judge. You and the Governor are going to back me on this, aren't you? The goddamn newspapers have been making up things left and right; none of it is true. None of it can be proven. If I could get the Governor to sign an affidavit on my behalf, with that man's popularity—

Walter leaned over the judge, eclipsing the other man's face. Fuck you, he said softly, and then continued on his way.

30

The Selbys had a boy, born early one drizzly April morning. The delivery had been difficult, it had lasted an eternity, twenty hours of labor, with Nicole's mother in from Charleston to attend. But when it was done there was a baby; they named him Frank, and wasn't he beautiful? Nicole could hardly believe she had carried such a thing; Walter could hardly believe they had made such a thing: a tiny prince for an age of optimism. Still, for a week or two afterward she had had terrible headaches, and for a few weeks after that, a despair, beyond tears, at being emptied, the motion gone from inside her, and she felt half as much alive. But there was an awful lot to do, and she didn't really have the time to feel bad. Walter was working, but he came home as early as he could, and he doted on the baby; he brought him a present almost every day, some little toy he'd seen in a store window, a windup airplane, a book he wouldn't be able to read for another half decade. Here you are, he would say. Here, my little boy, my Frankie, my son, and he leaned over the crib and dangled something down. The baby, not big enough to roll himself over, his eyes still watery and blue—later they would fill to a brown so dark it might as well have been black—would wriggle and squeal.

Walter rose again and went to Nicole. She was tired, he knew; at night she undressed slowly, drew back the sheets, and sat on the edge of the bed, not moving, her eyes downcast, before climbing in. He put his hand on her back and held it there, feeling the blind side of her warm rib cage expanding and contracting.

In the morning she stood naked in front of the mirror, examining what had become of her. Her breasts were heavy, and there was a fan of blue veins visible beneath the surface; her nipples were fat and dark. Her skin was no longer a single, pearly surface; now she looked torn and exhausted, chewed upon and then discarded. Who had ever convinced her that a woman was a pretty thing? There was something she loved about being used this way, and there was something that frightened her about it. How wonderful, that her body was built so that a baby would destroy it, thriving on a pool of blood in her belly and then draining her of milk. What a purpose to be proud of; but she didn't dare ask her husband if he still thought she was beautiful.

31

Dinner with the Whites and the Wannemakers. A November evening, a baby-sitter at home, the child, Jody Wannemaker, at the door of her parents' house, politely collecting the perfumed coats and carrying them off to her parents' bedroom. Thank you Jody; thank you ma'am. Mary Wannemaker came over and asked, Who wants a cocktail? Then she took Nicole briefly by the hand and led her into the living room. Together they stared into the open liquor cabinet, as if its contents had fallen from outer space.

1 fifth of Johnnie Walker, Red Label, two-thirds full
1 fifth of Cutty Sark, almost empty
1 fifth of Jack Daniel's, half empty
1 fifth of Jim Beam, almost empty
1 fifth of Jim Beam, unopened
1 fifth of Beefeater gin, three-quarters full
1 small bottle of Angostura bitters, full but for an ounce
1 fifth of dry vermouth, empty
1 fifth of sweet vermouth, three-quarters full
1 bottle of Pernod, unopened
1 bottle of L.B.V. port, unopened
1 bottle of Campari, half empty
3 bottles of Coca-Cola

We're running out of Coca-Cola, said Mary. She reached for a tray and began to place glasses on it, arranging them carefully in a star-shaped pattern. When they entered the living room again the men got politely to their feet; Ellen White smiled. Walter, my dear close friend, my unnamed source, come sit here, said T. J. Wannemaker, patting the couch beside him. He was a newspaper man, a little bit older than Walter and happy to act it. Come here and tell me what the Governor's up to with these labor bastards. Wannemaker was thirty-eight; his nose was taking on a purple shade, and his legs had started to go; he had missed a story about corruption in the Statehouse, missed it by a day or two and never caught up. Then he'd hesitated on another, and the paper had put him in an editor's office, where he could ride younger men, snap wisely, and rewrite.

Ellie White got to her feet and came over to Nicole. She was working now, Nicole remembered, but she had forgotten where. —The Museum? She was an educated woman. Working, because her husband had been drunk every day by dinner, lost his job at the advertising agency, and then became drunk by noon. Paul White sat on the end of the couch, leaning his slight frame toward the others, trying to listen in but too far gone to focus. Now goddamn it, Selby, Wannemaker said loudly, having stopped listening to anyone but himself at about the same time he'd been pulled from reporting. We've got a fucking colored man on the paper now, editorial. Do you know that? He only covers doings in Darktown, but there he is. The fellows in the front office are getting all progressive on us. Does the Governor have any colored men working for him? I doubt it.

Ellie was speaking too quietly for the others to hear her, but not so quietly that she could be accused of conspiracy. Dutiful Ellie, pink around the nostrils, lovely ivory hands resting on her midriff. She had miscarried twice, though her husband had only known she was pregnant once. The second time occurred on the very day when she'd called her doctor for an appointment; she called the next day to cancel and never told a soul. Now Paul leaned in on the couch and began to speak to Walter and Wannemaker, though the sentence he had was very heavy, and slow to start moving.

Mark this fellow, said Ellie, gesturing toward her husband with a faint fluttering of her fingers. The man I married and to whom I pledged the length of my life. Our season is ended. Mark him: His pin hath hardly prick enough . . .

Nicole put her hand on the woman's elbow and squeezed gently.

. . . And his prick hath no more pin.

32

There go the times. They had another child, a girl this time, they named her Gail. The girl was crawling, Frank was learning to read. For a few months they had stayed home every night; the baby was too young to entrust to a sitter; there was hardly a second, day or night, when she didn't need something, to be fed or changed, or comforted, or entertained. On television, Nicole watched the Carolinas coming apart, and Walter came home angry in the evenings, from meetings where everyone had a threat to deliver to the Governor.

He was working too hard, aiming too hard, every day was another revision to future history and none of them was good enough. They argued. Of course, everyone has the right to the same schooling, she said. Everyone has the right to eat wherever they want, go to school, of course, to vote, but . . . but . . .

But what? said Walter.

Tradition, Nicole said. I believe in it; I do. I want Frank to grow up with a sense of the past . . . and not just as something he reads about.

What's a tradition? said Walter, slowly and quietly, as if to himself. White women blushing?

That's not fair, she said.

Instead of answering he gave her a look of deliberate perplexity, let it last a little, and then said, What are you going to teach the boy?

About this?

Yes, about all of this. What are you . . .

Teach the boy, me? said Nicole.

That's right. What are you going to say to him?

I'll teach him to be good and honest. An honorable man.

Honorable? said Walter, and he laughed. Ten years ago I was as honorable as a man can be, ten years ago I was beloved because I pulled a trigger. Yes? Because we won the War, and weren't we wise and right. Weren't we intrepid. This afternoon a reverend from Collierville called me a disgrace to human history for trying to get the police to stop using the word *nigger* on their radios.

Nicole went red and narrowed her eyes. Why don't you get out, then?

Get out?

Why don't you leave? Leave and go up north. Why don't you go to New York, leave me.

New York?

Isn't that where you'd go?

. . . I never thought about it. Why New York?

Go on, then. Go.

Not without you, you three, you and the children.

I'm not going, she said, with a vehemence out of every proportion. God damn it all, I'm not going. If you want to go, go now. Go on. Get it over with.

What are you talking about? said Walter.

Nothing, she said. She was calm again, she sighed. Nothing. And she turned away and settled back into her seat.

33

Nicole's father died, quite suddenly one rainy Thursday afternoon, and the Selby family went to Charleston to his funeral, Frank hardly understanding more than the idea that he was supposed to be still, stand up straight, and say nothing, and Gail blessedly sleeping. When the ceremony was over, Walter took the children back to Tennessee, while Nicole stayed for a few days.

All these things, all these things, said Nicole's mother in a daze. My Lord, did you ever see a man who was such a saving fool? He never throws out anything, your father. They were going through his possessions, closets, boxes, drawers, chests, shelves, corners of the garage, files, albums, all these things. She could hardly explain them, Nicole understood, and often her mother would simply take some object up— a commemorative plaque, a photograph of college friends, a suit he hadn't worn since he'd retired—turn it over in her hands, and put it precisely back where she'd taken it from. A bitter marriage will still end in bewildered sorrow.

Later that afternoon, Nicole went for a walk around town; it had been a very long time since she'd been alone in Charleston, and it was the strangest feeling. The day was bright but it felt overcast, and all the sidewalks and houses, the gardens and the walls, were vibrating at some strange frequency, as if she were tuned all wrong: she had changed, they were the same, the city on its peninsula was some demi-Atlantis, isolate and preserved in time by the ocean.

She met a man in a tea shop. She was sitting at a table by the window, relaxing, and this fellow walked in, maybe a few years younger than she was. He had kind brown eyes and a strong mouth, and he wore his hair a little bit long, the way they did those days, but on him it looked nice, it looked romantic. All the other tables were full, and he came up and sat down across from her, asked politely if he could join her—though he already had—and then, all of sudden, they were talking. The man was easy, comfortable, interested in her, so that she really couldn't leave, not for quite a while.

Are you from around here? he asked.

From around here? I guess you could say that; I was raised here. I was a little girl here. I don't live here anymore.

He made the question with his eyes, he had already taken note of the ring on her hand.

Well, Memphis, she said. My husband works for the government down there.

And your children? he asked.

Now, how did he know she had children? Did her body make it

plain? She blushed. Does it show that bad? she said. Here she was, only twenty-seven years old; did she look like a matron already? A mother of two?

No, he said calmly. It doesn't show at all. I just figured, a woman like you, you look good at taking care of other people. —Now wasn't that a nice thing to say? So they sat for a while, and she felt fine about it. He was a student, he said—no, a scholar—of plants and flowers from around the world. He worked at a university in Philadelphia, dissecting, analyzing, reading reports.

Is there something so exotic in Charleston? she asked him.

He laughed. I'm sure there is, but that's not why I'm here. I had a week off, and I came down to visit a friend from college.

She asked him, and he told her, about what there was growing in the world: a flower with poisonous petals, for which only the petals of another flower were the cure; bamboo that could grow a foot in a single day; a species of orchid that bloomed every year on Easter; trees with bark that burned a vivid shade of blue. She listened to him with unfeigned interest, until she remembered that her mother was home alone, and she took her leave with a nice-to-meet-you smile. Later she would wonder how, after all, she had accumulated so much debt, that just talking to a man she didn't know would begin to pay it down.

That evening she called home to Memphis, and even then her temperature was a little bit high, and each breath was a transfer of heat from within to without. Everything all right? she asked.

Everything's fine, said Walter. Gail learned the word refrigerator today, she just up and said it when we were in the kitchen. Frig-er, she said. Other than that . . . I took Frank to his ball game yesterday afternoon. Can't say he did so well, but that's O.K., he's working at it. How are you doing over there? How's your mother?

Oh, she's all right, I suppose. She cries a lot. Nicole paused. I have a favor to ask of you.

Yes, he said. Whatever it is.

I want to stay here a little longer. There was a short silence, and then she said, I think my mother needs me right now.

Sure, of course. Stay there, he said. He didn't tell her that he could hardly sleep without her, that he hadn't slept in days, because the bed was cold and dry. Give her my love, tell her I'm thinking about her, and stay as long as you want. (I miss you and I'm going insane.)

34

Nicole stayed in Charleston for another week. By day she watched as her mother became guileless in her grief: distracted, changeable, grateful for every indulgence. At night she went walking. It was cool on the sidewalks, pleasant and slightly damp, and one night she wandered all the way down to the bay, listening to her own footsteps on the sidewalk, brushing back the boughs of trees that had grown well over the fences that were supposed to contain them. She heard the water a little before she saw it, or heard the quiet that the nearness of water created. In time she came to the battery, where she stood alone and watched the waves roll up to the wall. Bay black, star bright. . . .

Then there was a man beside her, the same man she had met in the tea shop earlier in the week. She stared at him, afraid even to acknowledge him with a word, until he spoke. Isn't it a nice night? he said, and he smiled softly, as if he knew something she didn't. The Morris Island lighthouse glowed and died and glowed again, as its beam swept the harbor. Had he followed her? For how long? She didn't know what she was supposed to say, so she nodded, and wondered if he was going to hurt her, as punishment for her wanting him to touch her, or if the keen pain of wanting him to touch her was punishment enough. She couldn't stand to wait, and she wished he would leave, but she wasn't ready to go anywhere else, herself. He said something, it sounded flattering but she wasn't sure, and she wondered if he had made her crazy, or what it was. Then he came up behind her, where she was always most open; it was wise of him to approach her that way and get it all over at once. How did he know that? She let him do whatever he wanted to do with his hands, while she watched the water, dozey now. Was her mother really in bed at home, alone and under her drugs? Was her father really dead and gone? Nicole, that was her name. Her husband, her children, were they really six hundred miles away? Were there really rockets in space, arcing over the continents and seas, with bombs on board to kill everyone below?

The man never told her his name, and he never tore anything, but he brought her down on a secluded patch of the shore. She had no idea, no idea at all, that she could behave like that; she made sounds she'd never heard, called him hateful names, she drowned his face against her shoulder. She could feel him driving her into the ground under her back, thumping her hips, beating her down even as she was rising, as if she were caught between the two, squeezed between the planting of his cock and the elevation of her desire, an exquisite frustration, like pain would be if pain would burst—and then it burst, all at once but again and again.

He lay there for a time with his weight on her. What could she say? Get up, please, get up, I have a husband in Tennessee . . . They were both breathing very hard, but out of rhythm, and she took it as a sign that they weren't together and never had been, his breath, hers, hers, —his: it was a senseless disorder, intolerable. The moon was down.

Then he rolled off her and all at once she could see where she was: in her hometown, in adultery. She hadn't meant anything like that, but what did that matter? She had done it, she could remember it, she could remember what she felt during it. Now came the calculations, the sums and subtractions, and she was too frightened, really, to be frightened by the result.

She pulled up her hose and smoothed her skirt as well as she could, and then, for the first time, she kissed him. She didn't know why; maybe to make herself feel better. But on the way home, as she hid herself and walked, she felt worse about the kiss than she did about the coupling; and in bed she cried and cried, under a spell that grew stronger and stranger, and more and more agonized all night, until morning came, and with it the exhausted resolution: She was going home.

35

CASEY STENGEL TESTIFIES BEFORE THE SENATE SUBCOMMITTEE ON ANTITRUST AND MONOPOLY

MR. STENGEL: I have been in professional ball, I would say, for forty-eight years. I have been employed by numerous ball clubs in the majors and in the minor leagues.

I had many years that I was not so successful as a ballplayer, as it is a game of skill. And then I was no doubt discharged by baseball in which I had to go back to the minor leagues as a manager, and after being in the minor leagues as a manager, I became a major-league manager in several cities and was discharged, we call it *discharged* because there is no question I had to leave.

In the last ten years, naturally, in major-league baseball with the New York Yankees, the New York Yankees have had tremendous success, and while I am not the ballplayer who does the work, I have no doubt worked for a ball club that is very capable in the office. I must have splendid ownership, I must have very capable men who are in radio and television. We have a wonderful press that follows us. Anybody should in New York City, where you have so many million people. Our ball club has been successful because we have it, and we have the spirit of 1776.

If I have been in baseball for forty-eight years there must be some good in it. . . . I know there are some things in baseball, thirty-five to fifty years ago, that are better now than they were in those days. In those days, my goodness, you could not transfer a ball club in the minor leagues, Class D, Class C ball, Class A ball. How could you transfer a ball club when you did not have a highway? How could you transfer a ball club when the railroads then would take you to a town you got off and then you had to wait and sit up five hours to go to another ball club?

How could you run baseball then without night ball? You had to have night ball to improve the proceeds to pay larger salaries and I went to work, the first year I received $135 a month. I thought that was amazing. I had to put away enough money to go to dental college. I found out it was not better in dentistry, I stayed in baseball.

SENATOR KEFAUVER: Mr. Stengel, are you prepared to answer particularly why baseball wants this bill passed?

MR. STENGEL: If I am going to go on the road and we are a traveling ball club and you know the cost of transportation now—we travel sometimes with three Pullman coaches. I found out that in traveling with the New York Yankees on the road and all, that it is the best, and we have broken records in Washington this year, we have broken them in every city but New York and we have lost two clubs that have gone out of the city of New York.

Of course, we have had some bad weather, I would say that they are mad at us in Chicago, we fill the parks. They have come out to see good material. I will say they are mad at us in Kansas City, but we broke their attendance record.

SENATOR KEFAUVER: Mr. Stengel, I am not sure that I made my question clear. (laughter)

MR. STENGEL: Yes, sir. Well that is all right. I am not sure I am going to answer yours perfectly either. (laughter)

SENATOR KEFAUVER: Very well. Senator Langer?

SENATOR LANGER: You look forward then, do you not, to, say, ten years or twenty years from now this business of baseball is going to grow larger and larger and larger? Isn't that right?

MR. STENGEL: Well, I should think it would. I should think it would get larger because of the fact we are drawing tremendous crowds, I believe, from overseas programs in television, that is one program I have always stuck up for. I think every ballplayer and everyone should give out anything that is overseas for the Army, free of cost and so forth. I think that because of the lack of parking in so many cities that you cannot have a great ballpark if you don't have parking space. If you are aged or forty-five or fifty and have acquired enough money to go to a ball game, you cannot drive a car on a highway, which is very hard to do after age forty-five, to drive on any modern highway and if you are going to stay home you need radio and television to go along for receipts for the ball club.

SENATOR KEFAUVER: Thank you, Senator Langer. Senator O'Mahoney?

SENATOR O'MAHONEY: How many players did the sixteen major-league clubs have when you came in?

MR. STENGEL: At that time they did not have near as many teams as below. Later on Mr. Rickey came in and started what was known as what you would say numerous clubs, you know in which I will try to pick up this college man, I will pick up that college boy or I will pick up some corner-lot boy and if you picked up the corner-lot boy maybe he became just as successful as the college man, which is true.

Now, too many players is a funny thing, it cost like everything. I said just like I made a talk not long ago and I told them all when they were drinking and they invited me in I said you ought to be home. You men are not making enough money. You can't drink like that. They said, "This is a holiday for the Shell Oil Company," and I said, "Why is that a holiday?" and they said, "We did something great for three years and we are given two days off to watch the Yankees play the White Sox," but they were mostly White Sox rooters. I said, "You are not doing right." I said, "You can't take all those drinks and all even on your holidays. You ought to be home and raising more children because big-league clubs now give you a hundred thousand for a bonus to go into baseball."

SENATOR O'MAHONEY: Did I understand you to say that in your own personal activity as manager, you always give a player who is to be traded advance notice?

MR. STENGEL: I warn him that—I hold a meeting. We have an instructional school, regardless of my English, we have got an instructional school.

SENATOR O'MAHONEY: Your English is perfect and I can understand what you say, and I think I can even understand what you mean. Mr. Chairman, I think the witness is the best entertainment we have had around here for a long time and it is a great temptation to keep asking him questions but I think I better desist. Thank you.

SENATOR KEFAUVER: Senator Carroll.

SENATOR CARROLL: Mr. Stengel, the question Senator Kefauver asked you was what, in your honest opinion, with your forty-eight years of experience, is the need for this legislation in view of the fact that baseball has not been subject to antitrust laws?

MR. STENGEL: No.

SENATOR LANGER: May I ask a question? Can you tell this committee what countries have baseball teams besides the United States, Mexico and Japan?

MR. STENGEL: I made a tour with the New York Yankees several years ago, and it was the most amazing tour I ever saw for a ball club, to go over where you have trouble spots. It wouldn't make any difference whether he was a Republican or Democrat, and so forth. I know that over there we drew two hundred fifty to five hundred thousand people in the streets, in which they stood in front of the automobiles, not on the sidewalks, and those people are trying to play baseball over there with short fingers, and I say, Why do you do it?

But they love it. They are crazy about baseball, and they are not worried at the handicap. South America is all right, and Cuba is all right. But I don't know, I have never been down there except to Cuba, I have never been to South America.

SENATOR LANGER: Do you not think these owners are going to

develop this matter of world championship of another country besides the United States?

MR. STENGEL: I should think they would do that in time. I really do. I was amazed over in Japan. I couldn't understand why they would want to play baseball with short fingers and used the same size ball, and not a small size, and compete in baseball. And yet that is their great sport, and industries are backing them.

SENATOR LANGER: That is all, Mr. Chairman.

SENATOR KEFAUVER: Thank you very much, Mr. Stengel. We appreciate your presence here.

(Stengel leaves, Mickey Mantle enters.)

SENATOR KEFAUVER: Mr. Mantle, do you have any observations with reference to the applicability of the antitrust laws to baseball?

MR. MANTLE: My views are about the same as Casey's. *(laughter)*

36

On a Friday afternoon later that season, when spring was hot enough for summer, Nicole stopped by Frank's school to pick him up. The boy came out of the front door holding hands with a rusty-haired pink-skinned girl; they were chattering to each other about something and making their way merrily to the curb, looking up only at the last minute, simultaneously, to discover Nicole and the girl's father, unknowingly side by side, their cars parked nose to rear. Frank and the girl looked at their parents, their parents looked at each other. Mommy, this is Tammy; can she have dinner at our house tonight? said Frank.

The girl's father smiled gently at her; he wore slacks and a short-sleeved brown-and-white dress shirt, and he had the girl's features mirrored to the male side and thirty years worn. I'm Tom, he said. It's all right by me, if you don't mind the extra mouth at the table.

No, she said, not at all. I don't know what we're having, but whatever it is I can make more.

I meant, talking mouth, actually. —He smiled. —Chattering

mouth, asking questions mouth. Food's one thing, I know, and thank you. Quiet is another, and you won't have much with my daughter around. —Now the little girl was standing beside him, head resting on her father's thigh, arm curled around her father's knee, silent to her father's fond admission but rocking slightly around the axis of his leg. Something about the motion charmed Nicole, and she smiled.

Walter was away in Nashville that night so it was just the four of them, and the little girl did go on some. Frank was in awe of her opinions and instructions, her comments on everything from the teacher in their class to the car her father drove, and Nicole sat smiling and listening to her, and wondering if this was what she had been like as a child, or whether it was some Modern Girlhood, the fruits of the century finally appearing on the highest, youngest branches of the tree.

After eating, the children rushed from the room, and a minute later she could hear them in Frank's bedroom, screaming with laughter at some new toy. Gail cried to see her brother go, and Nicole went over to her high chair to comfort her. There you are, said Nicole, and put a pacifier in the baby's mouth. She cleared the plates and left them in the sink, unwashed, thinking she would get to them later, perhaps even the following day; then she realized that Tom would be coming by to pick the girl up, and it wouldn't do to have the kitchen a mess. So she did the dishes and put them on the rack, and then went into the living room to watch the television, with Gail sleeping in her lap and her feet resting on the edge of the footrest before the big dusty sea-green chair her mother had given them when the house was new and the marriage was new.

Tom was supposed to come by at eight-thirty to get his girl, and she waited, as the earth slowly turned upward into darkness. It was a very warm night, and the city was stuffy. Outside the crickets were chirping, and when she brought Gail out onto the front porch for some air, a half dozen grey and tan moths immediately started fluttering against the light. She wiped her palms on the thighs of her slacks, shifting the baby from one arm to the other, even as she bounced her gently and rhythmically; and then she grew self-conscious, standing out there in view of the street, and she went back inside.

He came just before nine, feet on the walk, knuckles on the door, ignoring the bell. She heard his hand on her home and she jumped, flushed, strode quickly into the entranceway and hesitated. There was a mirror by the coatrack, and she did her best to smooth away the faintly stricken look she wore; there was a pane of opaque glass by the side of the door through which his shadow stood, then moved with shadow swiftness as he rapped upon the door again. She opened it and let him in; he was smiling. Hello again, he said, as he paused on the threshold and removed his straw hat. I'm sorry I'm late.

She waited for him to explain but he just shrugged, and she decided the fault was hers for being nosy. There was an awkward pause. —Well, come on in, she said. They're upstairs, playing.

Thank you, he said. And thank you for taking care of my girl.

Oh, it was no trouble, she said. She's an angel. —Which she was not, exactly, but Nicole had liked her and thought she was good for Frank, who was moody sometimes and quiet always. Let him learn about girls early. I'll go call them down, she said.

The two children were visible from the bottom of the stairs, sprawled out with splayed limbs on the second-floor landing, nego-tiating something as children would: the terms of a treaty between two Oriental monarchs; the foundation of a foundation for the world's tallest building; the surrender of Joan of Arc to whoever it was who had captured Joan of Arc. No, no, no, Tammy was saying. You have to go here. Here, and ask for permission.

Frank, Nicole called. Tammy's father is here. He was behind her, watching from the living room.

Mom . . . said Frank. For a few seconds there was no sound, as the boy drew himself out of his play world.

Frank. It's getting late.

We're not done yet. Please? We have to clear this place.

O.K., she said. But soon. Ten minutes. She hesitated for an instant before turning back to the man, while she chose an expression to wear.

He was standing with his back against the credenza, his arms folded on his chest. Did he ever stop smiling like that? I guess they'll be a few minutes, she said. They're just finishing up. Can I get you a drink? Iced tea? Or something harder? She was keeping her distance.

Just tea is fine, he said.

She fetched the glass from a cabinet; he glanced at the dining room through the door. This is a nice place, here.

Thank you for saying so. She paused. Lately, she confessed, I've found myself dreaming of a house out of town. Someplace in the country. But my husband needs to be near things. You know how it is: there's always some crisis, some problem, somebody who needs to talk to him. And I'd hate to make Frank start at a new school, just when he's learning to make friends. She gave him a smile to go along with the compliment for Tammy.

You must be very proud of your husband, said Tom Healy. That's important work he's doing.

I suppose it is, said Nicole. There was a moment of silence. —Yes, it is, she said. Do you live nearby?

Near enough, he said. My wife and I bought a place just a few miles up the road—he gestured with his hands. We came up here from Mississippi with the Army Corps of Engineers a few years after our girl was born. —Just then a streetlight beyond the window blinked off, and the room became slightly darker; Tom looked outside, the light blinked on again, and he laughed but made no comment.

That sounds like a good job, said Nicole.

It is, he said. That it is. She studied his hands to see what an engineer's hands looked like. He nodded for some moments after he was done speaking, suddenly looking exhausted and finished for the day, with only his head still moving. Well, we should probably be going now. We're keeping you up, he said.

No, she said. But you look tired. Let me go get the children.

She stood and started back to the foot of the stairs, but just then Frank and Tammy marched down, chattering about something; Frank made a noise with his mouth and ran for his mother. Tammy's dad is building a dam on the river, he said. They're building it now. Can we go to watch them?

We'll see, said Nicole, looking back at Tom, who shrugged and frowned, as if to say, Why not? We'll see, said Nicole again. There was a great bustling in the room, a wonder what a little boy and a little girl could do, talking over each other with their childish authority, —You're going to lose a shoe there, said Tom, and when his daughter paid him no mind he got down off the couch and knelt before her to tie her laces. There were a few more measures of busyness, and then they were gone.

37

It was late in the day and there was a knock upon Walter's door, his secretary opened it and stuck her head in a little ways. Mr. Selby, there's someone here to see you, she said. I told him to phone in for an appointment, but he insisted on talking to someone, and you're the only one around. She paused. —He's very stubborn.

Walter stared at her, still lost in the paperwork that lay before him on the desk: a budget for sanitation, numbers, dollars. He made a noise which meant nothing, and his secretary answered: I can send him away. His attention broke. No, no, said Walter. Let him come on in.

A moment later there was a shadow beyond the door frame, and in came a small compact Negro man. He was dressed in a blue seersucker suit and a white shirt with no tie, and a translucent slick of sweat lay on his forehead and the pit of his throat. He moved swiftly and confidently across the room, stopping at the far side of Walter's desk as Walter got to his feet. The man's hand was out, his face stern. My name is Mose Drake, he said. Mose Drake.

Walter smoothed down his tie and composed a solemn, expectant expression. He couldn't remember the last time a colored man had come into his office uninvited and without an appointment. Good afternoon, Mr. Drake. What can I do for you?

Ah, well, that's just it, isn't it? Drake smiled unhappily and then hesitated, as if his plans had just run out. Do you mind if I sit down?

Go on, said Walter, and the two men sat, the oak desk between them. Drake started to reach out to move a pen set that was blocking his view, and then thought better of it and shifted his chair to the right a few inches. A few seconds passed; Walter waited expectantly, uncomfortable with his expectancy, irritated at his discomfort, guarded.

A rich, rich pageant, isn't it? said Drake.

Pardon?

A rich pageant. Tennessee. I was born here, right outside of Hodgetown, a little town out by Crossville called Boo City, about forty-two years ago. —Here Drake unfolded his hands and laid them face up on his side of the desk. Where were you born? he said.

Walter was taken aback: who came to him for help, what man of ashes, and asked him such questions? Kentucky, he said. —Drake raised an eyebrow. —My mother's family came from there. She moved up to New York, then back to Louisville: I moved here, my grandmother was from here.

Drake smiled, a warm and real smile. Well, there you go. That's part of the pageant too. My father's father founded Boo City, back in the last century, he and some families he loved and trusted. It was a refuge, you see. The afternoon sun was slipping through the slats in the blinds, and Drake shifted again to keep the light out of his eyes. When I was a young man, I went down to Atlanta for a little while, did some day labor and all that. But I came back to Boo City. Just like you, I suppose. —Not at all like me, Walter was thinking, and he wondered if the Negro was thinking the same thing. Been there about fifteen years, now. Getting along all right. —Walter nodded and started to speak. —I got married, Drake interrupted him. I had a daughter and a son. My daughter's about twenty-two now, and I think she's going to be all right.

Lot of worry, said Walter. Bringing up children in this world.

They're O.K. They're living right near by me, safe and sound, until about a month ago. —Drake suddenly leaned forward, so that it seemed to Walter that the desk belonged to the other man, and he was the supplicant. I knew as soon as I saw them, two white men in suits, riding in a big black sedan. We don't get many white people out that way. We don't get many fancy cars. They pulled up before my house, I was watching them from my window, they had . . . briefcases, identification, they had papers . . . they said . . .

Walter waited while Drake frowned and his eyes turned to a corner of the ceiling and lost their focus, as if he were getting ready to recite a poem. —They said . . . we had to move. All of us, pack up and get out. They said we had no right to the property, and they're going to build a power plant right there, dynamite a place for it right out of the mountainside.

Drake was done, but he stayed forward in his chair. Walter picked up a pen and held it over a pad of paper. Who are they? he said.

Some of your people. Going to blow down my home and build right over it, the house my daddy built. The graveyard where I buried him.

He stared hard at Walter, and Walter stared back. Our power program is the cornerstone of the new Tennessee. . . .

Are you going to tell me there's nothing you can do? said Drake. I voted for this governor. Twice. I voted for your party for twenty years. I voted for you when I had to scrape for the money to pay the poll tax; I came into town and voted for you in the days when a colored man could have been killed for trying to vote at all. —Drake finally leaned back; his hands were calmly in his lap, his brow smooth. And now I'm asking you, he said gently. What are you going to do for me?

At last Walter put his pen down on the pad. I'll do what I can, he said. I don't know if I can do anything, but I'll talk to the Governor over the weekend and see if we can't get something going for you. —Here he stood and went to the window, adjusting the blinds until the room was dark. —Turned. Here's what I want you to do. Go back home. I'll see what I can get done from here. I'll call you.

But there was nothing he could do, not that he could find. He called the Governor, and the Governor explained: The land upon which Boo City was built had once belonged to a man named Rourke, and so had the Negro families. When Rourke died without an heir, the families had simply built their town; but the taxes had never been paid on Rourke's estate, the families hadn't realized it was necessary, and the property was so distant and isolated that the state had never gotten around to sending someone out there. Nevertheless, the land had reverted to Tennessee; so what if it had taken a century to collect?

Why don't we try and find someplace else for the plant? Postpone it for a while and do a study.

Can't be done, said the Governor. It's a whole new world, Selby. Don't you see? We have to keep ahead. Everybody's got a secret, everybody's got a plan. The tribes are restless, and we can't afford to inflame them any further. Kefauver's making a big splash in Washington, hot-dogging all up and down the Potomac. Did you read that stuff about the baseball monopoly in the paper? All of those senators and such getting up to their high jinks? All that hug-tight testimony. They're having a high time up there, having some fun with a bunch of ballplayers. Antitrust my white ass . . . They're talking about making him President of the United States someday, and you know he doesn't see eye to eye with me. We need something big and benign to throw back at him, something everyone can be proud of. We need to shed light on the hollows of Tennessee, not to wallow in the darkness. We need this project.

It doesn't feel right to me, said Walter. A hundred years is a lot of history, a long time to be on a piece of land. Doesn't he have some kind of common-law right? I ought to look into it.

—Look into nothing, said the Governor. If he can put up a case, all right. The courts will sort it out. But we're not in the business of providing legal advice to our opponents. Now, Selby, I know you had a problem with something like this when you were in the service.

Walter reddened on the line. That was very different, he said. The circumstances were different, and I was just a kid.

That's right. I never held it against you. I never told a soul. But this isn't that, and I don't want you trying to make up for it on our dime.

No, sir, I'm not. But we have a duty.

We have a duty to get that plant built. Illuminate this great state. Am I right? We can't be held up by a few stubborn families when, hell, we're going to give them some fine land just upriver.

Walter said nothing, the Governor was right and he felt unwell.

Tell me you agree with me. Tell me you feel it. Lie to me if you have to.

No, I agree. That's no lie.

Good, good, good, said the Governor. Then let's try and keep our eyes on what's important.

What do I say to Drake?

Is that the fellow's name? said the Governor. Just tell him his state appreciates what he's doing.

Yes, said Walter, even as he searched his desk for the telephone number Drake had left for him, a general store some twenty miles down the road from his house. He was there, as if he'd been waiting, and Walter began to improvise an explanation, but after a few seconds the other man interrupted him.

Forgive me for being rude, said Drake. But are you going to be able to help me?

No, said Walter, faintly relieved to have been run off his words. I'm sorry.

That's all right, said Drake softly. Thank you for trying. Thank you kindly. Good-bye.

38

From time to time, Nicole would ask Frank what had happened to his little friend, but it seemed he'd grown tired of her, or had withdrawn again, into a world with its own blunted laws of causation and consequence, and his answer had been boyish and obscure: an averted gaze, a shrug, a word: Nothing. He was an elusive child, a little bit mercurial, maybe; he was soft on the surface but he could be surprisingly hard beneath, and she wondered what kind of man he would become.

It was a month or more before she saw the girl again, and met her mother. Then Nicole was alone; it was a weekend, but Walter was in his office, and she was at the garden nursery, among the lattice frames and clay planting pots, looking for bulbs to go beside the path in the front yard—tulips, paper-whites, perhaps some southern dahlias. There was a little girl in a blue and white dress standing close beside her. The girl spoke. Are you Frank's mommy?

Startled, she turned. Yes, I am, she said. It was not so far from bulbs to girls, and she recognized the child right away. You're Tammy, aren't you?

The girl nodded vigorously. That's my mom, she said, pointing to a slim dark-haired woman in a blue crepe dress who was just then approaching. The woman was lovely and she moved by gliding, closing the gap between them swiftly but without any evident effort.

Tammy, she said, gently admonishing the child.

It's all right, we've met, said Nicole cheerfully. She and my son attend Trumbull together. The other woman smiled, emphasizing the dark creases under her eyes,—a subtle mark that might have been a flaw, but which instead made her look, not so much weary as appealingly impure. Nicole patted the girl's head gently. She came by for dinner not so long ago. Right? —Tammy nodded. With my son, Frank. She gazed at the woman again. I'm Nicole Selby.

Oh, said the woman, and reached her hand out to touch Nicole's shoulder. Of course. I'm Janet Healy. Tom told me about that. She offered no explanation for where she'd been that night, a subtle indifference that slipped past Nicole, though she registered something admirable in the woman's complacency and wanted to talk to her some more.

Are you shopping for your garden?

Yes, said Janet Healy. What little of it there is. We had a dogwood that Tom planted in the front yard but it didn't do so well, so we're going to put in something else and hope for better luck. —She turned to her daughter. Right? Tammy loved that tree. But not all things abide.

The girl frowned. I want to plant a potato tree, she said.

A potato tree?

Janet Healy smiled. We don't know what she's talking about, actually. Somehow she's gotten something in her head about potatoes and trees. What is it, darling? she said to the girl. What do you mean? She gestured around the nursery, to the tables of bulbs and potted flowers, the sacks of peat, the rows of saplings, their roots bound up in burlap; and the child looked, but she saw nothing that fit her notion of a potato tree and she made no response. We'll find something, said Janet Healy.

We—meaning the family altogether. Nicole would have liked to have questioned the woman, perhaps even to have asked for her advice: How does a wife make a family so that all become *we*? How do you mend what only you know is broken? Oh, well, said Janet Healy. I don't think we're going to make any progress today. Are you done? I could use a cup of coffee and some company.

I'm done, yes, said Nicole, though she had just gotten there. Let's go.

They sat for more than an hour. Was it hard moving up here from Mississippi? Nicole asked.

Oh, God, no, said Janet Healy. I couldn't wait to get out of there. What a backwater. No. Memphis isn't Paris, of course, but it's a damn sight better than Vicksburg. At least there's someplace to go at night, and the rudiments of culture: a library, even a museum or two. I told Tom I wasn't going to raise my daughter to be preyed upon by farm boys. Luckily, this new job came up.

Later, Nicole would remember how the other woman had talked as if her daughter simply wasn't there. It wasn't callousness or neglect—if anything it was a kind of intimacy: the child obviously appreciated it, and her attention would wander happily around the room and then fix again on her mother. From time to time, Janet would turn to her with a remark which meant nothing: Do you want some more ice tea? Or, Look, if you hold your glass up you can see a rainbow along the edge. It was something Nicole herself had always striven for and never quite attained—an ease and effortlessness, like that of the other woman's beauty, which was not, to be honest, as inherent as her own, but was the more striking for that, as if she had willed it, and the will itself was what made her attractive. They had traded phone numbers when they separated, and in days thereafter Nicole thought of Janet Healy often—how good it would be to have a friend like that. Maybe she could learn a thing or two about how to make her way through life; but she was intimidated, like a schoolgirl infatuated with a popular upper-classwoman, and she never did call.

39

A DRESS BALL AT THE GOVERNOR'S MANSION, ON THE OCCASION OF HIS REELECTION TO A THIRD TERM

All the men were handsome in their black tuxedos, the women beautiful in their elegant gowns, an honor guard stood at the entrance, and a policeman on the left with sore feet who took pleasure in his duty and his soreness. By the back door the caterers hastily unloaded ice from a late truck, while the Master of the Kitchen, a thin, small bachelor, muttered under his breath and hoped that not too many people were drinking yet. Ice, he said. God almighty, ice. Go, go, go. —Not you, he said, pulling aside a server who had held one of the metal tubs too close to his chest. Goddamn it. You can't go out there with your shirt wet. Change your shirt, you shitheel. Now. Go, go.

The Governor stood on the staircase above the entranceway, shouting hellos and beaming, with his plump silver-haired wife beside him, while below the incoming guests wandered in from the door, some with slightly dazed expressions on their faces, as if the election results—which after all had been very close—were not yet real, even though they were celebrating. Already a state senator had passed out drunk in a second-floor bathroom, and a reporter had asked a question and received only the Governor's inscrutable smile, and a furious wife had snubbed her husband's not-so-secret mistress, and muttered the word *trash* loud enough for both her husband and the other woman to hear.

The Governor came down the stairs to shake the hand of the state attorney general and kiss the hand of the attorney general's wife. Walter Selby was just then giving his car keys to a boy in a red suit outside; he paused on the curb and took a deep breath, craning his head back to stare up at the facàde of the mansion, which was glowing from every shined window with the light of good fortune and good sense. He turned to his beautiful wife, whose smile beat the windows for brightness; then he took her by the arm, the motion setting free some fragrant particle of her fine perfume, and together they started up the front stairs to the busy noise inside.

Beyond the threshold there were a thousand conversations, a vast babbling roar, broken now and again by loud laughter. The Governor had opened the house to every friend he could think of, and more than a few of his enemies: there were city lawyers, newspaper editors, hospital administrators, youth leaders; there was the owner of a company that published sheet music, who long ago had begun his career printing five-cent pornographic novels; there was a lobbyist from Standard Oil and another from a citizens' group that was trying to sue Standard Oil for price-fixing, a retired prostitute, now the proprietor of Memphis's largest brothel, a massive man bursting out of a massive blue uniform, who was the commander of the state's National Guard units, a dozen or so members of the Assembly; a woman in pearls, whose late husband had owned half the state's hardware stores and who now spent her time erecting and preserving dozens of statues of long forgotten local heroes; and county chairmen, and union officials, bankers, insurance men, Negro ministers representing powerful congregations, the University's first-string varsity quarterback, with his parents standing stiffly by his side; police chiefs from Nashville and Knoxville, Memphis and Chattanooga, a few prominent administrators of the TVA—and among them, all the women, wives and lovers. Two hundred gentlemen, and two hundred charming women, in a vast, continuous dance, in and around one another, like some ritual ball of old whose rules had been half forgotten, leaving only the impulse of movement, touching, gliding, smiling, and drinking down the Governor's cold champagne and his best whiskey.

The Governor spotted Walter and advanced upon him with a convivial expression. Selby, he said. Where've you been hiding? And where is—where is that beautiful wife of yours? There you are. Of course! Nicole smiled her smile, and even the Governor paused slightly, as if he were ready to drop everything he had to say and bask in her luminescence for a few minutes. Then he leaned in. You taking care of our Mr. Selby? he said to her. —Now Walter was distracted by a state senator, who had him by the elbow and was whispering in his ear. You know, he's a fragile man, said the Governor to Nicole. You and I, we have to take care of him.

Fragile? said Nicole.

In his way, said the Governor. Nobody knows it better than we two.

Nicole gazed at him, still smiling, but thinking hard behind her expression. Maybe, she said.

He's a true believer, said the Governor. Hard to find in these times and worth more than I can say. —Nicole nodded. —Be tender with him, said the Governor, and Nicole faltered for a moment and then nodded again.

I will, she said.

Now, Selby, said the Governor to Walter, who had just turned back to join them. I'm trying to figure this out: I know you're a smart man, and you've done me all the good in the world. But you aren't handsome and you aren't rich; so what did you do to land this lovely woman? I mean it. What did you say to her to convince her to come away with you? I want to know.

I told her I'd take her to fancy dress balls at the governor's mansion, Walter said with a smile, and the Governor raised his head and laughed quietly.

Is that right? Is that all it takes? I could have used that myself, a while back, before I met my own sweet wife. If I'd only known. If I'd only known.

A young man who had been standing silently behind the Governor took the opportunity to sidle in. Sir, he said. There's a woman here I think you should meet; and he pointed discreetly at an elderly lady who just that afternoon had made known her desire for an appointment to Parks and Recreation, in repayment for the thousands of contributions she'd collected from gardening women around the state.

I see her, I see her. I'll be just a minute, said the Governor. He

turned back to Walter with a crestfallen expression. See now, he said
sadly. I've got to go take care of this, or else I'm going to be hearing
about it for the next two weeks. And we have work to do, right away,
you and I, he said. So I'll go over there and give that lady something,
and you go around and enjoy yourself, and I'll see you in the office
tomorrow morning.

Suddenly there was a Western Swing band playing in a corner of
the dining room, and soon there were couples whirling around the
room, while the fiddler played his furious circles of white jazz. Come
on, Walter whispered to his wife. Come. But instead of leading her out
onto the floor, he took her by the hand and guided her through the
room, where the Governor was now dancing with a woman Walter had
never seen before; along the hall, where two lawyers were arguing;
under the stairs, where a young man was sitting alone with tears in his
eyes; through the kitchen, where platters of shrimp were reverting to
grey amid pools of melting ice; past the closed door of the maids' quarters, behind which the Master of the Kitchen was receiving hasty
sexual service from one of his hires; and out the back door, where he
seized her under the stars and kissed her laughing lipsticked mouth as
if he would smother its glitter, all at once. He stood back and looked
at her.

We really should go back inside, shouldn't we? said Nicole.

He turned his head, contemplated the back garden in darkness and
sighed. Yes, he said. I suppose we should. He stood back and looked
down at his pants, which betrayed a fondness for loving his wife. We'll
have to wait a minute.

She gazed down at him and smiled. —Oh, she said. How lovely.
Can't we take it inside? She reached out a pale hand and through the
fabric of his suit she briefly, gently, stroked the blunt, nudging head
with her fingertips. He sucked his mouth quickly. Boys, she said, in a
rather inept imitation of the Governor's voice. I'd like you to meet my
right hand man, Walter Selby. And Mrs. Selby, his lovely wife. And
Walter Selby's erection, which he often brings out for display on occasions of great political importance. She laughed, and bit him gently on
his underlip, inhaling at the same time, so that he lost one entire
breath, and it took him several more to recover. She stood and walked
a few steps out into the garden, and sipped at the sweetness in the air.
By the time she returned the hardness had subsided, with a memory

left behind. Come, she said. We'll be home soon, and in our own bed. He turned and followed her back toward the sound of the ball. Do you know how much I love you? he said, before he escorted her through the kitchen door. How much, really?

She didn't face him but she took his hand. Yes, she said solemnly. I know.

In the ballroom the Governor had stopped dancing and now stood at one side, whispering into the ear of his attorney general. Now there was a man at Walter's shoulder, Harvey Somebody, one of Boss Crump's leftover minions from Germantown, who had opposed the Governor in the primary and then supported him when it became clear that he couldn't lose. This is a great day for the state of Tennessee, whispered Somebody, the note of mockery almost lost in his murmur. Isn't it a fine sight? The Governor, there. His boys. You're one of his boys, aren't you?

Walter said nothing, nor even nodded, but he nudged Nicole a little bit away, not wanting her to be made unclean by this man. One of these days we ought to have a little talk, said Somebody. He rested his hand briefly on Walter's elbow. One of these days and soon, I think.

Walter smiled without looking toward the man. Why don't you give me a call, all right? No business tonight, but you call me in the morning, and we can sit down.

Yeah, I think I'll do that, said Somebody, and was gone again.

He turned, and Nicole was standing a few feet off, talking to a woman he'd never seen before, a dark, volatile-looking woman who just then was tucking her hair behind her ear, revealing a small white pearl in her lobe. She touched the pearl briefly and smiled at Nicole. Walter started toward her, only to be buttonholed again, in the new instance by a man who introduced himself as Tom Healy, an engineer just up from Mississippi. How're you doing? said Tom. You're Walter Selby, aren't you?

I am.

I've been waiting to meet you, said Healy. The Governor told me great things about you. I said to my wife—here he gestured to the woman with the pearl earrings—I hope somebody talks about *me* that way.

Is that your wife? said Walter. That's mine, that she's talking to.

Healy grinned. Yes, I know, he said. You're Frank's father.

Yes, said Walter, and tried to hide his surprise, and his irritation at the idea that some stranger should have an advantage of information over him. He didn't say anything more.

Healy picked up the loose end. Your boy and my daughter are in school together, he said. I guess they've become friends. Anyway, Tammy went by your house for dinner one night a few weeks ago. I met your wife when I came to pick her up.

Yes, right, said Walter. I was down here in Nashville. —I heard about that, he added, wondering why in fact he hadn't. I'm afraid your wife's name has slipped my mind.

She's Janet, said Healy. Janet Catherine Anne Duvall—that's her maiden name—Healy. Let's go get the two of them, you and me, and see if we can't get some dancing out of this evening.

But there was some argument playing between Healy and his wife—what it was Walter couldn't tell, but she didn't look at all happy to see him, and in fact she moved that much closer to Nicole when the two men approached. There was a blush in Nicole's cheeks, a bit of blood language, and then she leaned back just a little and smiled; and there it was again, that mad delight, that warmth of hunger. It never lasted long, but while it did, all men rode upright on their horses, and no bridge would fall. Hello, darling, she said. I see you've met Tom. This is Janet.

The other woman simply said Hello before her attention was taken by a newspaper reporter.

I was just telling Walter, here, that it looks like we're going to be working together, said Tom Healy, while his wife spelled their name for the reporter. Him and his people call it in to us, and we build it.

Walter nodded, Nicole smiled, not her full smile but the one she kept for manners. Darling, he said. Dance with me. Then she held out her hand and he led her away.

40

There was a message from the Governor in a mustard interoffice envelope, Walter's name typed on the front, the note itself written out in that familiar meticulous handwriting, the studied penmanship of the

South. *Come on down to Nashville tonight. I need you at the mansion at 9:00. I'll send a driver.* There was no more, and Walter knew better than to ask what the meeting might be about. The Governor wouldn't admit to having had an extra glass of orange juice at breakfast unless he was certain the time was right, and had some reason to believe that credit would accrue to him for his candor. Still, there were clues, and after a decade's service they were plain enough. The Governor didn't like to do business at home, except in instances where intimacy would be an advantage; someone was going to be snowed. Moreover, he frowned upon frivolous uses of public money where cheaper alternatives were available. The car and driver, then, meant that he wanted Walter to be happy and relaxed, perhaps even inclined to spend a little gratitude, and no less so for the fact that it had been manufactured in plain sight. Then again, everyone knew that a pool of newspaper reporters paid the State's drivers twenty-five dollars a week in cash to tell who came and who went, anywhere policy might be made. Thus the meeting was meant to be known at large, at least unofficially, and the Governor could appeal to the need for a unified front should someone object to whatever was being proposed. And 9:00 was too late for dinner and only an hour before the Governor's customary bedtime, so the night would be quick and frank. Walter smiled.

The guard at the door of the mansion nodded to Walter Selby, and the butler in the vestibule bowed a little. Good evening, he said. They're waiting for you in the library.

The Governor was sitting silently on a long, low leather couch; he looked up at Walter with almost childlike confidence. Beside him was a motionless man, grey-haired and wearing a grey suit; behind them both stood a young and plump and ruddy-faced man, who was silent, too, but smiling. Selby, said the Governor. Good. This is Johnson from the power authority, Bodean from the State Police. Let's make this a quick one. He nodded at Bodean.

The plump man spoke up. You been talking to this man out in Boo City, name of Drake? Yes? He mentioned you.

Walter had to think for a moment: Drake, yes, the colored man. He came by my office a little while ago, he said. Just before the election.

Son of a bitch, said Bodean. Nobody tells me nothing.

What's the matter?

What's the matter is, the man's holed up out there, and he's not moving. Got his wife and kids in the house, and he won't come out. He says it's his land, it's his home, and we've got to shoot him if we want him off it.

I've got contractors lined up out there, said Johnson. Laborers, engineers. It's costing the state two thousand a day.

Walter looked at the Governor. You need to get out there, said the Governor. See if you can talk to him before someone gets hurt.

Hurt, said Walter.

My troopers don't like to sit still for too long, said Bodean. They get itchy, if you know what I mean.

Yeah, said Walter. I think I probably do.

41

Thicket, trees, morning, highway. Boo City was farther than Walter would have guessed. Nicole was going to miss him for the day. Hot, the road shimmering even at dawn, the sky a pale yellow-blue, the crows themselves sitting motionless on the telephone poles. Bodean driving, the land rising and sinking and rising again, until it was enough to make a man sick and dull. Maybe that's where everything went wrong, back when the landscape was designed by some unlovely hand. Down an old dirt road, over a ridge, then over another, deeper in, an hour and a half without sign of settlement, just the trees passing, the air lying thicker. There was no breeze. Walter leaned up in his seat, staring down the lengthening road. Just another ten minutes or so, said Bodean. Sorry you had to come all this way. I told the Governor we ought to just dynamite the fucking house down around them all, but he said you could talk him out. Said you could talk a cat out of a drainpipe if you wanted to. The road narrowed to a single lane and became so rutted Walter was almost thrown from his seat. Sorry, said Bodean. I don't know why anyone would want to live out here, anyway. Then he said, Right around this bend here, and they came around to the sight of a dozen or so squad cars, parked in the grass by the side of the road. A little ways down there was a line of empty construction vehicles. Across a short field there was an old wooden house, with dark windows. Bodean parked and the two of them got out, stretching in the heat, legs a little slow. One of the troopers came down, carrying a cracked-open shotgun in the crook of his arm like a hunter. Well, nothing happened all night, he said. Couple of our guys sat out here. They sat in there. This here's Selby, from the Governor's office, said Bodean. You know this man? said the trooper, gesturing toward the house. I met him, said Walter. You go talk some sense in to him, then. My boys don't want to spend another hot day out here, still less another night. Goddamn mosquitoes eat you alive. Yeah, said Walter. What's it like up there? Don't know, said Bodean. One of the contractors went up there yesterday, and your man Drake chased him off with a hammer and then locked himself inside. Time was, a nigger took a hammer to a white man, he'd soon find himself doing a hornpipe on the end of a rope, said the trooper, and Walter gave him a look. I'm just saying, said the trooper. He got a gun up there? said Walter. Don't know, said Bodean. The contractor thought he saw a long gun in the corner of the front room, maybe just a .22, maybe a shotgun. Maybe nothing, just a length of pipe. Walter nodded. We got you covered, said the trooper. I've got a man behind that tree out there, another in the grass, and one more round back of the house, and all these boys down here. He didn't seem like a murderous man to me, said Walter, and the trooper said, Sometimes they don't. Go to, if you want. Walter nodded and started walking across the field, calling Drake! Drake! It's me, Walter Selby! Drake! Was there movement in the house or just haze shifting across the windows? In time he came upon a cinder block, which almost tripped him up, then a bicycle tire, a paint can: now the field was a yard. Drake! Still quiet from the house, and he was only ten feet away from the front steps. —Hold it. The front door eased open an inch or two, and Walter stopped. One eye in the gap. Who's that? Drake, you know me, don't you? You came by my office. What are you doing out here? said Drake. I just came to talk, said Walter. See if I can help any. —You couldn't help before. —No, I guess I couldn't. Things are a little different now, though. Can't hurt to let me in. I'm not here to arrest you, I've got no gun or anything. —What about those other men? —I can't speak for them, said Walter. Just don't open the door too far, and I'll slip right in. There was a long pause, some cicadas buzzing in the grass, sun directly overhead. Drake? Another minute to wait. Then, from behind the door: O.K. Come on in, then. Slowly. Passing into the shadow-bell of the short porch, Walter couldn't see. Behind him there was yellow noise; before him a dark wall. The knob was brass and cool to the touch. Drake? —Let yourself in. He did, and the house inside was even darker. He stood in the front room, blinking. Drake was at the other end, standing by the door to the kitchen with a rifle in his right hand. In the room behind there were two women, wife and daughter, staring out. Walter looked around. Where's your boy? Drake nodded with his head, and Walter saw him, standing hidden at the side of a front window, peering around. One in the grass and one behind the tree, said the boy. And one in back, said Walter. Just so you know. The house smelled of bacon and chicory coffee, and something sweet and powerful, soap, skin, and heat. What's your name, son? He's Charlie, said Mose Drake. Charlie, don't get too close to that window, now. The boy took a step back. How are you all holding up? said Walter. Got enough food? —Everything we need. —Good. We can take our time, a little. I sure am sorry it's turned out this way. Yeah, said Drake, I bet you are: And Jephthah said unto the elders of Gilead, Did not ye hate me, and expel me out of my father's house? and why are ye come unto me now when ye are in distress? We are all in the same distress, said Walter. You and me, and your family, and even those men out there. —Those men, said Drake. They're not in my distress, they're in their own. —No, I guess they're not. But no one wants to see anyone get hurt. —And you, said Drake. You are not in my distress, you're in yours. I tried to help you, said Walter. Maybe I didn't try hard enough. Drake nodded. Walter looked around the room: a tattered couch, a thick, clean table, some chairs, a sideboard. It's a good strong house, he said. We can move it, the whole place, over the ridge. Look here, said Drake, pointing out a side window. On a ridge above the house there were a half dozen gravestones, standing straight and tall amid the grass. Those are my people: I'm not going to leave them behind, and I'm sure not going to dig them up, disturb their resting place. Walter looked out at the grave site and paid it a moment of respect. Then he said, those boys outside aren't going to go away, either. And sooner or later they're just going to come in here and get you, maybe hurt you in the process, and maybe your wife and your daughter and your son as well. I can't stop them, and the Governor won't. So you'll all be resting out there, and then they'll move you anyway, and there won't be anyone living to pray for your soul, or theirs, or your father's. You want that? Here Drake shook his head and said, I don't have an eternal soul. *This* is my home. His wife stirred, but said nothing. The Devil takes it, Drake continued. You mean me? said Walter, and Drake shrugged. There was a long silence. How about you make up some coffee or something, we'll talk, said Walter. Drake's wife started to move, but Drake stilled her with a nearly invisible movement of his hand. You're not staying, he said. —God damn it, Drake. —A shake of the head, a shake of the rifle. No, said Drake. He grinned, unexpectedly. I appreciate your company, it was nice of you to stop by, but you should be moving along now. Walter gazed around the room once more, one, two, three, four black faces. I don't want to go just yet. Go on, said Drake. Go home and take care of your own. Walter nodded slowly. All right, he said, and started for the door, turning at the end to look at all of them one more time. This worth dying for? he asked, but there was no response, and he turned back and stepped outside, into heat so bright it almost knocked him down, he walked out into the yard, shrugged exaggeratedly so that everyone could see, lifted a *stay*-hand to the trooper in the grass, and headed back down to where the police cars were glittering by the road. What happened? said Bodean. Nothing, said Walter. Bodean nodded as if something he suspected had just been confirmed. He got a gun? Some old .30-06 said Walter. He's not going to use it, I don't think. Why don't you call your boys in? Bodean paused. I don't take orders from you. —It wasn't an order. Just an idea. Bodean thought for a second, then nodded, turned slowly to face the field, and whistled high and loud between his fingers. The troopers came in, and for a while the five of them just stood around in a group, kicking a little. I don't know, one of the troopers said at last. Maybe we ought to smoke them out. Smoke them? said Bodean. He thought for a moment. Who's got tear gas around here? —I can check down at the barracks outside Sparta, said one of the troopers. —Go on. —You better let me run this by the Governor, said Walter Selby. The trooper left for the barracks, and they got the Governor patched in on one of the police radios. His voice sounded old. Tear gas? said the Governor. You can't talk him out? He won't listen, said Walter. He's damn stubborn. Static on the radio. Governor? Shhh. Governor? You still there? Shhh. —I'm here, yeah. What do you think? —I'm worried that the longer this goes on, the more chance there is something's going to go badly wrong. . . . Yeah, said the Governor. —Bodean's scaring up some tear gas. —Yeah, said the Governor. I guess we should try and smoke him out. I think we should, said Walter. All right, if you think so, said the Governor. Come on home, Walter. Let the police do their business. —I ought to stick around. No, said the Governor. Come on back west. Back to civilization. —All right. He put the radio up in its cradle, and went to Bodean's side, the two of them looking out at the dark house as if they were waiting for it to start talking. The Governor wants me back in Memphis, said Walter. You got someone here who can take me? The Governor's a smart man, said Bodean. Sutter! He was a young fellow, no more than twenty or twenty-one, with red hair and pink skin at his throat from a bad shave. Yes sir. Take this man back to Memphis. Yes sir. And so they left, hours along the way, the road almost empty in the middle of the afternoon, silence in the car as they monitored the radio, the sky thick and hot, wind in the windows, so much land, land, land, a garden of distant neighbors. They listened together, Walter Selby and that young, uncertain officer, as tear gas canisters were fired into Drake's home, and Drake's wife and children stumbled out of the house and were handcuffed and hurried into squad cars, and then Drake himself emerged on the porch, carrying a long hunting knife, which he waved in the air and then seemed to hug, forcing it into his own chest and slowly sawing with it, as if he would cut out his own heart, though he fell before he could succeed, and was dead before anyone could reach him to hear what he had to say. There was a stunned silence from the troopers, and then the women's abrupt, macabre keening. Sutter pulled to the shoulder outside Jackson, so that Walter Selby could vomit in the bushes by the side of the road. Highway, afternoon, trees, thicket.

42

All the next day he sat alone and thought, though his thinking brought him nothing but more misery, as of a grinding in an engine when the oil's gone, and the gears are bound and fight themselves. Goddamn Drake for getting himself on the land, and goddamn Drake for bringing it to him. —As if he were responsible, for electricity or where it went. Goddamn the Governor, for giving in so easily. The world was just out of reach and traveling away; what good was it to be a man? There were always some who got to stay and some who had to leave, and he couldn't control which were which. The power plant and Boo City were elements of a common change, a common history coming to a common end, both signaling that there was no need for him in this world, except to go along, and be the mere instrument of history and its principles of punishment. He was tired: how did he get so tired? During the reelection campaign he'd worked fourteen-hour days, and he hardly saw Nicole anymore, his only pleasure; he hardly saw his children. They were growing up without him, and why? So the Governor could protect his mandate, squander his will, waste agreement, scheme to make nothing happen. You tell them Drake was a madman, the Governor had said. You tell them he was raving. Lie low; I'll tell them you did what you thought was right.

Are you going to sacrifice me? Walter asked.

I'm going to quarantine the bad cows, so the good cows don't get sick. Lie low, Walter. I'll talk to you tomorrow. —And with that, the Governor rang off the line.

Afterward, Walter sat squarely at his desk, drew a sheet of bond paper from the drawer at his side, and took up a fountain pen. The words came to him in murmurs; he just said what he knew he was supposed to say, and he hardly thought about it at all.

I hereby tender my resignation, effective immediately.

He signed and dated it, asked himself if he should get it notarized, and decided not; and then he folded it carefully and placed it in an envelope—noticing only as he sealed it that the return address had State of Tennessee, Office of the Governor imprinted on the upper left corner. He stood and stared at it. Well, that wouldn't do. The glue had already dried, so he took up his letter-opener and slit the envelope open again, and stuck the opener dagger-style into the desk, upright, with its tip buried half an inch into the oak. He began looking through his drawers for a plain white envelope, but there weren't any. He buzzed his secretary: Do you have any envelopes out there, ones that aren't official?

Her voice came back after a few moments. What size?

Letter size. Regular letter size.

Again a certain pause. I don't. Would you like me to go down the hall and see if I can find any?

He thought. It was an act of state, after all.

—Mr. Selby?

No, that's all right, he said. He found another envelope, and sealed the note up again, this time drawing his name in below the imprint, and addressing it to the Governor. Then he stood and walked out, stopped at his secretary's desk long enough to leave the letter in the interoffice pile and to wish her good night, and went home to his wife.

43

On the way home his city turned around him. Every street was a block of voters, layered downward into public works and floating upward into abstractions: religious faith, source of income, attitudes and alliances, a vast and infinitely complex system of wheels and weights, levers and gears, a fantastic rigging that was always on the verge of breaking down. It was no longer his concern, and he thought about what he could do, now that he was free of it. Go into legal practice for himself, as Nicole had sometimes urged him to do. There was John Harrison from Vanderbilt; every time they met the old boy would say to him, Whenever you're ready, whenever you're ready. We could use a man like you, a lawyer with connections.

Who would speak to him now; who could he count among his friends? He ought to call T. J. Wannemaker, try to put the best possible face on his decision as quickly as he could. He was uneasy. How much food did they have in the cupboard? How much money in the bank? How much time before Gail started school? And Frank was growing so quickly, going to be a big man just like his father; he needed new clothes just about every other month, it seemed. Suddenly Walter grew dizzy and he pulled the car over to the side of the road, although rather than loosening his tie he straightened it in the mirror and then pulled it a little tighter. A warm day, maybe it would rain, and wash away the century. He glanced at himself in the rearview mirror and then pulled out onto the empty street again, rolling down the window just enough to take in the smell of green.

He thought he might just keep driving and give himself a couple of hours to reflect and come up with a plan, rather than surprising Nicole with the fact that he was out of work and making her worry. No, better to be with her. Maybe stop and get some flowers? No, go home. Go home. Was he humiliated? Go home. Was he embarrassed at the waste? Go home. Were there speeches in his head still undelivered? Go home. Did he wonder what he was good at, aside from war of one sort or another? Was there anything? And the world was made of ashes. He went home.

Pulling into the driveway he honked his horn once, hesitated, then honked again just before he turned the engine off. Wind in the yard, the grass would have to be mowed, he had time to do things like that now. On the threshold of his house he paused: here was privacy, here was peace. He opened the front door—and there was the sound of the back door closing, its echo reaching him just as he'd shut himself in to the silence inside. Nicole, he thought, except she would have heard him pulling into the driveway and would have come to him. Nicole? he called. I'm home early. Nicole? Nothing, and no more sound. Nicole? again. Where are you? But there was no answer, so he strolled through the kitchen, and the back door was slightly ajar. Hello?

In the backyard, crouched down against the side of the house, bare knees on the damp ground, was Tom Healy, wearing only a pair of black dress shoes, his pale legs pathetically trembling, his member red, half-swollen and dangling, his expression grim and fearful, but frozen, as if by not moving his face might have no meaning. There was a long period when neither spoke, and Walter stood on the back step, asking himself why this naked man had broken into his house, what he had wanted to steal. Then it came to him: You're that engineer. —And for a second or two he thought maybe the man had been hired, by the Governor or the Governor's enemies, to wiretap the house, or unbrace the foundations. But what was the advantage of being undressed? —There was a noise behind him, and he turned and saw Nicole, standing in the door frame between the dining room and the kitchen, stricken in her blue nightgown, her mouth a perfect zero. And still Walter didn't understand. Now Tom had gotten to his feet, though his eyes were still downcast, and he said the oddest thing, in the oddest voice. My wife doesn't mind. She doesn't. She knows and she doesn't mind. And still Walter wondered: Doesn't mind what? He looked at Nicole again, her face damp, her breasts appearing behind the translucent film of her negligee—neglect, day-for-night, disgrace—and at once he understood. The city had left him, the people had left him, and his wife was leaving; and all that would remain would be a shame in which he was buried.

Walter Selby stood in the doorway staring, now at his wife, who a moment earlier had been inside their bedroom, now at this man, who a moment earlier had been inside his wife. Nicole's eyes were filling with tears. The water made him angry and he wanted to leave, but he couldn't go in either direction without passing one of them, and that was impossible. Tom Healy was on his feet, he shrugged, he tried to smile and started to say something and then swallowed it. Walter wondered if he should hit him, but it didn't seem fair, with the other man unclothed.

Nicole sat down at the kitchen table, gathering her nightdress around her legs, her elbows on the surface and hands shaking just above the table. Walter, she called in a strained voice. Come inside now. But he was sure he would die if he went inside. Will you please come in?

They stood that way for a long time, Healy against the rear wall of the house, Nicole inside at the table, Walter in the doorway with a view of them both. He made a small, meaningless gesture with his hands. The other man stepped back a few feet, but Walter stopped him with a glance. I think I ought to get my clothes and just get on out of here, said Healy. And then, meaninglessly: I'm sorry. Walter made no move to acknowledge the remark.

Come inside, Nicole begged him. Come in here, will you please?

Instead, Walter started directly out into the backyard, and only when he traveled as far from the house as he could go and still be on his own property, did he turn, walk the back boundary, and come around again until he reached the driveway. All the time he kept an eye on Healy. All along he heard his wife saying, Walter? over and over again, wanting and worrying the talisman of her husband's name, the right to say it with whatever sense she could give it. As he rounded the corner of his house the sound of her voice faded, replaced by blood in his ears, humidity, the earth springy underfoot, and he felt a dizziness whose content he could not bring himself to contemplate.

The car started itself and drove itself, but it moved through a foreign land, as if the Memphis he had shared had suddenly come to belong to everyone but him. He was gone from it, not even a ghost. There was the corner park, there was the diner, there was the cross-roads. He turned right someplace, turned right again, turned left and went on for a mile or so until he came to a T-junction, and by then he was tired of driving, so he pulled the car up to the curb by the corner and turned it off. There was a slick of rust on his tongue, which turned out to be blood; he touched his thumb to his lip and found that he'd bitten into it so hard he'd split the flesh. There was no place for him to go, no place at all, and nothing for him to do. Helplessly, he started the car again and drove around for a while, going ghostly through intersections and along boulevards, wondering if he would ever have another thought that didn't feel like it had been wrung from him. Here was another corner, and all these people.

44

AN INDIAN ON BEALE STREET

His name was Terrence Lee and he was pure Shoshone, one hundred percent; there wasn't a drop of blood in him that couldn't be traced right back to the tribe, unbroken and unchanged. Six feet three inches tall, he wore his hair, not long and black, but cut so short at the sides that his scalp was visible underneath. For three months he'd been working as a welder on an oil rig in the Gulf, two weeks out on the water, and two weeks off in New Orleans. Then he'd fought with the Driller over a tin of canned peaches each had claimed as his own, and the Company had sent him to shore for good, with his suitcase in his hand and his pockets full of cash.

He thought about Nevada. On the one hand, everything he came from was there—his family, his tribe, all of them living in a small town on the reservation—and the things he recognized, bits of landscape, riverbeds and dry lakes. But there was nothing for them there but a pale yellow poverty: no work, no place to go at night, nothing to see for the first time.

Why couldn't he travel the world, like any young man? How would they look at him, in China, in Palestine, in Paris? What would he see? He could join the Merchant Marines and ship out for the grand, parti-colored world, send a few dollars out of every paycheck home to his mother along with a postcard from wherever he might be. She wanted him to come home right away, she felt uneasy about his absence, as if any one man missing from the family meant the entire tribe was hob-bled. He didn't want to go. Was he expected to tread the same sad soil forever, just because he was an Indian?

New Orleans was hot and strange, with whores in the gardens and witch doctors in the back rooms, and all of them after the money in his pocket, reaching in with a broad smile and a wink, as if his penury-to-come was a joke they all shared. Where you going to go? a whore named Lila had asked him, one shiftless, rainy afternoon when he'd bought her for an hour and ended up spending half of it explaining his reluctance to return to the reservation. —Where you going to go that's finer than New Orleans? She was lying back on the bed, her shoulders against the headboard, and she waved one elegant, creamy black hand to the four corners of a crucifix: north, south, east, west. Where you going to go, Mr. Red Man?

Where would *you* go?

She licked the sweat from her upper lip. I'm not going anywhere, she said. I'm staying right here in this house. I've got pretty much everything I need right here.

But if you were going . . .

She thought for a moment, not about where she would go but about leaving at all. I'd go north, she said. Right up the river. I'd get out of this heat, see the snow. Do you know I've never seen it snow? Except in the movies. I'd go north until I got to where the Eskimos live. —She smiled without parting her lips, as if there was a secret she wanted to keep her tongue from telling. —Then I'd be tricking in a fur coat instead of these rags.

It had rained for three days after that, and he'd sat in his tiny immaculate room and watched the street from his window, the storm falling, the water rushing in the gutters, the hasty comings and goings at a café across the street, through the scarlet-curtained windows of which he couldn't see, leaving him to test his imagination on the tableaux occurring inside. When he woke on the fourth morning the rain had ceased, though recently enough that glittering droplets still hung from the wrought iron parapets, and the city seemed steeped in primeval steam. At midday he saw a fish truck pull up outside, and he packed his duffel bag, left his key at the desk downstairs, and went out to ask the driver where he was headed next.

Right up 55, said the driver, a bony white man in overalls, whose hands were laced with cuts and scars.

Mind if I ride along? said Terrence Lee. I've got gas money, if you want it.

My boss pays for the gas, said the driver. But you come along and talk to me, and I'll take you as far as Memphis.

Now he was standing on the corner of Beale Street on a Saturday night, there were lights shining and music playing everywhere, Negro women, Negro men, strolling up and down the sidewalk in their finest, and Terrence Lee felt a little bit ashamed to be so underdressed. He didn't have any good clothes. He ought to get himself some. Now here was a big man, purple-black on the surface, by show. He was wearing a cream-colored suit and a white straw hat, and he was coming toward Terrence Lee on the sidewalk, smiling so broadly that his face seemed split in two. Hey, Chief, what's the good word? he said as he passed, and Terrence nodded and watched him as he walked away. Once upon a time there were more killings here on a Saturday night than on any other street in the world; the lampposts had been hung with gristle and the sidewalk was littered with parts. Who knew the difference between murder and a good time? The police would post themselves on either end, and by midnight they would be reaching in to pull the bodies out.

The Shoshone claimed to know all there was to know about the country, the blood beneath the desert, the nation behind the nation. But while they'd dwelt on their long war with whiteness, the blacks had snatched the country out from under everyone. Just came right down and settled in, because the continent had a fondness for its own curses, and somehow elevated them to standards. What did they know in Nevada? The Negroes were the real Americans after all, the only ones: it was their century and it ran under the rule of their rhythms, launched off their drums. He looked down the block, letting his eyes lose their focus until the lights blurred and grew.

And now here came another man: white, one of the few whites to be seen on this street. He was all by himself, and not quite young any-more, either; he looked like a businessman or a bureaucrat of some sort, wearing the same clothes he might have worn to work that day. Terrence Lee watched as couples and stray men subtly stepped out of the white man's way without so much as a glance—not out of deference, but just because his very presence, by virtue of its pointlessness, was going to be trouble for somebody, somehow, and no one wanted to be the one. Besides, there was something not quite right in the man's gait; he wasn't weaving like a drunk, and he wasn't gesticulating, but he didn't seem to be quite balanced either. He didn't belong. It wasn't just his whiteness: there was a profounder strangeness to him, some sense in which he appeared to be entirely wrong all the way to the bottom. From a distance and at first Terrence thought it was the way he was dressed and the way he moved down the street; but as the man drew closer he realized it had something to do with his expression; closer still, and he saw that the man was weeping uncontrollably and so possessed by it that he didn't even bother to hide his face: he just carried his grief outright on his features. Terrence had never seen a white man crying before, and he stared; but the man didn't notice, he just walked right past, his countenance streaming with tears coming down.

45

Many millions of years previously, the Appalachians had been scattered with volcanoes and torn by earthquakes, as the continental landmass slowly pulled west, moving away as it would always move, and forming the Atlantic Ocean to rest in between. In time the mountains eroded, leaving massive deposits of silt in the Plains and along the eastern continental shelf. Then came the ice ages, sliding their frozen sheets down from Canada and melting into an endless cold pour, a vast rush of water down through the middle regions, drawn by gravity to the Gulf of Mexico and gouging paths for itself as it went. Those were the Mississippi, the Ohio, the Cumberland, and so on. Such long slow fury and foment, careless, unceasing, and immeasurable.

46

The pistol was in a box of old effects. It was a Colt .32 Hammerless, small and blunt but beautiful in its way. It wasn't a treasure, but it was fine. In the same box Walter found his discharge papers from the Marines, his medal, and some things of his father's that his mother had saved: a silver pocket watch, now so badly tarnished it was almost black, a few letters tied with turquoise ribbon, photographs, a marriage license. These are the materials we leave behind: filigreed metal, fine cut glass, and paper.

There was a thick cardboard carton of bullets. When he'd first bought them, some years ago, he'd shaken the box and heard the rattle of metal on metal, but he'd never bothered to open it. Beside it there was a small tin container of gun oil, and once or twice a year he would use it to preserve the pistol, shutting himself in the bathroom for an hour or two and carefully lubricating each of its parts. He'd never fired it, after the War he was tired of guns, but he liked to have it around; it went with having a house.

It was dark and no one had been home when he arrived. Nicole had left a note, explaining that she was taking the children over to Josephine's until tomorrow. She'd be back and they would talk, then. He was staring at the corner where the ceiling met the wall, his eyes periodically glazing over as he lost focus. Old Mose Drake knew what died when a home died. The telephone rang, rang again and rang again, until at last he answered it.

It was his secretary: I have the Governor here for you. Will you hold?

Yes, he said, and absently replaced the receiver on the hook. Another ringing, just a few seconds later. I'm sorry, Mr. Selby? said the secretary. We must have been disconnected. I have the Governor here for you.

Yes, said Selby, and a moment later he heard that whisper, the murmuring of the end. —Where are you, my friend? I've been trying to reach you everywhere. You all right? I'm in town. There's some kind of Midnight Boatride, a fund-raiser for the Mayor, I have to go. What time is it, now? —A voice behind the Governor's said, Ten. Ten, said the Governor. The Boatride's at Midnight. I want you to come meet me.

I'm sick, said Walter. And then, because there was nothing perfect in politics, —I'm leaving.

Leaving where? What are you saying?

I'm gone . . . Didn't you get my letter?

I got your letter. I ignored it. Selby, you know I'd be the very first to do something, if there was anything we could do. You know I would. But we're just going to have to ride this one out, side by side. They'll be some ministers, maybe some newspapers, looking for someone to blame. You stick with me and don't talk to anyone, and we can get through it. Reputations a little worn, maybe you'll never be President, but we'll be all right. —He paused, and when he began again, his voice was softer and more gentle. If you leave me, I don't know what's going to happen. There won't be much I can do to help you.

Walter had hardly heard a word, it was just sea-sounds in his ear, cold and grey and saline. Mose Drake was dead. —No. Listen here: I'm giving you my resignation, he said, in a voice that wasn't his and wasn't anyone's.

The Governor took a few seconds of careful silence before he spoke. I know you've been having some trouble at home, he said.

What's that? said Walter.

We've all got to take care of our lives, sometimes. Tend to the garden, you know. Keep the weeds from growing all in everywhere. Maybe you just need a break, a little time off.

I need . . . said Walter, and then he stopped. It was the first time he'd ever known the Governor to make such an error, to be clumsy and miss; it was a lapse in manners, in style, a misjudgment. Perhaps he had meant to sound sympathetic, or maybe avuncular; instead he seemed obscenely miscast, hollow after all; and he didn't know when to be quiet and keep his advantage. My garden? said Walter, but the Governor missed the small screech in his voice, the bald fury of a night animal rousted from its safe rounds. My family . . .

Your family, yes, said the Governor, now adding smugness to his mistake. Walter could hear him gliding along the floor of his office and then gliding right back again. Everything out his window had been planned: all the boulevards, all the monuments, all the views. Unreal city, with an evil purpose. Come on down and join me on this boat, said the Governor. We'll go off somewhere and talk about it. DeWitt Landing. Midnight.

All right, said Walter, and he hung up.

He stood, went into the kitchen, and fixed himself a drink; he felt thirsty and his limbs were cold, his fingers stiff, and some liquor would warm him. He was nervous, although he couldn't quite say why. It really would be better for him if he relaxed some. Later, the whiskey was a little lower, and he picked up the pistol from the kitchen table. It felt fine. There was his reflection in the window, with that strange metal thing in his hands; he turned this way and that, he aimed emptily at his own image. Walter Selby, the warrior and hero. Well, the gun wasn't going to be any good without bullets, was it? It wasn't going to be a real gun. So he went back to the table for the box of ammunition and began to load the magazine, then clipped it into the pistol and put the pistol in the pocket of his jacket, where it weighed against his hip.

47

SPEECH FOR WALTER SELBY: DRAFT

My friends, my colleagues, fellow statesmen, lawmakers, soldiers, lovers, husbands, fathers and sons; you teachers and priests, bosses and toilers, outcasts, prisoners, slaves; my detractors and enemies; and all strangers, travelers, philosophers and savages, stretching to the corners of the world.

I stand here before you, with my case to make, unbound by the contingencies, the singularities, of this mighty House we call the World. It's not the day that will judge me, but an endless night, the night into which our souls will venture, when the dream of day has passed from our eyes. I do not fear that judgment, nor do I seek it; but I offer myself to it, knowing that it will take me when it will, regardless of my little efforts to meet or avoid it.

I speak to myself when I speak to you; I preach to myself, berate myself, persuade and encourage myself. I ask myself: Who inhabits the farthest reaches of perdition? I answer: The traitorous, for there is no evil greater than that. —No death like the death of a principle mutually built, nourished, leaned against; and then dismayed, and then destroyed. The friend can flay those stored, tender parts that the enemy cannot reach. The friend: the mentor, the disciple, the apostle, the companion, the lover.

Nevertheless, we should not be cynical or quick to condemn, for that is to give away exactly the faith which the traitor would steal. Patience, forbearance, lenience, charity, are the qualities of the righteous man. We are not so dark that we cannot sense a light. Nor is our union so tentative and frail that it cannot withstand an occasional error on the side of forgiveness. The institution that it represents has been designed by wiser minds than ours, precisely so that it might survive even the bitterest disagreement. It dances to the thunder of the storm, and nourishes itself on the accompanying rain. There is hardly a good in this world that does not spring from an evil, hardly a growth that was not planted in death, like those rosebushes which, according to legend, grow wild around the grave of Saint Jerome.

But the wise man knows, too, that the face of the earth is populated with demons, adversaries and weird angels. They come with their soothing and musical voices, their passion indistinguishable from the passions of the saints; they plead with you for help, they beg you for understanding, compromise, mercy. They say they're merely the agents of a greater power, and perhaps they are. Perhaps they are, but their agency results in nothing but ruin.

I believe in myself, my family, my friends; I believe in my associates, in my state and my nation; I believe in you. And I believe in that demon that waves a blade, and threatens to sever the bond that joins us together, and rescues us from solitude and misery. I kill that demon to save myself; I save you, I save my children, and my children's children, and I refuse any mercy or reward in return.

48

Nicole came home, she opened the door slowly, hesitating slightly when she saw him there on the couch, staring at her. She stopped just inside the front room. Walter, she said.

Where are Frank and Gail?

They're at Josephine's. I told you that. Didn't you see my note?

He nodded. Yes, that's right, he said. I like Josephine. —He watched her a little longer. I guess we need to talk, he said at last, and she nodded. Come with me.

Come with you where? she said.

Let's go drive for a bit.

Drive? said Nicole. Why don't we talk right here? We're home, now.

Home? said Walter Selby. Not so much, not anymore, is it?

It's still our home.

Let's go, can we go? he said to her.

Where are we going?

Down to the river, said Walter. It's a nice night. We'll go down to the river and talk.

She was tired, she was in a daze; otherwise she wouldn't have gone. Besides, she wanted to do what he asked, just in case it was the last time he asked anything of her. Still, she was uneasy, the more so because he seemed to have nothing further to say. He led her to the car, he opened the door for her and watched her intently as she climbed in.

All along the way he never looked at her, and he drove slowly, as if it were only a frail command that he had on the car. Where are we going? she said again, although she already knew; she was trying to get him to talk to her. Instead he simply nodded out the windshield. The night was not too real to her. The moon was full and the shadows were dark, and all the countryside had been glazed so white it was almost blue: a negative day, where the sky was black and the landscape was luminous. Walter Selby pulled the car to the side of the road, parked on the shoulder, and turned off the engine. Here? she asked. You can't just leave the car here.

It'll be O.K., he said.

Where are we? she said.

By the side of the road there were some woods. Through the woods she could see a glimpse of something shining and undulating. Is that the river? she asked. What are we doing here?

I want to show you something, he said, and he took her by the hand and led her between the trees. Just once, Nicole held back, but he had a firm hand on her, and without being at all forcible he got her started forward again. She could hear the turning of the water, and shortly after that they passed between two pines and stood together in a small illuminated clearing, about fifteen yards wide, bounded by the forest on one side and a vast slow rushing on the other. Farther out there was a pleasure boat, some lights, a little jazz music and chatter.

He took her down to the riverbank and stood her against the silvery water. Walter, she said. I don't know how to explain this to you. We're modern people, aren't we? Do we have to make a scene about this? Don't, don't make this so that the children find out.

Shhh, said Walter. Just, shhh.

Walter, she said. Walter. You don't love me as much as you think you do.

Shhh, said Walter, but he had nothing to say instead. The speeches he had been working on all escaped through the holes in his head, leaving nothing behind but a phrase or two. Shhh. He paced ten or fifteen steps downriver, then turned and looked at his wife, white as the moon and madly more beautiful.

Behind her the pleasure boat was now closer to the shore, the noise a little louder. Walter, will you please listen to me? Please? We have to find a way to get around this. Get past this. —She started to walk toward him, her feet never touching the ground for the beams of milky light beneath them. —Tell me what you want me to do.

Please stay where you are, said Walter. The pleasure boat had turned broadside to the shore. He could hear someone say, Hey, now. Look there. Someone on the riverbank. Then there was silence again, as if the boat had disappeared.

Will you tell me why? said Walter to Nicole. She couldn't even say, No. Will you tell me why? So I can understand . . .

She shook her head. It's nothing to do with why, she said. It's just me. Me and my mistakes.

No, said Walter, now reduced to nonsense. It's the calendar, it's the sky.

We have children, said Nicole, but he couldn't hear her argument for the rods that burned behind his eyes.

I wish you would walk back to the river's edge, he said.

Lovers in the moonlight, said the voice from the boat. Ain't that nice . . .

Walter nodded to nobody. Back, will you? he said. To the water? Nicole. She took a few steps back.

This man who had slept next to her for so many years had a gun in his hand, and there was white light falling in soft shards around him. She said to herself, No, no, no, no, no. This is not how the tale ends. She said, Let me start all over again, I can get it right this time. She worried about her children and glanced up toward the car, as if she might find them there, waiting, and know that this whole scene would soon be done, and she could stay afterward.

This is not about me and you, said Walter, pleading his case. This is not about anything. He held the pistol safely at his thigh. Get ready, will you? Please?

For some reason she nodded, and at that he brought the gun up in one clean motion, paused to gather his rage into a stillness, and then squeezed the trigger. She nodded, but she wasn't prepared for eternity. The barrel was pointed at her face, and down the hole she could see a struggle, as several dark and invisible spirits wended their way against the bullet. They came out of the gun at an enormous, slow rate, flashing at the lip of the barrel as they struck against the air. Then she had been shot—she couldn't say where—but she was lying on her back, her head against the stones on the riverbank, and there was a great commotion in the water, other voices, making noises like upset animals. Her face was gone. Well, she thought, wasn't that the way it always was? Something going into her, and some blood coming out. The baby . . . and Frank in school, her little boy, how upset he was going to be. She was sorry for her children, and she wished very much that there was something left she could do for them, her mind hurt at the idea that she wasn't going to be able to comfort them, but beyond that it wasn't so bad. She could feel her limbs and the back of her head against something hard, unless it was her head that was hard, and she was feeling it through the ground? She said: ? . . . ? . . . ?

Walter stood by. This is what we get, he said to himself, for making love because we thought it should be simple enough to work. Nicole was silently appealing to the night: Oh, God, save something from all this. But God wouldn't come. He was watching very closely, but he wouldn't come. The treetops above her were dancing this way and that, and she heard another shot. She thought maybe it was a crack in the sky that signaled the end of the world, and she made a gesture with her hand, the sheer electricity of life. Oh, God, she thought. Have mercy and protect my children. She closed her eyes, and the Angel of Death came down and took her.

49

Walter Selby put the barrel of the gun under his chin, and he meant to shatter his own head; but the metal was burning hot, it seared his skin and he jerked back just as he pulled the trigger, and the bullet rustled the leaves in the trees above and disappeared into the sky. Then something hit him from behind and he was sitting down, sitting right on the pistol, which dug sharply into his thigh. There were men all around him, and someone was holding his arms at his sides, while someone else stood on one of his legs, the other was twisted beneath him, and his chest was pounding, whether from within or without. —Now there were a half dozen or more men on him, their clothes all wet from wading through the water from the boat to the shore, and they were offering suggestions: Hit the bastard! Hold him. Hold him. Watch he doesn't have another gun, or a knife or something. Get him by the throat there, and he won't give you any more trouble. Where's the Governor? —Someone had a hand around Walter Selby's neck, and they squeezed and squeezed. —Go see if you can help the lady. Go on. Get to a telephone, —no, see if the captain's got a radio. She all right? —There was no answer, and a sudden awestruck stillness began with the man standing by Nicole's body and came over everyone, a reverent calm, contradicted only by the hand at Selby's throat, which squeezed harder and harder, the only effort in the stasis, blessing him with breathlessness, blindness, with darkness falling in on him like rain, and finally with oblivion.

THE BRUSHY MOUNTAIN LETTERS

Dear Donald:

It is not so bad being here, and please don't worry about me. I have pretty much everything I need: cigarettes from the commissary, books from the library, work in the machine shop, conversation with the other men. Thank you for your offer; I'll let you know if I need you to send me something.

Anyway, what I need most you can't send—a little privacy. Most minutes of most days, there's another inmate nearby, and often enough a guard watching. I know now why our ancestors conceived of God as ever-attendant: to be seen at every moment is law enough for most men, regardless of what principles they believe they should obey.

I often wonder if Nicole is watching me too, from whatever vantage she may have. If so, I hope she doesn't hate me, that she understands why I did what I did, how much I care about her, and how much I miss her. I think someday we will be together again.

When they are old enough, I want you to tell my son and my daughter that I was not a bad man, but a good man who did a bad thing—whose passion killed his passion's cause.

Your loving brother,
Walter

Dear Brother:

I look out the window of my cell, and all I can see is a small patch of sunlight, not even sunlight, but the sky, blue if the sky is blue, or grey if there's rain. And I can see Nicole's face reflected in that, as if the heavens were not some further realm, but merely a mirror of everything the earth has lost. She's never going to live again, and I sometimes think I'm never going to die, and such will be my punishment.

This is hell enough for any sinner. I can't sleep, partly because all the other men here make noise, yelling out with nightmares, or else suffering their own insomnia and talking to be heard: Guard, they say, I need a cigarette. Give me a cigarette. —Guard, the bitch lied, I didn't do nothing. —Guard, my lawyer was incompetent, the judge was on the take, and the jury just wanted to get home before dinner. I lie in my bunk with a weight on my chest: my conscience, or maybe just the massing hatred of everyone she loved. My breathing gets shallow and my heart slows; and then I start traveling backward at a thousand miles a second.

You didn't know Nicole the way I did. You didn't see in her what I saw in her. Maybe she seemed a little bit naive to you, but I can promise you she wasn't that. She was many things, but she wasn't that. I could spend my rough old soul right inside her, and she never flinched, not at all. She just made more of herself from it.

Do you remember when I introduced you to her? That would be Christmastime, a dozen years ago, or maybe a millennium. Do you remember? You and Mary and your boys running around. Nicole and I had just met, two or three months before, and I guess she didn't know, but I knew, that we were going to marry. And we all went to the pictures, but I can't remember what we saw. If you remember, can you write to me and tell me?

I knew she had a life before me, but I couldn't stand for her to have a life after, just as a man fears the death-to-come, but not the eternity before he was born. When I'm lying in my narrow bed, I think of how time converged on just that moment when we two met. It used to bother me that I didn't know more about the way she'd grown up. You know, her parents lived so far away. That was sad to me, not because I liked her parents all that much, but because it meant I was farther away from her childhood. I used to like to visit them, down there in South Carolina.

Now someone's shouting again, down the tier a little ways. God and the God of all prisoners, I beg you: grant me just an hour to think.

I'm going now.

Your loving brother,
Walter

Dear Donald:

I'm not a tough guy, not like some in here. A new kid came in today, young, pleasant-looking kid. He was trying to ingratiate himself, and he was bragging to one of the lifers. I robbed a bank, he said. Just like Jesse James, except I got caught. What did you do?

And the old con said, I had sex with your mother. —But not like that, of course; and he went on in great detail, until it was clear that he wasn't just having a joke, he was trying to break a new man all the way down. There's a hierarchy here, of time spent and time to go. The kid didn't have much of a sentence, but it's going to be hard on him if he doesn't learn how to wear it. I would have liked to take him aside and tell him how, but I can't. He'll learn. Still, it makes me think of my son and how little I've given him, or will be able to give to him now. I suppose he's lost to me forever, as I'm lost to him. Frank and Gail: I know it's best for them if I let them go. But it causes me no end of emptiness.

Love,
Walter

Dear Donald:

I heard they killed King, in Memphis, my Memphis. I heard it, we all heard it, right away. Some of the White men were cheering, but I just sat back in my cell. Then, that night, the Black prisoners had themselves a riot, setting fire to toilet paper rolls and mattresses, until the block was filled with smoke. I thought I was going to suffocate and die, right here in my cell. Eventually the bulls came and pulled us out, one by one, saving the Blacks for last, of course. Five or six of them went to the infirmary; the rest were beaten for a little while and then chained up outside in the yard. I heard one of the guards was stabbed, but I don't know if it's true. I was vomiting from the gas on the deck.

I hear the Blacks talking in here, and I wonder what we thought we were getting away with, as far as they were concerned. They see everything, I can tell you that, and there's going to be a whole world to pay, I guarantee it. You be ready, and get your family ready, keep them safe, and teach them. You teach them to be good, and to prepare themselves. You teach them not to lose their hearts, their souls, and not to lose their lives.

I'm beginning to understand what I am.

Love,
Walter

Dear Donald:

What man can be told by the society that he has served that he has done something wrong, and not just wrong but unforgivable, and accept such a judgment? I mean, without making any excuses in his own behalf whatsoever, without saying, I was provoked, or Everybody does it, or even, That was not me, it was a lesser version, possessed by evil, or simply misguided? What man can say, I've done wrong, because I am wrong, and this sentence I'm serving is proper? —And not believe, at the very least, that his acceptance of such is itself enough to mitigate his crime?

To say I'm guilty, and mean it entirely, is equivalent to saying I do not exist. It refutes itself; and this, I believe, is the paradox of punishment: it is impossible for the criminal and those who imprison him to see matters the same. The world has to see the prisoner as a bad man, or else it cannot function. The prisoner has to see the world as unjust, or else he cannot live.

If there's some reason or reckoning, then I have to wonder what purpose is mine. This period of confinement, all right, I've made a friend or two, and some of them are good men, but all in all it's been nothing but time. When I think about it, I understand that the years before I met Nicole were much the same, so I can only conclude that the period that I spent with her was the only real life that I had. —A flash of light, during which I glimpsed the one thing I had to do. And that I did. I'm not saying that I shouldn't be blamed, but only that it was not something I meant, so much as it was something that was meant of me. This is not contrition. If the officers in the mailroom read this letter then they'll put a note in my folder, and the board will read it when I'm up for parole.

Love,
Walter

Dear Donald:

They're going to move me to another cell block in a couple of days. I don't know why; it's just something they do every so often, I suppose so you don't get too settled in to your friend-ships and enmities. They keep you moving all the time, that's their policy, at least until you get to be such an old-timer that they don't bother. I've been a good con, I didn't break too many rules, I kept myself in good stead, and soon I'll be an old-timer and they won't move me anymore.

It has now been more years than I care to count since I've seen a tree close enough to be able to distinguish its leaves. In the yard where we exercise there's nothing but hard packed brown dirt, and a little grass by the fence to remind us that free-dom is green.

Had you asked me, before I came here, I would have said that nature, as such, was not very important to me; now I find that I think of it often, and miss it very much. Most of the books that I take out of the library here are nature books of one sort or another: adventure stories, essays on wildlife, issues of National Geographic; and collections of poems, older stuff mostly, Wordsworth, Blake, where they consider it important to describe the world; and reproductions of Dutch paintings. Of course, the selection here is limited; most of the men only read to research their own appeals, so law books make up the largest part. If you should come across anything you think I might be interested in, can you send it to me? It may not get through, it might be stopped in the prison post office, so if you don't get a reply from me it's because I never saw it. But I'd appreciate it if you'd try.

Thanks,
Walter

Dear Donald:

I see on the television that the Governor died; or rather, I heard a reference to him as the late Governor of Tennessee. Now when did that happen? Yesterday? A few years ago?

I remember watching him down in Nashville, giving a commencement address at Tennessee State. I went to watch, and I remember every word, because I wrote it for him, late one night when Nicole and the kids were asleep and the house was quiet. I wanted it to stay quiet, to preserve their peace in perpetuity, so I wrote a real humdinger for the graduating class, full of guarantees that the future world would be ever-exciting and open to the exercise of their young powers in the renewal of state and nation. I handed it to the Gov. just before he went on, he glanced at it quickly, —and then midway through his allotted time, he simply put my speech down and started talking about his father, how he'd never gone to college, himself, but owned a dry goods store where he worked from sunup to midnight. He made the man sweet and funny, a dear old fellow full of a poor man's wisdom, who only wanted the best for his son. Oh, it was a wonderful turn, and the students smiled and applauded him when he was done.

Today the Governor is dead, and my wife is dead, and who knows where any of those young men and women are or what they're doing; and the Governor's father was a drunk and a bully, and the Governor hated him as hard as he could.

Your brother,
Walter

Dear Donald:

My occupation is called serving time, or doing time, but time won't be done, and everybody serves it. In here it's like a vast worming, inching: periods which don't pass so much as they shift, like great ice flows, and reduce months, days, years, as the ice reduces hills and mountains under its enormous, crawling weight, at the same time as it creates new features in the landscape. I need words no one has ever heard before to describe duration; words for irregular fissures that I have to cross with one long leap, or else fall and be caught forever inside their depths; for islands that lie scattered across a cold river, some of which are solid down to the bottom and some of which are merely illusions, sheets of ice resting on nothing. Yesterday morning a man half a dozen cells down from me was released after serving twenty-one years; by dinner last night another had come to take his place. I've seen entire decades slide out from under a man all at once, so quickly that even he couldn't account for them; and brief moments that dilated into periods so long that you wouldn't have believed there was any time left on the other side. These men, when they get out, they should all become astronomers, physicists, atomic engineers, because no one knows better how time shifts and changes. The scientists talk about the speed of light, the gravity of planets, the wheeling of the stars: I can tell them about a ninety-nine-year sentence.

> Yours,
> Walter

Dear Donald:

Well, we knew this was going to happen, sooner or later. So here it is: and I am frightened of what's to come.

> W.

PART TWO | STAY

PIED BEAUTY

GLORY be to God for dappled things—
　　For skies of couple-colour as a brinded cow;
　　　　For rose-moles all in stipple upon trout that swim;
Fresh-firecoal chestnut-falls; finches' wings;
　　Landscape plotted and pieced—fold, fallow, and plough;
　　　　And áll trádes, their gear and tackle and trim.

All things counter, original, spare, strange;
　　Whatever is fickle, freckled (who knows how?)
　　　　With swift, slow; sweet, sour; adazzle, dim;
He fathers-forth whose beauty is past change:
　　　　　　　　　Praise him.

　　　　　　　　　　　—Gerard Manley Hopkins

1

Frank, Frank. Frank. Where have you been? What have you done? Frank. It's been years, you're not a kid anymore, and what can you tell us? What have you seen? What are you sure of? Someone has your name, yes they do. Someone has your face, and what can you say for yourself?

You called it The Bounce, you and Gail—trying to make a game of it, to keep from letting all your worries overwhelm you, to keep from gnawing a hole in your own cheek. Bouncy-bouncy, Gail giggling, hand in hand and house to house, couple to couple and strange home to dirty home, there are no sugar castles in foster care. You didn't complain. There were two years here and a year and a half there; one couple was stern and distant, and the other always spoke to you as if they were children themselves, a habit you and Gail used to mimic brutally whenever you were alone. Then there was a man and woman named Cartwright in Washington, D.C., older and with two boys of their own who were grown and gone; a fine and generous couple, with a certain sadness attending the late years of their marriage and their lives, as if they had just begun to realize that they were running out of time together and wanted to get a start on another family before it was over. When they saw how tired the two of you were, how sweetly solemn, they decided to adopt you both.

You were relieved to have some safety at last, but you resisted giving up your father's name. Do you remember how it felt? You thought you were disappearing, didn't you? You thought if you lost the name you'd be No One, son of No One, and melt into the very air of the capital. But you wouldn't tell the Cartwrights what had you so distressed, now would you, Frank? Because that seemed ungrateful, ungracious, and perhaps even a little bit immature. Still, they figured it out eventually and they weren't offended at all; no, such kind people, they offered you your old last name as your new middle name: Frank Selby Cartwright and Gail Selby Cartwright, and you were satisfied. You pale-lipped boy, you tall, thin boy. You obstinate, fitful and fretful boy: when you were twelve or thereabouts you dropped the Selby yourself, you just didn't want it anymore. You changed your mind, didn't you? The sort of thing you would do. And when you did, you were plain Frank Cartwright, son enough of the man and woman who took you in.

See the little white house, see the short stone walk. See the dim small room, a little talk late at night between a seventeen-year-old boy and a girl of thirteen. Gail was just beginning to change; you didn't see what a beauty she was going to become, now, did you, Frank? You missed that, too. Not that it would have mattered; she was smarter about everything than you were about anything. She didn't need your help, she didn't need your advice: she just wanted to have you around. But you couldn't even do that, Frank, could you? You had a semester left in high school that you had no intention of finishing; there was a friend of a friend up in New York City, who knew of a job sorting luggage at the airport. You made a good-bye to Gail and you ran off into the night. You thought that was the way it was done: a bag of clothes, a little cash, no reason or mercy given to those who had loved you and taken care of you. You thought that was how a figure was born; and it was the only moment in all your life and all the world's time that your little sister ever hated you.

Far away, friendless, and without funds; and you had nothing of yourself to sell. Frank, oh, Frank. You got caught stealing from unlocked suitcases, didn't you? A little jewelry, a radio here and there. You pawned them in the city for far less than they were worth. And you were caught pretty quickly. How did it happen? You lifted a camera and you felt bad for a moment, you felt sorry, so you carefully unloaded the film and left it behind. You didn't want your victims to lose their vacation snapshots—but that was how they realized the camera had been stolen at all, rather than left behind in their hotel room. Good one, Frank, you were a goddamn mastermind. You're lucky they didn't take you to court, —God knows, you're lucky no one has found out about it since—but the airline fired you right away, didn't they? Well, you couldn't blame them.

Oh, oh, oh, Frank. You should have been a better man, you should have been a keeper, a maker, a millionaire, you should have been singing praise-songs to the days-to-come, you should have been the raised arm, the mighty sword, you should have been the face on the first-class stamp. Don't you see? You were put here on the chance that you could start something. But what? You were made to make them all jump. But how are you going to make them jump, Frank? With this business you're in now? This childish pretending? What kind of work is that for a full grown man? What will survive of it?

Remember when you loved Helen? Of course you do. You met her in Union Square one sunny July afternoon, you were just sitting there enjoying the feeling of one hundred dollars in your pocket and twenty-two years on your birth certificate. Helen, on her lunch hour; she took her shoes off and sat on a bench, barefoot on the concrete pathway. There once were famous days when a woman's ankle was the curve of desire, the perfect part for a perfect whole. So it was: she was a jewel of a girl, glittering in the cheap sunlight: her kiss-mouth, her brown eyes built to hold tears, her roundings; and the harsh cut of her shoulder-length hair, and her angry hands, always clenched in girlish fists. You asked her if the people in the office where she worked were going to notice when she came back with dirty feet, and she shrugged and said she didn't really care if they noticed or not.

You went back every day at noon for a week, until you saw her again; and then you gave her that smile you had practiced, the one that promised a conspiracy. Oh, you were a handsome man, weren't you? And you had that smile, the girls loved that smile. Helen herself didn't seem so happy to see you, but she let you sit with her; and later, a week or two later, she let you take her home. How long was it before you explained to her where you came from? What little you knew, what little you were willing to speak out loud. You were scared half to death, weren't you? Scared she was going to see the stain and shudder in disgust, and when you told her you shook and cried like a little boy. And she was just out of college and hardly knew what to do; but she stared at you wide-eyed and wet-eyed with sympathy. She was good, the way young women can be.

When did you decide you wanted to be an actor, Frank? Go on, tell us. At first it was like everything else you did: you just sort of wandered into it, thought you'd give it a try. And what do you know? Hey, you were pretty good at it. You were good. It was something for you to get inside: playing, pretending, —lying is it, Frank? Being someone else?

Following the lines you were given? Doing what you were told to do? It was the first thing you had found that you could take seriously and stick to. They told you who to be and that's who you were—and your voice, so strong and dark as coffee, and your balance, amid those words, words, words. People came to see you, Frank, to listen to you ring like a bell, to watch you step and stomp, trace the stage, stare at the lights, make feelings under a glass jar. Still, you sometimes found it embarrassing, didn't you? Standing up there for all to see, having language fits and well-timed tempers under the proscenium. Use that embarrassment, Frank. Exploit yourself. Use everything, and use it all up.

You were twenty-five when Helen became pregnant; it was right around the time you made that movie, what was it? Something silly, something you don't talk about. Yeah, and you were going to be a father. A father: You didn't know how it happened—well, you knew, of course—but not how it could be—how you found yourself sleeping next to a woman with a baby girl inside her. But you didn't get married, did you? Why not? You'd say it never came up, Helen would say you never asked. It was one of the few things you didn't talk about. Well, but you were together for a good six, seven years. That's better than a lot of marriages do, anyway. Don't you think?

You remember the feeling, those first months with your daughter Amy? How busy the world was, what a morning, what a day to come. Oh, to hold that baby in your arms, you thought you had solved all the problems of home, didn't you, Frank? Having a child seemed so romantic; just to look upon the infant in her crib was to see the sex that made her, all done up in an exquisite package of smooth and perfect flesh, the excruciating sweetness of it; it was so beautiful it was obscene. You thought love could only get fuller, the heart expand. And every day she became more beautiful, your daughter: so fair and pearly, with her fine dark hair and her sea-pink skin. —Where did that skin of hers come from, anyway? Helen was Mediterranean, and you were just a man, but Amy was opalescent, as if she'd transcended mere inheritance and had made herself directly out of the stuff of innocence.

Right away you were your daughter's servant, weren't you? She was the boss and you did whatever she ordered, you couldn't help it. Three years old, four years old, if she asked for something you got it for her; if she wanted to show you something, you would be her rapt and unwavering audience. Isn't that the way it's supposed to be? Little girls in charge, tiny musical despots with all the world to gain. It used to make Gail laugh when she visited, sitting at the kitchen table with Helen and watching as you fell to answer your daughter's smallest need.

By then you were making movies regularly, you made a number of them, which in turn made you money, and you made friends and admirers. It was a ridiculous talent to have, but even clever people, brave people, profound people loved you for it. Who could say why? How could you say No? They sent you roles and scripts almost every day, and they offered you extravagant sums of money, dollars which you consumed the way a whale consumes plankton, in a vast and prodigal rush, the excess discharged in senseless gouts.

Gail was just out of college, then. A true and rare young woman, comely and radiant (just like her mother), the men gathered around her, smiling awkwardly and showing off, but she didn't seem to notice, not long enough even to break a heart. She was too thoughtful, she was going to be a significant woman, the discoverer of something left to be discovered, a doctor of conflict, calm, sensible, and unafraid; she seemed to know what she had, and she didn't want to hurt anyone.

On winter break before her final semester, she had been traveling home from San Francisco to Washington, D.C.; but there was snow over the Great Lakes and she was stranded in Chicago when the weather closed O'Hare. She met a man there, a big fellow named Richard; he owned a construction firm in Kansas City. He was ruddy-faced and broad across his shoulders, and he had a big pink scar that ran down from his left cheekbone to just below his left nostril—a fearsome thing, but she could tell right away that it meant nothing, he was perfectly gentle. They started talking and they talked all night, and when his flight finally left in the morning he took her number.

That was the same winter the Cartwrights died, one right after the other: he had a stroke and collapsed suddenly in their living room, and soon afterward she came down with cancer. And you held her hand while she shook from the pain; she was trying not to make a sound, but every so often she would moan a little, and the softness of it spoke of her agony more urgently than the scream that deafens the Devil himself. But you couldn't do anything about it, you couldn't save her one moment of suffering, money meant nothing, your talents meant nothing, and you couldn't explain to Helen why you were so angry all the time.

One rises where the other falls, that's just the way it goes. Gail and

Richard talked on the phone all through those months; he came east to visit her, and after six months he asked her to marry him. She called you that evening to tell you that she was going to say Yes; you were her mother and father for that moment. And you were happy for her, weren't you? You liked that man, Richard. You hadn't met him, but you liked what she'd said about him, and you blessed her and sent her to him. And sure enough, when they came to visit you a few weeks later, you found her fiancé to be quiet and polite, his hand tender on her, and you trusted that he could take a husband's part of caring for her, and leave you the brother's part. You were proud of her for having such a wise love, and you told her so. And she moved out to Kansas City, she married. She was hardly a woman yet; but they'd stayed married all those years after, and in time they had two boys named Richard Jr. and Kevin.

Gather them around: sister, girlfriend, daughter. But, —Oh, Frank. You dangling nerve, you poor punch line, you dumb fuck. What went wrong? You and Helen started fighting about money, about schedules and times, about absurd things: the arrangement of the furniture in your apartment, the way she answered the telephone, about the traveling you did for work, about whether Amy's hair was auburn or brown; about the look a lovely woman in a dark blue business suit gave you when the three of you passed—as if you were alone and looking for someone like her. And you were hard, really hard to be with. It was as if everyone else knew something you didn't know, something huge about how to get along. You couldn't have it. Who cared? No one, Frank, no reason why they should. It was you, that's all. (And by the way, did you cheat on her, Frank? Helen? Did you?) So you left; you left Helen and Amy, and at the time you thought maybe that was best for everyone— or at least, that's what you managed to believe. Why should a little girl grow up amid such strife? Why should she hear such disappointment in her parents' voices? Amy's mind was as fine as confectioner's sugar; why muddle its sweetness with misery? So you gave them money and you left. Hell, you might as well have tried to keep them. Not that it was love, really, that had failed you in the first place. It was you who had failed, and the loss of love was what you paid. You had brought them to Los Angeles, but you couldn't bear the place anymore, so you left them there. Go. Remember birthdays, another school year done, remember Halloween and Christmas: call when you can, from wherever you are, and tell your daughter that she's your girl. Tell her you miss her as much as a ghost misses its flesh, misses life and all its alarms. Call her and say, Hello, sugar bear. It's your daddy.

Daddy! Where are you?

I'm in, —oh, let's see. I'm in Atlanta, Georgia.

There's a girl in my school named Georgia. She's got an all white dog. Whiter even than the skin in under my arm. Where's Atlanta?

South.

O.K. . . . Do you want to talk to Mommy?

Later. I want to talk to you.

O.K. —A moment, the girl breathing, thinking, her attention gathering. —What sound does a star make?

I don't know. What sound does a star make?

. . . I don't know.

Oh. That's not a joke? A riddle?

Not. It's a question.

What sound do you want it to make?

I don't know.

Any sound you want, it'll make for you.

Atlanta!

You want it to say . . .

I want it to go, Atlanta. Atlanta, Atlanta.

O.K., then. Atlanta it is.

Cool!

Cool? When did you start saying *cool*?

Cool!

Yeah.

Can I have a bow and arrow?

A what?

A bow and arrow.

I don't know what you mean . . .

Here's Mommy.

—And she was gone again, and there was Helen.

Hi, honey. I'm glad you called. You know how happy you make her when you call. —She was always affectionate, Helen, now that she didn't love you anymore. She was always polite.

What's this about a bow and arrow?

Oh, they've been studying Native American culture in school. She thinks she's found her calling: she's going to be a warrior.

A warrior . . .

I don't know. Yeah, that's what she's saying now. So she wants a bow and arrow. Which of course I'm not going to get her, so she figured you were a lighter touch.

O.K. . . .

Don't worry about it. It's a phase. —What about you? Are you O.K.? I heard Amy say something about Atlanta.

Yeah. I'm here.

What are you doing in Atlanta?

Oh, you know. Stealing hubcaps from Coca-Cola trucks. It's a phase.

Stealing . . . No, seriously.

Seriously? you said, as if you'd never heard of such a thing. That was around the time you lost control wasn't it? Drank too much, talked too much. Said things, you didn't know what you were saying; you didn't care who heard. Calling magic down, but the magic was always different from what you intended it to be. What did you do, Frank, oh, Frank? You only played monsters, and you played them too well: such a handsome man, with your black hair and pale skin, your pitch eyes and startling smile. Such a striking voice, and all you wanted to do was burn it away. And why, Frank? You hated the pleasure others took in your performances, and you hated the fact that you couldn't get them to hate you in return, like the man who jumps on a vaudeville stage to tell the audience that the streets outside the theater are running with fire, only to find that his performance inspires yet more laughter and applause. But why should they have listened to you, Frank? Why? You didn't have enough. What made you think it could have been any different? You were strange, that's what it was, that's all it was: you were strange.

Then you stopped speaking, that was even stranger. Did you want to be Valentino? Only taking roles where there was screen time but little dialogue, and insisting to the director that even those lines be curtailed, and when they couldn't be cut, you whispered them, didn't you, until the sound men complained. You wanted to be mute and luminous, an animal, a new image on color film, —The Last of the Silent Movie Stars, some magazine called you, and they were joking, but you weren't. And you might even have gotten away with it, Frank, oh, Frank, if you hadn't been so difficult.

Ooooeeee, Frank. Frank. Women used to tell you how you thrashed around in your sleep; they thought it was because you had nightmares, though you never remembered dreaming anything at all. No, it wasn't that: your violence, you were given it by vicious cherubs come down off their thrones to collect on covenants that you hadn't kept: to hold and care for the ones you love, to raise your child to inherit all this. Then you woke up ashamed, and what could you say about that? When you didn't even know for sure what you'd done. When you couldn't say what you'd seen or what you'd heard, there in your sleep. Well, you weren't too honest with them, anyway, the women after Helen. Oh, you were nice enough, and you seemed straight, but you never told them anything you couldn't take back. —Oh, what the hell, let's just say it: you lied to them, Frank. You were a dog and you lied.

Well, there were always women, Frank, of course there were, even in your merciless decline. And this is what you did: you lurked, stalked, traveled, fought; you seduced, surprised, betrayed, abandoned; you kissed, you came; you stared and were speechless; you held, you murmured, you slipped away. Frank Cartwright, Light of the Western Sky. Frank Cartwright, the Soft Hand. Frank Cartwright, Maker of Broken Hearts. Frank Cartwright, the Loneliest Man in America. How many women were there, in those days? Who knows? Isn't that the idea? To be profligate with love's design, because the world itself is spendthrift, and death happens every day to someone else.

But you stopped working, just about. You had enough to live on in every way, you left, you sank, you vanished, not all at once but soon enough, and so quickly that even those who remembered your name could hardly remember what you'd done. You still had the trappings of a career—a manager, union membership, scripts in the mail from time to time—but you always seemed to miss the calls, and you never got back to anyone. Dim the lights, Frank. Chase the evening. Disappear.

The only people you really kept with were your sister and your daughter, Amy. You were on the phone with Gail at least once a week, even if you had nothing to say—and, come to think of it, you almost never had anything to say, now, did you? But you liked to listen to her talk, you admired her, and you were never embarrassed with her. Here's what's strange, though: All that conversation, all those years, and you never really talked about your mother and father. —Not the Cartwrights, the Selbys. You weren't even sure what their first names were—Wallace, you thought. That was his name. Or Wilson; and Nadine. Amanda, for some reason, you thought about her, when you thought about her at all, as Amanda. She who put you down on the planet and then disappeared again. When you were a boy and the other kids asked you about your parents, you used to say that your mother was dead and your father was dead, and then you fought if you had to. But you knew that wasn't exactly the way it was. He had put her in her grave, that you understood; everyone around you had tried to keep it from you, but news like that makes its way. Like the smell of a fire, it gets into everything. They buried your mother in the ground, but they took your father away, and what had happened after that was a mystery. —Still, Gail was too young to remember, and you never told her any of it. Isn't that something? Well, what would there have been to say? *Oh, pity, pity, pity?* Maybe you thought you were protecting her, maybe you hoped the past could have no hold on a baby girl. Maybe you thought it was understood anyway, as well as it ever would be, and nothing would be served by cracking it open. It was like a Japanese gift-box: the wrapping meant more than the object inside. You just never discussed it, and she must have assumed they had died together, linked in some unspeakable accident, if she thought about it at all. (Did you think she never thought about it, Frank? Do you think she never wanted to know?) Well, you couldn't tell, could you, if she would have been any different, any better or less, if she realized that only your mother was dead for sure, and for all you knew your father was still waiting somewhere in Tennessee, that he'd been waiting since before the girl could say the word *daddy*, and would be waiting indefinitely, infinitely, forever, like a demon made of tin, half dead and half alive.

Your sister Gail, your daughter Amy. Anything more splendid than making them laugh? Anything more heartening than their confidence in this terrible world? No there isn't. And it wouldn't have been so hard to spend your days among laughing women. They loved you. Isn't that so, Frank? Isn't it? What more do you want? Frank. —Frank. Frank: you poisonous man, you misshapen lover, you creature of stupid bone, you destroyer of hours, Frank: you spoiler, you spill, you freak of culture, you barbarian and beast, you conqueror of the void, you faithless gibe, you dead slab of meat, you purveyor of sordid spectacles, you waste of a suit, you helpless donkey, you guttering flame, you last out, you parasite, you traitor to all that wise men hold dear, you worm in the ground, you emblem of the failings of the spirit and the body, shunned by the innocent and the good, reviled in heaven, Frank, you fucking asshole. Why don't you tell us now? Tell us all, so we'll know and we can stop wondering. Tell us: What's the matter with you, Frank?

2

TEN PERCENT OF NOTHING

Home through the handsome metropolis, through New York on a fall afternoon, the darkness just starting to come down on the Empire City, with intimations of the weight of an entire winter. He passed a lightpole, from the top of which a pair of basketball sneakers dangled by their tied-together laces, a taxi garage with two dozen bright yellow cabs parked outside, he passed a hair salon, where a row of three elderly women were being fussed over by three young black men. A bodybuilder walking a pit bull went by, and the dog stopped to stare at Frank, his sloe eyes focused, the beginning of a growl in his throat, until his master said Duke! and tightened his chain, and he trotted away. Then suddenly there were people streaming up from the subway stop on the corner, a scattering of souls, some stood blinking in the setting sun, some traveled the sidewalk with their heads down, a few waited on the corner for the light to change. A middle-aged man in a business suit, apparently very drunk, was standing against the window of an electronics store, watching everyone go by, while behind him a thousand lenses stared. City of delight, of wonder and awe: Inexhaustible City. It was the most magnificent object ever made by man, and no mind or eye could comprehend it, nor any philosophy explain it.

In the lobby of his apartment building there was a chirping noise, a smoke detector warning that its batteries were running down. The doorman appeared in front of him, nodding and smiling. Good evening, Mr. Cartwright, he said, and then he drew a rubber-band-wrapped pile of envelopes from a ledge behind him and handed them over. Frank nodded, thanked him, and crossed the floor to the elevator, the marble squeaking underfoot. In his mail there was a utilities bill, a flyer from a local pharmacy, a manila envelope from his manager, two scripts which had been delivered from the same producer's office by two different messengers, three catalogues, a letter postmarked Washington, D.C., no return address, and another that was meant for his neighbor, which he discovered just as the elevator doors closed and the car started to rise.

Inside his apartment the blinds were open and he could sense a rushing from the city outside. Shoes come off, jacket goes on the coat-rack, a glance at his own face framed in the mirror in the front hall, just to be sure that it was still there. He wasn't young anymore, but he wasn't old either. He carried the mail into his living room, sat in his armchair, and flipped through the envelopes again, but before he could open any of them his phone rang.

It was his manager, his voice immediately breaking with excitement. Thirty years in the industry, and still the man could find something extraordinary in a phone call. Hello Frank, he said. How are you doing?

Fine, said Frank. Good. Just out for a walk.

Where to?

Nowhere in particular, said Frank, and there was a moment of uneasy silence while each tried to imagine what the other was thinking.

Well, let me get right to the point, said his manager, whose day was punctuated by points of all kinds. I just got a very interesting call from a man named Richard Richards. Do you know who he is?

No, said Frank.

A producer, —now don't get all defensive. He's a producer, he's working with Lenore Riviere now.

Frank made a noise of assent. Riviere was a figure from another age: she had begun in Europe—France? the name was French, but maybe she was Danish?—decades previously, making strange little movies as if they were art: camera-dances, fairy tales, stories of brutes and beauties. Then she had moved to Hollywood and had a run at American moviemaking, even marrying a star—what was his name?—for a little while, before her talents proved too unpopular and she drifted into the weeds along the riverbank. Still, she was stubborn enough to have stayed alive all these years, stubborn enough to have made more good movies than bad ones and a few that were considered great. She had outlasted several more husbands, and studio executives, actors of all kinds, critics, cinematographers, editors, she had outlasted most of her peers and all of her audience, and now she was a hippogriff, a figure of ancient fiction living high in the hills, with God knows what surviving retainers around her, and who to visit her in the huge darkness of her home. Every ten years or so she had emerged with one more movie, a cast no one could possibly have predicted, a style so loose and yet so refined that it seemed to compete with the real, and each story more peculiar than the one that had preceded it.

O.K., said Frank. Lenore Riviere? I didn't know she was still alive.

She's still alive. She's still making pictures. Or anyway, she's making a picture, again. Evidently, she's convinced some studio to give her a few million dollars. —His manager loved the word *evidently*, because it was a sophisticated way of saying *maybe, maybe not*.

How old is she?

Christ, I don't know. Seventy-five? Eighty? —Anyway, she wants to talk to you. She wants to call you.

When? said Frank.

Now. When we're done.

It's ten o'clock at night.

There was a pause. . . . It's only seven here, said his manager.

That's still past working hours.

Are you saying no? I think you should take the call. She hasn't made a movie in more than a decade, you know. This may be the last one she has in her. I thought you might be interested. It's your kind of thing.

I don't want to make a movie. He rocked back in his chair and put his thumb to his lower lip. Then: What is it about?

I don't . . . his manager said. I don't know. You should let her explain it to you.

And another silence, representing six years of residuals and a certain resentment. All right, said Frank. All right. I'll talk to her.

Yeah?

All right, yeah.

Great, said his manager. Great. I don't need to tell you what this could mean for you. Get yourself back in the game. Have a good time talking to her.

Frank hung up the phone and almost immediately it rang again, so that he wondered for a moment if Riviere had been listening in on another extension.

How are you, Frank? the woman said. Her voice was clear as could be and retained a command as long and as dark as the last century, and an accent quite as complicated: her English was perfect, but there was a slight angle to her pronunciation, though nothing he could identify with a nation. It was like listening to a classically trained violinist play a fiddle tune: she was too good for the language, and yet not quite good enough.

Just fine, said Frank. And yourself? —He loosened his tie and crossed the room to fix himself a drink from the bar.

Decrepit, said the other. Quiet, curious, fond, quixotic. Do you know what that means? Quixotic? It's . . .

I know, said Frank abruptly, and Lenore chuckled.

Dancing. Can you dance, Frank?

A little. —He began a playful shuffle on the polished hardwood floor of his living room, holding the half-full tumbler of scotch and ice high in his hand. —Can you hear that?

Yes, good, she said. I don't need you to dance, but I wanted to know.

That's too bad, said Frank. If you'd wanted me to dance I would have done anything for you. Beyond that—my career as a hoofer—I'm not working much these days.

Yes, what *are* you doing these days, darling?

Not a lot, he said.

Why don't you come visit with me? she said warmly. We should meet. We should talk.

Oh, about what, Lenore?

About things, said the woman. I want to meet you, Frank. I have a part for you, a role, a position, a play. The play's the thing, wherein I'll catch the conscience of the King. Do you know what that's from?

Yes, said Frank. He took another sip of his scotch and lay down on his long black couch.

Yes indeed, said Lenore. Do you suppose anyone cares about conscience anymore?

Maybe.

Maybe, said Lenore. I have something, it's going to be the end of *maybe.*

Why don't you send me a script? said Frank. We'll talk about it. He idly picked off a piece of beige lint from the thigh of his dark wool trousers.

There is no script. There's a script, but it's no good, I'm not going to send it to you. I'm not going to insult you by sending it to you.

What's it about, then?

Meet with me. I'm in New York. —He was startled to realize she was not calling from across the continent but was near and by. He glanced out the window, half expecting her to be staring at him from some brightened window in the building opposite. —I don't like talking on the telephone, she said. I never have. Why don't you come by my suite?

I should probably see a script first.

Oh, bullshit, she said, pronouncing the word as if it was arcane and delicate. Bullshit. You do not need a script.

He reached for a silver pen that lay on the coffee table and began turning it with his long fingers. What do you want from me?

I've been watching you for some time now, Frank. You are beautiful on film; you know that already. You don't care. You know that's what makes you so appealing. Tell me: Why did you stop?

Acting? —He had become bothered by the light from a floor lamp in the corner, and he rose from the couch, crossed, and turned it off, leaving the room dim and populated by motionless belongings.

Why did you stop acting, yes. Why did you stop? When you were just about to become big.

I didn't stop, per se, he said. I just . . . don't do it much anymore. —There was mute skepticism on the other end. —I guess I stopped, O.K.

Why?

Because, he said.

Because. Thank you.

He pondered for a moment. All anyone wanted me to do was to run into a room with a gun drawn, he said. Have an argument over the telephone, drive a car too quickly down a narrow street, make love to a little bit of light. While they all watched. . . .

Asinine, said Lenore. Yes, I understand. I understand. Performing . . .

Performing, said Frank. Like a puppy. —He had come to feel a certain quick liking for this woman, odd and unusual as she was, old beyond discretion. There were directors who commanded and directors who ignored, young men compulsive with quick ideas, others so overtly lacking in responsibility that one wondered how they achieved their position, nervous men who wheedled and snapped, screamers, weepers, and one or two who were careful, thoughtful, and kind. Lenore was another: wise and weird, majestic and half-hidden. —Exhausting, isn't it? I know, she said. Emptying out, again. Saying something, again.

Listening, reacting, again. Waiting. And why? To lend a few hours to someone else's entertainment. Ah, but this is the part of a lifetime, Frank. What I'm working on. Come to my hotel and talk to me. Come and help me. Help me end my life with a little art.

Can I think about it? said Frank.

Think about it, said Lenore. Call me, yes, whenever you want. —She gave him the name of her hotel. —You will be proud of this when we're done, she said, and then she rang off the line.

3

Left alone again, he began to play with the mail, still lying unopened on the table before him. Lenore Riviere, he thought, and then he said the name out loud, just because he liked the sound it made: Riv-iere. She had come a long way to get to him. Idly opening the manila envelope, he found himself gazing at his monthly financial statement, a few pages of columns, numbers, dollars; it gave him forty more years to live, twenty in perfect comfort, ten in luxury, five in dazzling splendor. Did she really have a movie she was going to make, or was she merely exercising her eccentricities? He had liked their little conversation a great deal; she was frank and funny, and warm in her way. She was as old as oak and she had been flirting with him, if only for their mutual amusement. If he worked with her, it would be something to do with his time. He might spend a little attention, gain another story. And maybe she had a role that would be worth playing. Maybe it was something for him to take. —The letter had a card inside, or something small and stiff and nothing else. He tapped it on the edge of the table. If she had something good and they went into production, he could bring Amy out to visit him on the set; she'd like that, she used to love to see how it all worked, the cables and cameras, the crew busy, the occult instructions shouted, though once when she was very little he'd made the mistake of letting her watch a scene where he was pistol-whipped by a policeman with a rubber gun, and she'd gasped at the first take, burst into hot tears, and had to spend the rest of the day with the makeup artist, painting her face and playing with wigs.

He slid his index finger under the flap of the envelope, a puff of breath to bellows it open, a shake, and out fell a photograph of a little boy and a baby girl. He recognized it immediately, recognized and remembered the cowboy shirt he was wearing, —which was red though the picture was black and white—and his sister making the most of her infant smile. He was so startled to see it that he hardly wondered who had sent it, he just gazed on it for a while, as if it had materialized out of the silver of time itself. He had loved that shirt; the day it had been given to him, he had removed it carefully from the white tissue paper it had come in and hugged it to his chest, marching happily around the house with it in his arms before he could be convinced to actually try it on. He remembered the feel of someone tugging on the tail to fit it more securely to him, and then smoothing the cloth across his shoulders. That was in spring, and the air had been full of the sweet green sound of young things growing.

At length he turned the photograph over. On the back was written Memphis, 1966 in one thick hand, and then a later annotation below it, in more fragile penmanship: Frank, I found this and I thought you might like to have it back. Do you remember me? I'm O.K., as long as I take care of myself and take my medication. I think about you all the time. —Kimmie.

Do you remember me? All the years wanted his answer. He took another step back and said, out loud, Of course.

4

THE INVENTION OF PORNOGRAPHY

We will now sit silently upon the cliff and stare down on the darkening plain, the array of camps, the day's things put up for the night, the bonfires, and the wide-eyed bewildered boy standing before his tent; and we'll watch as a sickness among the stars causes misery on the ground, and weigh the little deaths of princelings and girls.

Frank Cartwright was sixteen, a junior in high school, too tall by about two inches, sharp-featured, smart, solitary by nature and sociable by default. Kimberly Remington was his first love and the last element of his childhood. This was in Washington, D.C., and she was in her senior year of a girls' school over the river in Arlington. Her father was a surgeon at Bethesda Naval and Kimmie was regard's desire, pale and keen; and Frank Cartwright had fought with her the first time he met her.

They were geniuses back then, every one of them; they knew dollars and days, they were getting bigger by the minute. On a weekend night in mid-winter, Frank and a boy he knew from school had gone out drinking down in Georgetown. Two places had turned them away for being underage, but at a third they'd slipped in, overtaking a trio of girls who had stopped just inside the door to remove their coats. Frank had found himself talking—some remark on the cold, a gesture toward the steam that fogged the windows—and soon the five of them had seated themselves, somehow: Frank, friend, tall girl, snub-nosed girl, girl with red hair, at a table in a back room with noise all around them. The red-haired girl undid the scarf from her throat; the sternum below the V-neck of her black sweater was eggshell; she shivered, pressed her knees closely together beneath the table, and smiled. From where Frank sat he could see the curved shadow where her blue-white breasts began, and he became conscious of his hands on the table, one of them idly worrying a bar napkin while the other lay wrapped around his beer. What are your names? he asked the snub-nosed girl, though already there was only one name he really cared about.

I'm Andrea, she said. She pointed to the tall girl. She's Terry. And that's Kimmie.

What's that? said Kimmie. What are you telling him? She smiled, revealing her tiny teeth and a flash of glistening gums. Her features were at once crude and delicate—sharp nose, reckless mouth—etched quickly from some fine-grained material; and her hair fell down her shoulders, glimmering with copper-red like nothing else in nature. She was small as a bulb, white like a pill, bitter as early morning, and Frank could taste her.

They sat and talked for a while and they drank a bit. There were three or four men in military uniforms standing by the bar, laughing and yelling; Frank wondered what he could do if they came back and tried to take the girls away, but they didn't come, and the music still played. With feathery fingers, Kimmie tucked her hair back behind her pink ear.

Besides which, the tall girl was saying, anyone can lie over the telephone, anyone can say anything they want to.

Was he lying? said Frank's friend.

That's just it, we don't know, said the tall girl.

Kimmie reached into her pocket and came out with a cigarette, which she studied for a few moments before lighting it. I can always tell when someone's lying, she said. In person or on the telephone, even on TV. I do it, and I've never been wrong. I can always tell.

You cannot, said Frank's friend.

I can, said Kimmie, nodding emphatically. She blew two pearl-grey plumes of smoke from her nostrils and sat back. Watch me. Try and tell me something, and I'll tell you whether you're lying or not.

Frank's friend sat still and silent, trying to see how serious she might be. The others at the table watched. At length the boy ventured a phrase, with as much confidence as he could muster. . . . My middle name is Orlando.

—Lie! said Kimmie, immediately and happily. That's a lie.

Frank's friend leaned back in his chair, in part from shame and in part in surprise at the vehemence of her response, but he smiled a little and nodded. O.K., he admitted.

Go on, she said. Try me again.

The boy hesitated, now a little longer. In my grandfather's house, he said, pausing cannily . . . There were four grand pianos.

Another scorekeeping second passed. True, said Kimmie. Absolutely true, that's true. The boy nodded again, more pleased that he'd been caught in a fact than perplexed by her ability. I told you, she said. I never fail. Your turn, she said to Frank.

He leaned back and looked at her, alive on the manifestation of her mysterious skills. I believe you, he said.

But she wanted to keep going, she wanted to snatch every phrase from every boy. Come on, she said, squirming a little and then briefly reaching over and tapping her finger on the back of his hand. Come on.

Now what was he going to do? He could tell a lie or tell the truth, in either order, or twice tell her the truth, or twice try to con her; or he could follow fate and chance a sentence, hardly knowing himself whether it was true, at least until he was done with it. —I was adopted, he said suddenly.

Kimmie looked at him carefully, and watched as he watched her. That . . . is . . . true, she said.

No it isn't, said Frank's friend, who wasn't friend enough to know for sure.

Yes, it is, said Frank. Then to his friend: It is, actually. I was.

The friend stirred awkwardly in his seat. Frank had some company he was trying on the red-haired girl, and no more company to give.

One more time, said Kimmie, and now her attention was entirely on this boy Frank, who was clever and open and might surprise her. She didn't move her grey eyes from his face, not one little bit. Tell me a lie or tell me the truth, she insisted.

He thought quickly, but far out into the reaches of his animus, seized upon a statement and then took a long period to work up his courage; he grinned slightly nervously, started to lean in to her, stopped, —what if he was wrong? —and then continued, because it was a winter's night, and he had nothing to lose but cold. He put his mouth against her ear and whispered very slowly, his voice trembling a little bit on the end of his breath. You are the prettiest girl . . . I've ever seen, he told her . . . And if I don't get to kiss you by the end of this night, my head is going to explode.

He pulled back and paused, and she stared at him, her features in a rage. She turned more pale, if that was possible, and her freckles seemed to dance upon the bridge of her nose.

What did he say? said the tall girl.

Nothing, said Kimmie, who was now staring at the tabletop. He said . . . Nothing.

What did you say? said Frank's friend, but Frank merely shook his head and stared at his beer.

Was it the truth or a lie? asked the tall girl.

It was a lie, said Kimmie quietly.

It was not, said Frank.

It was too, she said, and she got up from the table, tied her scarf around her neck, and walked quickly through the bar and out the front door. In the quiet afterward, Frank's friend and the two remaining girls sat motionless and showed as little as they could; but Frank was thinking about the girl in the snow, and he got to his feet, said, I'll be right back, and went after her.

5

No one sees how time will play: not ever, and least of all on a snowy night. There is the specific warmth of waist-flesh under woolen clothes, the astral appeal of city lights, the sidewalk slipping underfoot. No one sees the end of an action, and no one believes that there is one; the crest of the future is close, and over it lies anything: a plain, a cave, another crest. Kimmie was halfway down the block when Frank caught up to her; her thin shoulders were hunched as she hurried toward her car. He took her arm from behind and she spun around and twisted out of his grip; and as she turned a few of her tears landed on the back of his hand. They were cold, and they burned on his skin. I'm sorry, he said. She didn't say anything in reply, but she reached up angrily and brushed her hair back from her forehead. Tell me what I did, he said.

You were making fun of me. You were acting funny, to under-mine me.

I wasn't, he said.

You were tunneling under me. His words were telling her words what to say, whether to trust him and what to expect. She reached into her pocket, pulled out a cigarette, and found the last match in her only matchbook. If the match lights, she realized, and stays lit long enough to light the cigarette, then it was a flame of pure love and she was going to kiss him. If it lights and then goes out on the way to the cigarette, then he was another dead person that she had to avoid. The flame was yellow and flickering beautifully; she let it go on for a while, she liked the way it sounded. When it had burned almost up to her fingers, she lit her cigarette with it and then turned her face up, with smoke still on her lips, and kissed him.

Later, in her car, a yellow Toyota Corolla that smelled of stale per-fume, she left the engine running and the heat pouring out of the dash-board and they kissed away, her warm soft lips, her small tongue in his mouth, the faint drizzle of snow melting on their shoulders. She pulled back and looked at him with her starry grey stare. My father's out of town, she said. Why don't you come home with me? No sex, you can't fuck me, O.K.? But come home with me. Come be with me.

He nodded and she sat up and put the car in gear, little girl bossing the machine out of its parking space and down the street. Where are we going? asked Frank.

Arlington, she said.

What about your friends?

She was watching the traffic at the intersection. Oh, she said. That was a lie. They're not really my friends. No friends. Oh, well. Who needs friends?

The Francis Scott Key Bridge was closed for construction, so she steered down toward the Lincoln Memorial, the capital city wheeling by out the snow-slurred windows, the Potomac dark and cold. She didn't speak, but she was thinking very hard about something, she seemed to vibrate, like a bell after it's stopped ringing but before it's completely still. They crossed the river and glided away from the center of town, into what once had been gentleman's farmland and forest, before it was turned into gentleman's suburb; then they came to a main street, a few blocks of shops, all of them dark, the sidewalks empty, and at the end there was a tall white brick apartment building, latter-day International Style, with a half-moon drive leading up to the entrance. Beyond it was an iron gate; behind the gate was a passageway leading to an underground garage, where night was traded for garish fluorescent light and pitch black shadows, and she pulled into a spot between a Galaxie 500 and a Malibu. Out the windshield Frank could see the name DR. WILLIAM REMINGTON stenciled in yellow paint on the wall. Like the gun? he said.

Like the artist, said Kimmie. Horses, you know. Wild West. Broncos and . . . He was a painter, like I'm going to be a painter. That's what I do, you know? All day, I'm a painter. And so when I get old enough and good enough, I'm going to move to New York and live and be an artist. Like those women. So . . . O.K. . . . We're here, she said. Still, she made no move to get out of the car; instead she sat staring forward for a moment, and then turned and kissed him, kissed, longer and longer, the two of them twisted awkwardly in their seats. He could hear the sound of his own breathing, every sigh and rustle amplified in the confines of the car; the noise was unbearable and he was cold. Her tongue was cold. All right, she said at last, pulling away and looking at him frankly. Do you want to come up?

Yes.

In the elevator she stood in front of him and leaned back, the crown of her head pressing against his collarbone. Now it was midnight on the fourteenth floor, and she led him down the hall, around a corner, and to her front door. Shh, she said, although the quiet of the building was enough to keep him quiet.

The apartment was darker than the city outside, which glowed in the snow—so much glamour for a teenage boy: regent city, white night, vast apartment, brand-new girl in her secret bedroom. She had things: pictures on her mirror, scarves tied around her bedposts, books on the floor. On one corner of her dresser there was a small pile of her watercolors, but when he idly bent to look at them, she said, No, no, no. They're not finished, and she hastily closed them in a drawer. The door to her closet was open, and inside her shirts and dresses were jammed tightly together on the too-short clothes bar, fold upon fold of blues and blacks. He dropped his coat on the chair at her desk and glanced at a pegboard on the wall, and when he turned around he found her already undressing. He stared for a moment and then moved toward her. He didn't have a word to say. Tentatively, he touched a pair of fingers lightly against a bruise on the side of her rib cage. What happened here? he asked. Shhh, she said, and when he glanced back at her face she was looking right into his eyes.

There was something fresh and strange about the way she smelled, a combination of that perfume of hers—whatever it was—and her pallid health, an admirable and irreproducible artifact, the mark of a girl at once slightly sick and absolutely living, like the lewd smell of the air in a greenhouse. This is me, she said. Be nice. She made a come-hither motion with her hand and then pranced across the room to her bed.

He stripped off his clothes and got in with her, shivering, and then shocked at how hot her skin was. They kissed for a while, and then he went down. He'd never done that before, it was a divide he hadn't dared cross, on the few occasions—his first real girlfriend, a classmate named Trina—when it had been possible. But Kimmie had no parts; she was all one piece. She was all one skin, one surface and weight: neck, nipples, abdomen, haunch. She was perfectly enclosed upon the mattress, it fit her like a frame. She was insane. She made soft noises, her ass fit in his palms, with his fingertips touching the bottom of her spine. What was she thinking? His lips reached her navel and she flexed her belly involuntarily, bringing up the slatted curve of her rib cage. He nodded his mouth down a little farther, turned his head, and rested his cheek on her stomach.

What are you doing? said Kimmie. Are you listening to my insides?

He didn't answer but he raised his head and started down a little farther, and suddenly she opened her legs wide, startling him for a moment; he thought she must have done this before and he collected himself and bore down as he assumed he was supposed to. Her pubic hair was the color of copper wire, and the mouth below was miniature. Its secret was its gratuitousness, the abundance of ridges and seams, hoods and clefts—a tiny red palace for a tiny pink doll. He really didn't know what he was doing, how to make her happy or how much of her to take for himself. Where to go. He kissed at her for a little while, all along wondering what she was feeling; there was a dampness in her that had weight but no taste. She took the hair on the back of his head in her hand and gently pulled him up to her, awkwardly reaching between his legs with her other hand and taking hold of his erection so quickly that he flinched. She played with it a little, her thin fingers fluttering gently, and then she stopped. No more, she whispered. I'm sorry.

The rest of the night was no more. They kissed and turned and entangled themselves, but she wouldn't let him inside her—when he tried she just twisted her hips and kissed him again. Then it was early daylight and he was waking in her intricate world, alone in her wealthy room, with his clothes cast on the floor beside her bed. There had been the darkness of the theater, and then sleep, and now the lights were up, the illusion dispelled, the set was plain. This stuff of living, it wasn't going to dissolve in the daylight, no.

Soon Kimmie was back through the door, dressed in a flannel nightgown, her hair unbrushed, her smooth white skin bearing angry abraded patches from the rubbings of the night before. She held a finger up to her lips. My father's home, she whispered. He widened his eyes in alarm. Wait here, she said. And you should get dressed. She slipped out her door and disappeared.

Slowly, he drew on his clothes. More snow had fallen during the night, and while he waited for her to return he stood by the window, looking out on the city, its innocent drifts fantastically bright in the early morning sun, the more so in contrast with the taste of her mouth still lingering in his, and the sharp, bitter odor that she'd left on his fingers. He wondered if it was the same world they had driven through the night before.

She slipped back in the room, breaking his solitude. He just got into the shower, she said. You have to go. She wrote her phone number on a sheet of school notebook paper and then stuck her head out her door again. Now, she said, and she kissed him, exchanging her grimy breath for his. Go.

He barely noticed the apartment as he hurried through it. Skin-sore and fuck-dizzy, with a steely ache in his groin, he walked half a mile before he found a bus stop, stood shivering for ten minutes, and then rode a half hour to his own house in Silver Spring, where he slipped in the back door, climbed to his room, and fell into his bed, exhausted and still dirty, and then fell into dreams that were dirtier still.

6

There was another day, another day, and another after that. He was a wealthy man, when it came to time and diversion. In the bursary of her room, he counted her freckles across her flesh, the atoms of her inscape, in awe at their variety and the body they were written upon. Each time afterward that he saw something dappled he shivered and went, anywhere along the spots that he could go. The dark spangles that were cast over everything he appreciated in the world: the stars in the sky at night and the streetlights of the city seen from a high window, benday dots on a newspaper photograph, the spotting on the underside of a turning leaf, the spatter of mud on a winter windshield, flecks of cigarette ash on the cloth of a car seat, droplets of blood on a butcher's block, speckles of foam on ocean waves. Crushed glass in sidewalk pavement, pepper on a dinner plate, the stipple of city marks on a map: These things and his girlfriend were proof to him that to be in the right place was to be scattered all over.

On the telephone at night she whispered strange stories amid remarks of affection. Her mother had run off some years earlier with a man she called the Skipper; now they lived in Florida and Kimmie rarely heard from her. Her father worked long hours at the hospital. Washington was a museum full of mummies and old guns. She was tired of walking around by herself. She wished she could be with him all the time, every day and every night. Oh, Frank. She wished she could wear him like a big wool overcoat. He'd rescued her from the tedium of school, the horrors of her classes, where they fed her lies and tried to change the shape of her brain; from the comments she heard about her looks, her clothes, her voice, from schoolmates along the halls; and from the growing treachery of her friends. Someone—she didn't know who—had done something to her car—she didn't know what. She woke one Saturday morning and went to the bathroom in the hall by her door, rubbed her eyes, washed her face, saw her skin, a slight pinkening around her nostrils; she thought she really should try to stop rubbing her nose, if she could stop worrying about whether the bone beneath was real. She got dressed and went down to get her car out of the garage so she could come get him, and the car started, but the engine was making a strange noise. She sat in the garage and listened: It was something subtle, almost silent, a song, she thought, and she strained to make out the melody. The notes went: G-A-B-G. What was it, that gabbling? —Oh, Frère Jacques, of course, Frère Jacques. Are you sleeping? But she wasn't sleeping, she was wide awake; someone had decided she was too lazy in the morning, and they'd hidden a song in the engine of her car to tell her so. Someone jealous of her, because she had such a beautiful boyfriend. Let them be jealous.

She went back inside and called him. The car is broken, she said, without explaining why. She sounded mournful, and he wished he had a car of his own so he could take her somewhere. Instead, he rode the bus to her apartment house, and they stayed inside her room for the remainder of the afternoon. Outside it began to snow again, at first slowly and then faster, the pale blue-white flakes falling gently down onto the city and all its buildings. They got into her bed, the room was so bright. She was thinking *slow down* when he started going too fast, and *hurry up* when he went slow, —and then in mid-act she heard a voice say, *Light up a cigarette.*

She took his face in her hands. They're in the pocket of my coat, she said.

He hardly had the will to stop moving, and he kept on until he felt her go still underneath him. Looking down on her, he could see her expression: alert, intent, preoccupied. What are?

My cigarettes, she said, in a don't-you-know voice.

You want a cigarette now?

She thought about it carefully, because she wanted to be certain. . . .

No, never mind, she said, but by then all the concentrate of sex had been dispelled, and there was no way to get it back. She had wanted so badly for it all to go well, and now it was ruined, everything around her was ruined. I'm sorry, I'm sorry, I'm sorry, she whispered, and to punish herself she dug her nails into the side of her leg, leaving blue-white crescents that didn't fade from her flesh for a week.

7

For each sentence below, mark whether you (a) strongly agree, (b) agree, (c) agree somewhat, (d) disagree somewhat, (e) disagree, (f) strongly disagree.

1. People only like me if I tell them what they want to hear.
2. I often wonder if the government really has my interests at heart.
3. The color of the food that I eat is important to me.
4. No one can tell when I'm bored.
5. Lost things are always found in the last place I look for them.
6. I'm often much more unhappy than I think I should be.
7. There's no real difference between looking and watching.
8. My favorite song is about people I know.
9. I find it comforting to think that God has a plan.
10. On the whole, people don't treat me as fairly as they should.
11. Scientists know a lot more than they let on.
12. It isn't really stealing if the person you stole from should have caught you.
13. It surprises and upsets me when I learn that someone finds me frightening.
14. Sometimes my face just stiffens, like a mask.
15. Everything in the world has one and only one true name, and no two things have the same name.
16. The inside of my mouth often feels too hot or too cold.
17. Habits come in the front door, but worries all come in the window.
18. [This space intentionally left blank]

8

It was six in the evening by the time Frank got home. His mother was in the kitchen, busying up some dinner, and his father was in the garage, rewiring a living room lamp, but Gail was waiting for him, watchful because she had nothing in particular to do. She gave him five minutes behind his bedroom door and then she knocked politely. Come in, he said, and she opened the door and walked a foot or two into the room. His wet boots were standing by the door to his closet, and he lay shirtless and supine on his bed, his hands behind his head.

Little Gail, with her thick brown hair, too rich for such a young girl; with her wide eyes, dark as the corners of a cathedral; with her telltale mouth, as if she couldn't help but taste all her words before she spoke them. Little sister: she wanted to sit beside him, but she didn't dare. What's going on? she asked him. He shrugged, and the motion released some of Kimmie's scent from his skin; it drifted across the room and caught up to her. In the ordinary day he would have told Gail almost anything, but this happiness was all his, and he wanted to keep it for himself. I've met someone, he said. A girl.

Gail tried to be mature, and she nodded silently. She didn't want to ask him anything about love, because she was afraid that he would feel it if he said it. —What's her name? she asked instead.

Kimmie. I guess it's Kimberly, but she's called Kimmie.

Is she pretty?

He nodded, an awkward motion from his position. Oh, yeah, he said.

Is she nice? Gail was staring at the baseboard.

I like her, he said, conscious of the fact that it was cruel of him to be so terse, but unwilling to give up any more.

Gail pressed her left toe against the instep of her right foot. All right, she said. And then, because it seemed like the right thing to say: I'm very happy for you.

He turned his head to look at her and smiled. Thanks, he said.

Dinner's going to be soon, she said, and then she backed carefully out of the room, shutting the door gently, as if something was going to break.

9

March came and went, and April was midway through; and Frank and Kimmie's mutual devotion strengthened over the weeks. It was spring, and there was not a day without some discovery: a sentence one spoke that made the other smile, a trail of nerves not yet explored, a throb of feeling that passed from one to the other when a song they both loved started playing on the radio in her car. His birthday was on the twenty-third; she gave him a painting she had made, a busy little townscape fraught with inscrutable insignia and emblems, and one large black crow gazing out at the viewer from between two white houses. His father gave him a camera that had once been his own. It was a small Leica, a fine machine, sharp and elegant; Michael Cartwright was a machinist of Swiss descent, and he believed in the fundamental virtue of an intricate and well-balanced tool, but he'd long since run out of time to make pictures, and it had languished in a felt-lined case on a shelf in the basement until he decided his son was old enough to appreciate it.

To Frank the camera was weighty and grave, and while he loved the gift, it was a few weeks before he could use it comfortably. First he had to make it his and take the time, for time to take. He shot a half dozen rolls of nothing in particular: his bedroom, the facade of his school, a roll on a local playground, taking pictures of things to try to figure out what a thing was, and what a picture of it might be. Once he opened a fresh roll of Tri-X and ran his fingers down the frames, exposing the film and getting the oil from his fingertips all over it, just to see how it felt. He spent a few nights sleeping with the lens nestled against his chest until the metal warmed and he drifted off, half-hoping that the images from his dreams would somehow be transferred onto the film. He would roll over on it, or his arms would become entangled in the leash-like leather strap, and he would wake in the darkness, his eyes alive with blindness. The world was physical, the light was physical, the picture was physical.

Kimmie was physical. She was always talking, always moving, always touching, and she was so fair in any situation, fair and fragile, as she murmured, sweated under his hand, kissed him happily. Out her window there were microphones in the trees, transmitters at every window. Kiss, kiss, kiss.

An exhausted afternoon, with the sun in the blue sky and a breeze through the open windows of his bedroom. The house was empty downstairs; the Cartwrights were out shopping, and Gail was rehearsing an afterschool play. Moments earlier Kimmie had swallowed him whole, and her lips were blood red from the effort and glistening with the remains. She licked at the last bit softly and smiled. Breath-heavy and half asleep, still he wanted to know why she enjoyed him so deeply, what she got from him, who was nothing much: but a boy, and here was this supernaturalism visited upon him. What does that taste like? he asked.

Hard to say, she replied slowly. Hard to explain. —She thought carefully, because she really wanted to tell him about it. Like what you would taste like if you were an egg. But it's also a little bit . . . fizzy? She smiled at him sadly, because they weren't going to get any closer over that, were they? Words were willful, words were weird, and resisted being given. She ought to have a present for him, equal to the present he was. She sat up on the bed and looked slowly around the room, her ardent gaze turning past the neglected baseball bat leaned in the corner, the pile of books on his desk, her own blue jeans draped over the back of his chair, and coming to rest on the camera resting eye-inward on his windowsill. She rose, translucent thing in a transparent pond.

Where are you going? Frank asked.

To get this, she said. He watched her as she swam naked across the room and retrieved it. Is there film in it?

He nodded.

Do you want to take my picture? she asked.

Like that?

Just like this, she said. Yeah. Like I was a pussyfish.

He paused for a second. Really? he said.

She smiled bravely and held out the camera to him, leaning forward so that her breasts were slightly distended by gravity. He took it and she sat down on the bottom of the bed, her legs crossed, her hands on her thighs. She smiled mischievously; he pressed the shutter button, and her nakedness was his forever. He sighed and looked out from behind the lens. More, she said, and moved her hands back to her waist, bending back a little bit; she reached up and tucked a strand of hair behind her ear; she made a princess face; he took pictures.

He stood from the bed and she took a deep breath and stretched out on her back, her belly flattening, her breasts becoming apple-round. Everything, she thought. Everything. She spread her pale thin legs, and the clicking of the shutter, which had been regular until then, suddenly stopped. Frank? she said, and he lowered the camera and stared hard. There was a meanness in his expression, and something that meant that he loved her. Maybe they were the same: attention, appetite. She didn't know, she didn't think anybody knew, where devotion ended and destruction began. Go on, she said, lying flat, lying soft, and he paused for just another second and then brought the lens between them again. The camera was a magical machine that fixed her flesh in its seconds—one two three four—and allowed her spirit to wander. She could see herself posing, and then the lens went out of focus and she was lost. That was the way it worked, then, a test of their love and perfect intercourse, because if the camera blurred her then she would have no home to go to. She wondered if he could see how she was trembling, how hard she was fighting. He didn't say a word, but she could hear him talking to her, telling her what he wanted her to do. She opened her legs a little farther.

This is my cooch, she thought, using the only word she knew. This is my thing. This is what makes me hoochie-coochie. Do you love me?

He was seventeen, and he loved her; then she lost every embarrassment. She began to turn on the mattress, posing and opening, stretching, crawling; she blushed and laughed, sang something, kissed at the camera, which kissed at her in turn. Is this all right? she asked out loud, and over onto her belly she went, swinging her heels in the air. I want to show you everything. I want you to see everything. She rose up on her knees and raised her cleaved rear.

What did they make up that artless afternoon? The experiment grew harder and brighter, the girl grew bolder and the boy became bigger. Her lovely surface was revealed, —every element of her beauty, every ridge and lip, brushed with short soft copper hairs, and bare; every shade of skin from perfect white to mud-dark, every star and foxing; and her blades of bone, her shifting muscles, her gleaming eyes. She laid herself up against the lens as it bellied forward and back, reaching for a focus. He had fallen in love with the sight of her face before him and the feel of her body beneath him, but strange facts remained hidden: those bright red membranes, the glistening and gore within, all that witchery, it was now made plain. That was a moment, and then his whole mind turned over. —Ha! He was a man, and she was madder for her display of celebrity. He saw more, and more even than that; he moved in closer, and if he'd had some way of getting inside her entirely, exploring her right down into her viscera, he would have done it; he would have photographed her liver and her gleaming heart, pointed his lens down into her foamy lungs, gotten himself entangled in her red veins and blue arteries. She had become perfect, all on this afternoon, amid this sober daylight, on his obvious, unmade bed.

Then she was out of ideas and she said, I don't know what else to do. He was out of film, and he said, Are you O.K.? He sat down heavily on the edge of the mattress, even as his fingers reached for the back of the camera.

O.K.? Yeah, I'm fine. She watched as he removed the roll and set it carefully on his bedside table. What are you going to do with them? she asked.

He shrugged. He felt full and slightly nauseated, not from disgust but from satiety. Develop them, he said, stalling with the obvious. Save them. He only half knew the force of what they'd done, making these imperishable pictures, souvenirs of an hour that no one could deny or forget.

She sat back, happy and proud of herself. Will you give me something? she said.

Anything you want. But I don't have anything, he said, which was true.

A picture, said Kimmie. Pop for pop, picture for picture.

He thought for a moment and then rose from the bed, went to his desk, and took a small white envelope from the drawer. As she watched, he opened it, drew out a photograph, and looked at it for a moment. He glanced at her and then looked down at the photograph again, as if he was trying to memorize it. This is me and my sister, he said. When we were little. I'm not even sure how I got it; I've always had it. Will you take it? Hold it for me. He walked back to the bed and handed it to her gently.

She stared at it as if the image were animated, alive, and performing just for her. Oh, she said. You were so cute! —She brought the picture to her lips and kissed it quickly. She adored him: That was her power and she couldn't be convicted for it. She put the photograph carefully between the pages of her social studies book, because it was social, a study, page 55; then she lay back in bed, closed her eyes, and listened as he gradually fell asleep, lying beside her in his wonderland. Frank Cartwright, photographer, she said softly. Photograbber, famous, and his famous girl, Kimmie Remington, a painter by blood. Then she stopped to wonder whether she'd said *by blood* or *in blood*. Not in blood, she hoped, and then she started thinking of pictures in blood, until she heard the sound of the door opening downstairs and Gail calling to see if anyone was home, and then she leaned over Frank to wake him up.

10

MILLION-DOLLAR BARTENDER

He always liked working the day shift, though the money wasn't as good as nights. Joe the Owner wouldn't come in until five or so, and even then he'd just head downstairs to count the previous day's receipts and put in whatever orders were necessary, and then he'd disappear again, not to return until nine or ten. In the daytime, too, there were fewer hassles: no kids trying to sneak in for a Seagram's in a dark booth, no ladies yelling at their husbands, nobody looking for a fight— he was a small man, Harold, and he didn't like to have to step into a brawl—and there were no cops, come in to rule by chest, as cops will. By day the place was cool and dark, and all he had to do was pour shots of rock and rye for a half dozen or so old men, who sat at the bar, peaceably and within easy reach. If there was a ball game on the TV, no one played the jukebox. All was simple and quiet, and he'd be home at six with a pocketful of one-dollar bills.

He was feeling lucky one warm spring evening, a good job to get by on, a fine woman to come home to, a way of living that any man would envy; so he stopped off at Sid's Cigars and bought a lottery ticket, using the first five numbers that came into his head: his birthday, his mother's birthday, his home address, the address of the bar, and the highest score he'd ever gotten down at the lanes. He left the ticket on the kitchen table and woke the next morning to the sound of Yvette screaming, her voice like a fountain up over all of Newark; and when he rushed in to see what was wrong, he found her standing there, the newspaper open on the counter and the ticket clenched so tightly in her sweaty hand that he worried the numbers would wash right off. He checked it and then checked it again—Yvette wasn't always very smart—but the ticket was right and it was his, and a few days later he was posing on a dais in some dingy building, a filthy blue curtain behind him and masking tape X's on the floor. Stand here and smile, they said, so he stood and smiled, holding a big cardboard check made out for THREE MILLION DOLLARS and shaking hands with some man in a suit, while all those people took his picture. Look here, Harold, they said. Look this way. And the next day there he was on the front page of the newspaper, and MILLION-DOLLAR BARTENDER was the headline. He didn't even bother to quit his job: he just stopped going, and Yvette walked out of the parlor where she cut hair and never went back. Joe the Owner didn't call, either. He must have been scared to get a cursing out, as if riches were the opposite of manners.

Yvette, she didn't know what to do at first, being with a man so suddenly, magically, rich as the devil; it frightened her. And the phone was always ringing, a hundred times a day, from everyone he'd ever known, some of them wanting a handout, some just wanting to talk to a lucky man. Brother, a fellow would say. You remember me, don't you? I'm Sara Watson's son, Tom. You know Sara from Indiana? I'm her son. I've got this car wash I thought you might want to get in on. —It was always framed as a favor to him, something to do with his money, as if it were a burden and he needed relief.

Well, the phone calls were a burden, but the things he bought were a joy. A brand-new cream-colored Lincoln—not the most original exercise of his imagination, he knew, but it was beautiful and he bought it, and he loved that car. He bought a few new good wool suits, an alpaca coat, a soft grey felt fedora, a pair of pearl-colored snakeskin cowboy boots, and a matching pair of his-and-hers gold watches. Soon enough he'd start looking for a new house, but in the meantime there was better living to be had in the old one: he bought the biggest television he could find, a new stereo with speakers that came up to his waist and a shopping bag full of LPs to play on it, a recliner, a black leather couch, a rosewood dining room table and a matching set of chairs, a set of dishes for ten, and silver flatware so heavy you could have used it in a street fight. He bought new fixtures for the kitchen sink, and then new fixtures for the bathroom sink and the tub, a German-made electric toothbrush, Jacquard-woven towels. He always liked those little trees, those bonsai trees; he thought they were fascinating, and he found a store in the City that sold them and came home one afternoon with a Baby Jade, a Hawaiian Umbrella, a Brush Cherry, and a tiny little Juniper, which he placed on the concrete porch out back. Passing by a sporting goods store later that same week, he decided he needed to get out and play more, and he strolled in and looked around, wandering down the aisles, picking up things here and there. By the time he'd reached the checkout counter he'd gone into a daze; he looked down and found a cart full of merchandise: a football, a basketball, a half dozen baseballs and three baseball gloves for three positions, a catcher's mask, a hockey goalie's mask, a swimsuit and a pair of goggles, ski boots though not the skis themselves, and a heavy punching bag on a chain. When he got home, with the trunk of the Lincoln raised to hold the stuff, he unloaded it all into the garage, where it sat, unopened and unused, for a week and a half. Then he decided to hang the punching bag from a rafter, only to discover that he didn't have a drill to make the hole; so he went by the hardware store and came home with more inexplicable stuff. It was fun to get and spend, the more so when he was recognized, as he sometimes was. You're a lucky motherfucker, one thick-faced man had said to him in a liquor store parking lot, and Harold had watched as the man's eyes searched for the bulge in his suit where his wallet would be.

Yvette wasn't enjoying any of it, though she didn't say so. She stepped around the packages piled in the living room and she never did wear the watch he gave her. She wouldn't do anything for him at night, she sighed in bed and rolled her hard back to him. Take some cash and go out, said Harold. Enjoy yourself some. Call one of your girls and go have fun. She nodded but she made no move, and finally he had to press a wad of bills in her hand and push her out the front door.

He walked in the house later that day and she was sitting on the living room couch in a daze. I was walking down Center Street, she said, and I was thinking, I can buy anything I want. She made an opening, ta-da gesture with her arms. Anything, in all those stores. She looked at him as if he'd just hit her, and he thought she was going to start crying, but she started laughing instead, a cold, cracking laugh.

What did you buy, then?

Nothing.

Come on, you can tell me. It doesn't matter. We've got enough now to carry us through any kind of spending.

Nothing, she said, slumping back on the couch as if Nothing was the worst name she knew. The skin on her face had gone opaque, a trick she had for when she was distressed. —Not a thing. There wasn't anything I wanted, now that I could have it. Isn't that just strange? she said, but she looked terrified. She went on: I stopped outside the travel agency and looked at all the posters in the window, but there wasn't anyplace I wanted to go. Then I got tired and I came home. —She stared at him.

So what are you going to do? said Harold. Sit around the house all day? We've got all this opportunity, we can live as large as we want.

Opportunity? she said. There wasn't anything wrong with how we were.

God damn, said Harold. Well, God damn. If you're going to be so country, you might as well go back to Georgia.

Country was good enough for you a month ago, she said, still staring at him with her dark eyes.

He looked back at her hard. Well, a month is a long, long time, he said. Maybe that's all the time I need. With that he turned and left the house.

He took a walk over to his friend Bobby's, who'd known him and watched over him since he was a kid shoplifting fruit from Red Biggs on Market Street. Three million, said Bobby, standing in his living room, wearing nothing but a pair of white briefs. I saw you grinning on the television that night, and I knew you'd be down here, soon or late. You and Yvette have a fight or something?

Harold nodded sadly. These are joyous days, but she isn't living them, he said. She's bringing me down.

That right? said Bobby.

Ever since it happened. She won't get up from the couch. She's a good woman, but—I don't know, I think she'd rather I was still pouring drinks. Coming home with my feet hurting, like I used to.

You know she loves you, said Bobby. Through and through. She's just got to adjust. Give her time to adjust.

Adjust, said Harold, his voice pitching up to a squeak. I don't think so. It's money; what's the fun of it if she's always going to be complaining? Maybe it's time for me to move on.

No, no: you should go home. You've got to romance her, make her feel good. Make her feel like an African queen.

I don't . . .

Love her up with flowers.

I'm going for a walk. Maybe I'll just keep on walking.

It was night when Harold left Bobby's, and the streets were quiet, the day done; the windows of all the buildings were dark, and he wished he could use some of his money to light them again, just for an hour or two. Maybe I should go by Bo's house, he thought. Bring him a bottle of cognac, spread my good fortune around a little bit. But instead he wandered a few blocks down, passed under Route 21, and stood at the far edge of Riverside, looking down at the black Passaic and listening to the dark, oily waves gently breaking, the tendrils of things beneath. Then there was a man beside him, the same thick-faced man who'd told him he was lucky in the liquor store parking lot. Harold stared at him, unwilling even to acknowledge him with a word, until the other man spoke. Isn't it a nice night? he said, and he smiled softly, as if he knew something Harold didn't. Had he followed him? For how long? How you doing? said Lucky Motherfucker.

I'm all right, said Harold. He was calm, but he knew he might be walking home without his wallet. Why? It was like one of those stories out of the Bible, where good fortune is inverted into bad, just to illustrate how little difference there was between the two.

Good, said Lucky Motherfucker. He pulled a two-foot length of lead pipe from under his coat and brandished it a little. Good. —Now, you know you're going to have to give me what you got.

I don't think so, said Harold. No way. You can't take from a man what he's already won.

Watch me, said Lucky Motherfucker, and just like that he cracked the pipe up against Harold's temple, so swiftly and in such darkness that the man never saw what felled him: he just went blind and hit the ground, out of thoughts before he landed, and stripped of his wallet, his rings, his new watch and his alpaca coat, before he had moved from one column to the other in the Book of the Living and the Dead. Then Lucky Motherfucker rolled his body into the river, where it floated down to the bay and sank near a piling at the edge of the airport, only to surface again many months later, this sad unburied wraith of chance, so rotted by the time it was discovered that it never was identified.

11

In Kimmie's head the neurons clustered and fizzled in baths of sickly dopamine. Her words came loose from their moorings and wriggled on the floor of her mouth. At night she saw a purpose and a plot in everything. There was always a man's voice with her, and he would talk, talk, talk, as if he was trying to talk her to death. Just bothering her all the time, criticizing everything, threatening her with jokes. She wanted to know why she'd been chosen to be tested this way. Was it because her father worked at a hospital? Had he volunteered her for some experiment? And every day on television there were terrible stories: entire countries sacrificed, driven backward into history until there was nothing left of them but rusted scraps of metal on the roads into ruined villages; nice-looking men who broke into women's houses at night and raped them; forgeries on the walls of museums; cars that exploded at the slightest impact, and the company that built them knew, but they kept it a secret.

It was two or three in the morning, but she couldn't tell if she'd been up since bedtime or if she'd just woken. Or maybe she'd been asleep for days but no one had told her, and they came and changed the world. She flexed her fingers and watched as her fingers flexed; they were flesh but they weren't quite real, or they were real but they weren't quite hers; there was something repulsive about it. The telephone in her room rang, not the normal ring, but a lower, almost rumbling tone. It rumbled again and she reached across her mattress to the night table and answered it, but there was no one on the other end. Instead they had found a way to pipe in the thoughts of famous men—Jimmy Carter, who spoke without moving his lips: Johnny Cash, who had shot a man in Reno, just to watch him die: Jesus Christ, except he had breasts like a woman. They babbled to her on and on; she put the receiver down on her mattress, but the noise was excruciating, and as much as she wanted not to offend anyone, she had to hang it up again.

They sent signals to make her shiver, just because the sensation was so unpleasant. At seven in the morning she heard her father in the hallway outside her door; a little bit later he left the apartment, slamming the door hard because he wanted to make sure she stayed inside; so she drew the curtains closed in her room and didn't go to school that day.

Evening, when the dark spirits were free in Washington. Night in her room again, and again with no sleep. At two in the morning the phone was ringing—still? or had it just resumed?—this time with a high-pitched whistling noise. She tried to ignore it, but when it stopped she could hear the people on the other end laughing at her. She waited until they shut up, and then she picked up the receiver and dialed Frank's number. He had her picture, so he had proof of the way she used to be.

His father answered, his voice bleary, slow and hoarse. This is Kimmie, Mr. Cartwright, she said. Can I talk to Frank?

There was a long pause. Do you know what time it is? he demanded, and she tried to apologize, but she was already crying. What is this nonsense? What are you doing, calling at this hour?

Please, she said. It's important. Please please please.

It was a full five minutes before Frank came to the phone, and when he did he was still besotted with sleep. Hello? he said.

She didn't wait. Frank, she said. Are you there?

Kimmie? he said slowly. What's going on? Are you O.K.? I've been trying to call you, all yesterday and today. What time is it?

The voice in her ear startled her, super clear and so close. Were they on some special line? Do you still have those pictures we took? she asked. The ones we took the other day, in your room.

Can we talk about this in the morning?

You still have those pictures, don't you? I need to see them.

Of course I do, he said. I think you had a nightmare. Kimmie, did you have a nightmare? I think you did. You had a nightmare.

I've been wide awake, she insisted. Try to understand. —She began whispering. —They're probably listening now. I bet they are, listening on the phone. Frank, I'm going to hang up now. I'm going to go. Good-bye. Do you love me?

All the time, he said.

I'll talk to you tomorrow, she said, her voice suddenly thin. I'm sorry, good night. Good-bye. Good night.

For a minute or more he stood there in silence, wondering whether he should call her back again. Then the receiver was in its cradle and he was in bed, his hand on his bare chest, his eyes fixed on the ceiling, he was sorry she had dreamed so badly; he was sad, and then he was fast asleep.

12

They said to Kimmie, they said to her, they warned her: not to tell anyone, not to let on. They asked her if she knew what that meant: Don't let on. Don't lie down. They told her she could be an angel, one of the special few, if she listened and she did what she was told. Kimmie, they said. Kimmie. Kimberly. Everyone around her was dead and just pretending. They needed her thoughts. They were feeding on her thoughts, because they didn't have any of their own. They wanted to replace her with a dead person, bit by bit, they were going to use the number 5, because 5 was the shape of her body, and they were going to use words like salt, and snow, and shoe, because an s is like the number 5. They made animals out of little machines and put them in with the other animals, the rat with his sharp white teeth, the snake with his long forked tongue, the dog with his terrible claws. They wanted to frighten her so she would secrete a special smell, which would tell them what she was thinking. That's why she stank, that's how she knew. It came and went, the stink; sometimes it would be so overpowering that she could barely breathe, and she was embarrassed to stand near anyone; then it would go away just as quickly and completely, and everything would be O.K.

13

The Cartwrights left town one Friday afternoon, on a train down to Florida to sit in the sun. Gail and Frank stayed home, master and mistress of the little house and everything it contained. For some time the girl had wanted to be alone with her brother for a day or two, the way they used to be before the Cartwrights took them in—a period which he remembered only vaguely and she didn't remember at all, but which they remembered together through the stories they knew and told each other, accounts of homes and events emerging from the gloom before memory, way stations that survived and were recounted long after the homes and events themselves had been forgotten. They had been refugees, then, in the war for generation, and they were come-what-may; and Frank was always with her and always watching out for her. She was the littlest soldier, the point of promises, an acorn in a matchbox.

There's plenty of food in the refrigerator, Mrs. Cartwright had said as she was leaving. Use whatever you need, and just clean up when you're done. Now they were gone and the house was quiet. Frank was in his room, carefully polishing the parts of his camera. Gail was listening to the radio and reading a cookbook in the kitchen. In time he appeared in the doorway. What are you doing?

Can I cook something tonight? Will you eat it? I promise I'll follow the recipe all the way, I won't cheat, and I won't make anything up.

What do you want to make?

Chicken and basil, she answered right away. She pointed to the open book, where she'd found the recipe and decided upon it half an hour previously, returning to it again and again, despite faithless forays into beef stew and veal cutlets. Red meat was unhealthy; chicken and basil it would be.

Does Mom have basil? he said.

She nodded.

All right then, he said. Make a lot, I'm starving. —He slapped his stomach with a flourish: Starving! Starving! Starving! Gail giggled and began to get ready, laying the pans out on the countertop, setting the oven, taking butter and garlic from the refrigerator, rice from the cabinet, measuring cups and mixing bowls from the cupboard.

He sat at the table with a bottle of beer and watched her. Are you doing all right? he said, as she made a basting mix.

It's pretty simple.

He thought for a moment. No, I mean, are you getting along all right, in school and everything?

She nodded and hitched up her jeans. I'm Diana, the goddess of hunting, in the school play, she said. Are you going to come?

He'd tilted his head back to finish his beer, and hearing no answer she turned to look at him. Yeah, of course I am, he said, setting the empty bottle down on the kitchen table.

She smiled and turned back to her cooking, only to turn around again a moment later. Can you get the chicken ready for me? she said. He nodded, and she put a wooden cutting board of breasts on the table in front of him. You have to use this, she said, handing him a tenderizer. He gave her a questioning look. Just sort of hit it, she said. You have to soften it up. The meat was shiny and slippery; he took one corner and unfolded it, revealing striations of muscle and a few bright red clots of blood.

Just hit it?

Go ahead.

With this? He brought the tenderizer up—she nodded—and he brought it down again with a smack. Gail yelped at the sound, and little bits of chicken leapt from the cutting board.

Wait! said Gail, but he was already striking at the meat again.

Like this? Because I want it to be tender, he said. I think it's important. Anyone will tell you, when you're making chicken and basil— again he struck—that the chicken *has* to be tender. —Frank! said Gail. Now he was smashing at it over and over, reducing it to a small flat piece of pink pulp, while his sister laughed and brought her hands to her face, to protect herself from the flying odds that were showering up from the table. Frank! Stop! Please?

You think it's ready? He had the tenderizer raised over his head with both hands, as if he were getting ready to ring the bell on a fairground test-your-strength machine.

Yes!

All right, he said reluctantly, letting his hands drop. There was nothing left but a few shreds lying forlornly on the cutting board, and he gazed at them skeptically. I don't know, he said. I guess it's probably pretty tender, but there doesn't seem to be much of it left.

That's because it's all over the kitchen, said Gail, who had stopped laughing but hadn't yet regained a normal tone of voice.

Well, you better give me some more, then.

No way, she said, and snatched the tenderizer from his hand. It's just going to have to be tough.

Aww, said Frank. I was having fun. Cooking *should* be fun.

You're a menace, said his sister. Sit there and be good.

Bring me a beer from the fridge? he asked, and she was happy to comply, but when she set it down on the table she hesitated, then turned to the sink, where she started to wash the basil leaves.

Are you going to marry Kimmie? she asked.

Marry her? said Frank, and at once his little sister was looking at him over her shoulder, her expression of anxiety unmistakable. He shrugged. I don't know, he said. Not right now, anyway. Not anytime soon. Are you worried that I'm going to marry her?

Oh, she said. No. And then, Oh, again. I'm not worried. I'm not worried, at all. Then she frowned and lied. I'm happy for you. She nodded emphatically, as if the matter were thereby settled, and turned back to the salad bowl before her.

They spent the evening after dinner watching a movie on television, in a dark room in the dark house, with the dark night surrounding them. The used dinner plates were piled on the coffee table; Gail was contentedly sprawled out on the floor; Frank was curled up in a corner of the couch. As nine o'clock approached she rolled over onto her back and regarded him with eyes glazed and burned by phosphors. You can go out if you want, she said. You don't have to stay here with me. I don't need a baby-sitter.

I'm not going out tonight, said Frank. She showed no expression, and he hesitated. —But Kimmie's going to come over tomorrow and spend the night. You can't tell anyone. Is that all right?

She shrugged. Sure. I won't tell, she promised, but the rest of the evening was precious, because they were alone, and a ruin, because she dreaded the arrival of the other.

When Gail woke the next morning, Frank was gone, and he didn't return until early in the afternoon; she waited in her room, reading a book about a woman who made friends with a band of gorillas in Africa. She wondered when she herself would be some boy's girlfriend, and whether he would have a little sister, and if so, whether the other girl would be as unnerved by her as she was by Kimmie. She didn't hear the two of them come into the house, and it was only when she went down to the kitchen for an apple that she noticed the extra jacket on a peg in the front hall, and the murmuring of elementary voices in the living room. She went in and found them together on the couch, going through a book of photographs they had found on the bookshelf. Kimmie was curled up against Frank, her red hair falling in her face as she bent her head to look at a picture. Hello, said Frank, and Kimmie, startled, lifted her head and looked at Gail with her grey-glowing eyes; but she didn't sit up and Gail thought that was rude. Hi, said Kimmie.

Hello, said Gail. She was standing in the doorway and staring.

Do you want to come look at these? said Frank.

No, said Gail. I'm going to go over to my friend Patsy's house; she's going to teach me to roller-skate.

Do you need a ride?

No, said Gail.

Be back for dinner?

She nodded and left, though not to go to Patsy's house. Instead she walked down to the mall, where she pretended to shop and then pretended to be waiting for someone. A midshipman in his plebe's uniform came by and talked to her for a little while, but when he discovered that she was only thirteen he frowned, made an excuse, and left. According to the clock in the center of the food court, it was now three in the afternoon; she walked down to her school, but the school was closed. On the fields in back a half dozen boys were playing a pickup game of football, kicking through the patches of snow that still lay on the ground and sweating even in the cold. She stood by the fence and watched them for a little while, and then she walked home.

Kimmie was sitting alone at the kitchen table, with nothing before her. Frank's in the shower, she said softly, gazing keen-eyed at the younger girl. He should be done in a minute. How was the roller-skating?

Fine, said Gail. She didn't want to think about why he decided to take a shower in the middle of the afternoon, but she thought about it anyway. Kimmie was studying her own hands, as if she'd never seen such ingenious devices before. Are you going to stay for dinner? said Gail.

Kimmie nodded. Cannibals cook people in big black pots, she thought, the idea inspiring a thousand more in a second. They make soup or stews, right? She wondered if anyone had ever tried to feed her human flesh, if that was why she had thoughts that weren't her own. She didn't want anything like that to happen to Frank; she really should try to get him to be careful about what he ate.

Gail reflected; it was her house and her kitchen, and shouldn't the girl know that she took care of Frank too? They could be allies, since they both wanted the same thing. I don't know what to make, she said. I've been trying to get Frank to be a little more careful about what he eats.

Bop bop bop. —Kimmie's mouth started trembling. Maybe Gail

wasn't so young. Maybe she was very, very old but just looked young. How else could she have read her mind exactly, and where was her privacy? She wondered if there was a point to proving that she was transparent. It was a warning, or else they were trying to convince her that she was crazy. It was a mean thing to do. She stood up quickly from the table. You didn't have to say that, she said to Gail; and she ran from the room, taking the stairs two at a time until she reached Frank's bedroom, where she slammed the door shut, leaving her alone inside with her heart beating a thousand times a minute.

14

Oh, she could hear everything, couldn't she? All the radios and televisions, all the satellites in the sky, which was blue but would soon be black. She could hear the corpses singing to call nighttime in, the screaming of airplanes as they fell to the ground. She heard her name: Kimmie. Kimmie. Kimmie. She could feel a burning in her mouth, a strange taste on her tongue. She tried not to think about where it might be coming from. Her mouth was burning. There was a strange taste on her tongue. She could tell: they were getting to her everywhere, with aerosols that they sprayed through the air duct in her bedroom, with drugs that they put in her water, with invisible lights that they beamed through her window. Kimmie. Kimmie. She could tell: it was her job to program the radio, to think of a song, so they'd play that song. That was her sign, her message. She stared at the pattern of the wallpaper on Frank's walls: it was the letter s, it was the number 5. She marked the hour, just like they told her to: it was five o'clock in the afternoon, and it was always going to be five o'clock in the afternoon, always that twilight at the window, always that stillness on the earth, always now and evermore.

15

Frank came in the room and found her lying face down on the bed, with her head beneath a pillow; she wasn't moving and he thought she was asleep, so he quietly pulled on a pair of pants and a t-shirt and tip-toed out of the room. Downstairs, Gail was still sitting at the kitchen table, wearing a pained expression. What's wrong? said Frank.

She hesitated. I think Kimmie's mad at me, she said.

How come?

I don't know. I said something about dinner and she left. I'm sorry. I didn't mean to make her mad.

I don't think she's mad, said Frank gently.

She didn't say anything to you?

She's upstairs sleeping.

—But she was standing quietly in the doorway. What are you say-ing about me? she said, and Frank jumped and turned.

Just that you were sleeping, which I guess you're not.

Kimmie shook her head. I wasn't sleeping, she said. I think I should go home.

What do you mean?

I want to go home, she said. I don't want to talk about it. You already know what I'm going to say anyway.

Aren't you going to stay for dinner? said Frank.

Did I do something wrong? said Gail, but Kimmie shook her head at them both.

I want to go home, she said again.

There was a long period of silence in the kitchen, crumbled into seconds by the ticking of the grandfather clock in the hallway; none of the three broke their expressions, Kimmie adamant, Gail frightened, Frank vexed. At length he said, I guess I'll take you home then.

In the car on the way she saw houses that looked as if they'd been inflated, like balloons, and she noticed that they passed the exact same cherry tree twice. This isn't the way to my house, she said, and when he looked over at her she was shaking.

Are you all right? —She said nothing in response to that, but a few blocks later, when he pulled up to a stop sign, she stared at the white S, and then suddenly threw open her door and ran from the car, slipping back between two houses and disappearing into the neighborhood, and all Frank's calling and searching failed to find her, throughout the remainder of the evening.

16

Summers end in *tears* and decades end in *madness.* Cells *split* and *signal*, and a *fire* begins beneath the skull. There are *signs* in the *petals* of *wildflowers*, in the whispering of *cities*, in the *jingle of ice cubes in a glass.* Sex is *suicide.* Doctors *cut* into the skin, lawyers *lie*, lie, lie. The following day, a Sunday, Frank called Kimmie at home; her father answered. Hello, Dr. Remington. It's Frank. Is Kimmie home?

No . . . I thought she was with you, said Dr. Remington.

There are *pills* in the *cabinet, liquor* on the shelf, *rain on* the window-sill and music *everywhere.*

She left last night, she said she wanted to go home, said Frank.

There was a long pause on the other end of the line. She's not in her room, said Dr. Remington. Her door is open, so I know. I haven't seen her.

People choose the *clothing* they wear, because clothing *is a secret sign.* Only objects live with a reason; people are *machines.* They give out names so that they will *know who everyone is. Cocksucker.*

Kimmie didn't come home that day, nor the day after, nor the day after that. Weeks went by and she didn't come home. Frank would search the schoolyards of Washington, D.C.; he called hospitals and the police, watched television for any picture, and read the papers for any story. He half expected to simply run into her, on the street or in the lobby of a movie theater, on a bus, in a store. He had tears always waiting for the spasm that would set them off, a sob threatening behind certain syllables—words with *ha* in them, or *gr*, or any word that began with a *b*—and he had to be careful about what he said, sometimes planning sentences well in advance, so that he could avoid certain obstacles, and be prepared for any that remained. The camera went into a drawer; he didn't take any more pictures, but he studied the ones he'd made of Kimmie, again and again and again, and he began to tear others from magazines, anyone who looked like her, who had her skin or her shoulders or her smile. For several months he stopped masturbating altogether, because he couldn't find a fantasy that didn't feel poisonous.

From time to time he would stop by Dr. Remington's house, to sit with the man and wonder. Was she taking something? her father asked. Did you give her something, some drug?

Nothing, said Frank. No, no, no. We never did anything like that. —But they had taken those pictures, hadn't they, and he couldn't keep himself from wondering if there was something he had stolen from her in the event; and if her grief was for its loss; and if there was, or would ever be, anything that he could do to make it up—anything he could return to her, anything he could say, anything he could be, if not to heal her then to join her.

They have methods, *they* never tell. All *thoughts* must be written down, *so* that when they change them it is still possible to *know* what they were. *Solitude* is real. *Laughter* is an evil, dogs *are* an evil. We *are all* part of one consciousness, *which struggles* against itself.

Kimmie called her father from Santa Fe four years later; she had found a place on the edge of the known world, but she needed money to pay the rent. Dr. Remington's features turned to pewter when he heard her voice. Will you please, please, please come home? he said. —Home? she said. I'm on the planet. Mars, the planet of war, Venus, the planet of love, Pluto, the planet of cold. He flew to Santa Fe that evening, checked into a hotel, and consulted with the police and social services the following morning. They knew who she was, and with their help he found her, living in a small dark room by the railroad tracks. She had painted over the windows; beside her bed were three combination locks. She didn't know where they had come from, who they belonged to, or how to open them. A *bomb*, *A-bombs*, *candy* bombs. Her red hair was long and matted, and she had split her underlip by biting on it. *Look what they did to the aborigines, to the Indians, to the people of Tibet.*

He called for an ambulance. I guess I can go now, she said, nodding casually. I need some rest. That's true. She went to the hospital without resisting, and there they cleaned her up and put Haldol into her head, until her thoughts were muffled and her brain slowed down to a mumble. After a week her father took her back to Washington; on her chart the doctors had written a mirror-lettered couple, of curves half split and sharpened, the story of an S that gazed upon itself in a pond and saw within the ripples a fractured Z. During the flight home, Dr. Remington wrote the diagnosis over and over again with a ballpoint pen on a paper napkin while his sedated daughter slept beside him—a swirl of SZ's, inside, beside, bestride one another.

17

Frank Cartwright stood in his office, his broad desk bare, the computer screen dark, the telephone resting in its charger. A half-empty tumbler of scotch and ice sat next to the box in which he kept stationery, resting in a ring of its own condensation. It was night, and out the window he could see small white lights strung among the leafless treetops far below, holiday decorations put up months ahead of time. He lowered the blind and turned on the halogen lamp affixed by a metal arm to the bookshelf, and then aimed it at the wall.

There were three photographs pinned there, side by side. The first, on the left, was the picture Kimmie had sent him: dauphin cowboy and baby girl, gazing and grinning, —at whom? Behind the lens there must have been some absent authority, mother or father, and it frustrated Frank that he couldn't see who it was, he couldn't simply turn the picture over and find the back of its making on the back of the print; instead, all he found was that notation of a forlorn and romantic convergence of space and time. Memphis, 1966, when the shutter opened and the flash went off, and he and Gail were fixed in a world from which, shortly afterward, they would be expelled.

Then this: the first girl he had ever loved, the second thing he couldn't keep, the last time he'd spent as a boy. It was the only picture of Kimmie that he could find; the rest had been long since lost, and he winced to think of where and how, with the abashment of a man who's been helplessly careless with breakable things. She was standing naked at the foot of the bed, the mattress against the front of her thighs, and from years away she was tiny, she was just a child, hardly big enough to bear desire. Frank the Boy still stirred to look at her; Frank the Man found her so fragile and unformed: she was only Amy's age, and he could hardly contemplate her as a lover, even once upon a time. He wondered, was she better now, along with being a woman? And what did she want from him?

The third photograph was of Helen and Amy, the first standing in a kitchen, the second an infant in her arms, as she was and would never be again. These pictures of women—every picture in the world was a picture of women, even when there was a man among them—they represented the generations of Frank. But there was one picture missing, the earliest of them all. Come on: What did his mother look like? And what did his father look like next to her? What sizzling genomes made the boy, what pottage of soul and skin? He had nothing to do but finish his drink and think about it.

Frank Cartwright, the inimitable, the uncanny original, once the medium and the taste of his times, Frank Cartwright went out. There was a wild wind blowing down the avenues, and if wind was nature he would have felt like an explorer, or the monster an explorer was pursuing. His gait was lurching a little bit, but his mind was perfectly clear.

The avenue was fluttering with women's capes and men's coats; he wandered down the narrow streets, the sound of his own footsteps ringing back from the walls. There was a bar on every corner he passed, each a little stage set, carefully designed, distinct, animate. Some were filled with young businessmen in tight dark suits, in packs of twos and threes, drinking imported beers with ladies who drank sweet cocktails; some were filled with sports fans, every neck craned to the television screen in the corner, while from their throats came loud sounds of approval or disappointment; some were filled with drunken children, and some scattered with old men. He started south, propelled by the breeze.

Amy was in Los Angeles; what time was it there? He should call her, just to tell her he was thinking about her; but it was late and he'd wake her. He should give her sleep. She would be sixteen soon, and what could he send her? Pearls for his daughter, he thought. Presents all the time, a princessdom in a world so safe that even sixteen was safe. Confidence, when she lacked confidence; laughter whenever it was possible. Preparation—let it be a long way away—for loving a man, and being loved by a man in return. Beautiful things, the trappings of luxury, pretty dresses, happy birthdays. Married parents, that had been impossible, the one emblem of belovedness he hadn't been able to provide; but the rest. . . . Frank studied his hands. Down the avenue he could see the luminous mist of the New York City sky. Then it was three in the morning, his bed was white and bare, his sleep was stuffed with anxiousness and he traveled in his dreams, though to nowhere he could identify.

18

This is just so we can get to know each other a little bit, said Lenore Riviere.

O.K., that's fine, said Frank. He had arrived one afternoon at a vast and elegant hotel on Central Park South. It had been raining madly all morning, the day was dark, the streets had tides, the cab was a boat and the floor was wet. The doorman had come ducking out of the front door to shepherd him in, and together they ran back for shelter. Inside, the hotel's elevators were hidden from the lobby by halls that turned three different corners. On the eleventh floor he had found her door, knocked, and was greeted, a long moment later, by the woman herself.

He had seen photographs of her, but they were twenty years old, images from which this fabled dowager descended. Now she wore her white hair down to her shoulders, tucked back behind her faintly jaspered ears; she was clad in black trousers and a black sweater, and she was barefoot. She was tiny, but her posture was as plumb as a dancer's and she was swift on her feet. She'd watched him with hawk's eyes, the lines extending outward and the semicircles of flesh below framing them in an art deco filigree, as if they too were an artifact of design left over from the days when she was young. She put her hand on his shoulder blade and guided him into the living room of her suite, where she nodded to a middle-aged man—assistant, adviser, lover—who promptly left the room through a door on the far side. There was a pitcher of freshly squeezed orange juice on the table, a bowl full of plump, brightly colored strawberries, linen napkins and crystal glasses.
—You can just put your wet things down wherever you want, she said, and he removed his coat and laid it carefully over the back of a wooden chair placed uselessly against the wall. Do you want to take off your shoes? said Lenore. The carpeting feels very nice underfoot.

I'm all right, said Frank. Thank you.

She studied him for a moment. You're a big fellow, aren't you? she said, briefly taking hold of his upper arm and squeezing it. That's good. I like that. Sit anywhere, she said, and he took a white velvet armchair.

Do you have something for me to read? he said.

Let's just talk.

I still haven't seen a script, said Frank. I've got no character, I don't know . . .

You're a powerful man, said Lenore. How's that? A very powerful and ambitious man at the height of his achievement, at a moment when all may be won or lost.

Lenore, that's not enough. —He shook his head in exasperation. I came here, I thought you were going to give me something to read. I can't consider a part if I don't know who I'm supposed to be.

Be yourself. Be Frank Cartwright. We'll get to all of that other nonsense in due time. For now, I just want to talk.

The word *ready* came from the next room.

Ready? said Lenore, and she slowly stood and started for a door on the far side of the room.

Frank followed, muttering something soft to himself about this craziness. Through the door there was another, smaller sitting room; the middle-aged man had vanished through another door, into another, yet farther and more private room. There was a pair of dark brown leather chairs arranged to face each other across a table lit by a small pool of incandescent light; there was a 16mm camera behind one: Lenore motioned him to the second. He stood before it and then turned and slowly sat. The director handed him a clip-on microphone and he attached it to his shirt; then she reached back briefly and set the camera going, and sat across from him, her elbows resting on the table, a small and slightly haughty smile on her face.

I didn't know we'd be filming, said Frank.

This is just for me. Maybe for the studio. If I decide to let them see it.

See what? he said.

I just want to ask you a few questions, said Lenore. Simple things, about your life and how it's gone. Will you humor me? Frank hesitated, and then nodded. All right then, she continued. Let's begin with . . . Are you married?

Frank paused for a few moments. Not really, he said.

Yes, said Lenore. I know what that's like. Do you have any children?

Fifteen.

Boy or girl?

Frank stared at her carefully. Four of them are boys, eleven of them are girls.

—Oh, said Lenore. I thought you meant . . .

He stared a moment longer and then smiled gently. That was a joke, he said.

Oh. —She took it well, though he hadn't known if she would, and he felt a little bit ashamed for having fun at an old woman's expense. Tell me about her. Does she live here in New York?

They're around, said Frank.

There was an awkward moment, and then Lenore said, Very well. Tell me . . . All right, about the first woman you ever loved.

Her name was Kimberly, Frank said immediately. I was sixteen, and she was seventeen. She was perfect.

You've been thinking about her. —She said this as if she cared more for his musings than for anything else in the world, and he nodded. —What happened to her?

He thought for a moment. Trouble came and got her.

You lost her?

Of course, said Frank. Everyone loses the first.

Is that right?

Frank smiled. Am I ever anything but right?

Mm, said Lenore. That's what I'm looking for. That's why we're here. —She seemed to lean forward a little, though she hardly shifted her posture. —Tell me about your father.

Frank's smile contracted to respect. He was a good man, nice man.

What did he do?

He was a machinist. He was quiet. Generous. He took me in and treated me well.

Took you in?

Yes, said Frank. —Outside the rain had stopped, the air was still and cool, and a mist was over the face of the city.

From what? said Lenore.

He took me in, said Frank.

Took you in, repeated Lenore, as if it were a hypnotist's phrase. Took you in.

Yes.

Adopted you?

Yes.

Then before that? said Lenore.

Before that?

Yes.

It all seemed soft, the boundary of light, the faint reflection of the lens behind, the rain hanging just outside, questions. Was that the smell of hyacinth? It must be coming from a vase somewhere in the darkness beyond their cell of illumination. O.K. And the quiet. It's not something I talk about, he said.

Never? said Lenore. She sounded surprised by the notion, and slightly incredulous, as if he'd told her that he'd never tasted orange juice, or that he'd once gone a year without sleeping.

Frank shrugged, frowned, shook his head, wondering all the while if he seemed too casual, like a suitor whose utter nonchalance suggests an infatuation which mild interest might hide better.

Ah, said Lenore, and then there was silence, a showdown. She looked at him sadly but he couldn't tell if she was seeing a man or a film.

He gestured toward the camera. Can we turn that off? Lenore nodded, stood, switched off the camera and opened the case, exposing the stock inside, thus ruined.

There you go, she said. Better? Frank winced at the loss, however it may have been motivated. It's just film, she said gently. They make it by the mile. —And time, she added. They make it by the decade. Didn't anyone ever explain that to you?

Who could explain such a thing? he said.

Well, said Lenore, I guess it explains itself, sooner or later. She thought about that for a moment, and he could see her eyes glaze a little. I had a husband, you know, before I came to America. He was a lecturer at the university, she said. Architecture. I was one of his students. Quite a sad man, really. More than anything he wanted to build, but every time he submitted a design to a competition it was rejected. Then at last he received a commission; it was for a small apartment building on the outskirts of town. A nice design it was, too: lovely, simple. When they finished building it he was suitably proud, and then he went back to lecturing. —She paused and said, Hm. Five years later the War began, and that building was the first thing that got knocked down. By one of our own bombs, too, that had gone astray in battle. Poor man. I never did divorce him. Well, in those days one didn't, not very easily. Instead I came here and simply married again. —She smiled softly. —I suppose that makes me a bigamist, doesn't it?

A felon, said Frank, returning her smile.

A felon, yes. Now you have something on me. She turned a bit in her seat and leaned forward. Then: I have a story, she said. A young Prince—not a boy, but he has spent his life dutifully waiting—is newly appointed to the throne after the death of his father, and soon discovers evidence of a taint on the palace. There are rumors, then rumors confirmed, that his mother, the Queen, was taken by force when she was young and fair, just before the King had wed her. The perpetrator was a general in the King's army, newly returned from a campaign overseas, unaware that the maiden he raped was the Queen-to-be, and considering her—as beautiful as she was—his rightful reward for his sacrifices on the battlefield. Our Crown Prince, our inheritor, is the issue of that crime, a bastard unknown to his father. He seeks his revenge upon the general, who still lives. —You see? said Lenore. This is our dilemma. Now, what is he to do?

Frank thought for a moment, taking in the circumstance, confident enough to take his time. The Queen is still alive? he said.

Perhaps, said Lenore. And he regards her, as he does the late King, with great fondness.

He uses the power of his office to prosecute the general, said Frank.

A paradox, said Lenore, with an air of supreme interest. Such an act would undermine itself in the proof; for if he's not the King's son, then he'll never be the King, and he has no office.

Then he's doubtful, isn't he? said Frank. Our Prince: doubtful of his own powers. He's been waiting all these years, and now? Is he royal, after all, or merely another man? Can he assume the throne rightfully? The general could as easily expose him as the reverse.

Moreover, said Lenore, there's the humiliation of his mother to consider, and the reputation of the late King, even in his grave. And the security of his people; for the King has had no more heirs.

All right, said Frank. He confronts the general in private, and destroys him.

Patricide, said Lenore. No easy act, even if the father, thus understood, is hardly a father at all. Besides, the general's troops are more loyal to him than they are to the throne. And yet he must do something, she continued. It's his obligation, as he assumes the throne, to assert his authority and see justice served.

Frank nodded, now engrossed in the problem. There was a long silence while he pondered it. —Wait, he said at last. There are inconsistencies.

Go on, said Lenore.

The King didn't realize that his bride was broken?

The King was no more experienced than the Queen, said Lenore. It is easy enough to hide such a matter, especially on a night so momentous. Besides, his physicians had examined her before the assault, and found her fit to be his wife.

He wasn't suspicious of how soon his son was born?

A matter of a few weeks, here or there. A claim of prematurity.

The Queen had no compunctions about mounting such a deception?

Some, perhaps. But to see her child raised as royalty, rather than cast out into bastardy. . . . Quite a few blameless women have done a greater evil for a smaller good.

Yes, said Frank. I suppose they have.

So, said Lenore. What is he to do?

It took a moment to realize that the question required an answer. You don't know? he asked, and she shook her head.

Come, Frank, she said. I'm leaving it for you to settle. Solve for x and you can have the part. You can play it without a word, if you wish.

He was tempted, but he laughed and said, I haven't told you I wanted it.

That's true, said Lenore. But of course you do want it, don't you? My difficult man. My silent man. Come back and help me. Tell me how it goes, and we'll finish it together. Make this with me, darling.

I'll think about it, said Frank.

She stared at him for a bit, as if expecting that he'd finish thinking about it right there and then, and agree to join her. And in truth he nearly did, so compelling was this tiny woman, and fitting was the role, and flattering was her plea, and intriguing was the problem she had posed for him to settle. He wondered if she'd somehow discovered the story of his origins; with enough money and curiosity all things become public. She might have composed the plot just for him. He stopped and mused over the possibility that he should feel offended. But who could be offended by a tale so tenderly offered?

Solve this for me, she said.

I'll think about it, he repeated. He stood and thanked her, and together they started for the door, collecting his raincoat along the way.

Is it still raining out? Lenore asked the middle-aged man, who had appeared again from his exile.

The middle-aged man nodded. Still, he replied. Again.

Well, bundle up then, she said to Frank, and she took his coat by the lapels and pulled it more tightly closed, and then patted him affectionately on his chest. You think about things, she said. Call me if you want to, for anything: to talk, to ask me a question, to run a suggestion by me. Anything.

He smiled and said, I will.

19

THE BALLAD OF THE LITTLE SISTER

We were alone, I didn't mind,
Sprung as children from strife itself
Or Tennessee, or winter wind,
And set back down, together, safe.

—Or safe enough: in dreams behind,
The ogres squatted in the trees.
I looked back almost all the time,
He looked back even more than me.

Blue below and blue beneath,
Do as you say, and say as you do.
There's more to a marriage than wanting to leave,
Say as you do, and do as you please.

Oh, there are those who look abroad
For pornographic ecstasy
And there are those who don't, the brides
Of patience, good cheer, modesty.

Here I stay, for here I chose
To prove the choice, this song I sing
With verses long since memorized
—But melody's the tricky thing.

> Blood below and blood beneath,
> Say what you mean, and mean what you say.
> There's less to a marriage than absolute faith,
> Mean what you say, and say what you may.

The little sister knows these things:
A telephone ringing late at night
Should not be answered, bringing
As it might, news of death—or worse, of life.

So I will stay here with my boys
And make a house, and call it peace
And pass along my local voice
And die when living comes to cease.

> Love below and love beneath,
> Mean what you do, and do what you mean.
> Always a little is always enough,
> Do what you can, and mean what you will.

20

Lenore was a witch. —Sympathetic and endearing, but a witch; Frank soon found out, his days were hers, and he loved her all the more for it. The puzzle she had set him perplexed him mightily; its logic seemed locked down, the situation irresolvable, no action possible and inaction inexcusable. He couldn't escape it; for days he sat at his desk and contemplated it, sandbagged, so he thought, by his stupidity. The pressure on his imagination was intolerable. He jotted down thoughts, new characters, laws of nature to suspend, laws of human conduct, pleas to God and the muses who served him, curses upon Lenore, bits of business, scenes, slapstick, unanswered dialogue. This old woman had knotted him up in his own vanity: To be taken for a talent greater than vesselhood, wasn't that every actor's desire? And here it was: But now he didn't know if he was the player or the played.

Outside his window the city went on, so many thousands of thousands—what was the word?—*teeming*. He went and watched. What a view, what a world. A man could vanish in there and never be found, and his story would have to be invented after the fact, a pattern pulled from random events, a figure, like a constellation seen in a scattering of stars.

Just so: The whole of his life seemed a mighty flurry, an endless cataract of accidents and reactions, decisions made without reflection, amid which swirled scraps of paper, certificates, forms, pages of scripts, checks, and conversations ended before they were complete, goods purchased and thrown away, takes never printed, people hardly enjoyed before they were lost, moments slipping away before they could be calcified into experience. He stood from his desk and looked around the room, so tastefully decorated with ashes and the wages of ashes. Now he was pacing the floor, and he could feel his situation doubling up on him, a mirroring inside himself, the role and the real reflecting each other, the show and the circumstance, back and forth and back again, until he couldn't tell which one would prove the other. He felt an immense desire to please Lenore that he hadn't expected and couldn't explain, —she was a witch, a witch, and he wanted to help her, to save one, to make her proud of him, oh, to earn the part.

Then what did he have to do? There was no theory to cover this, nothing in a book, no advice to heed. He needed simply to be more himself, so he could be more another. He stopped his pacing and ticked his head, as if he were listening to a faint buzzing sound, the word to go. He laughed out loud; he had nothing to lose, and there on his feet, in a fit of ambition, he decided to pilgrim back to the kiln itself, the ember, the origin of his Franksomeness, the beautiful diligence of his daughter's face, his true part and portion at last.

21

Outside the airport in Memphis it was evening, and the air was sweet and warm and smelled faintly of perfume, or whatever it was perfume was made from: the lust of flowers, the promise that you've known a certain place forever and will know it forevermore. It gave him the sensation of having entered into some aboriginal scene, the stage on which, not just his origins were played, but the beginnings of the very world: so cheerful, so corrupt, all sex, and sung out loud.

There was a line of taxis waiting outside, and he hailed the first. It was painted green and grey, and there was an advertisement for a computer company on the door. I need a hotel room, he said to the driver.

Anywhere in particular?

Frank thought for a moment. You know where the main library is?

I've been pushing a hack for thirty-three years, said the cabbie. I know where everything is.

All right. Take me to a hotel within walking distance of the library. That'll do me.

A few minutes passed while they wheeled down Lamar Avenue: signs with pictures of Elvis Presley, neat little malls made of chain stores and car parts stores, old houses on new roads, and green growing everywhere. You need anything else with that room? said the cabbie.

What did you have in mind? said Frank, just to hear the list of available vices.

The cabbie shrugged. Maybe some company, he said. Maybe some medicine. Maybe some entertainment of some kind. Whatever you're maybe thinking about, I don't know.

No thanks, said Frank. I'm just thinking about getting a good eight hours' sleep.

There was another period of silence and Frank went back to watching out the window as the city turned by. Was it the capital, Memphis? Probably. Or was Nashville, or—what were the other cities—Chattanooga, that was in Tennessee, right? And the other one, that sounded like Nashville. . . . Knoxville. Memphis was for Egypt, Chattanooga must be an Indian name. He wondered who Mr. Nash and Mr. Knox had been, and what they had thought of each other.

Were they rivals in the city-fathers racket, or was one a disciple of the other? And what about their wives, their children? *Sir, I am Josiah Nash. —As in, the gnashing of one's teeth? —(Drawing himself up to his full height) Sir, as in Nashville.* What brings you to town, then? said the cabbie.

You've been doing this thirty years?

That's right. Thirty-three. Yes.

Do you remember, back then, probably just when you were starting, a story in the papers? Man named Selby did something to his wife. —He didn't like to speak the name out loud; it felt minatory and blue, as if it naturally went with his next line. Killed her, I think. I'm pretty sure. Anyway, she was dead, and he was put in prison.

When was this?

Back when I was a boy.

The driver tipped his head up and looked in the rearview mirror, studying Frank's face for a moment. Hey, he said. I've seen you. You're that man in the pictures. I used to see you in magazines too. Frank thought for a moment about slipping on the disguise which was no disguise; mere denial, he'd used it before—smiling: *No, that's not me, I get that a lot*—and often enough it had worked. There were many faces in this world, and it had been a while since he'd made a movie. Instead he nodded.

Are you down here for a movie? said the cabbie.

Something like that, Frank said. Do you remember the case I'm talking about?

Don't know for sure, the cabbie said. In those days, that sort of thing happened often enough. What was it? Wanted her money? Caught her in bed with another man? Couldn't take her nagging anymore? —He paused for a second and glanced at Frank again.

That's what I'm trying to figure out, said Frank.

And on the cabbie clacked and guffed: Well, Memphis was a sore town, Memphis was a foundry, where the fires of history once made a sound so new it stole the century. That was once upon a time; they had covered all that over, as if it was something they were ashamed of. Mud Island, that used to be nothing but a swampy mound in the middle of the river, mosquitoes there as big as a man's fist. Now it's all cleaned up, parks and promenades. Memphis has come a long way in the past two or three decades. Is it better? Better for me, the cabbie said. I guess. Families come into town now, vacation, bring the kids, nothing to worry about. It's like an amusement park—what do you call it?—a theme park. They don't put murders on the front page anymore. I'm not saying it doesn't happen, just no one wants to hear about it. You know what I mean?

Frank nodded silently, and the cabbie glanced at him in the mirror again. I'll keep quiet now, if you don't mind, said the cabbie. I won't say another word. No, sir. —And truly he didn't speak again, until they reached a cinder-block hotel on a strip of superstores, fast-food restaurants, a mattress shop, a sporting goods store, then a dry cleaners, then a car lot, and the city going by on the road beside. The cabbie pulled into the driveway of a concrete monstrosity. This isn't so nice, he said as he pulled to a stop, staring up through the windshield at the hotel as if he expected it to step off monsterlike down the road. We've got much better downtown.

We near the library? said Frank.

It's right down there, said the cabbie, pointing toward the setting sun.

Then this is fine, thanks, said Frank, and he settled on the meter and tipped too much.

Inside, he gave over his credit card and signed his name, and the plump woman behind the desk hardly glanced at him. The place was much bigger than it looked from the outside, and he got lost trying to find his way through the corridors to his room; the numbers, too, seemed all out of order, 2212 following right on 2207, as if there were some sickly motel algorithm at work, the calculus of middle management on a bad day. 2219 was beyond that, and then the numbers started going down again, until at last he reached his own room, 2205, waiting for him at the very end of the hall. Inside it was so cold he could see his breath; he crossed the room and turned the air-conditioner off, then collapsed backward in a perfect arc onto his bed. There was nothing but news on the television, nor anything to look at in the room. He went to the window and pulled the curtains back: traffic hushing by on the boulevard, and on the far side there were railroad tracks, an endless train passing, beating on the evening air with a familiar segmented sound, like that of rhythmically dropped ladders. Men getting home at night. The idea of it made him sad and a little bit frightened—the picture of the front door of some modest house, the dirty yellow light in the hall, the wife looking worn, hardly a woman at all, and no words spoken. In time he went back to his bed and went to sleep, where he dreamed of Kimmie coming on to him in tears, her little thighs shiny, as young as she was and as out of her mind.

The next morning everything was new again; out the window the city was young, the plastic signs clean and bright, the world was working. It stung in knots, to think that his prehistory, as little as he knew of it, was someone else's bright, banal present. He found the library listed in the blue pages of the phone book in his room, and called for a cab as soon as he'd finished his morning coffee. The day was overcast but it was warm, and by the time he reached the place his collar was damp and sticking to the back of his neck. He had expected the building to be some venerable mausoleum, a relic of upward strivings; instead, it was a deceptively small structure made of poured concrete, with posters taped to the glass beside the front door, announcing Book Week, lectures on local history, a short course on how to fix cars. There was a wire-haired terrier chained to the bicycle rack outside; he bounded to the end of his leash and snapped at Frank as he passed, missing by a yard and settling, instead, for a wet growl.

He found a shelf of dark-blue bound editions of the *Commercial Appeal*, took a carrel, and began turning through newspaper articles, starting from 1963 and making his way back; back to the old days, when they were just the days. Stories, stories; he was taken by the fact that so many things had happened, and had seemed new when they first occurred. Business, government, arts, sports, sciences made of glass, recipes, advice; and then so many killings; there were murders by the mile, once upon a time in Memphis; so many names, so many deaths, the police reporters and obituary writers chattering endlessly in flecks of ink, gibbering as if that made it better: a car crash, a bar fight, the Battle of Blueberry Hill.

STATE OFFICIAL SLAYS WIFE

Governor's Aide in Passion Murder Probe
District Attorney Prepares Indictment

He scanned the page and collided right into his name, or the name he had come with: Selby's six-year-old son Frank, who was at the home of the family housekeeper with his two-year-old sister Gail at the time of the killing. What? There was his father's name, Walter, and his mother's, Nicole, and there was an account of her end. —Shot, he flinched at the word. Was it possible? He read the whole thing again, but it was stranger the second time. Frank, Gail, Walter, Nicole. Shot. So it came to that: a pinch of gunpowder: she was shot, that was what happened. —And there was a photograph, not of his father or mother but of a riverbank, and beside it another of a nice brick house on a shady street, house empty, street empty, history blank.

He read the story again and again, and as the shock passed a peculiar feeling began to develop, neither fascination nor sorrow, but something that made him feel a little bit sick: the familiar humiliation of fame. Grotesque, he thought, that anyone should have ever peered upon his life and the life of his parents that way, made them into grubworms, blanched and soft and vulnerable to the careless tread of strangers. These things so easy to see. For a moment he thought about sabotaging the oversized book before him, if he could figure out how, and he looked around him to see if anyone was watching—there was no one—but such a gesture would be futile; there were other books, other libraries, microfilms, and diaries, memories, stories, stones: no way to make the past be past. He exhaled, and then slowly, reluctantly, he left the revelatory page and began to move forward again. There was no account of the trial, only the sentence of ninety-nine years. He went back before the event: a month, two months, three, four years; the governor was in the paper almost every day, Walter Selby about once every two weeks. A spokesman reported . . . optimistic . . . budget. Never a mention of his mother, and he felt a certain insult on her behalf. This politics, it was already forgotten; tell the story of the Ship of Love. Tell what shore it had wrecked itself against. He began to wonder if there really was an era that all these reporters were talking about, or if it wasn't simply a myth, to explain and then obscure the mystery of his own origins. A young Korean woman slipped behind him, leaving a scent of crushed walnuts. What else was there? In a story about the governor's triumphant reelection he found a reference to his father's war record, but when he searched farther back in the newspaper, the volumes covering the months just after the War ended were missing.

Time was too much. To be these containers: it was too much. He thought about Helen and wondered if he'd ever wanted to kill her. It hadn't been a graceful parting, though it hadn't been too ugly either; there had just been mean days, every one breeding misunderstanding, disappointment, a resentment more chafing for the fact that they'd had to hide them from Amy: days as bitter as captivity. Maybe he'd thought of killing her, then, and had since forgotten. Maybe he should have done it, if only to prove how much he had once wanted her alive. To be the passionate son of a passionate man. No? An executioner. No? He was an heir to something more sorrowful than that.

There were no photographs in the papers of his father or his mother; names were cheap, back then, and stories hardly more expensive, but pictures were rare and not wasted on those who weren't famous already. But there was this, in an article describing a dress ball at the governor's mansion, on the occasion of his reelection to a third term:

> Among the guests were Mr. Walter Selby, one of the Governor's closest advisers, and his wife, Nicole; and Mr. Tom Healy, of the Army Corps of Engineers, who is overseeing construction on the Euchee Dam, and his wife, Janet. "It's a lovely evening," said Mrs. Healy. "It's so gratifying to be here with our friends, celebrating the continuation of a great period in this state's history."

That was a start; he shut the volume and went to the main desk. Excuse me, he said to the librarian, a thin, elderly black man in a pale-green polo shirt. Suppose I were looking for someone who lived here a long time ago. . . .

The librarian looked up blinking, and thought for a bit. At length he said, Oh, O.K. I can help you with that. He thought some more, and when he spoke again he seemed to be talking to himself. Time was, he said, people came into a library to read—I don't know—novels, books of poetry. To look at plates in art books they couldn't afford. They came with their children; it was a luxury, don't you know. Leisure. Lagniappe. Now all anyone wants is information. Doesn't it seem that way to you?

I suppose so, said Frank. I'm looking for someone who once knew my parents.

That right?

It is.

Well, I'm sure we can help you, said the librarian. If they're here, if they're anywhere in the country, if they're still alive, we can find them. Yes.

22

COYOTE

Out there authority was like handwriting on water, just gone by nature. Cash was the only stuff that persisted, and even that had a tendency to disappear: seventy-five dollars per head of wet ones, maybe seven hundred and fifty dollars for a ride across the river with the van full, and much of that went back into expenses: gasoline, oil, and maintenance, mostly for the suspension on the Econoline, which was soaked when the water from the Rio Grande hit the U-joint, became caked with mud as the van hit the opposite bank, and then broke up as he bounced along the roads of Big Bend. One time he'd snapped an axle ten miles into Texas, and there was nothing he could do; the State Police didn't catch him, they just stumbled upon him standing by the side of the road, the doors open, the empty van still reeking of the ten men who'd sat quietly for the five-hour ride and then bolted as soon as they realized that they'd been dumped in this wealthy wasteland. How many had been caught, how many died in the heat, how many made their way to farms in Arizona or Florida he couldn't say. The State Police held him for a few days and then sent him home to Juarez in handcuffs. He'd spent a month digging drainage ditches south of town, just to earn enough money to cross the border again, get the axle fixed, and bring his van back home.

Anyway, seven hundred and fifty dollars. Take away expenses and that left five hundred dollars per run. No more than one run a week at best, the rest of the time spent keeping his connections open, haggling with the men who guided his customers to him, scouting for shallow spots in the river and trying to keep track of the Federales' habits. Not a fortune to take home, even if home was below the border. But he got to drive.

Oh, driving. Had he been born and raised two thousand miles north, he would have been a champion, he used to tell himself. He'd be at Indianapolis by now. Indianapolis: he liked the sound of the word, its double waltz across his lips. Indianapolis, where they burned gasoline like they were boiling water. He watched the races every year and dreamed of that overpowering noise, the high, quavering wave of fantastic engines flashing by. At the end he would have swaggered through the winner's circle and climbed onto the stand to collect his cup.

The Econoline was no race car but it was a good machine, just a big light box on four small wheels, with a stable transmission and a strong, reliable engine. When it was empty he could mash down on the accelerator at a stop sign and it would seem to hop straight up in the air a couple of inches before darting forward. When it was full it could roll down a paved road like a boulder coming down a mountain. It wouldn't outrun the Patrol in a chase, but he could dance it along the back roads for a few miles and hope whoever was behind him banged up in a ditch before he did.

He remembered when he'd first seen it, dark blue with tinted windows, sitting on a side street on the outskirts of Juarez with a FOR SALE sign taped to the back door. He went home that afternoon and counted out his savings, —dollars mostly, with some pesos mixed in—which he kept in an empty coffee tin, buried under the concrete slab that lay outside his back door. He'd haggled with the owner for an hour or more, until finally he'd drawn the roll of bills out of his underwear, where it had nestled and grown damp against his groin; then he fanned it out, and waved it in the man's face. Is that all you got in there? the man had jeered.

Take it or leave it, said the Coyote, and the man had hesitated, his fingers twitching, and then said, All right, all right, and snatched the money from his hand, as a last gesture of disrespect. It didn't matter. He drove home that afternoon, sitting high up in the driver's seat and honking at a pretty girl in the street.

He had no particular use for the van at the time; but one day a fat man called to him from his neighbors' porch. It was no one he'd ever seen before, but his neighbors had so many people in and out that he never did know who lived there and who was just visiting. A rich pageant, isn't it? said the fat man, gesturing into the street.

What?

A rich pageant, Mexico. That your van? the fat man said.

Yes.

It's beautiful. What are you going to do with that van?

A shrug. Drive it around.

Why don't you come over here?

He hesitated and scowled a little.

Come on, come on, said the fat man. —So he went, but shuffling a bit, as if slowness was enough of defiance. I had a van like that once, the fat man said when he was close enough. A jackrabbit. Comfortable. High off the ground, but not too high. —Sit down, the fat man said. —So he sat, and he stayed all afternoon, and by nightfall he and the fat man (he was the brother-in-law of the neighbors' niece) were laughing and complaining like old friends. Near midnight the fat man said, Ah, yeah, the world right now. A kid like you . . . If he was smart, he could make himself a lot of money. And that was how he became a coyote.

Eleven times he'd been across the border, and only that once had he been caught. Twelve was a May night, overcast and cool, as luck would have it, and the Coyote was restless all evening. At ten, he climbed in his van, filled it with gas, and started down, southeast along the river toward El Porvenir, stopping in two or three little towns along the way to pick up his charges, pulling into a gas station or the parking lot of a cantina in the darkness, pocketing his money, and then opening up the back door and letting them in. Two brothers carrying plastic jugs of water, a man alone, some more that he didn't see, because after a certain point he stopped looking at anything but the cash in the palm of his hand. At midnight he was done; it was a dark, damp night, and as he started down into Cajoncitos he had nothing to steer by but his headlights. Here and there on the far bank of the river the Americans had night-vision goggles, but the border ran a long, long way—over eight hundred miles to Matamoros and the coast—far too long for anyone to cover. His uncle had told him about the Gulf, how the sunlight glittered on the waves. One night he wanted to make that trip, all the way east through Mexico to the water's edge.

For tonight, his job was to get his passengers across the river and twenty miles or so up north, where a second truck would meet them and carry them deeper into the country, dropping them off wherever the driver decided to go: San Diego, Tucson, Houston. That was not his concern; he needed only to get there. The water was high, and he would have to run all the way down past the Rio Conchos to a small, desolate pass a few miles from any town, a little west of the Chisos Mountains, where the width of the river made it run shallow and slow. In the back of the van there was no noise; he wouldn't have known that the passengers were there at all, if it weren't for the weight under his foot.

The turnoff was marked by a wooden sign, though whatever had once been painted on it was now weathered off. It appeared out of the darkness, and the Coyote slowed the van and turned. It was ten miles to the river and the road was just a dirt trail, rutted and pitted and so serpentine that he couldn't see more than twenty yards ahead. The going was slow, the van's suspension complained, in the back he heard a thump and a curse as one of his passengers was thrown from his seat. He wished he were alone.

Then the bank of the river appeared. He slowed, halted, and turned the engine and his headlights off. Certainly there was silence then, not even breathing from the back, not even the sound of water ahead. He opened his door and stepped out into the cool mountain air, the smell of dust, a small breeze.

He'd only walked a few paces forward when he stepped into the water, soaking his boots. He swore. Either there was no light for the river to reflect, or it was so dark that everything was swallowed, from a glimmer to a brightshot. He turned around in a full circle and there was darkness everywhere: the van was gone, the hills were gone, the sky was gone. This was the spot he'd found a few days previously, but there was no way to tell whether the water had risen since then, and nothing to do but go across. He stood there for a little while, not thinking but waiting for a sign that never came; he sighed and walked back to the van, climbing in and starting the engine while he shook his head. A proper plea to the proper saint. Be quiet back there, he said, though there had been no talking.

He eased forward, lights still off, the vehicle not so much rolling as slowly passing through a void, calm in the conduct of panic. There was a slight dip as he started down the near bank, a drag on the wheels as the van hit the water. He braked a little and then let it roll, breathing shallowly and listening as the river sloshed against the bottom and the gravel slid beneath his wheels.

It was about thirty yards across, as he remembered it, but three quarters of the way the wheels of the van became stuck in the soft bed of the river; he could feel them turning without effect. He shifted the transmission into a lower gear and tried again; again the wheels spun helplessly. He said nothing, even to himself, but he opened his door and stepped out into the water, knee high in the Rio Grande. Obscure above, unfriendly ahead. He slapped his palm against the side door, making a loud bang that drifted away on the water.

The Coyote walked to the rear, opened the door and peered inside. Everybody out, he said. We're stuck. His passengers started to file out, stepping down on the rear bumper and landing in a foot or so of river. For a minute or so they all stood there, gathered in a semicircle at the back of the truck, blinking in the darkness. It was four in the morning, and soon the sky would lighten. He wondered if his meet would still be waiting for him, and if not, what he would do with these dozen souls, these cats in a bag. God has his fat cock out, said one of the men, a teenager, really, who was wearing a length of rope for a belt. He's pissing down on us.

Don't say that, said another, who looked enough like the first to be his brother or cousin.

It's true.

That's why you shouldn't say it.

Everybody find something to grab on to, said the Coyote. We're going to get this thing out of the river if we have to carry it out.

Together they tried to shift the van, tried again, pushing and rock-ing, and tried again, —until at last, just as the sun was beginning its rise over an eastern outcropping and the rock forms around them were try-ing to appear out of the darkness, they succeeded in shoving it forward a few feet. There the Coyote got back in and tried the pedal again, and the van jumped forward. He drove the rest of the way across the river, leaving his passengers standing knee-deep in the water. When he reached the far bank he stopped and waved out the window with his arm, and they all waded over and climbed back inside. By now it was morning, first day, new world, and they were late. Hurry up, he said.

He set off again with great relief; they were in the U.S. and no one was looking for them. About a hundred yards in, he scanned the hills and roads for a glint of metal, a pair of binoculars or the chrome on a truck; but there was nothing out there, so he stopped the van, got out, and checked the undercarriage. He whispered at it. You're doing good, he said. Holding up well. So why don't we just start driving again and hope for the best? As he was stepping back into the van he looked up at the sky: by then it was bright blue and very hot, such a pretty color, but it would kill him and his passengers if they got too far from water or shade, and the blue turned yellow, the royal color of we've-got-all-your-money.

He took off down the road on the other side, making his way through the morning dust toward his rendezvous, the schedule broken, though how badly he couldn't say, and perhaps it might be made right again. Now he was steering through the Valley of Lunatics, with the Bootleg Mountains overhead: Cancer Ridge, Christ-Is-Risen Butte, Dog's-Ass Pass. The heat was starting to affect his passengers, who moaned from time to time, most often when he hit an impact in the road and they were thrown against one another. The van was bouncing quickly and hard, but the moaning was slow and extended, and sometimes continued up until the next bad bump. He sped up a little more, until he was skittering along the vast, tawny lunar surface of Big Bend. —Nothing, but he came roaring around the side of a rock outcropping and descended upon a man standing by the side of a big blue sedan, —a white man, —with a pair of sunglasses, and he felt for one brief instant the glittering reflection of the glass in his eyes before he pulled his wheel to the right, causing the van to slide off the road and start frantically up the wall of the ravine, insanely climbing like some huge ungainly goat, skipping upward a few yards on the terraces of stone before it struck a wall of rock; and the Coyote's head burst through the windshield amid a corona of blue-white glass, and the van fell backward again, tipping sideways and rolling over and over, until it landed on the floor of the road on its back, where it lay, wheels gently turning, the moans of the men within emerging from a great cloud of tan dust.

Late that night, from a dark motel room, Frank called all the way up the country to his sister in Kansas City. It was the strangest thing I've ever experienced, he said. Just a few miles from the border . . . Those poor people stumbling around in the heat, that man with his mask of blood, and miles to get to the nearest town. I stood out there and I tried to help; finally a truck came by, and I flagged him down and got him to call the state police. But I still don't know who lived and who died.

Are you all right? said Gail.

I'm fine, he said.

What are you doing down there, anyway?

Just visiting somebody, he said. But I'm coming, he said. I'm coming to see you.

Coming here?

Yes, he said. Is that all right, if I come?

That'd be great, said Gail. Anytime, you know that.

It would be about a week.

A week, then. Anytime. Anytime. What's going on?

Just a family visit. I want to say hello, said Frank. And I haven't seen the boys in almost a year.

Come on, then, said Gail. I'll put Kevin in with RJ.

I'll get a room in town, it's O.K., said Frank.

It is not, she said with mock indignation. Me or Big Richard will come get you at the airport, and you'll stay with your sister.

23

The next day Frank woke to find a redness on his forearms and his calves, the back of his neck was stinging and the tip of his nose was about to blister. The hours he'd spent in the sun the day before had burned him badly; he started to take a shower but stopped when the pain proved too much to bear. He dressed again and stepped back out into the furnace of his room, and then into the further furnace of the world, through which he made his way to the little square that served as the town's shopping district. In the center there was a big red-brick municipal building: courthouse, jail, police station, records office. Around it there were stores, each with a weathered wooden awning to shade the sidewalks below. There was an old pharmacy on one corner, with advertising placards in the front window—for sun-glasses, a balm, a regional brand of soft drink—that were bleached so pale they were almost unreadable. Inside there was a dun-colored fan whirring noisily on a metal stand, then a rotating rack of greeting cards, a row of emollients, first aid, bags of shredded tobacco, round bars of shaving soap, faded boxes of ballpoint pens. An entire history of ancient ablutions, untouched and waiting. There was some kind of unguent in a tube and he took it to the counter.

In the back there stood an old man in a white smock, his thin black and grey hair slicked back so that his scalp showed beneath; he had been burning down, like the building was burning down, slowly over the years. Before the register there was a small shelf of cosmetics, tiny things with curious purposes, little bottles of nail polish in shades from incarnadine to pale, pale pink; and a rack of metal instruments for this or that betterment: clippers and tweezers, curlers, brushes for blushes, and perfume. What forgotten girl used scents like these, to make her feel pretty and clean? He could tell by the printing on the bottles' labels that many of them were almost as old as the store itself. Even their names—Arpege, Bellodgia, Coty, Fabergé—suggested a past that only the past had wanted, the essence of romance as conceived by the small American cities of the fifties. Perhaps he could send one to Amy as a present. She would like that, she could wear it or just keep the bottle on her dresser.

He paid for his tube of ointment but instead of leaving he stood before the rack of fragrances, and his hand reached. —Do you mind if I smell these a little? he asked the druggist. The other man nodded. Go right ahead, he said, and disappeared back behind his cabinets of medications. One bottle was squarish, and the fluid inside was almost transparent, with just the palest trace of purple. At first the pump had no effect at all: then a fine mist, and the scent of violets, with a riverine sweetness behind it. The next bottle held something light and tart; the next was light and rose-like. He paused there and was going to stop, when he spied a final bottle at the end of the rack, faintly frosted and cut in a shape that was reminiscent of the underside of a swan's wings, the sepal of a flower, the tender curve of nightfall. There was no atomizer, just a silver cap, beneath which lay the thick lip of a small opening, designed to release one drop at a time; he placed the pad of his index finger over the hole and tipped the bottle once, drew the scent to his nostrils, and there was the smell of a familiar voice, a face bending over him in the dark, half hidden in shadows and swooning forgetfulness: goodnight, goodnight, sweet boy: his mother.

It was just that sudden, and he shook his head and took a step backward, holding the bottle out at arm's length as if it were something so violent that he could neither allow it near him nor let it go free. He looked away and drew one hand up to touch the tears in his eyes, as if he wanted to see if they were real, rather than a reaction to the sheer force of the impression. Slowly, he brought the bottle to his nose again. This time the sensation was merely a wisp, and he couldn't be sure that it meant anything at all; the presence was faint and sculling backward, a shy ghost, drawing away to meet the demands of its own dominion. Twice more he passed the perfume bottle under his nostrils, but each time there was less to be sensed; and at last there was only perfume, and even that was hardly distinct from the front room of the pharmacy, the smell of the sun, the day. The druggist came back out. You all right? he said.

Can I buy this?

That's what it's there for, said the druggist.

How much? said Frank. There's no price anywhere.

That's fourteen dollars, said the druggist. Any one of those, fourteen dollars. Those are old prices.

Do you have a box or something?

I ought to have something, back here. I think I do. The druggist bent down, disappearing behind the counter and rising with a small beige-and-brown striped box. He measured it against the bottle; it was too small. That's not right, now hang on, now, he said, ducking down again and emerging this time with something off-white and covered with a thin film of dust. Here we go, he said, blowing on it briefly and coughing once at the result; then he took the bottle from Frank's hands and laid it inside, turning it until it fit. Fourteen, he said again, and Frank paid him and took the package back to his motel, where he packed it carefully among his clothes.

24

Is this Tamara Healy? he asked the woman who answered the phone.

Who's calling? There seemed to be a note of suspicion in the woman's voice.

Frank Cartwright. I called from Memphis, about Walter Selby, he said. I'm afraid I got delayed a day.

There was a bit of silence, and then the woman said, Where are you now?

Del Rio, said Frank. I got a little lost. But I think I'm just an hour or two away.

All right, said Tamara; and now he was sure she was uneasy. Got a pen? I'll give you directions.

In time he found her driveway, a pale brown dry dirt road marked

by a mailbox. Then it was another three miles to drive; at last he came
to a frame house with a large screened-in porch and an old Lincoln and
a new Mazda in the driveway, both of them dulled by the dust that covered them. There was a pen made of cyclone fence in the yard; inside, a
patchwork mutt trotted threateningly along the edge of his domain,
then went paws up on the diamonds, wordless as Frank went wordless
toward the house. On the porch there was a woman sitting, about his
age; she wore blue jeans and a light blue chamois shirt, and she had
long brown hair and large, sunburned features. She stood and said, I'm
Tamara. Tammy.

The woman was broadly built, not heavy but athletic, her shoulders
wide, her face open and already creased by years in the border sun; she
was still young, but there was a screen of age over her, and it was possible to believe that she had looked just like this for decades, and would
look just the same for decades more. —Pleased to meet you, she said.
—It's funny: I saw you on television, not two days ago. —He winced,
but she didn't notice. It was quite an interesting movie, too. You were
in Rome; you were an ex-patriot, —an exile, I suppose. No, that's not
right. You were an archaeologist, and you were trying to smuggle arti-
facts out of the country. Or trying to prevent them from being smug-
gled, I don't remember. You didn't talk much. There was a woman; she
was dark, Italian, very beautiful. Of course, I didn't know it was . . .
you. —She paused, staring at his features, as if they were not the bear-
ers of his being but merely goods to be appreciated. It was a look he
was familiar with, from makeup artists, cinematographers, publicists:
an evaluation of his mask, his cover and his cost. Do you want something to drink?

He nodded. That would be great, he said, and she was gone, leaving him alone on the porch within a massive silence, all sound on the
wing and a wind that had nothing to bend. In time Tamara returned,
carrying a tray holding two tall ice-filled glasses and a sweating pitcher
of amber iced tea. She placed it on a wicker table and sat. Thanks for
your time, he said.

Time's cheap, she replied. There's plenty of time in a day.

I guess there is, said Frank. Can I ask you a favor?

Mm, she said.

I'm sorry, this may sound ridiculous, and please don't be offended,
—he looked down —but someday there may be a way for you to profit

from all this. Money, from a magazine, if you tell them what we talked about. It doesn't happen to me so much anymore, but you never know.

I won't tell anyone anything, said Tamara. Don't worry. She smiled confidently. I wasn't even sure I wanted to talk to *you*. There was another extended silence. She was gazing out into the landscape, though he couldn't tell in what direction; the sun was directly overhead.

How'd you end up down here? he said at last.

The woman ignored him, or perhaps she hadn't been listening. You and I used to play together, she said. When we were little children. Did you know that?

He looked at her and shook his head.

We were in that school together. What was the name of that school?

I don't remember, said Frank.

She snapped her fingers a few times, calling the name in. . . . Trumbull, she said at last. It was a good school. We were five or six years old, then. And now look at us. —But she was still looking out into the desert. She spun around another notion. My mother wanted grandchildren before she died. Didn't happen. Do you have children?

A daughter. Going on sixteen, he said.

Sixteen. . . . How is your sister? She was just a baby.

She's doing well. —He didn't want to talk about Gail; it would have been too much to tell. Tamara looked down at her shirt and plucked a stray hair from her abdomen with no expression at all.

Is that how our parents became friends? said Frank. We were in the same school?

That's how they met: my parents and your parents. That's how my father and your mother met, and then the rest of them. The two of us used to play together, and there they were, young parents. —She paused, breathed a few times, and started again. My mother told me all about it, about a year before she died. Because I asked her, she told me. —She died two years ago, right here in this house. That's what you came for, isn't it? To find out what she told me? —Frank mimicked her motionlessness, her quiet and calm regard.

Nicole, your mother, was very pretty, said Tamara. Beautiful, that's what my mother told me. And always well dressed. A sweet woman. She was a little bit younger than my mother, you know.

Then she was . . . said Frank.

Maybe thirty-two, said Tamara Healy. My parents came down here right after it all happened. They sent him down here to the border. Army Corps of Engineers, they were going to build a fence all along the way, from Brownsville to Tijuana. Keep the Mexicans out, and they sent him down to help. It was an experimental program, and they tried everything: cyclone fencing, barbed wire, reinforced concrete, steel. They built a few miles of it, right down there. —She pointed out onto the land. —But nothing worked, nothing worked at all. The illegals cut through the fencing, they cut the wire. They made holes in the concrete with pickaxes; they dug tunnels under the steel. My father sat up here and watched them come. I remember seeing him, in the evenings; he'd be up here with his binoculars, and they'd be walking down in groups of five and ten, as if nothing had been put up to stop them at all. Drove him crazy to see. Not that he hated Mexicans so much. He liked Mexicans, he really did, and he loved the U.S., and he thought everyone should be able to come, share in the . . . you know. Share the wealth.

Just there Frank would have said something sympathetic, but the woman had closed her eyes, and he didn't want to wake her from her story. At length she spoke real words again. Nicole was lovely. That's what my mother said, and she wouldn't have lied. Lovely. Dark hair, pale skin, smile. She and my mother were going to be friends. And your father was an awfully nice man. A good man. You want to know that. It may sound strange to say, but he was. He cared about things. —She paused there, as if she was waiting for Frank to ask her a question; and he had a question, so he asked it.

I was wondering if you happened to have a picture of them, he said. My parents.

A picture?

A photograph. I don't know what they looked like.

Oh, no, said Tamara Healy. I'm sorry, I don't. Nothing like that. Have you asked her family? Or his, I suppose.

Frank cocked his head and frowned: a gesture of surprise, ignorance, and coated embarrassment. Family.

Their parents are probably gone by now, said Tamara, but you might have an aunt or an uncle around somewhere. If so, I'm sure you can hire someone to track them down pretty easily.

I never even thought to check, said Frank. He stared incredulously at the floor. —I just assumed, there he was, and there she was, and the whole thing started and stopped right there. It never really occurred to me that there might be more of them. Of us. How could that be? Christ, what if they're all out there?

Tamara laughed once. I'll tell you, I don't know, she said. I wish I had some more of *mine* out there. Look at how old we're getting. And wise? You came all this way, and I'm not going to shit you, Frank. I don't understand a thing. —She stopped to watch a big black crow that was stalking about the yard and then fixed Frank in her sight again. After what happened, my father felt so bad. My mother felt bad too. Because she knew, you see, and she didn't do anything about it.

The sun was very bright, and it was making a faint, high-pitched whining noise, like an engine at its limit. Knew, said Frank, too softly for Tamara Healy to hear him.

She went on. They thought they were being so modern and so chic, up there in Tennessee. What was a little playfulness between friends? Who could say? He might even have been in love with her.

Frank sat back. It was your father?

What was my father?

With my mother. The one she . . .

Now there was the silence again, of a great still atmosphere over useless land. I thought you knew, said Tammy at last. Isn't that why you came?

I saw your parents' names with my parents', in a newspaper story. That's all, said Frank. When they wrote about the trial, they said she'd had an affair, but they never said who it was with. I didn't know. . . .

People were discreet in those days, said Tammy, without making it quite clear whether or not she thought those days were better than these. Frank felt slightly nauseated, it was the heat, and his sudden hatred directed at this innocent woman, for living with his mother's perfidy for so long. She was looking at him with the same flat unapologetic gaze. He wondered why she had agreed to see him, what she wanted: exoneration or to help him away. He stood.

She wanted to finish her story. She said: Your mother was young. And my father was very charming. He was always very charming, my father.

Tom, said Frank, still standing. O.K. Tom. What happened to him, anyway?

Sit, said Tamara Healy, and Frank sat down again. He wanted everyone to play by the rules, I think, after that. After what happened to your mother, he thought everyone should play by the rules. Including Mexicans; and he was down here trying to keep them out. Oh, he wanted a way to keep the Mexicans out. It became an obsession for him. It was all he could think about, and nothing was working. I mean, it wasn't his responsibility, really, if they got in. He had a job to do, and he was doing it as well as he could. But that wasn't enough for him. He wanted to get it right. I guess, finally, he thought maybe a scarecrow of sorts would do the trick. My parents sent me away to school when I was eight; my mother drove me up to Virginia. I'd never been away from home before. While we were gone, my father hung himself, —she pointed to the roof of the porch—right from that beam there. Facing south. My mother came back, he'd been hanging there for days. He must have looked a fright. —She paused. —Didn't stop the Mexicans, though. They just kept right on coming.

25

OPTIONS

1. Kill the General in private.
2. Kill the General in public.
3. Suicide.
4. Abdicate the throne.
5. Prosecute the General.
6. Disband the Army.
7. Do nothing.
8. Forgive the General; greet him warmly; retain the throne.
9. Marry the daughter of the General's enemy.
10. Blackmail.
11. Resurrect the King.
12. Turn over the throne to the Queen.
13. Exile.
14. Institute democracy.
15. Crown the Fool.
16. Etc.

26

Oklahoma City, Oklahoma, where everything was either brand new or very old, —old in that city, in those days, being thirty years or more, time enough for cheap design to change, for the edge of a car hood to square up or round off again, the cross on a church lawn to acquire neon or lose it, a phone company's logo to convey sex and speed rather than home and a bell. Yes, and in those days a sudden bang—the hatch on a pickup dropped, steel struck on a construction site, or an event as innocent as a child stepping on a milk carton— would make someone walking nearby flinch and start to cower, then quickly stand at full height again, maybe smiling with embarrassment, or looking around to see if anyone else had flinched as well (and often enough someone else had, and they would glance at each other and then quickly look away), or maybe just resuming the ordinary course of his or her gait, but with a certain darkness of spirit superimposed upon it, an imagination of death or disfigurement from shards of metal and glass; a fine dust of shattered concrete; heat and noise; and how-could-this-happen, when we have been so good to our friends and so friendly to Jesus Christ?

There was Frank, emerging from the airport terminal and saying to himself, Here's where the spark meets its kin, with the smell of airplane fuel all in the air, and that old Indian in walking shorts and no shirt, but with a woman's straw hat placed carefully on the back of his head, and the speed bumps in the parking lot, so that no one can come hurtling up to the entrance in a car. On the telephone Donald Selby had said he'd come to the baggage claim station and find Frank on that afternoon. Now the day was upon them, but there hadn't been anyone around who might be his uncle; so he walked outside, and the few people who were nearby were looking at him with a sort of sunny suspicion, as if they wanted to like him, maybe some recognized him, or maybe they couldn't help wondering why a young white man was coming into a city all alone, —wondering what, after all, he intended to do. A police car cruised slowly by on the road beyond the lot; there was a German shepherd in the backseat which began to howl and scratch at the window when he laid eyes on Frank, but the policeman behind the wheel ignored him. There was an elderly woman walking toward him, slowly, because of her age and her weight: she was grey-haired and massive. You must be Frank, she said, and he thought, I must be, and then he nodded and held out his hand for a shake, not knowing what other greeting would do for the occasion. I'm your Aunt Mary, the woman said.

27

I was standing next to him when the judge passed down his sentence, said Donald. I was there to help him; he was my brother. There was nothing I could do about that, and nothing I would do, even if I could. The house was large, the lot was shaded, the living room was penumbral and painted sea blue, as if in honor of oceans a thousand miles away. On the floor there was a thick shag rug, a dark shade of something; dim light came from a brass floor lamp; there was a small shelf of leather-bound books, a few Western prints in metal frames, a crocheted blanket folded neatly and draped over the back of a recliner, a large, dark television on a console in the corner. In the center of the floor sat a glass-topped table; on it there were white flowerpots with no flowers inside, a glass cat, a dish that may have been an ashtray or just a dish. A round mustard-colored upholstered footstool lay in the center of the room, where no feet could be rested upon it. Plants in pots on the mantelpiece, candy in dishes on the side table, the faint, heady smell of senescence in the air. Donald Selby and his wife were sitting side by side on an enormous blue corduroy couch, so deep in its cushions that they'd taken a good while to settle in; watching them, Frank couldn't help feeling as if it was incumbent on him to be gentle with them, these giants, these living witnesses. You have a sister, you know what it's like, said Donald. I worried about him for thirty years, and then when he got out I took care of him as best I could.

They let him out, said Frank.

Parole, said Donald. A few years ago.

Parole.

He served his time, said Donald, and then he held his hand up peremptorily.

28

When they released Walter, —said Donald, —it had been eleven years and three months since we'd seen each other. In the beginning, I used to go down to Brushy Mountain and visit him as often as I could. Every couple of months. Every six months, maybe. But the years went on and I saw him less and less often.

Not because he didn't care, you understand, said Mary.

It was just that neither one of us enjoyed the visits, said Donald. He found it humiliating to have me see him like that, and he felt guilty, I think, for the distance I had to travel. Instead, he wrote me letters regularly, and I wrote him back—less often, but often enough. We sent him packages, when he asked; Mary sent him things to eat, and we mailed books to him. Sometimes they let him have them, and sometimes they didn't. It was like that. I suppose we both were waiting for the day he would be released, when we would resume our brothership.

Brotherhood, said Mary.

Brotherhood, O.K., said Donald. And the years went by. My two boys grew, —did you know I had two boys? Your cousins, I guess. One of them is a captain in the Army, based out in California.

The other one died, not so long ago, said Mary.

He was a troubled boy, said Donald, frowning frankly. Always troubled. Drugs and such.

He died in a car accident, said Mary, and there was a moment or two of quiet.

. . . I guess we never really thought about what would happen when Walter was let out, said Donald. And then the day came. When he called to tell us, he sounded so sad about it, I couldn't understand why. I got off the phone and I said to Mary, Walter's getting out.

We were living here, said Mary. Right here in this house. We had all this room. I said to Donald, There's no question about it. He's going to come stay with us.

It was May when he was . . . *set free*, said Donald. I guess that's what they call it. *Released.* I never thought of it that way, especially when I saw Walter. He didn't look released from anything.

It was already hot up here, said Mary. Oklahoma, it gets hot midway through the spring.

Anyway . . . said Donald.

Anyway, said Mary.

They gave him a bus ticket, a Trailways bus ticket, said Donald. It stopped right at the gates of the prison. It was fifteen hours to Little Rock, and then another nine hours to get here. It was eight o'clock in the morning when he arrived. I remember that morning.

It wasn't raining, said Mary. We were all glad for that. Imagine getting out of jail, and it's raining.

Prison, said Donald.

Imagine getting out of prison, in the rain, said Mary.

He stayed in one of the boys' rooms upstairs, said Donald. A nice room, sunny room. He had trouble sleeping at night, though. It was too quiet for him, and the bed was too soft.

We went and got him another bed, said Mary. A harder one. That seemed to make him happier.

I told him he didn't have anything to worry about, as far as money was concerned, said Donald. And he didn't. He had some savings when he went in, and I'd invested them for him. Conservative stuff, you know. Certificates of Deposit, a mutual fund. I took care of all that.

Donald was always very smart about money, said Mary.

It was only a few thousand dollars, at the start, said Donald. But it had been growing for a long time. All by itself. It was a considerable sum. The first night Walter was free—no, maybe it was the second night—I sat him down and showed it all to him: all the papers, the passbooks. All that. It came to about three hundred, three hundred twenty-five thousand. And you know what? He started to cry.

We didn't know what to do, said Mary.

We didn't, said Donald. I figured, I might cry too, if it were me. But I didn't know what to say. Well . . .

How old was he? said Mary.

He was sixty-eight, I think, said Donald. But he couldn't do anything for himself. Almost nothing. You know, at that age most men are thinking about their retirement. I retired when I was sixty-six. But with Walter it was almost the opposite. What's the opposite of retiring?

Not retiring, said Mary.

He found it very difficult, I think, said Donald. He didn't talk about it much, but I could tell. What he had known, he had forgotten; and there were new things to know which he couldn't understand.

He wanted a new outfit, said Mary. Clothes, you know. He'd spent three decades wearing those prison uniforms, and he couldn't stand another day. I had saved some of his old clothes for him, but they wouldn't do. They wouldn't fit, for one thing. He'd gotten so much . . . I don't know how to describe it.

Harder, said Donald.

Stonier, I was going to say. Harder, yes, said Mary, while he was away. He was older, but he was harder, like old wood, if you know what I mean. I should have known that. I don't know why I saved them, anyway, they were so out of date.

I told her she might as well throw them out, but she wanted to keep them, said Donald.

Anyway, he went shopping one day, said Mary. But he had no idea what was fashionable in the world outside, and he was afraid to ask the salesgirl for help. He came home from the store in white jeans, brown shoes, and a red cowboy shirt. He was a sight, and he must have known it, but he didn't know what to do about it.

He used to sit at the dinner table and tell us all the things he didn't understand, said Donald. Ask us questions, What's this, what's that. How does this work.

He was like Rip Van Winkle. —Do you want some more water? said Mary. Frank shook his head.

He used to tell us: call waiting, contact lenses, price clubs, cell phone towers, said Donald. Words like *Ms.* on envelopes and *motherfucker* on cable television, all those wires and radio waves, all these plastic bags, men and women exercising, corporate parks, organic foods, signs in Spanish, video everywhere, radar guns, no one acted their age, there were so many messages from everyone to everyone, all those things flying around in space while all the streets below were empty, reminders and alarms of nothing more important than the day ahead.

He couldn't understand the names parents gave their children, said Mary. Brittany, Blue, Serenity, Rain. I remember that. What was wrong with the old names? he asked me.

It bothered him that there was pop music playing in every store, music coming out of every car, said Donald. The numbers all over everything, he said to me. The numbers. It seemed to him that half the nation was high on something the other half had never heard of, and he couldn't get over these debates about abortion on the radio, about cigarettes and guns. So many pairs of sunglasses, he said. So many sets of headphones, so many magazines, men in love with other men, monster trucks, movie stars he had never heard of, motion detectors, and the young were so beautiful. Vietnamese immigrants, twenty-dollar bills dispensed from street-corner machines, medicine cabinets full of prescription drugs, single mothers, sullen glances. He couldn't fathom all the signs and photographs; he called it, The world given over to advertising the world; and everyone was an entertainer.

I found him sitting on the back porch one evening; he was holding a glass of whiskey and his face was flushed, said Mary. A lot of things are different, he said to me. I suppose that's to be expected, but . . . Oh . . . I can't figure out which button lowers the window in the car. —I told him it would take some time to readjust, and you know what he said? —Adjust? he said. I don't think so. I'm a bad radio, a thousand miles from any station. And the program is old and faint; and the announcer is sad and tired. —Isn't that an interesting way to put it? He was always good with words, Walter was.

One afternoon he called from the street, said Donald, and Mary answered. He said he was in some kind of trouble, and he asked her to help him.

He was speaking very quietly, said Mary. But he really seemed to be panicking. I have to say, it frightened me. I didn't know what had happened. Donald was somewhere, I don't know where.

I was walking around the reservoir, said Donald. My doctor told me I should.

He was in a state, Walter, said Mary. The poor man. He really didn't know anything about how to get along. He said, I'm on the street. On the corner, at a telephone, on the corner. He said, I was in the store, and I wanted a little can of beans, I got it out of that refrigerator there. And then I found this little oven, and I pulled the top back and put the can in and turned the dial. And then I went looking around the store a little bit. There was this girl in there, also, and she was wearing hardly anything at all. —He noticed that. —So I came back, he said, and the beans were all over the place, I mean the can had exploded. —And he didn't know what to do, he didn't know what he'd done wrong, so he just walked out of there. He was convinced that somebody was following him, and they were going to have him picked up for something: shoplifting, he thought, or destroying property. He was down on the corner, a couple of blocks away. He wanted me to come down and get him.

It was a microwave oven, said Donald. That's all it was. Mary explained it to him, that it cooks things very quickly and all that, but you can't put metal in it. He'd never used one before.

I told him I'd come down, said Mary. I told him we'd go back to the store and get it all worked out. They won't be too mad, I said. —You know, it'll be pretty easy to clean it up. —I told him, If you offer to pay for the food, they won't try to have you arrested or anything. So you just sit, I said, I'll be there in a minute. And down I went. He was still standing in the phone booth, holding the receiver like he was talking to someone on the other end, but as soon as he saw me he hung up. I don't want to go back in there, he said. I'm just going to do something else wrong. I told him it was all right, said Mary. I told him I'd go back, if he wanted, and take care of everything. I said, I'm sure they won't be too upset about it all. But when I left the car he slumped down in his seat until he was hidden by the dashboard.

It took Mary about five minutes to get it all straightened out, said Donald. Right?

Three minutes, said Mary. He jumped when I opened the car door, and he looked like he'd been waiting for days. He asked me if they were looking for him. I said no, they weren't, that they'd already cleaned it up. It was just a couple of dollars for the food that got ruined. I paid it. He asked me how much it was. —He was a good man; he wanted to pay me back. But it was nothing, I told him it was nothing. Just a couple of dollars. When we got home he went to his room and stayed there for the rest of the day, thinking God knows what.

She didn't even tell me until later, when I got home, said Donald, and then only because I asked her why he was in his room.

I didn't want to worry him, said Mary. But he asked, so I told him. I said, I don't know if he's going to make it, like this.

I said to her, Well, he's going to have to, said Donald. Because he's not going back in. I know he's not, and he knows he's not, so we're just going to have to do the best we can to help him. But there was no way to know how he would react, or even what he would react to. He would stare at anything, trying to figure it out. Just a casual remark, something simple a clerk in a bookstore said, or the hostess at a restaurant, was so difficult for him: he didn't know how to respond, what was a joke, or maybe an insult, what required an answer; and when they were done talking, he didn't know whether to say good-bye or whether he should just turn around and walk away.

I tried. I really tried to help him. We both did.

After a while, though, he began to feel like he was a burden on us, said Donald. And one weekend he mentioned at dinner that he was ready to move out.

I asked him if he was sure, said Mary. I tried not to make it sound like I was hoping he was. But I'll tell you the truth: I was hoping he was. It was hard having him around.

It was hard on Mary, said Donald.

It was hard on me, said Mary. I did the best I could.

Walter said he was sure, said Donald. So I asked him where he was going to go. He said he remembered California from his days in the service, and he'd always wanted to go back. He thought he could afford a little place by the ocean. Someplace he could live. He had already checked with his parole officer, and they had approved it. I wanted him to stay nearby, where we could help him if he needed it, and I told him so, but he didn't agree. So he left one Saturday in September, with just a suitcase full of clothes and a box of mementoes that I'd been holding for him for thirty years. He found a condo in Oxnard, near the water, and spent his days reading histories of the World Wars and gardening a little bit. We talked on the phone. He learned to swim at the local YMCA; that was something he'd never attempted before.

I don't think he ever did open that box, said Mary.

No, said Donald. I don't believe he did. Still, we talked a lot, then, Walter and I. More, even, than when he was in the penitentiary. He told me: there were days in the years, occasions in the days, when he would suddenly up and tell a new acquaintance that once, a long time ago (But you know what? he would say, leaning in closer: it might as well have been yesterday), he had shot and killed his wife. He would say that to storekeepers, to postmen, to strangers he'd just met, finding some way to bring it into the conversation: He'd say, Well, that was when I was a con, so I only heard about it secondhand. —Or he'd say, My late wife used to say exactly that. —Or, I once went thirty years without putting down cash for a glass of whiskey.

I suppose he just wanted to tell his story, said Mary. Whatever it was in his head.

There were other times, said Donald, when Walter would skip the fact that anything had happened at all, pass over his marriage, his three decades in prison, pass over his wrongdoing and lie. I don't think he convinced anyone, though, said Donald. I don't think he wanted to. He didn't want people thinking he was innocent. He was just . . .

Exploring, said Mary.

Pushing at things, said Donald. But he told me that now and then he would see Nicole in a vision, and every time he did he was right back where he started, all over again and going down.

29

Donald leaned back farther into the great blue couch and yawned, not because he was tired, still less because he was bored, but as if in corporeal sympathy for what he was about to relate. Then Walter started feeling run out, he said. Exhausted, weak. Well, you know, we're all running out at our age. Running down like those toys they give to children. Those robots and games, when the batteries start to go. Walter went out to Oxnard. But he hadn't been there very long before he started feeling like he was breaking down. And so a little later he found a doctor. He used to call me, I guess I was the only person he felt like he could talk to. He said his doctor was a young Bengali man, a nice man, who told him he had a cancer, and he had only a few more months to live. He said this with great restraint . . . great grace and dignity. He called me, and he said, Donald, you should know that I'm dying.

Just imagine, said Mary. Him knowing that, and being able to tell someone else, so that they knew he wasn't long for this world. A few months.

He called me, said Donald. He said the doctor had a clipboard; he said the paper, there, had more on it about him than he'd ever know himself. He thought that was funny—you know, strange and amusing both. Still, when he asked the doctor how it would go, the doctor couldn't say for sure.

He was a very strong man, said Mary. Except in the ways that he was weak. He wanted to know if he was going to be in a lot of pain, but he wasn't frightened. He asked us not to go to see him, just to remember him. But . . .

The doctor said they'd do everything they could. Walter said that was good, but he didn't want to be so drugged that he didn't know what was going on around him. He said he would take some pain if it came with consciousness. He said that was very important to him. He said, I'm hoping that my children will be coming by to visit me. I haven't seen them in a long, long time, and I want to be able to speak to them.

Donald and Mary were watching Frank, and he caught their stares and sat up, a strange rictus upon his face, a sudden coldness under his skin. He's still alive?

Oh, yes, said Donald. Not for long.

He wants us to visit him?

More than anything on God's earth, said Donald. He's been waiting for you for thirty years now. We've all been waiting for you, Frank. Wondering who you were.

And here you are, said Mary.

30

Big Richard was waiting at the airport in Kansas City, parked at the curb in a brand-new Dodge Ram 1500, a shiny black hulk that idled like a lioness. He stepped down from the cab when Frank came through the glass doors, took his bag, and placed it gently in the bed, a gesture of sheer innocence. Trip O.K.? he asked. His face was red from the sun, making his scar stand out in pink relief, that great and mysterious cut, its color an indelible reminder of the violence that must have made it.

The plane was almost empty, said Frank.

Climb in, said Big Richard. It's just a few more miles to go.

The highway north out of town was long and flat, and everything was new: the sweeping concrete curve of the road, the cars beside them, then land on which nothing was growing, with here and there a long, low warehouse. Big Richard never said a word. They passed an enormous restaurant on the edge of a field. It was the size of a feed store, and a sign by the road said ALL YOU CAN EAT: STEAK AND SHRIMP—$12.95. He wondered if Gail had ever taken the boys there; little girl she was once, she would have giggled at the very thought of All She Could Eat. A hot dog and a little cup of ice cream would have been just about it. —He flinched. She was going to be upset when he told her about their father. About that man. She was going to be angry, confused maybe, sad, maybe scared; she was going to be concerned. Or maybe she wouldn't care at all. Still, he should have warned her, somehow, let her know what he was coming with. He should have taken some time to come up with a plan, he should have explained it to her on the phone. But no, better to be with her; why make her think about it any longer than she had to? As a child she'd had a ruthless side, exercised mostly on herself. If he had a loose tooth he'd rock it back and forth with his tongue for days, listening to the shreds of tissue gradually separating and tasting bits of blood; she would reach into her mouth with her own tiny fingers and twist the tooth until it came out, then smile redly and display the prize proudly in the palm of her hand. Shame was never sharp enough for her, nor discomfort a solace.

Now they were emerging out of the city, or it was sneaking away behind them, like an ocean wave pulling back from a swimmer. There was a construction crew working to widen the road; orange cones and sunburned men out in the pitiless day, putting down an extra two lanes of blacktop. Big Richard drove through slowly; then they took a turn to the right and they were on a wide, pleasant, tree-shaded street, with shallow curbs and short houses; he took another few turns, glided the truck halfway up the block, and pulled into the driveway of a large white ranch house. Frank gazed down the side to the yard in back, where there sat a painted red swing set that he himself had helped Gail and Big Richard raise, back when Kevin and RJ were too young to go down to the playground by themselves. Now they were, —what? Fifteen and thirteen. Kids, just ponies. Big Richard honked his horn, and Gail was the first one out the door, the two boys behind her, and both of them a foot or so taller than she was; but she led them, nonetheless, to their Uncle Frank, and made them wait just behind her while she reached up and gave him a strong hug, then turned him, still in her embrace, first one way and then the other: *Ohhhh!* she said with rough delight. Then she laughed, just because her brother was before her. Hello, hello, hello. Kevin and RJ stepped forward to shake his hand, with a mannishness that they seemed to find awkward themselves, though Kevin, the younger of the two, was still child enough to smile. His brother simply nodded. Hail the day: these were the grandsons of Walter Selby. Come on inside, said Gail, and she smiled again, this time just to herself.

The two boys went to a bathroom in the hallway to wash their hands, while Gail showed Frank into Kevin's room, which was decorated with a simple, solid bed and desk, some sports posters on the walls, a blanket too brightly colored for a teenager—it would be gone in a couple of months, replaced by a solid blue or green—and lamps which the boy had rearranged so that they cast as little light as possible, giving the whole space an air of some burial ground for childish things, from which a thus far undescribed adulthood would someday soon emerge. Frank unpacked his bag carefully, not wanting to disturb the subtle incubation of the place. He left his toiletries in the dark-blue canvas bag in which he carried them, placing them on a corner of the sink top, among the fluorescent toothbrushes, the tri-colored toothpaste, the tubes of acne medication, the bright little tubs of hair groom, the sporty, sweet-smelling antiperspirant. All his clothes were dirty, but for a pair of jeans and a white t-shirt which he'd saved; he took the rest down to the basement, threw them in the washer, and wandered barefoot back up through the house. On the walls he noticed pictures: framed prints, a carefully chosen painting or two, and photographic portraits of Kevin and Richard Jr., the boys and Big Richard, Gail and the three of them, and one of himself, taken the last time he'd been in Kansas City; but nothing older than these.

Gail and Big Richard were in the kitchen. Are you hungry? she said. We're going to eat soon. Her husband opened the door of the oven and gazed in at a slab of beef. There was a bustling throughout the house, Kevin setting the table and joking about something, while RJ brought an extra chair in from the back porch; there was a collie running back and forth, barking intermittently at the excitement and entangling himself between Frank's legs. How long had they had a dog? Gail gave her brother's arm a squeeze.

Later, they all sat at a big wooden table in the dining room. For a moment there was no talk, just a certain stillness and silence, that ingathering of the senses before dinner, the clearing of spirits, the moment of devotion to evening-fall and appetite. Then Kevin said grace and the meal began. There were steaks and greens, coleslaw, mashed potatoes, loaves of hot bread, iced tea for the boys and beer for the adults. The boys were quiet, deferential; by now they would be interested in girls, and they would see their Uncle Frank, the movie star, as the most magical of womanizers. They ate, and the food never seemed to diminish: as soon as Frank finished a serving his plate would be refilled. More steak, more slaw, and the boys were matching him portion for portion, Gail and Big Richard eating more slowly behind them, watching them with the amusement and satisfaction of those who have provided. There was a peach cobbler and ice cream for dessert, so sweet and rich that it made Frank's teeth ache. There was rusty cinnamon and vanilla, and a sprig of mint-green mint, all the spices and fruits of the earth, drawn from distant lands to this Kansas City dining room and laid before them like a bounty. Afterward the boys cleared their dishes, loaded them into the dishwasher, and then went out into the blue dusk, while Frank and Gail and Big Richard sat in the living room, sipping whiskey from thick glass tumblers, adults out of children.

I don't know how you eat so much and stay so skinny, said Gail to Frank. You just burn it off, somehow, don't you? —She turned to Big Richard. When we were kids he once ate an entire cooked ham that our mother had made for dinner. Ate it in an afternoon, and when she went to get it out of the fridge there was nothing on the plate but a bit of the rind.

A leg of lamb, said Frank. I started it—what can I say?—I was only going to have a little, but it was good. So I just kept going, and the next thing I knew . . .

She made him, —

She wasn't happy. I was sixteen: she made me make dinner for the whole family for the next week.

She could be tough, said Gail. Not so much on me, but on you. Not in a bad way. Right?

Yeah, said Frank. No, not too bad. If she'd known how terrible a cook I was, —I mean, I didn't know how to boil an egg—she probably wouldn't have made me do it at all. We almost starved to death that week.

You were just a kid, said Gail, as if she herself had always been an adult.

Frank hesitated. Outside the night was coming down, blue and darker in subtle increments, like layers of ink wash on a drawing of the neighborhood.

What? said Gail.

Nothing.

What?

We were younger than that, once, said Frank. She looked at him as if he'd said something oddly incomplete, the very grammar of his point unresolved. —We were younger. I have something to show you.

. . . O.K., said Gail, drawing out the syllables skeptically.

He leaned forward and reached into the rear pocket of his jeans, drawing out an envelope. It's a photograph, he said. Do you remember, when I was in high school, a girlfriend I had, named Kimmie? —You remember her: small, red hair. She went . . .

I remember, said Gail, nodding gently.

I gave her this, back then, said Frank, removing the picture and glancing at it for a moment before handing it to his sister, who took it and set it on the coffee table before her, as if it were a specimen of something rare and demanding. —She sent it back to me a few weeks ago.

Gail lifted her gaze from the picture long enough to give him a concerned look. How is she?

She says she's fine, he said, and she lowered her eyes again. Pause. That's you and me.

I know, said Gail, still engaged in her toneless study. She leaned back a bit and motioned Big Richard to take a look. I don't have anything like this. When do you suppose this is?

Turn it over, said Frank, and she did, scanning Kimmie's note quickly and then fixing on the older notation. Memphis, 1966, it might as well have said Shangri-La or Heaven Itself. —I brought that for you, he continued. I thought you should have it. Maybe show it to the boys.

Gail nodded solemnly, and for a moment Frank wondered if she was angry. But no, she was trying to recollect. Do you remember this? she said.

I remember the shirt I'm wearing. I don't remember the picture being taken. Or, —and here he hesitated again, and then hated himself for being so actorly—who took it. Gail looked up at him, again with no expression. He couldn't tell which of them was leading the other; did she want him to continue? Was that dread or openness upon her still features? —They weren't really our parents, he said. The Cartwrights.

Big Richard made a noise, almost his first expression since Frank had come into the house, and it was meant, as they all recognized, to protect his wife with sound.

Of course they were, said Gail.

O.K., said Frank. Real, they were real. They weren't the ones we were born to. They weren't our parents when that picture was taken. I'm sorry, we never talked about what happened. We should have. Maybe we should have.

—Gail had no expression at all. All right, she said.

We never talked about this, —her name was Nicole—how she died.

I know, said Gail.

I've been looking into it. Listen. I think I ought to tell you. Listen. He drew a breath, and now Gail was staring at him with a dark burning expression. He killed her, said Frank, sounding the words out for their mystery. His name was Walter Selby. They put him in prison.

No, said Gail. I'm saying, I know. He's been out for five years. He's living in California. I know. I looked it up years ago—now Frank was staring—I looked it up when I was in ninth grade, I think. —Her gaze was fixed on the floor in front of her. —Kimmie, exactly: Kimmie. I watched you fall in love and lose her, and you changed. I thought about the whole thing; you left and I wasn't sure if I was ever going to see you again. Because I was thirteen, fourteen years old. You were gone. I wanted to know where we came from, so I went down to the library and looked up whatever I could find in the newspapers. —She leaned forward and licked her lips, as if that were a form of remembrance too. Do you remember when I went to Memphis, that summer after my sophomore year in college? I did a lot of research. I talked to some people. I went to see her parents' graves, in Charleston. Our grandparents.

I . . . said Frank. I . . . Then he shook his head. Go on.

I've been keeping track of him ever since. Frank, you were a long way out of the house by then. You were always busy with something. For a while I worried that someone writing about you would find out, but it never happened. And I didn't want to tell you if you didn't know.

She spoke quickly and with great earnestness, but when she looked up at him he was laughing softly. Of course, he said. Of course, of course. All this time.

I thought, if you brought it up I'd tell you. But you never mentioned it. Are you mad at me?

Frank shook his head, still smiling. No, he said. Not at all. I'm . . . —He turned to Big Richard. Did you know? he asked.

Big Richard shrugged softly and nodded faintly. A little. Not all of it.

I found a bottle of perfume the other day, the same brand she used to wear, said Frank. Do you want to see it? —Gail shook her head emphatically. —He wants us to go visit him.

Who does? said Gail.

Him, said Frank. He's in a hospital. Will you come?

She shook her head again. You're going, then?

I think I am, said Frank.

Why?

Don't know. I'll go, see Amy, see him, take care of some business.

How much time does he have left?

I don't know. Maybe a long time, maybe a few days.

So you don't know how dead a man you'll see.

He shook his head, sat back, and thought for a moment, then looked to Big Richard, who was watching his wife. Are you sure you won't come?

One hundred percent, said Gail. You go, if you want.

You don't mind?

Mind? said Gail. Frank . . . She sighed, by way of explanation. I think you should go. Be the son.

Not the son, said Frank. Just . . .

You remember him.

A little. What I remember, I think it's him.

Well, said Gail, I don't remember anything. I can't even imagine. You go, and tell me what happens. I've got pretty much all the family I need right here with me now.

He shook his head. I don't know if there'll be anything to tell. It won't be like that. What am I going to say to him?

I don't know. Ask him . . . Ask him where our mother is buried; that's the only thing I couldn't find out.

I'll ask him.

You go, then. —She nodded. —Now, she said, I can tell you what I know; if you're going to go, maybe you should hear it.

He made a bring-me gesture.

More wine, she said. Honey, that bottle we put away for a special occasion.

Big Richard returned with the wine. This is between you two, I think, he said, and he set the bottle down and vanished into the back of the house.

Are you ready? said Gail, when they had been alone for a little while.

O.K., said Frank, and she began, using a tone she might have used to recite tales to her boys when they were younger, or to read aloud from a sacred book whose contents she had long since memorized. She nodded to mark the beginning beat, took a breath, and began, saying, There was a woman named Kelly Flynn.

31

The hotel was quiet in the early afternoon, the dark lobby was shadowed from the sun of Los Angeles, the woman at the front desk was friendly and confident. How can I help you?

I'm Frank Cartwright, he said. I think you have a reservation for me.

Yes, she said. She turned and drew a bright brass key from a cubbyhole behind her, handed it to Frank, and then checked the computer screen on the counter before her. —You'll be in Room 702. And I have a message here for you. She looked down at a piece of paper.

Thanks, said Frank. He took the paper and his key and started for the elevator.

In his room he dropped his bags on the floor by the bed and immediately went to turn on the television. Some sporting event: they were parachuting onto skis, and then skiing down to a lake, where they swam, all the while the cameras following in great arcs beside. The message in the envelope said that Lenore Riviere had called; how had she known he was coming to town? And she had sent him a bouquet of flowers, a great to-do in a big glass bowl, not just blooms but buds and leaves, some seed pods still on the twig, even a few long blades of mountain grass. He went to the window; outside lay Sunset, down which the bright cars brightly passed. He stood there for a few minutes, watching them and wondering where they could possibly be going, on such a day in such a city.

32

God damn this hotel, and all the years she'd spent in it. Pushing her cleaning cart up and down the carpeted hallways, wearing her white uniform, always the same. Just like her husband, floating in the river; except she was floating on wage work. By now she knew every fixture in the place, every sconce on the walls, every tear in the carpet, every burnish on every brass doorknob, where the forks lay in their drawers in the kitchen, deep in the bottom of the basement, where in the laundry the sheets and pillowcases were kept, every paperclip in every desk drawer, every inch of wainscoting, the homes and trails of mice. One of the night managers had a collection of pornography on his computer, black girls all bent over, which he supplemented over the hotel phone lines whenever the night grew slow. One of the operators cried in her little cubicle every afternoon; cried and cried, but kept the tears out of her voice so that no one she spoke to ever discovered. No comfort on this cold planet, no there wasn't, but the brief joy of a sunny day and the hasty friendship of hard times. It was strange. No wonder so many ghosts spent their dwelling time screaming; no wonder no one ever heard them.

She never knew what to do with herself, what to say when she encountered a guest, though often enough it didn't matter: she went unnoticed, she might as well have been invisible. Sometimes she wished she could vanish for real, just disappear, like her husband did. Just like that: walk out and never come back, but she had no place to go, and no one who would miss her if she did. All she had was time.

She had only been eighteen when Harold left; she didn't know the man that well, he was older and they hadn't been married very long. So she didn't even know where to start looking for him. Left her with a lot of junk he'd bought, and she just went back down to her ma's house, down in Georgia, out in the country. All those times she dreamt he'd come and get her, she had dreamed that he was rich and kind, and hadn't abandoned her so much as he'd lost her, and would come for her as soon as he could; but she'd long since realized he couldn't come for her anymore.

The room was empty, immaculate to the casual eye—though she knew there were wet paper towels clotted in a corner of the cabinet under the sink. The bed was made, the sheets and comforter smoothed, the drapes pulled across the window so that only a bright pillar of light fell a few feet onto the carpet. The dead in their dust drifting aimlessly on the air; she ran the tips of her fingers over the surface of the dresser.

She missed the sound of the turtles in the Georgia creeks at night, she missed making cobblers and pies with her ma every morning and taking them over to the neighbors' houses. What do you want to go to Los Angeles for? her mother had asked her. You've got everything you need right here. But her ma was just scared of being alone to face the stars at night. Did she fall on her knees, did she pray? Did old Mrs. Jordan come around, clucking and comforting?

She glanced at herself in the dark screen of the blank television, convex, black, unlit and unelectrified; there was the maid's uniform of white and pale blue, a distorted black face above, luminous brown where the sunlight hit her, bright yellow at the edges, a spark for her eye, then a melancholy curve, fading back into the room behind her.

Oh, this hotel. In came the movie people, businessmen, musicians, all that publish upon the world. They stayed, they laughed, they made love to one another, fought on the telephone, they sat alone on the edge of their beds, spent and still high. They ordered liquor from distant room service, spending money they didn't have on things they didn't want; they watched themselves on the television. She slipped in and out of their rooms, pulling their soiled, spotted sheets from the bed and replacing them with fresh new ones, restocking the tiny bars of soap in the shower, the little plastic shampoo bottles, miniature props for three-day lives, more paper in the desk drawer, fresh flowers in the vase. It was the same every day, and every day was the same.

She could hear a man coming up the hallway, his tread heavy, grateful for the darkness. There was something on his mind, some problem he had to solve, or work he needed to complete. She liked him by the sound of his footfall, and she turned, listening, when he stopped outside the room. There was a pause, and the door swung open.

He was tall and white, handsome and graceful, and for a moment he seemed not to notice her, standing there—well, they never did, and she watched him sidelong as he walked softly to the bed and sat on the edge. Then, —Oh, I'm sorry, he said. I didn't see you.

She didn't answer him.

Were you cleaning the room? said Frank. She shook her head no, then nodded, so that he didn't know what she was trying to say and he smiled.

It was a good, warm smile and she spoke for the first time in years, without even wondering if the instrument would work. I'm not here to help you, said Yvette.

All right, said Frank.

I think I'm here to help my husband.

Frank misunderstood. It's hard to find work these days, I guess, he said. You have to take what you can.

She nodded.

What does your husband do?

Oh, I don't know, said Yvette. He was a millionaire: lottery, you know, and he left the house one day and never came home. I do believe he died—she gestured to the window—somewhere out there.

I'm sorry, said Frank.

I waited, and I waited, and I waited, said Yvette. Oh, I loved that man. Isn't that what you wanted to hear? I loved him so, I could hardly breathe without him. But he never came home. And now I know: His soul is still looking for its resting place.

Mm, said Frank. I hope he finds it.

I haven't been right since the day he left, said Yvette. My soul is still looking for his.

33

Amy on the beach, sixteen and fair, in her shorts and sleeveless t-shirt, they passed men who eyed her and he wished they would stop, but not even his glaring got in their way. He had no authority next to that of desire, and he mused for a moment on the fact that no man is famous next to a lovely young girl. He wondered if she noticed them. Of course she did. He wondered how she felt. By her side she held her shoes, with the perfume bottle he had brought her from South Texas lodged inside one of them; it was too big to fit in her pocket. When he'd given it to her, she had opened the stopper and sniffed at the lip, and then looked at him with a question.

The waves were slamming into the shore, and he had to speak more loudly than he would have wanted. It's not for you to wear or anything. It's just for you to have.

She nodded; she knew that. This thing you came to town for, she said. You told me your father had died.

Different father, he replied.

Different? Her hair was long, light brown, and carefully cut, and her hand was awkward as she brushed it back from her face, as if even that gesture was caught between childhood and maturity. When he'd picked her up at her mother's house, he'd noticed immediately that her features were thinner; she was losing the last of her baby fat, and he was sad, and a little bit frightened to see it go. Helen had said she worried that she was too short; she wanted to have longer legs, she wanted to have larger breasts. —She's getting to that age, you know. She spent a lot of time at the beach; she wanted to be a marine biologist, these days. The down on her arms was translucent. Across the continent in one generation, and she bore it all without even knowing.

It's a long story, he said. It's not important.

He could feel her looking at him skeptically, though the sharpest edge of it was drowning in the sunlight. O.K., she said. My *other* grandfather: Not important. Got it.

I'll tell you someday. How's school?

She sighed, at the dreariness of the question or the dreariness of her classes, he didn't know which. —Fine.

Just fine?

Fine, she said again, and set her mouth with a girl's secrets. The wind was ripping at his jacket, and he buttoned it all the way up, knowing it made him look silly, but knowing, too, that she liked it when he looked silly, though she would never admit as much. Let her be barefoot and uncovered. He felt an urge to say her name, over and over again: Amy, Amy, Amy, Amy. —Your mother said there were boys in your life now. Cars. Boys in cars. California.

She nodded by way of admitting nothing.

You're careful?

Dad. . . . She was battling him, not angrily, but time was a tug-of-war, he trying to rein her back with it, while she wanted to run on, older, farther forward. Oh, dear daughter, he said to himself. Please enjoy your April.

Are you really going to make another movie? she said.

I don't know. I think I might. She had never asked him about work before, and this new interest, too, seemed to be a bid for adulthood.

Good, she said firmly, staring down at the sand.

He was surprised. I didn't know it mattered to you.

It doesn't, she said, and then she cut him, the more deeply for the fact that she meant nothing cruel by it at all. It's just that me and Mom . . . she said. We don't want to have to worry about you anymore.

34

THE DEATH OF WALTER SELBY

Here comes Nurse Linen, with her pinned-up hair and her cool strong hands, come to roll him over and change his sheets, just like he was an infant. Are you ready? she asked, her mouth fixed, the drawstring on her smock tied tight. Are you ready? Here we go. He was never ready, really, but he did what she told him to do: his body went limp, and he let her push him onto his side while she tugged at the bedclothes beneath him—a poor bit of jostling that sent him on a long long journey through a cloud of pain, inside him or outside him, who could tell the difference? He tried not to make any sound, but a cry came, and it took him two or three minutes to get his breath back again. I'm sorry, said Nurse Linen. We'll be done here in just a moment. Swiftly, and with a confidence and dexterity that never failed to impress him, she pulled the worn sheets from under him and replaced them with freshly cleaned ones. Then, as always, he was struck by her strength and her health. She had a kindness that wasn't so kind, but it had been more than thirty years since he'd touched another human being with love in his heart, and this was close enough. Her almost caring questions: How are you feeling today? Have you eaten? Have you eaten everything they gave you? Have you had a look out the window? It's a beautiful day. He was seldom able to answer her, but he was comforted by her asking.

He began reeling in time, closing generations. He said hello to his own mother, a woman he hardly remembered but who was now so close that Walter could smell her, could brush his fingers across her features. She was a young woman, she wore a lacy dress and black ankle-high shoes, and her eyes were a penetrating brown. I put you in this world, she said, and maybe I'll be waiting for you when you leave it. And maybe I won't.

Now, as he slept morphine sleep in his hospital bed, the strains of waltz time made their way into his dreams, as if it was the rhythm that would lead him all the way down to the end, wherever the end might be. He remembered watching the Governor gently feeding a sugar cube to a beautiful brown and grey stallion during a review of the state cavalry. He remembered Nicole, drawing circles on his back with her index finger while he lay half awake on a Sunday morning.

Are you going to heaven or are you going to hell? asked Nurse Linen.

—Is that right? Is that what she said? Impossible. What a question. He really wanted to laugh, but laughter was well beyond his powers. Instead a red orchid bloomed inside of him, the petals unfolding and expanding, opening outward in a glorious stop motion. He was astonished, and all he could do was lie back and wonder at it. Slowly, the flower faded and he came back to his senses; Nurse Linen was gone, and he was alone again.

He stirred and opened his eyes. Gazing down the length of his sheet-wrapped body he could see his hands, spotted where the pigment had collected, the sediment of age. There were spots, too, in his vision, dull, milky bits that floated in one direction or another. In each lived a memory that was eluding him. His veins were plastic, sweet and old, and they ran with salt. He couldn't divide his life; it had been one container, one measure, a unit of being, perfectly circumscribed. One woman, one act, one sentence.

Nicole came to him, sneaking through the tangle of drip lines and monitor wires to hover above his bed and sweetly sing:

When it's peach-picking time in Georgia . . .

He was a four-year-old boy in a backyard, a summer home his mother had taken up near Newport. Behind the edge of the lawn there was a line of towering trees. It was a Saturday morning, just after breakfast, and his mother was inside the house, talking to a man he'd never seen before and would never see again. The back door was open, but the screen door was still closed; he could smell the metallic flavor of the screening and feel the rough surface on his fingertips. Now he was wandering, tiny through the great yard, tiny under the sun. He noticed every feature of the ground, where there was a depression, a dandelion, where, at the base of the single tree that stood about fifty yards from the house, the grass was growing long because the mower hadn't been able to reach between the roots. Maybe he was four years old, maybe he was only three. The big house behind him was noiseless, and so was the sun. Only the atmosphere made a sound, and that was just the hush of heat in the morning. He could see his feet, and that was about all he could see. Then he was in the trees.

The floor was soft and the needles smelled sweet, and the air was cool and damp. He felt a kind of dizziness, nothing unpleasant, he enjoyed it. He walked along, turning one way and then the other, as something caught his eye—a stalk of tiny blue flowers growing in the half darkness, the breeze through a patch of ivy, the warm glittering gold of sap appearing on the side of a tree. He craned his head back and looked up through the branches to the sky, which appeared here and there, neither blue nor grey, but a strange sort of milky white that came from the clouds being illuminated from behind. He couldn't say that he was afraid, not at all; he liked the feeling of being lost very much, with no place to be and everything to see. Here was a mossy log, flaking pieces of itself off in the gloom. Here was a little brook, visible only because of the soft sheen of water that it left among the rocks. Then at last he came to a small meadow, with grass almost up to his waist. On the other side the trees began again. It was there that he sat, watching the clouds pass by overhead, on their way from where to where, so slowly. It was there that his mother found him, three hours later, the woman taking him by the arm and lifting him to his feet, at first roughly, so that the boy wondered what was wrong, and then gently, with a look of fear and tenderness which he had never before seen on her face.

Well, how long ago was that? And in a boyhood he had left so far behind, lost in the noise of years. He wondered if that was what dying was, still more what living was: endlessly remembering the boy you were, the adult you wanted to be, the old man you became. And then there were the other children, the ones he'd made: Frank and Gail. He hadn't been a good father. He hadn't been a father at all, except to make them; and here on the edge of always, he wanted very badly to know how they were faring, the two tiny lumina he had cast into the world.

35

How are you, Frank? said Lenore Riviere. You know how I feel about telephones; why don't you come by? We'll have breakfast.

Already eaten, thanks, said Frank, and absently shoved a forkful of home fries from one side of his room service plate to the other, as if in proof. The window in his room was open, and a warm, flower-fragrant breeze seeped in amid the air-conditioning.

Very well, then, said Lenore. How has your stay been?

So far, so good, said Frank.

What have you been doing? —She made it sound like such a grand question.

Taking care of things, said Frank.

Yes, said Lenore. Westward is an escape for most people, isn't it? Westward is toward the new.

Not for me, said Frank.

No, not for you. Have you thought about our problem?

I have, said Frank.

In the distance a car horn blew, that lovely summery sound. He imagined Lenore sitting by a window high in the hills, looking down on all the business below with her air of fond amusement. Good, she said.

And I've decided, said Frank. I'll do it. We'll do it together.

Hooray, said Lenore.

On one condition.

Which is . . . ?

He smiled, he hoped she was smiling too. I won't play the Prince, he said. I want to play the King.

There was a pause on the other end of the line. He could hear her breathing; an old woman breathes like she's reaching into her purse. But the King is dead, she said.

I know, said Frank. Long live the King.

36

Late the next morning, after coffee and croissants in his room, Frank opened his address book and found the name and number of the hospital, muting the television as he dialed. A woman answered, an administrator. Hello, he said. My name is Frank Cartwright. There's a man there, in intensive care. —Strange locution, it seemed overly dramatic; he was afraid that she wouldn't believe him and he began again. I'm inquiring, I want to visit a patient in the intensive care ward, a man named Walter Selby. I was hoping you could tell me when visiting hours were.

Walter Shelby? the woman said.

S-E-L-B-Y, said Frank. Can I see him tomorrow?

The woman seemed to have put the telephone down; anyway, he could hear the sound of a chair rolling across the floor. On the television a man was standing at a kitchen sink, washing his hands. Walter Selby, said the administrator. I have him here, Room 304. Tomorrow, you want to come?

Yes, said Frank.

It's relatives only, said the nurse.

I'm his son, said Frank, for the very first time.

All right, said the woman, her voice absent any inflection. If you want to see him, visiting hours are nine in the morning to nine at night. You can just come.

The phantom approached, the obligation faced, Frank hung up and sat on his bed, while through the windows, the sunlight of Los Angeles exercised its unreasonable influence. The television had become repulsive to him, the combination of colors so harsh that it caused him physical pain, and he found the remote and switched it off.

37

Nurse Demerol came by with her sweet slow smile and refilled the bottle on a stand by Walter's bed. He wondered whether she was ministering to him or to his disease: they were hardly separate entities anymore, and serving one was serving the other. The doctors had stopped talking about recovery, or even treatments; instead, the nurses came around and tried to make him comfortable, keeping the body alive so the disease could stay alive. He had the button in his hand all ready, and before she was gone he had pushed it. The love manifested by the fluid made him think of the love of his wife, and how fine the line was between poison and cure.

God, it must have been about a thousand years ago, Walter had read some book, or maybe just the title. He could see the spine, it was green and the lettering was gold. God, where did that book come from? Had someone lent it to him? He remembered the title: *How Much Does It Cost If It's Free?* But he didn't know what it meant, so he couldn't have read it, after all, and now he was never going to be able to. Never, never, never. It might have been the one that would tell him that small thing he needed, the sentence that explained everything. The idea terrified him, and he began to shiver under his bedclothes.

Here came Miss Demerol again, what was she saying? He stared at her blankly, not sure if she was speaking at all. If she was, she'd do it again, and he'd try to catch it that time. She said, Mr. Selby, you're going to have a visitor, and then she went about primping his tubes.

He thought, No one's coming to visit me. There is no one to visit me. There is no one. The fact that there was no one made him want to cry, but he didn't have any tears. Who is it? he said, and the effort of asking caused another great flower of pain to bloom in his chest.

Nurse Demerol smiled. What's that? she said. Who is it? It's your son. I didn't know you had a son. Walter murmured something. He'll be coming by tomorrow, she said.

His life was absurdly weighted: all his years, of youth and marriage, of violence and penitence, all laid out at one end, and the last empty days at the other, with this visit weighing the final hours down. He waited, it seemed a balance, with himself at the fulcrum.

The window darkened and it was night. He was remembering the future—had Frank already come and gone? No. He thought he recognized a face in his fantasies, but when he tried to scrutinize it further, the features became clay and smeared. So he didn't know what his son looked like, so he hadn't come, so there was still tomorrow, and he wasn't dead yet. He wondered if he would know when he was, or whether always was just this.

38

At ten o'clock on a bright, bright Wednesday morning, Frank was driving on a highway heading down to the ocean, with the sun still rising huge behind him, causing heliotropic spots to drift across his field of vision. On the passenger seat there was a plastic quart of water, which he'd picked up in a convenience store before he got on the highway, and which was already too warm to drink. There were cars all around him, but he couldn't imagine where they'd come from, midmorning on this weekend; the brown hills around them were bare, the highway went nowhere. As he watched, the traffic separated and reconvened, pointlessly slipping from side to side on its way down to the ocean; in time he began to cross the broken line himself, pulling left and speeding up to pass a particularly slow station wagon, or right again to avoid the idea that there was no way to go faster still.

Suddenly he was over the last hill and stretching before him was the Pacific, the new-old ocean, vast and blue and grey. The wind buffeted his car, and he straightened it and then peered down at a sheet of directions on the passenger seat. And there was his exit, the last in the nation, a long curve down through hills covered in scrub, with no houses.

The hospital lay at the bottom, an enormous winged white structure, glittering and floating in the sun. Before it there was a vast parking lot filled with blinding acres of shiny cars, their reflections ringing in Frank's ears. He parked a mile away from the front entrance and started walking. It was too bright to breathe, too warm to think, there were no birds in the sky and he could hear the distant noise of the ocean. And a heart is red and beats music all day long. And . . .

Just then, Walter was journeying outward, hurtling through concentric, spreading rings of stars. He could tell that when he reached the last ring all that would be left was a darkness, and he would be done. So many men and women had preceded him, known and unknown, admired and despised—millions upon millions, and each with a face. And the one he had loved, whom he'd sent. Does anyone know how lonely this is? Where was that brightness he'd been promised? Where was the rising? The universe convulsed in a moment of panic, a surge of energy, life, pity, and if those had been enough, he might have stopped the entire process. No. No matter: he was calm again.

Then there was someone near, he knew that, some male form hovering, just beyond his reach; he could hear the murmur of an attending voice. Here he is, the nurse was saying, as she escorted Frank into the room. He isn't awake, I don't think. —Mr. Selby? she said loudly. No, I guess he's sleeping. He's on a lot of medication. Is he really your father? We had no idea his son was an actor. Usually we know, because someone will call and tell us. And you have different names. Did they make you change your name? But Selby is a perfectly good name. . . .

Frank nodded at the tone of her voice, but he'd stopped listening. Instead he was looking down at the body of the aged man in the bed of white, a once large man, now so shrunken that he was almost swallowed by the sheets, his head sunk in the pillows. Hello, he said, because that was the beginning.

I don't think he can hear you, said the nurse.

He nodded. Can you leave us alone for a little bit?

The nurse complied, and the room was empty of everyone but the two: Frank in the sunlight at the foot of the bed, Walter supine upon the sheets; the one gazing at a corner of the room, collecting himself to look down, the other gazing, eyes closed, upon the universe. Frank searched for some form of address: *Father* would not do.

Can you hear me? he asked.

Can you hear me? said a passing dark planet to Walter. And then it was gone. He smacked his lips a little, in search of a taste on his palate, —another thing he couldn't speak, but which spoke to him of days and life.

Frank wished that his sister were there with him. He wanted to show her what their father had become and to contemplate him together with her. Years of treating the old man as a ghost, with no powers in this world save the occasional haunt, had left him little prepared for a meeting. He wanted to reach for Walter's hand, to hold it in his own and scrutinize it, for a sign of his own history, an estimation of his own qualities, a figure of his own powers. He didn't dare, he was afraid. You're Walter Selby, said Frank, still looking away but helplessly addressing this half creature, whose other half was already a prize promised to oblivion. The man below him made no motion at all; there were no more lines, and Frank's last remaining questions echoed softly. Can you tell me what it was? he said. What you saw . . . What you did . . . Walter Selby's breath came through a reed, wavering and faint; he opened his eyes but saw nothing but the ceiling; then he focused, just for a second, on the man standing above him. A tall man with familiar features. A doctor? He wasn't dressed like a doctor, and he didn't have a doctor's demeanor. Something sad was happening. What was it? —There. In Frank's face he saw the heartbroken face of his wife, wavering like a slide projected on flesh: Nicole, then she wasn't dead and would never die, because her features lived on in the features of his children, and would live on still longer in theirs. Just then Frank looked down and took in his father's form, —there, —he suddenly saw himself: himself, his countenance, something of his own expression. There was the sharp shape of his nose, there the slight downcurve at the outside corner of his eyes, the same brow with its suggestion of curiosity and care. It was like gazing into a magic mirror, which aged the face of any who dared stand before it. This is my father; this is me. He recoiled from the effect, but he couldn't look away. The two of them studied each other, perched together upon some vast and intricate structure, a latticework of years and all the hours within, —which shook and creaked and moaned, —and separated slowly, one rib from another, —and then collapsed majestically, falling inward and downward, while the two of them, man and son, tumbled down help-lessly, still locked in their mutual observation. One long moment of recognition passed between them, a thought without content, and then Walter Selby closed his eyes.

Where does a man go when his life is done? What does he know? What are the letters of Sheol, and what do they mean? The syllables sounded in Walter's ears like a trumpet, like a flash of light; but he didn't know if it was the summoning sound of death or merely the last cry of his consciousness. He was frightened, but it was like no fright he'd ever felt before; it was soft and didn't cut, and his heart had long since stopped beating. Then his fear left him and he waited.

Frank was going through his father's material. It was afternoon, and the condominium, one of a dozen in a hillside complex, was bright and plain. There wasn't very much to see: a few paperback books, a closet with some clothes, a few CDs of country music—what was that? T for Texas: what else was T for? There was a bar of soap and a bottle of shampoo in the bathroom. Neither souvenirs nor luxuries: no pictures on the wall, no candles on the table, and only one set of dishes in the cupboard. In the sole drawer of Walter's desk there was an envelope, and in the envelope were a few papers: his will, a bank statement, the title to his car, and one small photograph, wallet-sized, showing a young man and a young woman on their wedding day. The woman was young and so beautiful she seemed unreal, and the man was tall and handsome, and gazed on her with immeasurable adoration. But there was something in his posture: he was leaning, one chuck away from this worldly mob. Walter Selby was a lonely man, and Frank was his son. He stared.

Walter had left such things behind; he was dead and waiting for death to begin. Where does a man go, if he's done wrong? Time had ended for him; it had stopped, divided and stayed. It became an intoxicant, on which he was drunk, not just now but evermore. What law held? He had memories but he was mindless, and whatever he had once so briefly sensed—the smell of a living room, a woman's hand on his arm, his young son and infant daughter, a scrap of sky blue cloth—flashed and was gone. There was a long period of absolute silence, an absence of any motion, the world gone empty and therefore still all around him. He was cold. He was an atom, alone and without context, without movement, indivisible, and then he began to divide. A sensation started—not a sensation, but a recognition in reverse, as parts of his history began to peel off, one by one, flying away to join some distant source: an unwrapping, an unbinding, layer upon layer swiftly lifting, the corpus of his life all leaving, and beneath it there was nothing. Every thought of self had dissolved, his name expiring on the last remembered sound of its last remembered syllable. He was dead, and at last all-time had begun.

Frank was on an airplane, winging over the continent. Beneath him ran the green-brown fields and silver rivers of the Plains. At the apex of his parabola over the nation, suspended high there over the earth, he felt an equal pull from every direction, a massing all around him, something like clouds would be, if clouds had content instead of rain: the people he knew, and those to come, all of the dead and dying, and the ones who wanted to die, and the ones who weren't yet born: the ones who wanted to save others, and the ones who lied their whole life long, the ones who could cry at the ends of movies but never at real life, the ones who just wanted to have a little fun, the ones who sold themselves for nothing, and the ones who couldn't stop doing whatever it was that gave them pleasure, until all the pleasure was gone; and the ones who listened but rarely spoke, the ones who loved the sound of people cheering, and the ones who always ended up trusting the wrong people, the ones who made everyone around them feel stronger, wiser, more beautiful; and the ones who never seemed to have enough money, and the ones who felt joy unexpectedly, and the ones who lost something dear to them and then found something yet more dear, and the ones who traveled through life touched by the divinity of devils, the desperate, the bad, and the ones who smiled at strangers because they, too, were strangers once, and might someday be strangers again. It was evening, and the sky was darkening, the sun burning the Western horizon orange, the stars emerging overhead.

We say, Ah, but a life is short: a shout, a kiss, a bell. So it is, and the instant shutters, the life is done. What survives? Not Walter Selby, not himself, but some ecstatic mark of all he had known, which exploded outward, forever bursting, to be food for the stars, the burning ether, the fluid plenum, forever and without end, amen.

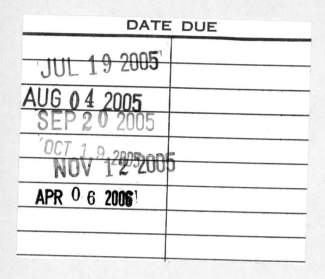